Mr. Wrong

Books by Liz

Countdown To A Kiss
A New Year's Eve Anthology

Playin' Cop
Heroes of Henderson ~ Prequel
Previously published as
The Keeper of the Debutantes in
Countdown to A Kiss

Good Cop
Heroes of Henderson ~ Book 1

Bad Cop
Heroes of Henderson ~ Book 2

Taming Molly
Heroes of Henderson ~ Book 2.5
A DuVal Cousins Quickie

Top Dog
Heroes of Henderson ~ Book 3

Tempting Vivi
Heroes of Henderson ~ Book 3.5
A DuVal Cousins Novel

Kissing Cooper
Heroes of Henderson
A Christmas Quickie

Under Dog
Heroes of Henderson ~ Book 4

Mr. Wrong
Heroes of Henderson ~ Book 5

Sign up at www.LizKellyBooks.com
to be alerted when new books are released.

MR. WRONG

HEROES OF HENDERSON: BOOK 5

Liz Kelly

Published by Kelly Girl Productions
©Copyright 2016 Liz Kelly
Cover design by Tammy Kearly

ISBN: 978-0-9860864-6-5

For more information on the author and her works, please see www. LizKellyBooks.com

For my brother Mac and his daughter Molly
A helluva Father-Daughter Team.

Go Blazers
Beat McDonogh!

Who's Who in Henderson

Should you like a review, here is a reference to
the primary characters you've met in previous books.
See a complete list of characters at www.LizKellyBooks.com

Thurgood Lewis Watson III a.k.a. Thor

Army Ranger back home in Henderson, now owner of a large plantation passed to him upon his father's untimely death.

Missy McReady

Imported from Baltimore by Davis Williams to be Henderson High's ladies lacrosse coach as well as the town's Marketing and Event-Planning guru.

Davis Williams a.k.a. Pinks or the Ninja

Originally from Baltimore and a childhood friend of Missy McReady's, Pinks is now heavily involved in Henderson's economic recovery plan. He's also heavily involved with *Red*, a.k.a. Scarlett Langford.

Scarlett Langford a.k.a. Red

A Henderson native in the middle of her senior year at Ole Miss. Unaware of her involvement with Pinks, her mother arranged a blind date between her and MLB pitching phenom Cal Johnson. She passed that off to her roommate, Natalie Houser.

Cal Johnson

Rookie MLB pitching sensation who showed up in Henderson last Christmas to help sort things out for his third base coach, **Cooper Crenshaw**. He came back in March to help promote Henderson High's Baseball Opening Day Spectacular.

Natalie Houser

Scarlett's roommate at Ole Miss. She's the daughter of Hall of Fame pitcher, Nate the Great.

Brooks Bennett (Good Cop)

Henderson's Golden Boy. He's determined to bring economic prosperity back to town and stop the mass exodus of younger generations. He's running for mayor and is madly in love with **Lolly DuVal**, who is at N.C. State finishing up her Masters in textiles and design.

Vance Evans (Bad Cop)

Part owner of E&E Investments and high school baseball coach, he's also the mayoral campaign manager for his best friend, Brooks Bennett. He recently married **Piper Beaumont**, defense attorney in Raleigh and his fourth-grade savior.

Hale Evans

Vance's father, who has recently married Lolly DuVal's mother, **Genevra** (pronunciation Gen-ev-ra), and is part owner of E&E. His mother, **Emelina Flores**, originally from Spain, also lives with them.

Duncan James

Fraternity brother of both Brooks and Vance, Duncan is a corporate attorney in Raleigh. He's presently engaged to **Annabelle Devine**, Henderson's own Keeper of the Debutantes.

Harry the Bartender

Mysterious young country club bartender with an uncanny knack for knowing your drink and reading your mind. His tequila shots have a way of bringing couples together.

Rye Langford

Third-generation Hendersonian and commercial real estate tycoon. Married to **Garland Langford**, Henderson socialite and former Miss North Carolina. They are the parents of **Tansy and Scarlett**.

Crain Carraway

Dallas business tycoon and star Texas A&M athlete who found his runaway bride, **Tansy Langford**, in Henderson. He's teamed up with E&E to create the coming sports academy.

Cash Carraway

Crain's younger brother—a cowboy in Ft. Worth, Texas—who romanced Missy McReady during his brother's wedding reception.

Josh McCourt

Assistant football coach, computer science teacher, member of Team Henderson, and dating the infamous **Molly DuVal** (Lolly's cousin, Genevra's niece, and creator of the Big Pie Plate.)

Vivi DuVal

Another cousin of Lolly's, presently in her first year teaching statistics at the high school in neighboring Oxford. She's also the advisor to the cheerleaders there and is keeping a really big secret.

CHAPTER ONE

March
Evening of the Opening Day Baseball Spectacular

Marcie Watts's shrewd and calculating mind had been hard at work since ten that morning. Twelve solid hours of watching … weighing … *strategizing* all while hiding in plain sight. All while the man she'd planned to marry presided over this horrid little Podunk town which, had given him his start.

Henderson.

Just the name Henderson, North Carolina caused her to grind her teeth. And that was before she'd driven five hours south to do personal surveillance. Before she'd come to realize that she'd been thrown over for nothing more than a mousy little do-gooder, fresh air, small-town baseball, and freaking apple pie. All of which had served to turn her lingering heartache into outright rage.

She'd been mere weeks from announcing the merger she'd toiled over for a solid year. Weeks from becoming engaged to the Orioles' frank-but-likable third base coach. And that press release she'd all but typeset? It would have been the equivalent of trumpets blaring. The lineup she'd arranged to broadcast her engagement to Cooper Crenshaw would have catapulted her into celebrity status within Baltimore. Her public relations firm would have toasted her ties to the Orioles organization, and her own star would have risen in the field because her name would now be recognized inside and outside of the industry.

But all those plans had come to naught.

Standing in the shadows of a clichéd honkey-tonk where the jubilant party carried on around her, her eyes swung toward the men responsible for her undoing. Brooks Bennett—Podunk's Golden Boy. Brooks *should-have-minded-his-own-damn-business* Bennett and his home-wrecking sidekick Vance Evans. The two of them were nothing but polished-up rednecks smart enough to use a shovel to force-feed their agenda down Henderson's collective throat. Their preachy-preachy town revival crap was the reason Cooper had extended his stay when he'd come down to handle the sale of his grandparents' farm back in December. Apparently Cooper had swallowed their rubbish, joined their team, and showed up today for the freaking high school's opening baseball game, doing his best to pump some life into the dying town by bringing Orioles no-hitter Cal Johnson along with him.

Well, Marcie thought as she pulled out a mirror and applied more lip gloss, she'd give them all this much. This ridiculous Opening Day Spectacular had hit its mark. And if all had gone according to plan and *she* was now Cooper Crenshaw's fiancée? She would be jumping on board to PR the hell out of this rural cowtown. She could do it too. Had she been in the right frame of mind, she could have thought up a dozen simple, cost-effective campaigns to promote Henderson near and far. She had the ability, and she had the contacts.

But thanks to Brooks Bennett and Vance Evans, Henderson would not be getting the benefit of any of that. In fact, over the last dozen hours, Brooks and Vance had acquired an archenemy. An eager, vengeful, stop-at-nothing, take-no-prisoners supervillain. One who had stood back, watched the dynamics, and cased the situation, and who now knew exactly where their unsuspecting Achilles' heel stood.

All by himself at the bar.

As Ms. Watts stepped from the shadows, her lips twitched in anticipation. Courting the light had been pleasant, she conceded. Cooper Crenshaw and his upstanding values were rare and unique in this day and age. Plotting to win his heart had been a pleasant, if not fruitful, endeavor. But stepping over to the dark side? There was something about taking down the town he loved that promised to be even more satisfying.

"Mayor Stevens?" she purred, catching the attention of the man who stood alone in the crowd. "I'm Marcie Watts. Your new best friend."

Thurgood Lewis Watson III, better known by his nickname, Thor, sat on a worn and cracked vinyl barstool just a few steps away. He was struck by the realization that this was the first time he'd been caught up in a crowd this thick in months.

Maybe longer.

Probably a lot longer.

And he couldn't deny how much he was enjoying the scene even though his body ached like a sonofabitch. He'd been up since the butt-crack of dawn, lifting and toting and hoisting everything from blue-speckled donuts to over-teeming cans of trash. But damn if that crazy cult known as Team Henderson hadn't gone ahead and pulled off a true *Spectacular*.

Watching the rowdy crowd on the dance floor, Thor would have bet good money the place hadn't been this jacked up in years. In fact, his hometown had seemed on the brink of falling off the map the day he'd received his commission. Hardly a soul from his graduating class had stuck around. Now, after six years of service and a thank-you-but-no-thank-you to the Army's offer to reenlist, he'd come back to what, in comparison, seemed like a thriving metropolis.

Okay, that might be a little extreme. *Today* Henderson seemed like a thriving metropolis with all the locals, past residents, extended family, and every goddamn baseball fan from here to Raleigh swarming around. But Thor was happy to give credit where it was due. Thanks to Brooks Bennett and his team of crazy-ass do-gooders, Thor's hometown was turning itself around. And everyone was celebrating because of it.

Thor watched the antics as he sipped his beer ... his second beer. Well, make that his third beer since the party started. He wasn't tipsy. At six-foot-four and well over two hundred pounds, he was too damn big for a couple of beers to fuzz him up. But the alcohol certainly seemed to be easing his muscles. And maybe he wouldn't admit it out loud, but Pinks and the Outlaw's little band rocking out on that makeshift stage was reviving his spirits. That, along with all the soft and pretty he couldn't drag his gaze from.

Yep. There were a lot of girls in the room tonight: Old friends he'd attended school with who managed to make that impending thirty-year mark look good. Young cuties he hardly recognized after being abroad for so long. Plus a whole new gaggle of women he assumed had worked their way into Henderson from neighboring Oxford. Probably hoping for an up-close-and-personal with Cal Johnson, the young, deadly handsome major league pitching phenom who'd put on a helluva demonstration this afternoon.

Yep. Lots of good-looking girls. Damn if he couldn't drum up interest in more than one.

His obsession with Melissa McReady started the moment he'd set eyes on her two months ago. Didn't make a lick of sense either. The twenty-four-year-old overachiever had corporate America written all over her. Of course, he'd been sitting at rock bottom for a helluva long time when she'd come into town to interview with Team Henderson. No doubt one look at her was the equivalent of a breath of fresh air to a man who'd been trapped inside an overflowing shithouse.

He'd seen things in Afghanistan. In Iraq. In Kuwait. He'd seen all kinds of things. Felt the euphoria of victory and tasted the agony of his fellow Rangers' defeat. But nothing had swamped him nearly so much as being home a total of two stupid weeks last spring and then having his widowed father—a healthy, strong, ox of a man—drop dead from a sudden brain aneurysm.

"Just his time," the doctor had said. "No good explanation for it, and nobody could have done anything. *You* couldn't have done anything," the doc made a point to tell Thor. "This is just how it happens sometimes." Because his pop was fit. And young. So damned young.

And happy to have Thor home.

So happy to have him back that Pop hadn't gotten around to bringing up the subject that had kept the two of them at odds for most of Thor's life.

Fuck it, Thor thought. Not going there. Too much fun happening right under my nose. *I am not going back there.* He was grateful when the man of the hour chose that moment to sidle up to the bar and take a load off.

Brooks Bennett was nothing but a positive flow of sunshine when he was in public. Thor had known the guy forever. Had followed a year behind him all through school. Brooks was the star pitcher of their high school baseball team—and that would be *The* baseball team—the team that handed little ol' Henderson its first state championship. Ever since Brooks's freshman year, he'd been the poster boy for all things good in Henderson. And it was probably a real pain in the guy's ass, but he'd handled it with finesse and a whole lot of grace.

"Nice job today," Thor said to Brooks while trying to get the bartender's much desired attention. "Allow me to buy you a beer."

"Not necessary," Brooks said, easing onto the barstool next to Thor and wiping his hands over his face as if trying to transition out of campaign-for-mayor mode and into just-another-guy-at-the-party mode.

Good luck with that.

Although, Thor supposed, that *was* the beauty of Henderson. Still the favorite son, Brooks had served as today's master of ceremonies and was about six months away from being the town's new mayor. *The Spectacular* was his idea. Bring people back to Henderson at the start of baseball season and celebrate all the championship-winning teams that had come before. Thus creating an opportunity for Team Henderson to show off where the town was growing, improving, and giving residents hope for the future. Taking the opportunity to shine a light on the field of dreams Brooks thought Henderson to be.

"You deserve a beer and then some," Thor said, pointing out to Ed—the owner of The Situation—that Brooks needed a beer and for him to put it on Thor's tab. It wasn't twenty seconds later Ed had an ice cold, longneck bottle sliding into Brooks's empty hand.

"Thanks, Ed." Brooks motioned a toast. "And thank you," he said, turning back to Thor.

"My pleasure. What do you make of all this?"

Brooks shook his head in awe, taking in the spread of bodies before him. Tucked against the bar and up on stools, the two of them had a clear view of the crowded—meaning hardly any room to move—dance floor. The entire place was packed and everyone was having a good time.

"Another dream come true," Brooks said after taking a long guzzle. "A damn dream come true." He smiled, knocking his beer against the glass in Thor's hand. "Big win for the baseball team. Even bigger crowd. And word is getting out. Henderson has plans. Big plans. People are signing up right and left for the digital newsletter. I'll tell you, this event is turning into a hell of a springboard."

"You're a good man, Brooks." Thor took a moment to pat him on the back for real. "Good for this town. The right man at the right time. The difference you and your worshipers are making here is real—"

"My worshipers?" Brooks interrupted.

"The Evanses, the DuVals, the whole Team Henderson crew. Which now includes the Langfords apparently. Did you have any idea Rye Langford was going to get on his soapbox like he did this afternoon and light a fucking fire under generations of Hendersonians?"

"No idea at all," Brooks said. "None." He turned and gave Thor his full attention. "But I gotta tell you, it's about damn time our parents' generation joined in the fight to save this town."

Thor gave him a slow, knowing grin. "That torch you've been carrying starting to feel a little heavy?"

"For about ten years, it's felt like a damn pipe dream. But after the turnout today? And with what we've got planned for the future?" Brooks shook his head. "Getting Rye and his cronies onboard was just the first domino to fall. Mark my words, now things are really going to happen."

"I believe it. *Now.* Because I did not see this coming. I thought you'd get a nice crowd of townies. Maybe a couple fanatical baseball fans coming in to see Hall of Famer Nate the Great and good ol' Cal over there. But this? This is like a high school reunion on steroids. And after Rye Langford's Knute Rockne-style rah-rah speech, I'm tellin' ya. I'm a believer."

"Good. Team Henderson meets Monday mornings at ten. Put it on your calendar."

"What? Oh, hell no," Thor declared.

"You just said you're a believer."

"Yeah. I believe you and your followers are gonna get this done. Put Henderson on the map. And I'm happy to drink a beer at any and all of your future Spectaculars. But I'm done with the teammate thing."

"Bullshit. You were all over the damn place today helping out. Don't think I didn't see you holding the day together with a bit of twine and some chewing gum, MacGyver style."

Thor snorted. "I wasn't doing that for Team Henderson."

"I know exactly who you were doing it for. Which is why your ass ought to be in E&E's conference room every Monday. That little number from the north runs our meetings."

"Yeah," Thor said, taking a good, long drink from his beer as his eyes slid to the little number in question. *The* girl. The one who'd put the spark back into his life.

"Be a great way to get more face time with Missy."

Thor shrugged.

"Tell me you aren't panting at her heels and I'll call you a damn liar," Brooks argued. "Now that Pinks and Scarlett have been outed— and don't get me started on *that* by the way—you've got a clear shot at sealin' the deal with one very fine-looking lady lacrosse coach."

"Seal the deal?" Thor huffed out a sarcastic laugh. "I guess you haven't heard."

"Heard what?"

"Well, according to her childhood buddy, Pinks, Missy has put a deadline on all things Henderson."

"What!"

"Apparently the girl who helped you knock today's Spectacular out of the park is not as enamored with Henderson as Henderson is with her."

"Well, why the fuck not?" Brooks shouted.

"Dude." Thor held up a hand. "Do not kill the messenger. Although I'm happy to learn from your reaction that you aren't interested in seeing her leave town either."

"Hell. We need her. Pinks needs her. We are getting too damn busy, and she pulled this event off in a month's time practically by herself. Made it bigger and better than I ever imagined it could be. No." Brooks shook his head. "She can't leave. In fact, I am putting you in charge of making sure she doesn't. Seeing as you're a former member of America's legendary 75th Ranger Regiment, I have complete confidence in your ability to survey the situation, plan out an attack, and execute domination. I am counting on you to come through victorious. And you can count on me and all my *worshipers* to give you whatever support you need."

Thor chuckled. "Fine, I am on the job."

"All right then." Brooks seemed relieved.

Thor watched him check his watch. "You got a late date?"

"Matter of fact, I do. Most likely in about … thirty minutes."

"Really? Because as sure as I'm sittin' here, your little Lollypop is on the dance floor screaming her lungs out for the drummer in the band. A.k.a. her *ex-boyfriend*, Pinks."

"All part of the master plan," Brooks said into his beer, but his eyes were stuck like glue on Lolly DuVal.

"Seriously?" Thor reared back. "I have seen the veins in your neck pulse whenever the guy so much as breathes in Lolly's direction."

Brooks waved that off.

"All right. If watching her go crazy for the Dynamic Duo gets you off, you are a better man than I."

Brooks leaned in conspiratorially. "I have learned from past experience that Lolly getting all riled up on the dance floor leads to a lot of hot and heavy breathing. The kind that's been known to steam up the windows of my truck."

"Well, don't look now, but I think Lolly just took off her sweater and threw it into the crowd."

Brooks rubbed his hands together. "Means it's only a matter of time before I get to haul her ass out of here."

Thor stared at Henderson's future mayor a little in awe.

"It's how she rolls." Brooks shrugged. "At first I took issue, until I figured out it was all foreplay. Suffice it to say I now look forward to the times Lolly is under stress and Pinks and the Outlaw start up the band. That combination has worked out very, very well for me."

Thor shook his head. "Are you suggesting I tamp down my unmitigated jealousy that Missy is out there screaming for Pinks right along with Lolly?"

"Man, I'm telling you, just let it go. The Outlaw and Pinks can light their fires or even fan the flames. You just want to be within arm's reach when things start burning out of control."

Thor let his gaze settle back on the one he desired. She couldn't get lost in that crowd. Not from him. His internal homing device could pick her out of the throng at any given moment. He'd been aware of Melissa McReady all night. All day actually. Well, hell, for two damn months.

From the moment he had laid eyes on her, his world lit up. And up to that point, his world had been crap. Deep crap. Something about the girl from Baltimore got him turned around, in spite of him scaring the shit out of her the first time she'd seen him. And wasn't that a fine howdy-do?

Thank God Vance Evans had the sense to intervene, ordering Thor to get himself cleaned up before he was properly introduced to Missy. Because once Thor got around to taking a look in the mirror, he hadn't recognized the man reflected there. He hadn't shaved since his pop's funeral. Looked like one of those Unabomber types holed up somewhere off the grid. Definitely not the impression he wanted to make on a city girl.

So he got out his razor and then headed into Raleigh for a decent haircut. Two days later he presented himself at E&E and *poof.* The dang girl was gone.

So he waited.

Waited for her to move from Baltimore and into her new job in Henderson.

Didn't take him long to make his move after that. Though it had proven to be an uphill battle. Yeah, he might have gotten a taste of her supple pink lips fairly quickly, but she'd been tipsy on champagne at the time, and it had become darn obvious she was hankering after the Pride of Baltimore. Pinks. The Ninja. Fucking Davis Williams who could be or do or have anything he wanted.

Even Melissa.

But as it turns out, even with all the shit that had been thrown at him during his lifetime, Thor was starting to consider that there might be a God after all. Because for some unfathomable reason, Davis—Pinks—did not want *the* girl.

No, Pinks had been all caught up in young Scarlett Langford, and thank God for that, because he was welcome to her. And as Missy had become increasingly aware that Pinks's attention was elsewhere, she'd also become more aware of Thor.

And his somewhat unwelcome situation.

Especially in her eyes, apparently.

Whatever.

She was in Henderson for the next three months. And as Brooks had decreed, Thor's mission—and he had no other choice but to accept it—was to get the girl so enamored with Henderson, her job, and more to the point, *him*, that she wouldn't want to leave after her coaching foray with the high school lacrosse team ended.

Thor remained undaunted. He'd been working on a long-term plan all along. That pretty girl over there, laughing and dancing and carrying on with the rest of this town's debutantes, was going to be wearing his last name if he had anything to say about it. Because underneath the competent, corporate, competitive persona, there was something so soft about her, something that drew him in like no other girl ever had. He hadn't quite been able to put his finger on it because she also had this way of pissing him off on a regular basis. So yeah—he couldn't exactly say what he was so attached to.

Of course, there was her hair. Well, yeah—crazy long when she wore it down, which was like never. Shades of buttercup mixed with honey and brown sugar. And curls. When she wore it down, the damn stuff fell in waves over her shoulders and the ends curled up in a way that made his nuts ache. There were her eyes. Not blue, not green, but that perfect Caribbean Sea color right in between. *Soft.* Those eyes possessed a determined glint when she was coaching her posse and had a twinkle in them when she was running the show over at E&E. But he sure didn't miss how they'd turned soft and misty when she pulled back from kissing him.

And, oh God, that smile. That sweet little grin she liked to toss at him like it wasn't going to set him on fire.

The woman was living dangerously, truth be told. Thor had restraint. Plenty of it. Being an Army Ranger, he'd developed a discipline he didn't forget and probably wouldn't likely overcome. But those times when Missy let go of her give-'em-hell, competitive persona, those times when she'd give him a glimpse into the soft underneath the tough. Ahh. He'd wait a lifetime for those moments. And yeah, at first he simply enjoyed them. Revisited them in his bed each night. Did his best to plant himself into some part of her day so he might be lucky enough to glimpse it again.

But now? Recently? Discipline was slipping from his grasp as if it were a toddler's balloon being coaxed by the wind. That sweet little zephyr was slowly building, bringing on the occasional gust. Hell, he wasn't above pressing the issue with Missy, but that wasn't going to get him where he ultimately wanted to go.

He'd heard the stories from Pinks himself. In high school, college, and the three years since, this crazy female with all her feminine accoutrements had laid waste to many a man before him. So he'd been playing it differently. He hadn't minced words, but he'd been taking his time. Following her lead.

As he contemplated this, watching his girl—well, *the* girl—he saw Lolly rip off another article of clothing, causing Brooks to groan next to him. And then Thor noticed Melissa's eyes searching the room and then … yep, land right on him. He literally wanted to clutch his heart because that sassy, little grin she shot him felt so good it hurt.

He licked his lips as she started heading his way.

"Hey," she called, squeezing through the crowd to reach him and Brooks.

"Hey, yourself," Brooks responded.

Those blue-green eyes flashed in Thor's direction before she and Brooks started chatting. Thor wouldn't call her voice soft. No. But it was definitely pleasant. Feminine without being too high-pitched or babyfied. Apparently, she convinced Brooks that Lolly had shed just about all the clothes he wanted to see her take off in public, so off he went, vacating his bar stool.

Thor nodded his head to the empty stool, indicating Missy should have a seat. Maybe if he started plying her with alcohol, she'd forget all about his rural lifestyle and why she probably didn't want to kiss him tonight. But low and behold, she surprised him by doing one better.

She brought on the soft.

Woman snuggled herself in between his knees. Worked her way right between his thighs and leaned in like he was her man. And damn if his body didn't respond as if he truly was. Without giving it a thought, he lowered his chin and kissed the sweet-scented hair on top of her head as her arms wrapped around his waist and her upper body sank against his chest. He could feel the stress and adrenaline of the day draining from her.

Feel her go soft.

"Proud of you," he whispered. "What you did today. Never losing your cool, no matter what came up." He caught the eye of the bartender and ordered her drink. "Vodka, water, and lime for sweet Melissa over here."

Her head popped up, her brows pulled together over a cute little smirk. "My dad calls me that."

"Sweet Melissa?"

"Melissa. As an endearment. Everyone else calls me Missy, but my dad … and you—" She shrugged.

"Pretty name for a pretty girl," he said, taking the drink from the bartender and handing it to her. "To you—*Melissa*—and to a job well done."

Her lips started moving, but she was smiling through the words so he didn't hear them, too caught up in the feel of her standing between his knees. But when she set her drink down on the bar and deliberately rubbed her hands along the tops of his thighs, he tuned in. Big time.

"Thank you," she said sincerely. "For backing me up. Today and over the last several weeks. I needed it, and I appreciate it." She glanced over at the stage before bringing her regard back to him. "I'm sure you've noticed that my infatuation with the Pride of Baltimore has died a slow death." She grinned bashfully. "The two of us are close friends, and I have fully resolved he's not my Mr. Right." She tilted her head and gave Thor that soft smile that shot right to his heart. "And then there's you," she said, her brows lifting. "My strong, all-purpose, no-cape-necessary hero. With your big red truck."

He laughed at that. It was no secret she liked his truck and all it could do for her. Toting lacrosse goals and equipment when she'd needed. He was wondering what it would take to get her out of the bar and into said truck when she lowered her voice, her mesmerizing sea-green eyes locking tight with his own when she admitted, "I'm worried about leading you on."

Well. *Damn.*

Thor held her gaze, wondering if she was aware that her Pinks had tattled and given Thor a heads up. Had told him in no uncertain terms that when it came to Missy, he was on the clock. And now, well, she'd just confirmed it.

He glanced over at the band, wondering how to respond. Christ, he was putty in her hands. Because honest to God, he had no choice. If she was interested in a casual relationship—well good, fine, great— he'd take advantage of that and see where it got him. He had three months to make his case—to change her mind and make her his—or watch her walk out of his life.

So he let the need his body felt for her fill him. Let the desire he tried to keep at bay show in his eyes and in his grin as he looked back at her. He took his time clasping the back of her head, leaning his mouth up against her ear. The words he spoke came out exactly the way he felt. Heavy. Ripe. Eager.

"Pretty Girl, I am *begging* you to lead me on."

It might have taken her a second to think it over. But there was no mistaking her let's-get-out-of-here grin as she took him by the hand and pulled him from the stool.

Thor set his beer on the bar and followed her through the dense crowd, eyes trained on nothing but her ass in those faded blue jeans.

Holy shit, this day was indeed turning out to be spectacular.

CHAPTER TWO

As soon as they stepped into the night air, Missy felt Thor latch on to her hand and take the lead. They weren't friends, really. Weren't lovers—yet. But it had never been a secret how he felt about her.

And over the past month, with all the people she was getting to know here in Henderson, the only one who had really cared about where she was, how she spent her time, or what she was thinking about was Thor. So sue her if she wanted to spend a little quality time celebrating the day with the same outdoorsy hunk whose Southern-boy accent had started working its way into her dreams. As long as *Mr. Wrong* knew where she stood, she was willing to throw caution to the wind and indulge.

So yeah, when he swung her around and then deliberately backed her up against his truck, she did a very un-Missy like thing and giggled. And she didn't hesitate to smile up into those stunning, yet completely unnerving, neon-blue eyes.

Over the past several weeks, Thor had earned her trust and her admiration. Tonight, she'd be giving him a whole lot more.

She watched him move in slow, with an amused expression and a whole lot of intent. "You finally taking yourself off the clock?" he asked.

She nodded, lifting her chin to keep eye contact as he loomed over her. "If The Situation runs out of beer, they're on their own."

"Good." He turned her around abruptly. With two hands he managed to untangle the large clip from her hair before she was able to reach up and thwart his efforts. The messy knot she'd created early that morning fell, cascading over her shoulders as she spun around in time to see him toss the thing over his shoulder.

"Thor!"

"You wear your hair up when you work and when you coach."

"Yeah, because it gets in my way."

He shrugged. "I don't mind it getting in my way." As if to prove his point, he plied his fingers into the depths of it, helping to sort it out. "I like it down," he whispered, distracted as he watched it fan out.

Her mouth slapped shut with a quiet, "Oh."

"You had it down for your interview," he said quietly, still fooling with it. "Wore it down with that lavender dress at the wedding your first night here. Maybe you didn't recognize me without the godawful red beard and long hair," he said bringing his gaze back to hers, "but I couldn't take my eyes off you."

Missy bit her lip. He looked so different from the first time she'd seen him. Two months ago, his big imposing form, unkempt hair, and Duck Dynasty beard made him look like some sort of mountain recluse. His clothes had hung on him, making his appearance even more haggard. The GQ pinup she encountered at the Langford wedding a month later was polished and sexy, with his thick rust-colored hair styled and his gorgeous angular jaw closely shaved. No way had she recognized him. But the man who was stepping into her personal space right now was so much more *Thor* than either one of those variations. She continually likened him to an L.L.Bean model. Robust and handsome, dressed in flannel, denim, and work boots.

"You wore your hair down the night I picked you up and took you to the Evanses' for dinner." Thor continued, rubbing the ends of a curl between his fingers. His gaze landed on hers with a weighty stare. "I like it down."

"Good to know." She swallowed, suddenly feeling nervous.

His large hands eased up the sides of her face and tilted her head back, positioning them forehead to forehead. "Been a good day," he told her, his words falling down in a heated whisper across her lips. "Just wanna take a moment and make sure you and I are on the same page. If it's not how you see the night playing out, we can renegotiate."

Torn between giving him a green-light kiss or one of her flippant comebacks, Missy found the idea of needling him just too tempting. "Renegotiate?" One brow rose in question.

Thor took a slight step back, causing the cool night air to slip into the space between them. "If need be."

"Like a contract?"

"An understanding," he said, wrapping one arm around her waist, pulling her away from the truck and up against him. He stole a quick kiss and then brushed her hair from her face. The twinkle in his neon eyes wasn't guarded or hesitant. It might have been aroused, but mostly Missy thought it was amused. And that mouth of his was sporting a sexy smirk the likes of which he'd yet to expose.

"Are you laughing at me?" For the first time, she felt like she was losing the upper hand.

But he shook his head and gazed toward the heavens. "No, Pretty Girl, I'm not laughing at you." He brought his eyes back to her. "If anything, I'm laughing at the Cowboy."

"The Cowboy?" Missy thought back to her first night in Henderson. "Cash Carraway? At the wedding?"

"Yeah. The Cowboy. Who I'm fairly certain thought you were a sure thing when he locked the two of you inside that cloakroom."

"Oh, yeah. Cash was definitely putting on the full-court press. Until that bartender came to the rescue."

"Yup, Harry. Harry was on my side," Thor claimed.

"Your side?"

"Who do you think sent him down there to knock on the damn door?"

"*You?*"

"Of course, me. Somebody had to save you from yourself."

"Save me from myself?" Missy playfully pushed Thor's broad chest and leaned back against his truck, crossing her arms.

"Pretty sure the way the guy was pawing you all night he wasn't planning to build in any time for negotiations."

"No negotiating necessary. If Cash went too far—if *you* go too far—trust me, you'll know it."

"How?" he asked, making a show of his size by stepping back into her personal space.

"Because I will not hesitate to smack you upside the head, that's how."

"Yeah?" he said, wrapping her up in his arms. "See, I'm not interested in getting smacked upside the head. Or you pushing my hand away when I get the urge to touch you somewhere I haven't had the pleasure of touching you yet."

Missy grinned against his shoulder, remembering swatting his hand the first time he'd put it on her knee. He'd been nothing but a gentleman ever since.

"No doubt the Cowboy was struggling with a case of blue balls at the end of the night. While I had you in my truck, on my lap, with my tongue down your throat."

"Mmm," she hummed. "That *was* quite a night."

"Damn fickle woman."

She chuckled. "Are you ever going to let me live that down?"

"Nope. So let me open negotiations by saying that I have zero interest in standing in line for your attention ever again."

"Good Lord." She pressed back enough to make a grand show of ticking off her fingers. "Davis is with Scarlett. The Cowboy is in Dallas. And *I* practically propositioned *you* back in the bar."

"I accept." He leaned in, all grins and swagger, and laid a sultry kiss on her lips at the same time asking, "My place or yours?"

There was a knock on the tailgate causing both their heads to turn.

"Pardon the interruption," Brooks said, still tapping on the truck while he had one arm firmly wrapped around Lolly.

"This better be good," Thor griped.

"Tell me about it," Brooks said doggedly. "Lolly and I were right where you two are headed when my phone blew up. Come on," he said, backing away and pulling Lolly with him. "Turns out, Cal Johnson can sing. He's on stage and apparently good enough to leave what you're gettin' to until later. I've got over twenty texts telling me we do not want to miss it."

"Happy to miss it," Thor said, at the same time Missy ducked under and out of his arms.

"What? Cal's on stage?" she asked, skipping after them. "Singing?"

Thor stomped after her. "Don't tell me you're into Cal Johnson. What the hell did we just negotiate? I swear to God, you are the most fickle woman ever to walk the streets of Henderson. Are you hearing me?" he shouted from behind as Missy followed after Brooks and Lolly.

She turned, walking backward, shooting him a cheeky little smile. "I'm not into Cal, and I'm only a little fickle," she promised.

His long legs caught up, and he grabbed her around the middle, pulling her with him so they could catch up to Brooks and Lolly. "You kiss Cal tonight and there will be hell to pay. It was your idea to drag me out here," he reminded her. "I left half a beer sitting on the damn bar."

Lolly turned to Missy, rolling her eyes. "Brooks was acting the same way. But seriously, it's Cal Johnson. None of us are going to want to miss this."

Cal Johnson wasn't from Henderson. But he'd managed to shake things up good when he'd stumbled into town looking for his coach back in December. Right after he'd won the *Rookie of the Year* title for his phenomenal season in the Orioles pitching lineup. Possessing the vigor of youth, striking good looks, and crazy sexy hair, there wasn't a sports fan in the country who didn't know his name. He was darn good at throwing a baseball over the plate, and as the four of them shoved their way back into The Situation, it was shocking to hear that he was also darn good at singing.

The packed house sat mesmerized and silent as Cal sang a ballad a cappella, down on one knee in front of Nate the Great's daughter. Brooks scanned the crowd, taking it all in before turning and dropping a dumbfounded look on Missy. "Are you thinking what I'm thinking?" he whispered.

Missy licked her lips, noticing all the phones recording the moment. "Henderson's going viral," she whispered, bringing her gaze to Brooks.

The two of them broke into huge grins.

"Damn if this doesn't have Pinks's fingerprints all over it, and frankly, for once, I could kiss the son of a bitch," Brooks said.

"As long as *you* don't kiss the son of a bitch," Thor whispered over Missy's shoulder.

She burst out laughing and turned toward Thor as the entire place erupted in shouts, cheers, and applause. When the band started playing Maroon 5's "Sugar," she grabbed Thor by the hand. "You're the only one I plan on kissing," she promised. "But first we're celebrating." She pulled him through the crowd onto the already overcrowded dance floor, the party picking up as Cal Johnson hung on to the microphone and rocked out like he'd been born onstage.

"What if I don't dance?" Thor protested, making a great show of lagging behind.

When she had him positioned where she wanted, Missy swung herself up against him good and tight. "Fake it," she insisted.

He grinned down at her, snaking his hands over her hips and settling them into the back pockets of her jeans. "Now *this* works for me."

"See, I can negotiate," she teased with her lips up against his chin. "I don't want you upset about being back inside."

"Well you're not up on stage sucking face with Cal yet so, so far so good."

She laughed. "I'd say I'd give up men, but I guess that wouldn't really do you any good."

"As long as I'm grandfathered in, I'd be all for it."

Her brows rose. "You really are quite the negotiator."

He took her hand and spun her under his arm, dancing them forward toward the band as some room opened up on the floor. "And I can dance when I have to."

He could. As the party raged on toward midnight, Missy discovered that the God of Thunder really could dance.

Thor probably should have seen it coming the moment Brooks brought shots out to him and Missy on the dance floor. Well, that was all right, he figured, because damn if there wasn't reason for Brooks and Missy to celebrate. It was later, however when Missy and Lolly decided another shot sounded like a real good idea and took their shapely little behinds off toward the bar that Thor began to see the writing on the wall.

Tonight was not gonna be the night.

Sure, he was happy to see Missy bonding with Lolly. He just needed to tamp down Little Thor's expectations. He tried to convince himself that as long as he was the one taking her home, he could bide his time. After all, he'd done it for over two months now. First waiting on her to come back and then waiting on her to get over the Pride of Baltimore. And as Brooks had said, Thor now had a straight shot at convincing Missy he was worth her time and energy. Worth extending her stay in Henderson indefinitely to see what the two of them could work out.

As he watched Missy and Lolly live it up over at the bar with Cal Johnson, who thank God, had his hands all over Nate the Great's daughter, Natalie, and not *his* Melissa, a familiar baritone captured his attention.

"Who's the babe?"

"Thatcher." Thor's broad grin greeted his childhood friend. "Damnit, man." He pushed himself off the wall he'd been leaning against, grabbed his buddy's hand, and went in for a bro hug. "How the hell are you?"

"Great," Thatcher Jones said on a laugh. "And damn glad I decided to stop by now that I've run into you. Sure good seeing your lame ass showered up and that Grizzly Adams beard gone from your face."

"Yeah, I was going through a rough patch."

"Can't blame you. You shipping out soon?"

"No. I've decided I'm done. Served my time and then some. Figured there's gotta be more to life than taking orders."

"Yeah? I'm not so sure about that."

"Sounds like you're still working for your pop."

"Always, although at least we've diversified."

"Diversified?"

"He still grows sod, but when everybody started building artificial turf fields, I learned how to do that. Now, as the pendulum swings back and the trend is to reinstall grass, we're good coming and going."

"So you know a thing or two about building athletic fields?"

"I know everything there is to know about athletic fields. I build 'em and maintain 'em. Although I don't have a damn bit of time to play on one."

"I hear that. Hey, you happen to talk to Brooks Bennett today?" Thor asked, patting Thatcher on the shoulder.

"Couldn't get within ten feet of the guy."

"Well, it'd be worth hanging around and having a word. From what I understand, Henderson is looking to build a sports academy in the very near future. An academy with nothing but athletic fields from here to Oxford. You may want to remind him what you and your pop are doing these days. Get in on that deal early."

"Damn. A sports academy? Right here in Henderson? We sure could use that kind of business."

"You and everyone else."

"So is that your deal? Your part in this *Save Henderson* movement?"

Thor shook his head. "Not me. I mean, I totally support it, but I'm not involved in the sports academy. Truth be told, I'm having trouble sorting this civilian shit out. Definitely trying to figure out what I'm gonna do with all the land I've been saddled with."

"What'd ya mean, figure it out? Your pop had a helluva sweet deal renting out that land to big tobacco. Re-up those contracts, sit back, and watch the money grow."

Thor shook his head. "I'm not growing tobacco."

"Grow sod," Thatcher suggested.

"Thatch, I'm no farmer."

"Yeah, but you've got land. Farming land. Something sure as shit ought to be growing on it. How 'bout I stop by. Talk to you about the sod business. Give you some food for thought, as they say."

"Why the hell not? Lord knows I need to talk to somebody," he mumbled. "You still living in Chapel Hill?"

"I am. Great little town. Everything at your fingertips."

"So you aren't planning to move back to Henderson?"

Thatcher shook his head. "Not me. I come back regularly to see the folks, but there's nothing in this town for me. Although I might be rethinking that now that I've seen the fine piece of ass you had your hands all over on the dance floor."

"Yeah-no. You and your blond-haired, blue-eyed baby face can just hightail it back to Chapel Hill. I've been working long and hard for that one."

"From the way your fangs extended when ol' Neil tried to cut in, I figured you were feeling territorial." Thatcher grinned. "Who is she?"

"Newcomer. Works for Evans & Evans Investments as a consultant. Marketing and Event Planning. She's the one who put today's gig together."

"She got Cal Johnson and Nate the Great to Henderson?" Thatcher asked in awe.

"It was a team effort."

"Good team," Thatcher noted.

"Yeah, they did all right. How 'bout I buy you a beer?"

"Save your money. Just introduce me to your girl."

"She's not exactly my girl. Yet."

"Hmm. So if I went over and introduced myself?"

"You know that sod your daddy grows? You'd wind up six feet under it."

"Dude." Thatch laughed. "Sadie Love aware of this newcomer?"

"Sadie and I have not consorted in years."

"Seriously? Because while you were fondling your foxy blonde, I was watching Sadie watching you." Thatcher held out his arm indicating Thor's ex. Thor swung around just in time to see Sadie and Carla Christensen scuttle up to him and Thatcher.

"Ladies," Thatch said, reaching out his arm to give Carla a hug. "Long time no see."

"Thor," Carla said.

"Carla. Sadie. Good to see you two. Still thick as thieves?" Thor asked.

"Oh, we hardly ever get to see each other," Sadie pouted. "Carla's over in Oxford now, and I'm stuck here working at the hospital."

"You a doctor?"

"A nurse practitioner. I actually love it. I just wish that the three of you and the rest of our old gang would move back to town. It's lonely."

"Well, Thor's back," Thatcher helpfully supplied with a grin.

Sadie looked surprised. "I thought you had left shortly after your daddy passed."

"No. But I did hole up pretty good for a while."

"Understandable," Carla said. "That was quite a shock. My mom had my dad in for a physical the following week. Your daddy was in such good shape no one could reconcile his passing."

"Least of all me," Thor said.

"You doing okay, sugar?" Sadie asked running her hand up his arm.

Thor glanced over in Missy's direction, and yep, there she was, not missing a bit of the Sadie Love show. He sent Missy a wink and a smile, grateful when she smiled back.

"I'm still shook up," Thor answered honestly. "Miss the man every day. Now that he's gone, I've got a million questions I need to ask him." When there was nothing but silence, Thor went on. "I appreciate y'all remembering him. I really do. And I sure like seeing all of you back here in town. But if you'll excuse me, I've got to get back to my date."

"Your date?" Sadie asked.

"Melissa McReady."

"Do I know her?"

"She's new in town. I'll be happy to introduce you. Missy," he called.

And over she came. On her tiptoes. All smiles underneath unusually rosy cheeks. Must have done another shot by the tipsy little grin she was sporting. She stopped at the edge of the gathering, clasping her left elbow with her right hand, swaying a little but looking cute as shit as she did. The competitive athlete had retired for the night, leaving nothing but soft.

"Missy, these are some of my old friends. Thatcher Jones, one of my longtime buddies. We played football and basketball together all through school. And since he grew up on a farm just like I did, we were both stuck with the same *hick* label."

Missy shot him a guilty little smirk before addressing Thatcher. "Nice to meet you."

"And this is Sadie Love," Thor went on. "She grew up privileged."

"What?" Sadie said, aghast.

"Hell, you lived in the biggest house in town. Right next to the country club."

"Okay. I did. But, yeesh," she said, smiling at Thor instead of greeting Missy. So Thor moved on.

"And this is Sadie's old partner in crime, Carla Christensen. The two of them were as inseparable as Siamese twins back in the day."

"We were," Carla told Missy. "And now I live over in Oxford, and it seems we never find time to get together. Where are you from, Missy?"

"Baltimore."

"Oh, so you know Cal Johnson?"

"Only as a fan. I had the pleasure of meeting him in person just this morning."

"I like him," Carla said. "I mean he's young and all, but come on. That hair? Those eyes? That voice! I'm a baseball fan from way back, but I didn't know he could sing."

"Nobody did. Tonight was his big singing debut," Missy said. "So you're the first in on the scoop."

"Henderson having any sort of scoop would be a first."

Missy held up a finger. "Hang in there. There's a team of us devoted to making sure Henderson not only *has* the latest scoop but *becomes* the latest scoop."

Sadie sighed. "Good luck to y'all. I'll believe it when I see it."

"They gotcha Cal Johnson, didn't they?" Thor pointed out. "What more could you want?"

"Touché," Thatcher said. "Come on, girls, I'm buying."

Thor grabbed a hold of Missy's arm, holding her back as the others headed toward the bar. It caused her to stumble into him, and when she giggled about it, the sound lit up his world. That and the way she had her hands splayed against his chest. The heat of her touch always jacked him up. But feeling her fingertips test his pecs made his brain focus on one thing only—getting the two of them naked.

"You really are quite stunning," she sort of whispered as she watched her fingers poke and prod his chest.

He swallowed thickly, thinking about how much fun it was going to be when he got to return the favor. "I'm glad you think so."

"Everybody thinks so. According to Lolly, you're the second biggest topic of conversation—after Cal."

"I highly doubt that," he countered, taking up her hands in an effort to stop himself from picturing her writhing beneath him.

"That's what she says. *All* the girls want to know what you're doing out there on that big ol' plantation all by yourself," she teased. "And they think your new look is all that."

"All that?" He raised a brow.

She nodded, wrinkling her nose and grinning real cute. "All that."

"And what do you think?" he asked, unable to resist the urge to wrap her up in his arms.

"I think you are yumm-*mee*," she squealed as he squeezed her around the middle.

"You ready to go?"

She shook her head. "Nope. I have it on good authority that the band is playing yet another set, and anyone who is anybody is going to be dancing the night away."

"Including you."

"And you," she insisted. "We can't leave now. Now that Cal's singing, and Brooks is buying, and Davis is with Scarlett, and you and I are …"

"You and I are what?" He lowered his chin and stared directly into her eyes.

"Seein' what's what," she said saucily with an exaggerated Southern accent.

"I'd prefer to get you out of here and *show* you what's what."

She swayed to the side a bit, grinning. "You would?"

"I would."

"Pick up our negotiations?"

"At this late hour, I'm thinking we'll just wing it."

"Okay." The word came out as a pent-up breath through her cute little smile.

He couldn't help it. He smiled back before pulling her in and kissing the top of her head. "Come on," he said into her hair, glancing around the room before grabbing her hand and easing them both toward the door.

Surprised at the clean getaway they managed, Thor felt refreshed by the cold air. The temperature had dropped, reminding him it was March, and although the parking lot had emptied a good bit, there were still plenty of vehicles left to prove the party inside was riding out the late hour. He had a little bit of déjà vu as he opened the passenger door and helped Missy climb inside.

Though he hadn't exactly received a full-speed-ahead signal during their earlier negotiations, once his ass was in the driver's seat, he suspected Missy crawling across the center console and into his lap was as good a sign as any. It took him about a half second to find the lever and slide his seat away from the steering wheel, giving the blond-haired temptress plenty of room to straddle his thighs. The unfamiliar sensation of glee caused him to grin—big—as Missy set about on a mission to plant kisses all over his face. Now *this* was a first.

"Feeling frisky?" he teased.

She pulled back, all sleepy-eyed and cute. "You complaining?"

"Nope." He threaded his fingers into that luxurious hair of hers, easing her head gently in the direction he wanted it to go. "Gotta say, I kinda like it." That last part was mumbled up against her lips.

Lips that were plump—probably because she talked too damn much—and sweet with the taste of some silly girl-shot lingering in her mouth. And as much as Thor thoroughly enjoyed both the feel of her tongue against his and the weight of her body snug up on Little Thor, he was hyper-aware that the two of them were plastered together at the back of a public parking lot.

Apparently, his hand wasn't a bit concerned about the potential lack of privacy because it found its way under her flouncy little see-through top and then slipped under the white tank hugging her torso. "Damn," he whispered, enjoying the feel of her bare skin at last. He purred his contentment into her mouth.

When he felt her hands clutch and release his biceps and the not-so-subtle pelvis-to-pelvis grind she pulled, the pent-up lust they'd both been sittin' on erupted into a fiery make out session. One that involved a lot of noisy lip smacks and a few muted expletives. Christ, he loved having her hands on him.

"Under ... put 'em ... Hell—" He dragged his long-sleeve T-shirt over his head and tossed it into the passenger seat. Then he placed both of her palms solidly against his chest. "Have at it." He cradled her face, pulling her lips against his but leaving enough room for her hands to explore his upper body. Nothing had ever gotten his motor running like the touch from this one. Nothing. And he'd been waiting a long, damn time for it, panting after her like a puppy after its momma.

He didn't want to question too closely how this prime piece of femininity had landed in his lap. Choosing to believe his force of will was so strong even she couldn't escape the single, narrow focus he'd developed the moment he'd laid eyes on her. That deep, inspired desire to make her his. And damn if he wasn't doing just that.

The tipsy babe who'd crawled into his lap was a surprisingly new dimension to the capable woman and dedicated athlete he'd been crushing on. Her playful mood pulled at a part of him he'd practically forgotten. Unearthing it from the rocky debris of loss and anguish that had been weighing him down. Breathing life into the part of him that clung to the idea that life was bigger than the sum of your losses.

Now that Missy was in his arms, with all her defenses abolished for the moment, she seemed somehow smaller, more delicate as he maneuvered his hand back under her clothes to capture a breast and—*shit*—talk about soft. As much as he'd fantasized about this very moment, he certainly didn't anticipate the degree of pleasure touching her so intimately would give him.

And hell if he didn't hear her purr.

He could think of a whole lot of ways to get the two of them off while sitting like this. He just didn't trust that Brooks or somebody else wouldn't come knocking on his tailgate again.

"Pretty Girl," he whispered, as his lips traced a path to her ear. "Let's you and I take this some place more private."

"I'm good," she whispered between kisses.

"Yeah," he said, choking on a laugh while kissing her back. "You are. You're definitely good. But I'm fixin' to make both of us feel a whole lot better."

"Fix it here," she demanded before doing her best to suck his tongue into her mouth.

He groaned. Indulging her. Until it hurt. Until he either had to stop them now or see it done in the parking lot. He tried to kiss-talk some sense into Missy. "Come tomorrow, you aren't gonna want people speculating about—"

"Fiiiine," she said, flouncing back from kissing him—exasperated—as if he were somehow throwing in the towel.

"What?" Thor was stunned. Apparently trying to shield her reputation was costing him points. "Oh, hell no on the fii-ne. We're just going to see about that fii-ne." He pulled that feather light excuse for a shirt over her head and laid the back of his seat flat before the brooding seductress in his arms had a chance to backpedal.

There would be no backpedaling.

Backpedaling was now off the table.

And although Thor knew he was too damn big to be fooling around in a truck, even if it was a helluva big truck, one thing he knew even better? Where there was a will, there was a way. It wasn't graceful, but he managed to pull himself and Missy's sweet body into the back seat of his cab, flipping her underneath him only to groan at the sheer pleasure of finally being exactly where he longed to be.

Missy chuckled softly. "Just when I thought you didn't have game."

"Oh, I've got game. I'm just not usually a player in public," he growled, pulling her tank top and no-nonsense bra down under her breasts so he could kiss the flesh now spilling out. His dick grew hard with that first taste, grazing her pert nipple against his tongue. Make that, his dick grew *harder,* because he'd been sporting a rather lengthy stiffy since she'd crawled onto his lap. And now that the girl who generally couldn't stop talking had been rendered speechless—except for a few pants of desire as he sucked and played and all but swallowed her fabulous tits—started grinding her pelvis up against him, his ability to control himself or the situation was likely to snap.

He dragged his mouth off of what was giving him such pleasure and looked up at her. "That first night I drove you home?" he panted, his voice hoarse to his own ears. "Where I fell asleep beside you?"

"Yeah?" she breathed, not even trying to untangle the fingers she had in his hair.

"I dreamt of us, like this. Right here. In my truck." He kissed her neck. "So I think it's only right that I demonstrate"—he kissed her breast—"exactly"—he kissed her sternum—"what I"—he kissed her belly button—"was doing." His lips landed in the center of the tender flesh just above the waistband of her jeans.

"Wait."

Due to the large chunk of his hair she abruptly tugged, Thor did as she asked and glanced up.

She was smiling. Sweetly.

"Tomorrow," she whispered.

"Tomorrow?"

She nodded. "I'd really like you to … ah … demonstrate what you were dreaming about … tomorrow. Tonight …" She started to scramble up, pushing at his shoulders and guiding him into a sitting position as she came up on her knees, "I had something else in mind." She looked him over, seeming to assess their cramped quarters. "Can you …um… sort of flip us around?"

"Flip us around, how?"

"Ah, you lying down." She directed with her fingers. "And me on top."

"Not a problem." With an arm around her waist, he pulled her tight against him and scooted himself underneath, his left leg bent with his foot on the seat while his right leg sprawled over the reclined seat back and into the front. Missy tucked herself between his spread legs with a generous portion of her weight snuggled right up where he could enjoy it. Whatever play the lady coach had in mind was okay with him because she'd used the word *tomorrow*. And since he was after as many of her tomorrows as he could collect, he was more than willing to follow her game plan. Especially when her fingers went to work on his fly.

Seriously, at this point, all he could do was grin.

He noticed she grinned back, definitely bringing on the playful, as she wrestled with the button on his jeans and tugged at the zipper. She didn't take her eyes from his. "You look like you're enjoying this already."

"What gave me away?" he asked, clasping his hands behind his head, intent on watching whatever she was gonna do. He was only too happy to straighten out his leg and lift his hips as she tugged his jeans down far enough to expose most of his ever-expanding cock.

Then she let out a sound he tried hard to reconcile. "Did you just … *giggle*?" He was incredulous. "At my—at Little Thor?"

"Little?" She blinked. "*Little Thor*? You call this monst—" She stopped herself. "Master—" She stopped herself again and shook her head, not taking her eyes off the exposed half of his dick. "Honestly, I don't know whether to call it a monster or a masterpiece."

Springing up to a sitting position, Thor clasped a hand around the back of her head, guiding her lips to his mouth while his other hand guided her palm to his monster masterpiece. "Masterpiece," he whispered, barely getting the word out as his whole body shivered with that first *holy-shit-that's-amazing* touch of her hand. "Call it a masterpiece"—he panted—"and the two of us will love you forever."

He was in no way kidding.

"Mmmmm," she hummed against his lips as her palm stroked slowly down the tip of his shaft all the way to the base of his balls. He felt her fingers wrap around the girth and squeeze. His hips jerked forward.

"Damn that's good," he said on a deep inhale, wanting to pull her closer. Wanting his pants off. Wanting her naked. Really naked. Wanting her naked, on top of his naked. Really wishing like hell he wasn't *stuck in this goddamn truck*.

"Relax," she whispered, stroking the side of his face with one hand, while stroking his … *masterpiece* with the other. "Lie back. I want you to enjoy this."

Enjoy this?

Enjoy *this*?

He fucking *enjoyed* pizza. *This* was more like the rush of pulling all sorts of G-forces in an F-18. The fact that it was Melissa volunteering those G-forces was messing with his head, giving him something akin to vertigo.

So no. He wasn't enjoying this. Hell, he was trying to survive it.

"Miss … Mel … baby," he pleaded against her mouth, wrapping both arms around her and pulling her against his chest as he laid back. What he was pleading for? Hell if he knew. Maybe this, he thought as his fingers, hands, and arms all coordinated themselves to strip the stretchy little tank top off her incredibly luscious breasts. With her hand still stroking his masterpiece, he was surprised there was a part of his brain that had the agility to get that done. Because the majority of his brain was a drooling, humping, sexual beast with only one laser-focused thought.

And that was before he'd managed to get off her fucking sports bra, or whatever the hell the godawful thing was, and feel—*sweet nectar of the gods*—her soft, full tits against his chest.

"Condom," he grunted. Like a Neanderthal.

"You don't need a condom," she soothed.

He started feeling for his pants pockets. Even his inner Neanderthal knew he needed a damn condom.

"Not tonight." She bit her lip and smiled as she slid those gorgeous breasts down his chest and onto his stomach. As she continued to sneak backward, he cupped those fabulous tits with his hands and luxuriated in the feel of them until they slid away. Until he felt Missy's lips place a kiss on the top of his masterpiece.

He craned his neck to watch as he felt the soft, hot pleasure of her first, sweet taste.

"Jesus, Missy." His eyes closed, and his head dropped back.

"You deserve this, Thor."

He felt her palm smooth a slow stroke up his shaft. Felt her mouth cover the head of his dick. His hand reached out to tangle his fingers in her hair while his mind quickly sorted itself into two teams and began a lethal tug of war.

Team *Goddamn-This-Is-Good* gave into the bliss, not giving a rat's ass why he was getting what he was getting. Team *You-Are-A-Fucking-Pussy* worried itself to death that Missy was using her mouth for nothing more than to thank him for toting trash at her Spectacular.

But holy fuck, it didn't take long for the sensations rocketing out from the base of his spine to narrow his focus down to his epicenter— essentially yanking Team Pussy face first into a mud puddle, shutting down any and all thoughts in his head.

The words, "Dear Lord," slipped out of his mouth when Missy slid her knees off the seat and onto the floor, giving herself leverage to tug his jeans down farther. He pumped his hips, stroking himself into her mouth, everything caught up in that sweet, sultry pleasure and his intense desire to make it last. At some point, he pulled one of her arms straight up his body, flattening her hand against the pounding of his heart, trying to anchor himself while the rest of his body took flight.

There couldn't have been any mistaking when he was ready to explode. He sure hadn't been quiet about the buildup. But once he was there, once he didn't know whether he was going to live through the release he was teetering on the edge of—right there where sensation became so intense that pleasure resembled pain—he seized up, grimaced tightly, and let go ... again ... and then again.

Ho-ly shiiit.

She swallowed him down. Every last drop. Then soothed him with her mouth until there was far less of him to soothe, and maybe, probably, he'd accidentally fallen asleep. When she crawled up onto his chest, he welcomed her with a, "Pretty Girl," while encasing her within heavy limbs. "I don't think I can move."

"Then my work here is done," she whispered, snuggling her cheek against his shoulder.

His last thought before he passed out was that *his work* was just beginning.

CHAPTER THREE

Thor threw open his front door, certain some kind of catastrophe had managed to transpire during the two hours he'd been asleep. The constant banging put him on high alert, so he stared at his buddy Thatcher and then searched behind him and around him, waiting for the enemy to emerge or for a round of shots to spray them. He pulled Thatcher into the house and shut the damn door feeling wild-eyed and muddled. His heart pounding the shit out of his chest as words apparently eluded him.

"Not wartime, Tank. No code red," Thatcher said, moving past him and into the kitchen. "Just me."

"Christ. What the fuck?" Thor followed behind, scrubbing his hands over his face.

"Sorry, man. Thought I'd stop by on my way out of town so the two of us could take a look at your property."

"Yeah," Thor said, gathering his bearings. "Yeah. Yeah. It's fine. I just … I think I just fell asleep like an hour ago."

"Sorry. I shouldn't have come by so early. I just thought …"

"No. We're good." Thor checked out the clock on the wall oven. "I had to get up soon anyway. Let me pull on some clothes, and we'll do this. You know how to make coffee?"

"I am handy in the kitchen," Thatcher declared.

"All right, then. Fine. Help yourself while I jump in the shower."

Twenty minutes later and with two Yeti tumblers filled with hot coffee, Thor and Thatcher climbed up into the large, climate-controlled cab of his daddy's prized tractor and managed to squeeze two large bodies into a space designed for one. Thatcher gave Thor shit for having such a fine piece of machinery and not having the first clue how to use it. But together they managed well enough and were soon rolling along a flat expanse of land to the north that stretched out for a good couple of acres behind the old farmhouse. The ground began to rise, and once they were up and over the ledge, the view spread out for miles. Sweet, rolling farmland, just sitting there eager for something to grow.

"So, no tobacco this year?" Thatcher asked.

"I can't see it." Thor shook his head, his eyes spanning the scene before him.

"How about all your daddy's growers and customers counting on this land?"

"Lawyer contacted them after his death. The contracts were terminated at the end of the year. I've got offers galore waiting for me to look at, but everyone's been informed that I'm considering going in another direction."

"What direction?"

"Hell if I know." Thor looked over at Thatcher. "Sod is as good idea as any, I suppose."

"You've got the irrigation for it. I can't foresee any real problems. What else you gonna do with it? No use growing corn. Not much of a demand."

"Been reading a little bit about organic farming. Seems to be a trend along with all of that 'buy local' propaganda being spouted about."

Thatcher shook his head, laughing at Thor's choice of words. "You are so not a farmer," he said. "But organic's a thing. A big thing. A big, hard, you-gotta-really-be-into-it thing. Not a lot of farmers in the area are doing it, so there's a market. But it's work. It's a whole lot of work. So, if farming isn't your passion ..."

"Yeah," Thor said, feeling a bit defeated. "You know damn well it's not."

"Which is why sticking with tobacco is a no-brainer. You'd be the owner, manager, and bookkeeper. Not a farmer."

The two of them bounced along in silence for a while before Thatcher asked, "How are you, man? For real?"

Thor shot him a brief look before returning his gaze to the landscape. "I miss Pop. Far more than I would have imagined. Truth is, I find myself out here most days marching around his property just to feel close to him. Trying to see all of this through his eyes. And it's working. A little. Most days, a good walk will give me solace. Sometimes I imagine the pride he felt seeing the seeds take root, grow, and become a landscape of hearty green plants. I swear to God, sometimes it's like he's tugging on my attention. Because I'll look to the left or down this knoll, and I'll discover something in that moment. A fox and her babies. Deer. A tree I'd never paid a lick of attention to before; but in that moment, it becomes crystal clear that it meant something to somebody because it's still standing right in the middle of a field. I feel Pop out here. Almost like he's talking to me. Now, there doesn't seem to be a day that goes by I'm not out here talking to him. Hoping like hell he'll return the favor and just tell me what I'm supposed to do with his property."

"His property? Don'tcha mean *your* property?"

Thor twisted his neck, letting that four-letter word sink in.

A moment later, that word set off the equivalent of a nuclear blast inside his head. It was as if he actually saw the flash of blinding light and felt the subsequent explosion disintegrate all his confusion. "Damn." He jostled his head because the clarity was frankly jarring after all the months of foggy confusion. "Honest to God, I've never once looked at it that way." He laughed at how foreign the concept felt to him. "It *is* my property."

"Damn right, it is," Thatcher said, nodding. "Appreciate the gift, my friend. Land is the one thing God isn't making any more of. But do yourself a favor and do not feel bound by it. Your father's dream was to carry on the tobacco plantation, but he damn well knew that wasn't your dream."

"True. But he didn't like it."

"Yeah, and I know how much you'd like to have him back to give you his blessing. I really do."

All Thor could do was nod with the way his gut seized up in a wave of grief. Shit, did he ever want his pop's blessing. He felt Thatcher's hand on his shoulder.

"He was a good man, your dad. A fine farmer and a productive citizen. And he loved you. He was so proud of your ass when you became a Ranger. One of the Seventy-Fifth," Thatcher stressed. "In fact, the whole town was proud. Your pop didn't pay his own bar tab for a year. And every time he'd see me, he'd stop and tell me the latest news he'd received from you. I'm tellin' you, man, he loved your letters."

"Really?" Thor blinked. He had to force the words up and out of his throat. "I didn't know."

"Well, you do now. Your dad loved you and was proud of you. He got over his need for you to be a farmer. Having to carry on the Watson tradition. He was thrilled you were serving your country. But I'll tell you. He never missed a Sunday in church either. My mom can attest to that. She'd have him over for Sunday supper every few weeks and tell him how impressed she was with his faith. I remember him joking about how his faith grew exponentially the moment his only son was deployed."

"Damn." Thor chuckled. "I never knew."

"That's why I'm telling you. And to be honest, it's what prompted me to get my ass out of bed early and hightail it over here. You need to know the truth in all of this. That he loved you. That in the end, he wouldn't have changed one damn thing about you. So if you aren't a farmer, I know he's all right with that. And if all this land lies fallow for a season or two, who the hell is gonna care? This is your turn with it. Your chance to dream a dream, just like your forefathers did. Just like your pop did. Only this time, the dream has to be all yours."

Thor nodded. Too full of emotion to convey the level of appreciation he was feeling for Thatcher at the moment, he simply patted his buddy on the shoulder. Then he turned the monstrous tractor around and headed for home.

Missy woke up wearing Thor's Go Army sweatshirt she'd commandeered last night, and not much else. She rolled over to find the other side of her bed empty. Not even an indentation.

Really?

She hadn't anticipated that. Or the heavy sense of disappointment that engulfed her.

Because the first time she'd fallen asleep in Thor's truck after too much champagne and a really good make out session—where Thor had been more irritated than turned on—she'd woken to find him asleep next to her in this very bed. The two of them fully clothed.

Sinking her nose into the scent of Thor's sweatshirt, she replayed that morning in her mind. She'd been so worried about the rumpled mess she'd created by sleeping in Lolly's one-of-a-kind design that she'd whipped off the dress, stripping down to her bra and underwear in front of him. When Thor started yelling that he was still in the room, she tossed off her lack of modesty by saying he'd no doubt seen lots of women in their underwear.

"None that I haven't slept with," he claimed, stomping over and grabbing his suit coat. "But now that I know you don't mind me seeing you in your skivvies, next time I won't hesitate to undress you."

"There's not going to be a next time," she'd claimed.

"Oh, there will definitely be a next time," he promised.

And darned if he hadn't been right.

Last night, she'd gone ahead and fallen asleep in his truck all over again, leaving him to have to hoist her body up the stairs. She wasn't exactly a featherweight, so it wasn't out of the realm of possibility that the man would have been worn out to the point he'd have joined her under the covers and collapsed into sleep. Or at least use it as an excuse to stay the night.

But apparently he'd headed home.

Out to the backwoods.

Way out yonder.

To the *plaaan-tation*.

She wasn't sure what to make of that.

Gratefully she found that on the pillow where his head should have been, one of her lacrosse team's pink paper rosters had been folded into an airplane. Inside was tightly scribbled handwriting that was surprisingly easy to decipher. "Pick you up at eleven," it read. "Brunch at the Evanses'. You won't want to miss the debrief."

No, after all that went down yesterday, she definitely did not want to miss the debrief. She'd had the pleasure of dining at the Evans estate once before. Thor had invited her as if he were one of the many people who called the place home. He wasn't, but apparently he was welcome there any time. As was she, Hale had told her after her first foray into the highly entertaining Evans family dining experience.

But the Evanses were her employers. Well, not all of them. Hale was. Sort of. Hale Evans—truly one of the most gorgeous men on planet Earth—ran Evans & Evans Investments with his son, Vance. Vance, who was no slouch in the looks department either, was the voice of E&E for the most part. But Hale was the patriarch. The silent team leader. He didn't say much, but when he did, everyone listened, no one disagreed, and his word was final. But Hale preferred to work at home (probably to be closer to his new wife), so he didn't spend much time in the office on Main Street. Right across from CC Henderson where Missy had been given an office in which to work.

So Hale was her boss, and Vance was her boss, and even Davis, who lived in the pool house on the Evans estate and whom everyone called Pinks, was her boss.

Technically. *Technically*, she revised as she got out of bed, *she was her own boss*. Because, per her father's suggestion, she'd had the foresight to work out a sweet consulting deal for herself when she'd interviewed with E&E. So for all intents and purposes, E&E was actually her client—her *only* client. But they sure were a good start, she thought, giving herself a mental pat on the back as she stretched. If she actually wanted to stay in Henderson, E&E was a very good start.

If she actually wanted to stay in Henderson, she thought as she headed to the bathroom, she could probably pick up CC Henderson as her second client and then add Duncan James, Attorney at Law easily enough.

As she brushed her teeth, she considered that if she were planning to stay in Henderson, she'd head over to Henderson Country Club and ask what she might be able to do for them. Or Henderson Bank and Trust. She'd met Christy-Lynn Brilhart yesterday, and she ran the whole kit and caboodle over there.

If she wanted to stay in Henderson, she'd have plenty of prospects, even with the town itself struggling in rock-bottom mode. Because things were definitely on the upswing if yesterday was any indication. The Opening Day Baseball Spectacular had hit a high note, thanks in large part to her.

Yeah, if she wanted to stay in Henderson, yesterday was a very good beginning. And that thought had her stopping abruptly right after she'd turned on the shower.

Did she want to stay in Henderson?

Because up until this moment, that was not her plan. Up until this moment, she'd purposely put a deadline on all things Henderson.

After four weeks of having the God of Thunder and his big red truck save her ass more ways than she could recall, it was hard to ignore that the man liked her. A lot. Once she got her head out of her ass and realized her longtime buddy Davis had enticed her to Henderson solely to help him coach lacrosse and save the town he'd fallen in love with—not so she could fall in love with him—well, her heart had easily opened up to the possibility of Thor. Too easily.

Way too easily.

Because long term? Their romantic Farmer's Almanac forecast did not appear promising.

She knew, even if she was learning to live without a Starbucks or Target, she was definitely not cut out for life on a farm.

She might possess a long list of skills and interests, but not one of them fell within the domestic category. Her father ran a Fortune 500 company and was a mover and shaker in the business world. The life she'd grown up in was one she understood and planned to emulate. This small-town life she was trying to fit into here in Henderson was new and different and though not without its charms, well, farming was another matter entirely.

But then, you know, last night happened.

Last.

Night.

A frisson of desire hopscotched within her torso as she remembered *last night.*

Thor's kiss.

His arms.

That body.

Holy Mother of Zeus. Missy started to sweat.

He was big, and he was hard. Except for his smile, which—when it wasn't teasing or goading—was a lethal combination of delighted pleasure and wistful surprise. And boy, was it contagious. If he pulled a grin, she followed suit. There was simply no help for it.

And last night, Thor had grinned. A lot.

And then there was his touch, which frankly should be classified as a contact drug. If he trailed a fingertip down her arm? Tingles. The kind that lingered. Like … forever. His knuckle rubbing along her chin could cause acute shortness of breath. His palm to the back of her head? Forget about it—her legs went numb leaving her wobbly. A full-on assault from his hands anywhere on her body stoked the fires down deep in her core, radiating a heat that slow roasted her from the inside out.

That moment on the dance floor where he'd put his hands into the pockets of her jeans and pulled her up against him? Hotty McHot-Hots. There is no way a big white farmer boy should be able to bring that kind of sexy to the dance floor. But the way Thor moved, tight with rhythm, dancing in close—she'd wanted to jump him right there.

Which was pretty much why she jumped him in his big red truck.

Damn, she loved that truck. And him. And …

What?

No. No-no-no-no. No. She didn't *love* Thor. She wasn't, you know, *in love* with Thor. She just … was sort of … a little crazy for Thor. At the moment.

Because he was Mr. Wrong. As in, all wrong. Even if he *was* severely awesome. *And* a hunk-a-doodle. *And* he was interested in her when good ol' Davis hadn't been.

So … Missy sighed. Her crazy for Thor was probably more like a Davis rebound. Which was why she'd gone ahead and warned him. Warned Thor about not wanting to lead him on.

Right?

I mean …

When Missy realized she didn't remember stepping into the shower or how long she'd been standing under the water's spray staring at the godawful avocado colored tiles, she could only conclude one thing. Army Ranger-ready, super-sweet, super-strong, *super-hot* Farmer Thor had indeed started tugging at her heart.

So, oh yeah, she remembered. That's why she needed a deadline. She needed to get the hell out of Henderson before she became too attached to Thurgood Watson III and found herself scattering chicken feed and milking cows.

Ah … a big fat no on that.

So she would finish out the lacrosse season. Finish the Henderson website start-up. Get the networking database up and running. Carry out whatever parties and events Team Henderson could throw at her over the next three months. Because by the end of June, she and her fondness for rusty-haired, built-Ford-tough, L.L.Bean models needed to be good and gone.

Land.

It was worth something, Thor thought as he exited his truck.

Even during an economic downturn, or situated on the outskirts of a struggling little town, it was worth something. And at the core of Thor's being, he felt it was something worth holding on to.

His stomach twisted when Missy opened the chipped and peeling front door of Genevra's old cottage and then held open the screen door in welcome. Because here was something else worth holding on to, his dick assured him. He watched as she said, "Good bye," and clicked off her cell, standing there in a long, body-hugging sweater the color of cream.

"Your dad?" he asked, his eyes drawn to the denim colored spandex covering her legs. Lord knew, the girl was constantly talking to her dad.

"Filling him in on yesterday."

Thor's gaze drifted down to her cute feet with pale pink toenails tucked into fancy-girl flip-flops.

She must have caught him staring at her toes because she tried to hide them by placing one foot behind the other. "I had to paint them myself," she confided. "My fine-motor skills leave a lot to be desired."

See, he thought. He had no idea what the hell she was talking about. He didn't understand toenail painting. Why it was done, and why you wouldn't have to do it yourself. He only understood that something about Missy's painted toenails turned him on. Or maybe it was her feet. Or those ankles, he thought as his gaze started retracing its path back up her body. His thoughts wandered to slipping his hand up the hem of her sweater and what he'd find underneath.

Damn.

He should have jacked off before seeing her again. His body spontaneously remembered the feel of her ass in his lap last night, the pleasure of her mouth as he—yeah. All morning long, he'd tracked back to that. His brain being short circuited by his body, which was targeted in on Missy. Mel-is-sa.

He licked his lips.

As usual, her mouth was moving. But he wasn't listening to anything but his pulse points pumping along with the beat of his heart. A deep rhythm that broke out whenever the two of them were in close proximity. And it was probably way too early in the day to be starting up any of that skin-on-skin nonsense.

Hell.

Grabbing hold of her arm, he scooted her right up against him— looking over her head, glancing anywhere but down. Didn't distract him a damn bit though. He certainly wasn't immune to the soft feel of her body.

And then she laughed into his chest, and he cracked a smile at the memory of when she'd done it last night.

Dear Lord, if he thought he was a goner before? The sound of her laugh, the feel of her skin, the smell of her hair, the fucking heat of her touch—right through his damn shirt. The woman's hands sought him out whenever they were close and maybe that was the real reason he'd gone and tugged her into him.

Because he was addicted to her touch. And after last night, her mouth. And the way she was eager to put it all over him. *Hell.*

He made the effort to clear his throat. "I'm sorry about falling asleep in the truck."

"We both fell asleep. I was a little surprised to wake up in bed alone," she told him. Said it like it was nothing. Like she hadn't considered the strength of will it took him to strip her out of her jeans and then leave her alone. The woman slept like the damn dead. Not that she hadn't earned the right to it after running the show like she did yesterday. Which was the only reason he'd done his best not to wake her. It was near three in the morning when he finally wrestled her into bed. If she'd woken up, he'd have done his very best to keep her up for another hour or two.

"Well, I thought about crawling in with you," he lied. "Then I remembered you aren't much of a morning person."

She smirked. "Thanks for undressing me this time," she whispered, going a little bit shy on him.

"My pleasure," he said, feeling his way back to the top of his game. He smoothed her hair back from her face and touched a finger under her chin. "Just sorry I didn't have a chance to collect a good night kiss."

His lips brushed over hers, causing her to grin. He grinned back, touching her cheek, licking his lips, going in for more. There was something about taking his time with Melissa that was seriously satisfying. Soul satisfying. He didn't want to rush things. He hated being on the clock. Christ, he was trying to negotiate a relationship. A long-term relationship. One that Missy actually wanted to be in. Not one that had her running for the hills.

Or Baltimore.

He felt her hand wrap around the back of his neck, pulling him in, shutting off his brain, and stroking his desire. He wrapped her up in his arms and tilted his head, his tongue scooting in for a sweet lick. Her mouth felt so good. No wonder he liked starting their dates off with a good night kiss. "Why wait?" was now going to be his motto. Kiss first, ask questions later.

While his mouth was busy working on staking his claim, his hand slipped up the back of her sweater, searching for soft. Running his fingertips up her spine, a little *mmm* slipped out of her mouth and into his, stirring his desire like a phantom grip stroking his cock.

This girl right here was the little bit of paradise that had seeped into his colorless world. Every bit of his body longed to be saturated in a shade of Missy. There wasn't a part of his life that couldn't be enhanced by a blush of her pigment. Since she'd moved into town, happiness had settled into him quietly, unseating grief and depression. Dissolving remnants of guilt and loneliness. In a matter of weeks, Thor's life had changed for the better. And he was well aware that the catalyst for it was in his arms.

He simply couldn't afford to let her go.

It was no secret he had his work cut out for him. Especially with the stakes so high. He wanted to be happy. He wanted his life to work. He'd been floundering darn good after Pop died until this sweet wisp of a dream surrounded him, emboldened him, awakened him so he'd want to buy stock in his own life.

Missy pulled back from their kiss, tapping her hand gently against his chest as she was wont to do. She let her forehead rest against his sternum as if searching for equilibrium. "You sure can kiss," she whispered, turning from him slowly and reaching for her jacket. "You think I'll need this?" she asked, holding up a white down vest.

"It's fairly mild for March, but bring it along. Never know when you'll be caught out in the elements."

"Is that a Ranger-ready thing? Like the Boy Scouts? Always be prepared?"

"More like a little bit of small-town common sense."

CHAPTER FOUR

Missy hadn't yet attended brunch at the Evans estate, but she'd heard enough stories from Davis to know it was going to be entertaining. She just didn't anticipate that *she'd* be part of the entertainment.

Thor opened the Evanses' ornate front door as if he lived there, ushering her inside with a quick smile before leading her up to the main level with a decided spring in his step.

For all his denial about being a part of Team Henderson, Thurgood Watson sure didn't mind acting like he was a member of the Evans family. It struck Missy as curious when he high-fived Mr. Evans—Hale—and kissed Hale's wife, Genevra on the cheek and then headed directly to the kitchen sink where he began to wash his hands. He'd left Missy at the entrance of the enormous and elaborate kitchen anxiously watching as he blended into the dance being performed before her.

Genevra, a knockout brunette who looked far younger than her actual age of forty-three, stood at the center of the great island chopping vegetables, her pregnant belly covered by an apron. Davis was at the bar, squeezing multiple limes into a pitcher as sure as he was squeezing Scarlett around her middle. Scarlett—who Missy had met for all of five seconds yesterday—looked like a redheaded doll in her Sunday school best, making Missy feel woefully underdressed. Hale stood at a cabinet pulling out dishes and glassware, whistling a happy tune, a dishtowel tossed over his shoulder. And Emelina presided over all of it on a tall barstool with a Bloody Mary that had been so thoroughly garnished it looked like an entire salad had been pinned through with a toothpick.

Through the French doors, around the pool area, she could hear the muffled voices of Brooks and Vance laughing as Vance hovered over the grill, appearing to diligently scrape it clean. The two of them were already drinking a beer, and it was only … Missy checked her watch … eleven thirty.

Well, it was brunch, she thought. And boy, did those two have reason to celebrate.

"Missy, dear." Vance's grandmother Emelina drew her attention. "Join me?" She patted the seat next to her.

Grateful for direction, Missy crawled up onto the stool.

She could boil water. She could bake chicken, open a can of soup, whip up a box of mac and cheese, and definitely pour pre-washed salad out of a bag and dress it with a store-bought dressing. Other than that, she was a fish out of water in the kitchen.

Especially this kitchen.

With all these people who apparently knew exactly what they were doing. They were all moving around, talking, getting things done without bumping into each other or spilling anything.

"Would you like a cocktail?" Emelina asked.

Lord, yes. "Sure," she said.

"Pinks," Em called.

"Coming right up," he said over his shoulder.

Missy watched as Davis made a great show of putting a silhouetted glass containing a frothy yellow concoction on a silver tray. Scarlett eyed Missy briefly before she carefully lifted the tray and headed in her direction. With a shy smile, Scarlett whispered, "He made this special for you. It's a Southern Belle. Sweet Tea Vodka, lemonade, muddled strawberries and pineapple." She placed the tempting drink before Missy and said, "You did a great job yesterday with the Spectacular."

Missy wasn't sure she was ready to actually *like* Scarlett, but her guard was dropping. "Thanks," she said, offering up a genuine smile.

"I know you and Davis are old friends. Close friends. And … I was hoping … well …"

Missy felt compelled to hand Scarlett an olive branch. "If Davis loves you, that's good enough for me. Seeing as I really enjoy working with your mother and her henchmen, I'm guessing you and I will be able to find common ground, other than Pinks over there, on which to forge a friendship."

"He would have told you about me sooner if I hadn't asked him to keep us a secret," Scarlett confessed.

"I understand."

Scarlett nodded, checking back over her shoulder to see that Davis was hard at work at the bar. She lowered her voice. "He wants you to stay in Henderson. I want you to know that I want that too. He's convinced me to come back home after graduation, and it sure would be more fun if you stuck around. Do you like wine?"

Missy cracked a smile. "I guess. I don't buy much of it, but I usually enjoy what's being served."

"I could teach you about wine," she offered, extending her own olive branch.

"Do you play sports?" Missy asked, searching for a connection.

Scarlett wrinkled her nose.

Missy choked on the sip she'd been taking and laughed in shock. "No? Nothing?"

Scarlett shook her head vehemently, holding up her perfect nails. "But you should meet my roommate, Natalie. She's on the golf team at Ole Miss. She can talk your ear off about sports for hours. I know you're a soccer coach."

"Lacrosse coach."

"Right. Lacrosse." Scarlett leaned in. "Maybe you can teach me something about lacrosse before Pinks realizes I have no idea what the hell he's been talking about."

"I'd be happy to. Though, if you ask Davis nicely," she teased, "I'm sure he'd be more than accommodating to share his sports obsession with you. You are aware he's heavily involved with the creation of the sports academy, right?"

"The what academy?"

Missy and Em exchanged a look.

"Give her a break," Davis chimed in from halfway across the room, his back to all of them and his hands busy at work. "She's been on Mississippi lockdown for the past three and a half years."

"Have the two of you ever held a conversation?" Missy asked.

"Not about Henderson," Davis said, throwing a smile over his shoulder.

"Oh … right," Missy said, as understanding dawned. Although Scarlett and Davis had been in a long-distance relationship for months now, it had been conducted under their own brand of "Don't ask, don't tell" which had truly blown up on the two of them this weekend. Missy looked back at Scarlett with a little more empathy. "Wow. You two have a lot to talk about, don't you?"

"We do," Scarlett agreed. She leaned in and whispered, "I found out two nights ago that he slept with my sister."

Missy rolled her lips trying to cover her shock that Scarlett had brought this up. Here. Now. "Mmm-hmm," she murmured, hiding her angst within a sip of the delicious concoction. "And how'd that go?"

Scarlett gave a little laugh. "Honestly, I'm still trying to wrap my head around it. Because it seems like so much has happened in the last forty-eight hours."

"Darling," Emelina said, grabbing on to Scarlett's hand. "If I worried about who the loves of my life had slept with before they found me, I'd never have had any fun. That boy over there"—she tilted her head to indicate Davis—"is the catch of all catches."

"Tansy is her sister," Missy felt compelled to say.

"Who is in love with Crain. End of story. Now let's all move on. Sí?"

"Sí," both girls said at once.

"What's Thor doing?" Missy whispered, notching her chin in his direction.

Scarlett and Emelina shifted their attention to the far end of the kitchen where Thor was spoon feeding Genevra something from a freshly opened mason jar. Genevra was so enamored by the taste she grabbed on to Thor's forearm, not letting him get away. She tasted it again, licking her lips and moaning softly.

"Oh—" Emelina snapped. "Those two. We have yet to figure out if the two of them were lovers."

"Thor and Mrs. Evans ... I mean, Genevra?" Missy stumbled. Even eight months pregnant the woman was glorious. No way was she competing with all that, she thought frantically. *Thank God Thor didn't end up in my bed last night.*

"Are you serious?" Scarlett whispered in shock.

Emelina shrugged, adding fuel to the fire.

"Madre." Hale's call of warning poked through their conversation even though he appeared to be highly engrossed in running a dishtowel over several delicate champagne glasses, determined to make them shine.

"My son doesn't appreciate me speculating about his wife's past," Em whispered to the girls.

"No need to speculate," Genevra piped up as she continued to do what she was doing. "When any of you gets up the nerve to actually ask me that question, I'll be happy to put your curiosity to rest."

"I have a question," Missy said. "Do you all possess the power of super hearing? Or are the acoustics in this kitchen outrageously good?"

That brought on the laughs.

"Here," Thor said, coming at her with a fresh spoon. "This is the last of the peach preserves my mother made. Still good. Real good. Taste."

Missy's gaze drifted from the spoon held out in his hand to the neon-blue of Thor's eyes as he fed her the bit of marmalade. It was sweet, fruity, and a little tart. But that was hardly noticeable up against all the what-the-hell thoughts scrambling her brain. At the moment, she felt completely overwhelmed.

"Well?" Thor asked expectantly.

"Oh. Yes. It's good—delicious, I mean."

"You okay?" He narrowed his eyes, searching her face.

She shook her head in the negative but said, "Yes, of course."

He mimicked her by shaking his head no and saying, "Yes?" He turned and shouted at Davis. "What'd you put in my girl's drink?"

"A whole lot of Southern lovin'," Davis responded, still busy at the bar with his back to them all.

"Is this what he does?" Scarlett asked, looking over at Davis.

"It's what he does during brunch," Em reported. "And I, for one," she said, holding up her drink and shaking it, "truly appreciate his efforts."

Scarlett wandered back to Davis where he immediately had her taste-testing whatever he'd been concocting over there.

"Should I be helping?" Missy asked Thor.

"No need. Sit back and relax," he said, strutting his brawny self back over to Genevra.

"His mother made jelly," Missy whispered very quietly to Em. "My mother buys jelly at the store. *Grape* jelly."

"This concerns you because?" Emelina asked discreetly behind her Bloody Mary.

"He lives on a farm. Is threatening to grow things. I hate weeding, and I can't cook. He loves Genevra's fried chicken, and to be quite honest, I didn't know anybody still *ate* fried chicken. Hasn't it been declared a health hazard since like the 1980s?"

Emelina patted her hand. "Drink, darling. And rest easy. Fried chicken is not on the menu."

Missy did as she was told. Well, the drinking part. The rest-easy part, not so much. As much as she liked every one of the people gathered here, she didn't fit in at all.

At least not in this kitchen.

At work, yes.

Last night at The Situation—sure.

But here in their home, all working together and preparing food? All with intimate knowledge of each other? Less like a fish out of water, Missy felt like she was swimming in murky seas, searching for sunken treasure without benefit of an air tank.

Her gaze slid to Thor, who shot her a wink. Genevra was busy rolling some sort of mini pizza cutter along a stretch of dough and then dropping Thor's mom's marmalade into the middle of each piece. She motioned for Thor to go to the cabinet-encased refrigerator and fetch something, which he did without pause. Then Genevra proceeded to demonstrate what she wanted him to do. Fold the dough pinwheel style over the pastries while she cracked and separated eggs. She whipped the whites with a fork a few times and then handed a small brush to Thor and told him to paint the pastries with it. He looked up at Missy briefly. After saying a few words to Genevra, he proceeded to bring the tray, egg whites, brush, and all over to her.

"You want to help?" he asked.

It wasn't that she lost her voice or the ability to speak. It was more that words—all words—had scattered. From her head, from her throat. Leaving her mute and gripping her drink.

"Here," he coaxed. "I'll show you the way Genevra just showed me."

"Do you cook?" she blurted.

He shook his head as his big hands managed to gently wash the pastry with egg white. "I'm learning."

"From Genevra?" Her voice squeaked the name.

Thor's head snapped up. His stare intent as he searched her face.

He set down the brush, wiped his hands on the bar towel he'd tucked in his belt for a makeshift apron, and then turned and addressed the group at large. "I have an announcement to make." His voice boomed around the kitchen. "Mrs. Evans and I did not sleep together. Ever."

"Yessss," Hale hissed with a modified fist pump.

Genevra giggled over the sausage patties she was forming. "Really, Hale," she said, shaking her head.

"Stranger things have been known to happen," Scarlett added on an eye roll before taking a sip of her drink. Davis pulled her into him and kissed her cheek before going back to work.

Thor's head swung around to Missy, and he captured her gaze. "Just wanted to clear that up," he said firmly.

"Thank you," she mouthed at him.

He held out the pastry brush. She took it, eager to feel useful.

Brooks and Vance pushed their way through the French doors, ending a conversation. "All ready for the sausage," Vance announced just as his phone went off. He pulled it out of his pocket and put it up to his ear saying, "Yes, Baby Doll." After a moment, he looked at Genevra. "Okay, I'll tell her." Then he turned toward Scarlett and Davis. "All right. I'll tell her too." Then he began nodding his head, looking around. His eyes lit up when he saw Missy. "Yes. Will do.

Anything else?" He ducked his chin, smiled toward the floor, and then said quietly, "I love you too." He smacked a kiss into the phone and disconnected. "It seems Little Miss Bedrest is getting antsy with you all in her kitchen," Vance said.

A voice drifted down the staircase adjacent to the kitchen. "I heard that."

Vance raised his face to the ceiling. "Do not. Move one foot. Out of that bed," he ordered.

"Is that Piper?" Missy asked. "She's on bedrest?"

"Vance, Jr. tried to make an early appearance Friday night," Vance explained. "Lady Doc has ordered her off her feet for one week to see how things settle."

"Oh. How's her blood pressure?"

Vance's eyes went wide, and then he shot a disgruntled look at Davis. "*She* knew about Piper's blood pressure?" Vance asked.

"She had to know," Davis confessed. "In case I needed backup."

"What's the matter with Piper's blood pressure?" Hale asked.

"Nothing," Vance stated. "Thank God, it was nothing."

"Good to hear," Missy said, sheepishly throwing an apologetic look toward Davis. He simply shrugged.

Vance looked at Brooks. "It seems the Circle of Trust is ever expanding."

"Ah—that would be a no," Brooks replied. "Because clearly you and I have been shoved outside the Circle. I didn't know about the blood pressure thing either."

Vance gave Brooks a fist bump.

"What are y'all talking about?" came Piper's voice from beyond.

Vance stared at the ceiling and sighed heavily. Then he lowered his voice and addressed the girls. "Scarlett, Missy, I beg you. In an effort to save my own blood pressure, would you mind granting Piper's request for an audience? The two of you probably need a little bonding time, and the Lawyer Beaumont desperately needs a mission to keep her mind busy while her body is cooking up Vance, Jr." He took the volume down even lower. "So if things aren't truly awkward between you two, can you at least pretend they are so she feels like she's doing something?"

Missy shot a glance at Scarlett. "Are things supposed to be awkward between us? I'm the girl Davis *didn't* want to sleep with."

"I did when I was fifteen," Davis threw over his shoulder without missing a beat at the bar.

Both girls' heads spun toward him. "Seriously?" they chimed.

Davis didn't spare either of them a look. "There will be no skeletons left in my closet," he promised. "Finding out Scarlett was Tansy's sister and carrying the weight of *that* around for a month just about did me in," he said while slicing up a lime.

Vance slapped Brooks on the back. "Got any skeletons in your closet?"

Brooks scoffed. "Plenty."

The entire room grinned at that.

"What? Y'all don't believe me?"

"Good Lord, Brooks," Missy said, scrambling off her stool. "Even I can tell you are Mr. Straight and Narrow. Come on, Scarlett. Let's go bo-ond," she exaggerated.

The two women headed out of the kitchen and toward the curving staircase. "Drinks will be waiting," Davis shouted after them.

When they were out of hearing distance, Missy leaned her head toward Scarlett and whispered, "He was not nearly this popular in high school."

Scarlett laughed so hard she tripped up the stairs. "Oh, man." She grabbed Missy's hand. "Best icebreaker ever."

Missy laughed with her as they climbed the staircase. "Seriously, I grew up with Davis Williams the mortal. This superhero Pinks thing he's got going on is new to me."

"Me too," Scarlett confided. "I mean, the guy running around with his hair on fire saving Henderson one day at a time is not the Pinks I fell in love with. I don't even know *that* Pinks."

"You'll like that Pinks," Missy assured her as they stopped at the top of the stairs.

"Probably. My mother likes that Pinks. My sister did not like that Pinks, but clearly lost her shit over Pinks the Rock Star Drummer, and after last night …" Scarlett shrugged underneath a big sigh. "I get it."

Missy shook her head and laughed. "Superhero or no, that drummer thing I simply cannot explain. I'm still having trouble reconciling it. And how you two managed to get Cal Johnson on stage to sing?" Missy said as if it were a miracle. "Brilliant."

"All Pinks," Scarlett conceded. "Though we're plotting to get Cal to do an album. And that is *my* idea."

"If he'll make the videos in Henderson, it would be a huge boon for the cause."

Scarlett looked Missy over. "Those were Pinks's thoughts exactly. Hmm. Maybe the rumors are true," she said as she started walking down the hall.

"What rumors?" Missy asked, following in her wake, having no idea where to find Piper.

"That you're actually Pinks's twin."

"Do not say another word until you're in here," they heard Piper order as they found the open door to her bedroom.

Missy thought Piper looked as healthy and cheerful as ever. All blond curls, pink cheeks, and bright blue eyes. She was propped up by a ton of pillows in a huge bed. Her laptop was tossed to the side as she clapped her hands at the sight of Scarlett.

"Vance tells me everything is okay between you and Pinks. Is that true? Please tell me it's true," she begged. "That man is the best thing that ever happened to Vance and me. I need him to be happy. And to stay in Henderson."

"Then you're in luck," Scarlett said with a broad smile. "He seems quite happy."

"And you?"

"I'm happy he lives in Henderson and is already able to handle my mother. And father. As for the sister thing ..." Scarlett shrugged. "I'll get over it."

"Yes, well, your sister loves Crain. I can attest to that. And you— you—are perfect for our Pinks. Isn't she?"

Thankfully, Missy was exempt from answering that awkward question because something so much more interesting appeared in the doorway.

Cal Johnson, in all his wrecked and rambling glory, partially in and partially out of the room, had one hand holding on to the wall as if he needed it to steady himself. His gorgeous long hair was disheveled. He was bare from neck to hips, showing off some seriously hot muscles and mouth-watering skin. His faded jeans were pulled on but left unzipped, exposing his black boxer-briefs and a well-defined bulge. Magnificently droolworthy, he had taken on the persona of a calendar pinup god, except for the fact that he was clearly in more pain than his deep-set baby-blues could handle. Piper's room wasn't particularly bright with all the heavy silk drapes outlining the windows, but it appeared to be way too much for the superstar pitcher to handle.

He smoothed a hand from forehead to chin before grunting, "Where's Nat?"

When Missy checked with Scarlett, she noted a sinister glare in her eyes as she responded. "Nat? Are you sure you aren't looking for *Kat*?"

When Cal stood there unable to comprehend, Scarlett went on. "What exactly do you remember from last night, Cal?" Her tone held no mercy for his obvious suffering.

Cal rubbed the back of his neck, grimacing. "Last thing I'm clear on, we were all doing shots at the bar. Toasting Maroon 5 when I finally got the nerve up to pull Natalie in for a kiss. It all goes a little blurry after that."

Scarlett scoffed.

"Cupcake," he pleaded. "Where's your roommate?"

"Visiting with her parents."

"Where?"

"Over in Oxford. They wanted to take her out to breakfast before we headed back this afternoon."

Cal took a moment to look at the floor beneath him, scratching the back of his head. Thinking. "Pretty sure she asked me to join them."

"Hmm. Was that before or after you called her the wrong name?"

Cal abruptly stopped all movement. "What?"

"And just when I was beginning to think you weren't *anything* like I'd imagined."

"What did you imagine?"

"A spoiled, temperamental player."

"Let's not throw stones about spoiled or temperamental, Cupcake. Glass houses and all. But I am a damn good ballplayer, so I'll own that."

"Not a ballplayer, Fabio. A playa. A love-'em-and-leave-'em manslut."

"Hey. That is old news. I am now a one-woman man. Natalie's man."

"Sorry. She's done."

"Done?"

"Done."

"What do you mean, done?"

"She's done. Done with you and your playa ways."

"She can't be done. We haven't even started."

"Good thing, too. 'Cause I'd kill you if you broke her heart. It was good she found out exactly who you are before she fell head over heels for a playa like you. I tried to save her the trouble, but she just had to come and meet hotty-toddy Cal Johnson."

"Scarlett. Stop. Tell me what the hell I'm missing here."

Scarlett huffed. "I don't like that you got so drunk that you can't even remember the gross faux pas you delivered."

"Yeah, well, believe me, I'm suffering for it having to listen to you prattle on while I'm trying to figure out where the hell my girl is."

"Natalie is not your girl."

"Hell if she's not."

Scarlett shook her head and glanced at Missy and Piper. "Celebrities," she scoffed.

"Where is she?" Cal demanded.

"I told you. Over in Oxford at the diner. With her parents."

"Why didn't she wake me? Call me? Something? This is not going to look good in the eyes of Nate the Great."

"Is that what she is to you? The daughter of a Hall of Fame pitcher you want to get close to?"

Cal stared at Scarlett, his handsome face mired with disgust. "Be serious."

"I am serious. You can have any girl. Why Nat?"

"She hot." He said it like that was the stupidest question in the world. "And she's sweet. Simple." He cocked his head and squinched his eyes together as if he knew his words were going to be misconstrued. "And I don't mean simple as in mentally deficient. I mean simple as in easy. Easy to be with. No pretending. Just … Nat."

Missy watched the wind come out of Scarlett. Watched her go from angry to heartbroken. "Then why the hell couldn't you remember her name?"

"I remember her name. Natalie Anne Houser. Named for both her father and mother. What are you talking about?"

"You called her Kat. Right after you kissed her for the very first time, you called her Kat. As in Kathy or Kathleen or Kate or something other than Nat-a-lie."

It was as if Cal were struck frozen. His eyes blinked, still trained on Scarlett, but nothing else moved. He shook his head. "I didn't. I couldn't. That would be"—he altered his stance—"terrible."

"Yeah. It was. Pretty much," Scarlett said quietly, as if transmitting Natalie's pain.

"Scarlett," he breathed. "Scarlett," he pleaded. "I didn't … it was a slur of words. It had to be. I'd been calling her Nat for two nights. I knew who I was with. Damn well knew who I was kissing. *Finally!* The girl was no pushover. I fucking got up on stage and sang for her. *Her*," he insisted. "Not you. Not Pinks. Not fucking Henderson." He backed away from the door. "Oh my God," he said, running his hands through his hair. "I cannot win in this town."

"Not true," Scarlett said. "Tell me the truth. Is there a Kat or Kath or any some such K name in your life?"

"No. Nobody. I mean, yeah, there've been girls. Lots of them. Because, yeah … But I wasn't kidding about y'all coming down to spring training during your break. I like Nat, Scarlett. You know that. And you have to help me fix this."

"I do not have to help you fix this if I'm not convinced it's in Natalie's best interests to do so."

"I've told you. You know it. If I fucked up her name, it was because the big sunshiney one was buying too many shots."

"Brooks?" Missy offered.

Cal pointed. "That's the one. Look," he pleaded, "I'm not usually overserved. I can hold my liquor with the best of them. But last night? Hell, once I got on stage, it all got away from me. I liked it. Singing. Who knew? And I really liked that Nat liked it. Me singing on stage. And then I fell in love. With Henderson and this sweet, no-shit girl by my side, whose dad—yes whose dad—happens to be Nate the Great, so she understands me a whole lot more than all the usual panty-dropping honeys I'm having to deal with." He stopped a moment. His expression truly compelling as he said, "She took me seriously. Me. The human being, Calvert Johnson. Not that Rookie of the Year Cal. Nat got me. Like, right away. And I got her. So help me fix this, Cupcake, before I do something stupid like cut my hair."

Missy was appalled at the thought. "Why would you cut your hair?"

Good ol' Cal's devilish grin made an appearance. "I'd resort to anything to get Nat's attention."

"Fine. I'll help," Scarlett said. "I sure don't want to be responsible for you cutting that hair. But it's going to cost you."

"I'll fetch my wallet."

"Not money, baseball boy. Time. Talent. Your endorsement of Henderson. And your voice."

"My voice?"

"You will be cutting a record. Here in Henderson at your first available opportunity. Like the All-Star break."

"Like I'm not going to be pitching at the All-Star game."

"Oh. Yeah. Right. But at the earliest opportunity you have, we are cutting your first album."

"How are *we* going to do that?"

"I'll figure it out."

"You gonna write the songs?"

"If I have to."

"Scarlett. Even though I ended up not minding that little karaoke stunt Pinks pulled last night, I'm not a singer. I have a reputation to uphold, and I don't know the first thing about cutting a damn album."

"That's why you have Pinks and me. We'll figure it out. We'll find the right songs. We'll take care of everything."

"Including getting me face time with Natalie today."

"I'll see what I can do."

"I am on the clock here. I have been furloughed from spring training until tomorrow morning at nine o'clock. I need to speak to Natalie before she flies out of town."

"I will do my best."

"If you want your damn album, you'll get it done." He looked at Piper and then Missy and said, "Sorry, ladies. I'll go … get in the shower. *Shit*," he whispered as he headed back down the hall.

"Wow," Piper said, doing her best not to smile. "Imagine if I'd happened to have my phone on video and recorded all that."

"You didn't," Scarlett breathed in horror. "You wouldn't?"

"Yes I did, and you're right, I wouldn't. Would you?"

"Put it on YouTube for the world to see? No. I'd never," Scarlett proclaimed.

"Good. Then I can give it to you to use as leverage when he backs out of the album thing."

"Piper, you are bad."

"Not *that* bad. I will be working up a legal document you'll have to sign before I hand the recording over to you. I am a lawyer after all, and I have to protect this town's assets."

"You mean Cal?"

"From what I've been told about last night, Cal has become one of our biggest assets."

"True that. In fact, get on your computer and pull up YouTube. Let's see if anything has been posted."

"I've been looking at it all morning, sending the best videos to everyone I can think of."

"Did you send it to the network news?"

"No." Piper blinked. "I swear, being pregnant has made me soft. I'm losing my edge."

"There's your project," Missy interjected.

"What project?"

"Vance said you needed a project to work on while you were stuck in bed. Here it is. You make sure every news organization in every major league city gets the best video you can find of Cal on stage last night—promoting Henderson as you go—and let's just see what happens."

CHAPTER FIVE

Vance clapped his hands together. "Pinks, Brooks, Thor … outside. Team meeting." He held the door open for the men to walk through.

"Be right with you," Thor said, fooling around with the pastry dough and going over to ask Genevra another question.

Vance rolled his eyes at the two of them and followed his bros out the door, shutting it tight. "Did any of you buy that bullshit about Thor and Genevra never sleeping together?" he asked. "Dad can believe whatever the hell helps him sleep at night, but I, for one, am not buying it."

"They sure are cozy," Brooks said.

Pinks stood eyeing the two in question through the length of glass windows. "I just think he's the son she never had."

"Until Brody," Vance said.

"Are they seriously thinking of naming the baby Brody?" Brooks asked.

"I'm calling my baby brother Brody. So if they don't want the kid to be all messed up, they'll do what's good for him and name him Brody."

"What if they decide to retaliate by calling your kid Francis or something?" Brooks retorted.

"Ahh, Vance, Jr. will not be known by any other name."

"What's up?" Thor asked, coming through the doors and wiping off his hands.

"That was bullshit, right? You and Genevra have been intimate. Tell the truth," Vance urged.

"You heard what I said."

"I heard what you said in front of Missy."

Thor's face twisted. "Are you seriously standing here asking me if I've slept with your father's wife?"

"Nope. What I'm asking is if you got it on with the Widow DuVal back when we were in high school?"

"If I wasn't enough of an asshole to brag about it back then, what makes you think I'd start now?"

"So you did," Vance concluded.

"I didn't say that."

"You and Genevra seem overly close," Brooks observed.

"She's good people," Thor said. "The best people. Speaking of, where, may I ask, is Lolly?"

"Sleeping it off," Brooks said with a greedy grin.

"A few too many shots?"

"Not the shots she's sleeping off."

"Pardon me?"

"The woman was insatiable. Kept me up all night."

"Jesus," Vance mumbled.

"Yeah, still too soon for me to stand around listening to this," Pinks griped to Vance. "And I'm guessing you didn't bring us out here to get to the bottom of the Genevra/Thor debate either. So, what's up?"

"All right." Vance scratched at his brow before he started talking with both hands. "Here's the thing. Yesterday went well. Better than well. And a lot of the credit goes to Missy."

"Absolutely," Thor agreed.

"So, this nonsense Brooks just shared with me about her leaving Henderson has got to stop, and it has got to stop fast. There is a lot we are depending on her to keep on top of. Pinks can't do it all anymore. Not with Brooks's campaign and the sports academy. We need Missy on board and committed. Which means …" Vance dragged out as all eyes turned to Thor. "It is up to *you* to keep her here."

Thor blinked a few times as comprehension dawned. "Just so we're clear. I'm not interested in keeping Missy in Henderson so you yahoos can work her to death. I have my own agenda, and trust me, I'm working on it."

"Work on it harder."

Before Thor had a chance to blow a gasket, Pinks stepped in and tried to soothe things. "The three of us, along with Hale, Em, and Genevra, are offering our full support."

"Exactly." Vance smoothly ran with Pinks's lead. "That's what we did for Carraway when he was trying to win Tansy. That's what we're going to do for you."

Thor looked skeptical.

"We are here for you, dude. Now, what's your game plan?"

"I'm working on it."

"Whatcha got so far?"

"Not much. Happy for any and all suggestions except,"—Thor abruptly held his palm out halting Pinks—"I've already heard what you have to say, Mr. Multiple Reasons. I'd like to hear what these two have up their sleeve," he said, pointing between Brooks and Vance.

"Fine. But I've got an idea other than ... you know ... the orgasm thing," Pinks insisted.

"Orgasms are good," Vance said. "Never can hurt to know what you're doing there. I'll lend you my secret weapon."

"Lend me what?" Thor choked.

Brooks rolled his eyes before he said, "Don't ask. Just ... let's hear Pinks out, shall we."

"Shit," Thor huffed. "I'm sort of dying to know about the secret weapon."

"Later," Brooks said. "Pinks, whatcha got?"

"Well, look who's suddenly interested in hearing what I have to say?" Pinks teased.

"Trust me," Brooks growled, shaking his head. "You do not want to hear what I have to say about you and Scarlett Langford."

"Scarlett and Pinks are great," Vance defended. "Couldn't be better for Henderson."

"I think so, too," Pinks said with a big grin.

"Hell," Vance went on. "The traction that story got yesterday about you sleeping with both Langford sisters—that's the stuff that is going to make Henderson legendary."

"Jesus," Pinks cursed.

"Seriously, dude. Couldn't have worked out better. Timing or otherwise."

"I'm so glad my worst nightmare has served your purposes of putting Henderson on the map."

"Ah—back to Missy?" Thor interrupted.

"Yeah, yeah, back to Missy," Pinks said. "We expand her business. Make it so big and enticing she can't go home."

"How do you mean? She's already busy," Vance warned.

"We expand the event-planning part of her business. You said it yourself. Yesterday was a huge success. We do our best to spread the word that it was all Missy."

"I like it," Brooks said.

"It's a start," Vance agreed. "Thor? How can we help you?"

"Hell, after Tansy's wedding and the party last night, it's clear the woman enjoys a good time. I'm toying with the idea of hosting some sort of blowout at my pop's place. Something fun. Outdoors. Get her to see the land as something to appreciate, not be afraid of."

"Afraid of?" Brooks wondered.

"Missy doesn't think she wants to live on a farm," Pinks informed Brooks. "She's worried about falling for Thor and then waking up one day wondering how she ended up a farmer's wife."

"What's wrong with being a farmer's wife?"

"Nothing. She just doesn't see herself tending the fields or feeding pigs."

"Since when do you own pigs?" Brooks threw a bewildered look at Thor.

"We don't. Never have. It's been tobacco for generations. I'm not sure what she's afraid of exactly—we've yet to have a heart-to-heart on the subject. It's only been a couple of days since Pinks made me aware of all this. Although she sort of confirmed it last night, telling me straight up she didn't want to lead me on. Right before the damn girl jumped me in my truck and did exactly that," Thor grumbled before sucking in a breath and letting it out on a sigh. "So yeah, with all her not-wanting-to-lead-me-on-stuff, I think she's got it in her head to hit the road as soon as lacrosse season is done."

"Well, then," Vance said. "Our mission is to change her mind. Show her how much fun being part of a rural community can be.

Spring is upon us. All we have to do is put our heads together and come up with a few social events to entice Melissa into staying. Show her why we all love Henderson."

"I'm on it," Pinks said. "But with Piper on bedrest, Genevra about to give birth, and Scarlett and Lolly heading back to school, we are going to need reinforcements of the female variety."

"That's probably what she needs," Vance said. "A best friend. I mean, Em is great, but Missy needs somebody her own age to show her there's more to Henderson than just work, the Old Guard, and the four of us."

"Fine. Who you got in mind?" Thor asked.

There was silence.

"Okay. So we think on it. Hell, let's see who Scarlett recommends and then put Garland on it. Until then, we keep Missy busy all week and make sure Thor shows her a good time on the weekends."

"Would a trip into Raleigh be counterproductive?" Thor asked Pinks. "Or would it help our city girl to know that her natural habitat isn't too far away?"

"Couldn't hurt."

"I'm heading there to see Lolly next weekend. Y'all could join us and double date," Brooks offered. "Give the girls some bonding time."

"We've got options," Vance said. "And we've got some time. It's good she tipped her hand though. Gives us the opportunity to head all this off for Thor's sake as well as for E&E."

"All of this could be a moot point if Scarlett and Missy don't find a way to get along," Thor said. "Honest to God, I don't know a lot about women, but I'm relatively certain that's something that could make or break us."

"They'll get along," Pinks promised.

"Says the man who had no idea Missy moved down here and took a job for him."

"Trust me. That was short-lived," Pinks told Thor. "And yeah, it would really suck if Scarlett and Missy didn't get along. But Missy actually likes and gets along with Scarlett's mother, and trust me, Scarlett is a whole lot easier to handle than Garland."

"Seriously? Easier?" Thor argued. "Scarlett didn't give you her last name, her hometown, or where she attended college. If you hadn't shown up at her sister's wedding and figured it all out on your own, she'd still have you dangling in the dark."

Pinks's head snapped back.

"Don't look at me like that," Thor told him. "You know it's the damn truth."

Pinks stood there a good long moment, chewing on the inside of his cheek. Then he turned, threw open the French doors, and barged back into the house bellowing, "Scarlett!"

"Nice, asshole," Vance said, pushing at Thor. "The Ninja hasn't been through enough? You gotta go and pull the rug out from under him?"

"I was just pointing out the facts," Thor said, feigning innocence.

Brooks chuckled, knocking his beer against Thor's glass.

Vance looked between the two of them. "Honest to God, I don't get it. What the hell do you two have against Pinks?"

"Oh, jeez," Brooks said, eyeing Thor. "Where do we start?"

"Probably with Lolly and Missy screaming their heads off over him playing the drums last night?" Thor offered.

"Exactly." Brooks nodded. "And how about when he paraded his lacrosse team all over the damn place yesterday when Opening Day Spectacular was supposed to be about *baseball*?"

"Don't forget he drives Hale's One-77 around here like he owns it."

"Not to mention he now gets far more of your time than I do," Brooks told Vance.

"Oh, boo-fucking-hoo," Vance retorted. "Pinks and I work together. The guy's going to get you elected mayor in a landslide. You think you could show a little gratitude."

"He's getting me elected mayor by putting out his *own* fucking agenda."

"And what part of *his* agenda do you not agree with? Face it. The Ninja has picked up the ball—*our ball*—and is running with it. Which frees you up to spend your weekends chasing Lolly around Raleigh and me to get to know my wife. If it wasn't for Pinks, Crain Carraway would never have made it to Henderson, there'd be no sports academy in the works, and I'd still be putting up with Tansy in the office. And the fact that he's fallen for Scarlett Langford is the best damn news you two are ever gonna get. Because, one"—Vance pointed to Thor—"it means he's not interested in your Missy. And, two"—he told Brooks—"now he has an even bigger reason to stick around Henderson and see all of this through. You being mayor, the sports academy, Harvard Michael's brewpub, and whatever the hell else he's got up his sleeve on behalf of Henderson. Trust me, you need to do yourselves a favor and stop messin' with the Ninja."

When Vance received nothing but a couple of smirks, he said, "Seriously. You two need to stop giving my boy a hard time."

"We will," Brooks promised, grinning.

"Eventually," Thor agreed, grinning back.

CHAPTER SIX

"Baby, I thought Cal was joining us for brunch." Nathaniel Houser, a.k.a. Nate the Great—legendary Hall of Fame pitcher—sat across from his daughter in a tidy little booth inside the bustling old-school diner.

"Mmm," Natalie responded vaguely, acting fully engrossed in the overlarge menu. "Must have slept in."

"Really? Well, that doesn't seem like Cal."

Natalie flipped down her menu. "Daddy, you just met Cal Friday night. How do you know what he's like?"

Her father's head popped up, eyes wide and mouth slack. After a couple of blinks directed at his daughter, he turned a questioning glance to his wife. "What'd I miss?"

"I'm not sure," her mother replied slowly, eyeing Natalie. With a furrowed brow, she leaned over the table. "Sweetheart, when we left the party last night, it certainly looked as if you and Cal were hitting it off."

Glancing between her parents' concerned expressions, Natalie did her best to tamp down her disappointment and assume an air of casual nonchalance. "We did. Yesterday was a lot of fun. I just thought it was a little much, expecting him to show up for brunch with my parents. So I didn't bother him with a wake-up call. Besides, I haven't had a moment to catch up with just you two. If Cal were here, the talk would be nonstop baseball."

"Since when don't you want to talk baseball?" her father wondered.

He sort of had her there.

"Did something happen? Because when Cal wasn't pitching or signing autographs yesterday, it did not escape my notice that he couldn't keep his hands off you."

"Nothing happened," she blurted, worried over the concern in her father's voice. "I promise, Daddy," she soothed. "Cal was a gentleman. A truly great date." *Until he wasn't.* "But, you know, he is superstar *Cal Johnson*," she said waving her fingers in the air. "It's not like I'm ever gonna see him again—"

"Hey. Sorry I'm late."

And there he stood.

At the end of their booth.

His sexy hair wet and slicked-back like he'd just walked out of the locker room after a game.

Ho-ly shi…

It was as if his broad, well-defined chest—that was stretching the crap out of an Under Armour PROTECT THIS HOUSE T-shirt— had materialized out of nowhere, at eye level, and well within stroking distance.

Natalie sat mesmerized. To say Cal's presence had taken her by surprise was an understatement. To use the term "delectably tasty" to describe him would also be an understatement.

She licked her lips as Cal put a hand out toward her father. "Nate," Cal said, calling her father Nate because everyone called him Nate. Her father stood in greeting, shaking Cal's hand. "Mrs. Great—I mean, Mrs. Houser." Cal waved a hand at her mother. "I've taken to calling y'all Mr. and Mrs. Great. I certainly don't mean any disrespect," he told her and looked so adorable doing it there was no way her mother could possibly take offense.

"I'll own Mrs. Great," her mother said, smiling. "So glad you could join us, Cal."

"I was looking forward to it. Eager for the opportunity to get to know the entire Houser family better before I have to get my head back into spring training." He turned and laid a blistering stare on Natalie. "That still okay with you … *Natalie Anne?* Or should I start calling you Miss Great so there will be no further fu—mess-ups?"

She didn't say anything. Mostly because the moment Cal and his hot Under Armoured chest had appeared at her side, her stomach had flipped sideways. And then when he'd gone and been adorable on top of all that holy-crap sexy, her heart had twisted itself into a double knot. And now that he'd made a show of saying her full name—which is why he hadn't gotten that wake-up call she'd promised and apparently he knew it—her nervous stomach had pushed her twisted heart up into her throat, allowing no room for noise to escape. The most she could do was divert her gaze from all that temptation and scoot over in the booth.

"I'm sorry," he whispered in her ear as he took a seat beside her. And then he continued to stare at her profile as she looked everywhere but at him. She could feel it. The heat of his gaze. Feel those gorgeous blue eyes marking her. Just like they had in the hot tub the night they met.

"Natalie?" he called softly. Although it wasn't like her parents couldn't hear it. The two of them were sitting right across the table, engrossed in studying him. She knew this because she was studying them study him. Because she couldn't chance a look at him if she didn't want to fall back under the spell of Cal Johnson.

"Nat. Look at me."

This wasn't spoken soft. Not that it was loud, it wasn't. But it was sharp, and it was demanding. Her head snapped around following his order before her brain had a chance to process it.

His eyes went seriously blue. "There is no Kathy, or Kathleen, or Kaitlyn, or any K—or C for that matter—in my life. Nobody but you." And he'd said that sweet. That last part. The kind of sweet that had her stomach melting and her heart untwisting, allowing her throat to let out a breathy little squeak.

Dang.

And then Cal Johnson, centerfold material and MLB Rookie of the Year, turned his head toward her parents and told them—*admitted to her parents*—that once he finally worked up the nerve to kiss their daughter last night, he apparently messed up the pronunciation of her name.

What the hell?

Which, he went on to say, was probably why he didn't get the wake-up call he'd been promised and ultimately why he was late.

Her mother glanced over at her and grinned.

Her father thought it was so damn adorable he snorted.

What the hell, some more.

"You called me Kat," she accused.

"Which rhymes with Nat," he said, like that explained everything. "Just like Great rhymes with Nate."

"What does that have to do with anything?"

"It doesn't. Unless you've had three shots after pounding too many beers. And you've sung on stage to a girl you've been killing yourself to impress. And the night just keeps getting better until you finally do what you've been dying to do since you laid eyes on the girl forty hours prior to all of that going down."

"W-w-what?"

"Nat. I like you. I like you so much I'm making an ass out of myself in front of Nate the Great and Mrs. Nate the Great. Because, God's honest truth, if I called you Kat instead of Nat—which I *do not* remember doing and, may I add, in a loud and crowded bar, it's very possible you misheard me—but if I did it, it was because I had one too many while on a high enjoying the night and your company."

Yep. There it was. Her heart re-twisted and lodged back up in her throat.

When she did nothing but stare at his gorgeous face, her mind replaying the sweetest words within his convoluted explanation and not really processing anything at this point, he said emphatically, "Come on, Nat. Do not bench me for this."

"Bench you?"

"Bench me. Delete my number. Let me sleep through brunch with you and the Greats."

The way he continued to use that name struck her funny bone, causing her to burst out laughing. She told her parents, "He truly has been calling you that all weekend. The Greats. Like it's our last name."

"Are you ready to order?" a waitress interrupted.

"Am I staying?" Cal asked Nat.

Feeling light hearted and happy—probably way too happy—Natalie flicked an index finger at him. "Far be it for me to bench you during brunch with the Greats."

"Thank God," Cal breathed, clapping his hands together and rubbing them over the table. "So I'm buying," he said, holding his palms out to the table at large. "And because I need a little hair of the dog," he went on, turning his attention to the waitress, "we'll start with four Bloody Marys." That bought him a wink and a smile from the waitress. After she moved off, Cal turned back to the table, ran a hand through his hair, and confessed, "Jack Daniels kicked my ass last night."

Thor sat near Vance and Brooks at the end of the Evanses' large patio table astounded by what was happening. Missy, *his Melissa*—the girl so adamant about leaving Henderson that she didn't want to lead him on *(even though she damn well had)*—was holding court.

At the Evanses' table.

With all hands on deck.

He wasn't sure how it started, wasn't clear when it began, because Thor tuned out the moment he'd sat down to brunch and Missy had picked a fight with Pinks over the one and only lacrosse field both of their teams had to share. He'd heard it all before, ad nauseam, and he wasn't interested in letting their grade-school drama ruin his meal.

But now, between Missy, Scarlett, and Pinks, no one else could get a word in. Not that either of the Es of E&E Investments or the town's next mayor wanted to interrupt. It wasn't often you witnessed genius at work.

And that's what was happening. Pure genius.

This conversation was the equivalent to a no-hitter in the making, and no one was about to thwart the flow.

As Thor glanced about the table, he sensed the dynamics shifting. Genevra, with her hands folded over her pregnant belly, sat enthralled by the conversation, her eyes wide and focused on each speaker in turn. At some point, Emelina started taking notes with the seriousness of a court stenographer. Hale was in full tycoon mode, heavily intent on the conversation, his hands clasped, his forearms firmly set on the table in front of him. Brooks looked stoic. He had his arms crossed over his chest and his eyes downcast, as if he were blocking out distractions so he'd be able to retain every word.

When Thor craned his neck to look back at Vance, well, that almost made him chuckle. Pushed away from the table, Vance sat casually with one foot crossed over a knee, jiggling a fast beat. His expression was one of prideful delight. As if he were the proud papa of all that was being born before him.

And maybe he was.

Maybe Vance was the true genius. Having the ability to hold onto a vision and then bring in the right people to make it happen. Because it was obvious by the rocket-fire escalation of ideas being bantered between Missy, Pinks, and Scarlett, that Vance had done his job.

Thor had tuned back into the conversation when Missy explained that Piper was promoting Henderson by sending a video of Cal's performance last night to the ends of social media and beyond. That had led to a discussion about the overarching vision they—*as in the three of them*—should now focus on for Henderson. Missy's creative marketing skills fueled Pinks's business insight. Pinks's business insight fueled Scarlett's unique hometown-girl perspective on boosting Henderson to a new level, while mindfully keeping the small-town feeling alive. This in turn had Missy creating an impromptu "hometown, small town, you want Henderson to be your town" marketing campaign, and so on, and so forth until a— frankly brilliant—step-by-step, month-by-month, year-by-year plan for a re-envisioned Henderson had been set forth.

More topics had been discussed than Thor had the brain space to recall, which, as it turned out, was exactly the ability that set Missy apart.

Her uncanny knack for being able to hold all of Team Henderson's projects in her mind, in addition to E&E's separate interests, Brooks's mayoral proposals, the many ventures being suggested for Main Street, plus her own vast and varied marketing strategies, not to mention her ability to refer back to each throughout the lengthy discussion, no doubt turned E&E's head. When she began reorganizing all of it—shuffling the order of projects—and succinctly detailing reasons for the shift and why they were necessary to achieve smooth, steady forward progress, Brooks definitely took notice.

And through every bit of it, little Miss *I-don't-want-to-be-stuck-in-a-small-town* was fully engaged in the process, enthusiastic about the outcome, and lit up like she was living her own personal dream. Right here. Right now.

Thor had a sneaking suspicion why Missy was so close to her big deal, business-executive father. She was probably just like him. On fire when running the show.

He leaned back and whispered to Vance, "No way is she leaving."

Vance slid him a smile. "Nope. Especially not after I offer her the title of CEO."

"You want me to do what?" Missy asked, stopping dead in her tracks.

Thor kept going, pulling her along with him. It had taken way too long to get her out of the Evans place, and during that time he'd managed to come up with his own agenda. "I want you to drive my truck."

"Why?"

Why? Because right now you're totally juiced about work, and I want you juiced about me. So …

Thor deliberately slowed his pace, turning to link their free hands so that he now had a good hold on both of hers. He sauntered backward, keeping them moving, but doing his best to block her view of anything but him. "You love my truck," he said quietly, putting voice to the secret they shared.

A sexy spark lit up those sea-green eyes, adding a little more color to his life. "I do love your truck," she acknowledged, scooting forward a few quick steps, closing the distance between them and turning herself into his kind of sweet. "That doesn't mean you have to let me drive it."

"But don't you want to?" He egged her on by opening the driver's door and sweeping his hand inside.

"It's awful big," she said, not looking at the interior at all, but sneaking that sweet of hers past all his defenses. Not to mention the fact that she was now firmly pressing some of his favorite memories from last night right up against him. Soft.

His arms closed around her, his hands sliding down over her ass while he grinned into her upturned face thinking, *I seriously wanna keep this one.* And then he kissed her, because how could he not? But before he got carried away, he twirled her around, focusing her attention back on his truck. He tucked his chin and whispered in her ear. "The fact that it's so big is one of the reasons you like it."

While she nodded absently, Thor took the opportunity to release the hair clip she'd utilized during that impromptu audition for CEO and tossed it behind him.

"Hey," she scolded, whirling around.

"You're off the clock," he said, dropping his voice into military-grade authority. "Get in."

An eyebrow rose in response. "Next time, just ask me to take my hair down. I'm starting to run low on clips."

"No promises," he said, giving her a hand up into the cab and shutting her inside.

Thor's instincts had proved correct. As soon as Missy turned the ignition, she giggled—very unbusinesslike—melting into the soft, feminine, hot little number his hands had strip-searched last night.

Although Missy's CEO persona was impressive and Thor felt a good deal of pride watching her coach that lacrosse team of hers, when it was just the two of them, he wasn't interested in her "take-charge" mode.

And if truth be told, as much as he enjoyed last night—and he'd enjoyed the hell out of it—he wasn't exactly comfortable with how it all went, ah … *down.* He wasn't certain how the next few hours were going to play out, but he was clear on one thing. That heart-to-heart they'd yet to have? Second item on his agenda.

As he directed her toward the lake, Missy's confidence in driving the big rig revved up. Once there, she insisted they get out so he could teach her how to skip stones. Apparently, this was something of a novelty to the city girl.

As he took her hand, walking them back to the truck, he told her, "Getting to the lake was just your warm up. Now you're going to put Big Red through its paces."

"Big Red?"

He shrugged. "Seems fitting."

She tossed him a girly grin of approval before climbing into the cab. "All right. Where to next?"

"See that dirt road?" He pointed to a small opening within a stand of pines.

Missy McReady did not disappoint. She clapped her hands in glee. Thor chuckled to himself as he buckled his seat belt. "Somehow, I knew you'd be up for this."

"Will I need to put it in four-wheel drive?" she asked, hitting the gas. "Please tell me I get to drive through a creek, or over a log, or something."

"Just make sure you keep both hands on the wheel," he told her. "Things are about to get bumpy."

Cal drove *Natalie Anne Houser* and the Greats to the private airport outside of Henderson in his rented SUV. After helping extract their luggage from the back, he appreciated how the Greats thanked him, said their goodbyes, and then headed inside the tiny building so he could have a few minutes alone with Natalie.

He took her hand, pointing at the sleek-looking jet that sat, steps down, on the tarmac. "Your father and I are world-class athletes, yet the Cupcake is the one with the private jet."

"Her mother likes to travel first class."

"Her mother isn't on this flight. I dare say Mighty Pinks has his work cut out for him."

Natalie shrugged. "It's fun being Scarlett's roommate. I flew private and"—she leaned in—"I got to meet *the* Cal Johnson."

He took advantage and slid an arm around her waist, keeping her close. "Well, speaking for *the* Cal Johnson, I'm pretty damn happy I had the chance to meet *the* Natalie Houser."

"And my dad."

"Your dad's cool. Without doubt one of my personal heroes. Still, not interested in sticking my tongue in his mouth."

"That is disgusting," Natalie laughed.

"And true. You gonna let me kiss you goodbye?"

"Probably," she hedged. "Showing up today at brunch was quite …"

"Desperate?" he finished.

"I was going to say, ballsy."

"Well, I've got a pair of those. Wasn't sure if you were going to kick them if I showed my face, but I was willing to take the chance."

"Cal."

"You get that, right? Liking you has nothing to do with your father. And stumbling over your name had everything to do with being love drunk after our first kiss."

"C-aal," she whispered. "Stop."

"Stop? It's the truth. You gotta know that."

Natalie shook her head, her brown eyes twinkling, her dark hair coming loose from behind her ear and falling into her face, making her look young and shy. "I enjoyed being your date this weekend."

"So what about Spring Break? Can I count on seeing you in Sarasota in two weeks?"

She quirked a brow. "You think you'll remember my name in two weeks?"

"You think you're funny?"

"You're Cal Johnson. You have women hanging all over you. I don't want to show up at spring training and embarrass myself, having been forgotten in fourteen days' time."

"Not gonna happen."

"It could happen."

"You're gonna have to trust me. Trust that whatever we've got started here is gonna stand the test of fourteen long days."

"And nights," she said.

"No. Not the nights."

"What do you mean?" She started to pull out of his hold.

"You're a senior in college. It's your last semester. I don't trust you and Cupcake not to be out carrying on, dancing topless on bars, and picking up men. Your nights are mine."

"What?"

"Oh yeah. We're Skyping. We're texting. We're having a whole lot of phone sex. No way are you two girls gonna be left to your own devices. I'm totally bringing Mighty Pinks in on this."

"You're bringing Pinks into our Skyping, texting, and phone sex?"

"He'll be taking care of Cupcake so I can take care of you. Now kiss me before Nate the Great comes out here and puts me in a chokehold."

CHAPTER SEVEN

Big Red exploded out of the forest path and into a vast, open space that gave the false impression it was suited for smooth passage. After managing to hit every deep divot and going airborne twice, the two of them were laughing so hard tears were mucking up their vision. "Stop. Stop. Holy shit," Thor squeaked out between guffaws. His head had hit the ceiling twice in the last thirty seconds. The truck, the terrain, and the speed had clearly gotten away from Missy.

"Okay. Okay," she cried through hysterical mirth, spinning the wheel, kicking up dust, and bouncing them to a jarring, albeit spectacularly cool, skid at the crest of a bluff. After a few deep breaths, she used two hands to put the gearshift in park, shining glistening eyes, flushed cheeks, and a dazzling smile in Thor's direction. "Most. Fun. Ever."

"Ever?" he questioned, raising a brow. He didn't try to deny the impulse to reach over and pull her to him. And just like last night and several times before, she came willingly into his lap, crawling over the console. "Better than this?" he asked, palming the back of her head, bringing her lips to his. He then proceeded to kiss the shit out of her.

Making out wasn't exactly next on his agenda, but hey, he was flexible like that.

"*Almost* as good," Missy declared once he let her up for air. "Ba-hahing in Big Red is *almost* as much fun as kissing the God of Thunder."

"God of Thunder?"

"Your name *is* Thor."

"My name is Thurgood."

"Yes-yes," she said, sitting up, striking a haughty pose, and pulling out her over-the-top Southern accent. "Thurgood Lewis Watson the Third. Still"—she leaned in to press her lips against his—"you do roll like thunder."

He grinned at that. "So you think I'm a god."

"It's what I've called you, in my head, since day one. Since you roared as loud as thunder and scared the bejesus out of me."

"Oh, like you didn't scare the shit out of me just now trying to topple Big Red. Damn girl." He shuddered at the thought, hugging her tight. The compulsion to keep her safe swamped him. He had trouble letting her go.

Yep. Definitely time for that heart-to-heart.

"So where are we?" Missy asked, pulling back to look around.

Tilting his head, Thor studied her beautiful face, wondering how a creative genius had not seen through his very obvious—at least to him—agenda. He licked his lips, stared into the tropical pools of her eyes, and made his decision. "Hop out. I want to show you something."

Missy grinned, twisted, and in an overzealous maneuver, flung the door open so hard that she lost her balance and tumbled into the evening air. It was the second time he'd witnessed the Division 1 athlete turn into a klutz. Only this time, Thor managed to catch her before she did a header, holding her steady long enough for her to wiggle her legs out and get her feet beneath her. Once certain she was okay, he let go, giving her all kinds of grief before he reached for the down vest she'd tossed in the backseat. "You might need this."

She slipped it on, flipping her hair from the collar and then running her hands down her leggings and smoothing out the long sweater she wore. "Wow," she said as she turned around.

Yeah, wow. Exactly what he was thinking as he stood there checking her out. Finally, his one-track mind caught sight of *her* wow. The sun was sinking toward the western horizon, tinting a long stretch of clouds a glorious spectrum of pink while gilding the colors of springtime that surrounded them.

In that moment, standing beside Missy, Thor saw the sprawling landscape breathtakingly full of opportunity. Felt the infinite possibilities he suspected his great-great grandpappy had tapped into the first time he laid eyes on this land. But realizing that—no ... *expanding* to that, because it was as if blinders had been removed and he now had a broader, expanded view—well, that just brought on its own sort of pain. He dearly wished he'd been able to see those possibilities while Pop was still alive.

Hands in his pockets, head bent, he scuffed the ground and told Missy, "My pop would have liked you."

"You think?"

He nodded, lifting his gaze toward the horizon.

Missy bumped him with her shoulder. "Why don't you tell me about him," she coaxed. "Lord knows, I continually talk your ear off about my father."

"Ahh ..." he drawled out, rubbing a hand behind his head. "Pop was a good man. Solid. Strong. He and I did all right together. Well, except right after my momma passed."

Missy circled her arms around his waist. "Him losing his wife, you losing your mom. It doesn't get more stressful than that."

Thor looked down, taking in her plump lips and those heart-halting eyes underneath a troubled brow. He smoothed a thumb over her forehead as he admitted quietly, "I made it more stressful for him."

"How's that?" she whispered.

"I never actually said the words out loud, but I blamed him for her death."

"You said she had cancer."

He nodded, wrapping an arm around her. "Lung cancer," he said absently, looking back toward the setting sun.

"Did your dad smoke?"

He shook his head.

"Did she?"

He nodded.

"But you blamed your dad for her lung cancer?"

Thor's arm squeezed her to him, though his eyes were on the horizon when he answered. "My dad, my grandfather, my forefathers, they all grew tobacco. For hundreds of years, my family grew tobacco."

That's when he dropped his chin and locked eyes with her.

"Wow," she said quietly.

"Yeah," he said back.

He stroked his hand over her waist. "I get that it was her choice to smoke. As an adult, I understand that she knowingly put herself at risk. I'm also aware of the highly addictive nature of cigarettes and that most people cannot break the addiction. But back then"—he shook his head—"as a kid in high school? Really needing my mom? I was devastated. And so angry at the world I took it out on my grieving father."

"Thurgood," she whispered, tugging at him. "You were a kid. I'm sure he understood."

He shook his head. "I was relentless. I acted out, making sure he and everyone else around me was as miserable as I was. I got in trouble at school, on the football field, and in town, but no more trouble than I got into with Pop. Back then the man had the patience of a drill sergeant—which is to say he didn't have much. Less so when grieving for his bride of twenty years. Things got so bad, he tossed my ass out of the house."

He felt her stiffen.

"I deserved it. Trust me. I was nasty."

"What happened?"

"Mrs. DuVal—Genevra—took me in. I'd been doing lawn work and odd jobs for her as part of my service credits for high school. She'd been through hell herself, her husband being killed on their honeymoon and all, so I guess she recognized inconsolable grief when she saw it. She took me in, gave me a bed, fed me. Told me it was okay to hate everybody and everything for as long as I needed to. Funny thing that. Once she gave me permission to act like an asshole, I stopped wanting to be one.

"She made no apologies about aggressively monitoring me for drugs and alcohol. But it only took a few weeks of her kindness, her home cooking, and her soft way of handling me to ease me off of hating my life and everyone in it. She pulled out the stinger, allowing me to get on with mourning my mother in a more appropriate way."

Thor took a deep breath before saying more. "Eventually, she negotiated a truce between Pop and me. Talked me into sticking around Henderson when all I wanted to do was run away from the pain. Saved me from dumping more heartache on a good man who'd done nothin' but love me.

"And now, life has come full circle, because after my pop passed, in my efforts to search for you, I ended up on the Evanses' doorstep. And there was Genevra, soothing me with that same warm smile, gracious heart, and delicious, delicious food. Hale Evans is a man among men, willingly sharing his regal home, his beautiful wife, and his dinner table with the likes of me. I will forever be obliged."

"So *that's* why you and Genevra are close."

"That's why. But don't go ratting me out to Brooks or Vance. I've got them on the hook when it comes to my previous relationship with Genevra, and I'm not letting them off. Of course, she wasn't *God*. She couldn't fix everything. Because the backbone of our father-son relationship was the plantation—the Watson Legacy Pop wanted to pass on to me. Like his father had and his father before him. Only I refused to take it."

"Of course, you did," Missy said staunchly.

"What do you mean, of course?"

"You certainly aren't going to grow tobacco when it was most likely the culprit in your mother's death. That would be emotional suicide."

Thor's free hand slid over his mouth, probably in an effort to contain his response. Because later, Thor would compare the sensation he was feeling to a time-rusted lock being severed from the chain strangling his insides. But standing there, falling into the spellbinding pools of Missy's eyes, he felt … ease. From the inside out.

To have someone, *anyone* understand? Nothing short of joy. And this one—*The One*—had come to it so simply. So easily.

Damn.

He pulled her in and kissed the top of her head. "Thank you for that," he whispered, feeling her hands smooth over his back.

"How were things between you and your dad at the end?"

His gaze drifted as he sighed, appreciating the brilliant colors for the first time since he could remember. "That's kind of miraculous, actually. We spent our final days together in camaraderie. There was one night where the two of us were enjoying a drink on the back porch, sharing the quiet. We started talking about Mom. How sweet she was. How much we loved her. How quickly she'd been taken. And how much she was still missed. We joked that for such a large plantation, it never seemed wasted on just us three. I remembered how big the place felt when it was down to just two, but I didn't have the guts to ask him how it felt once I was deployed. When there was only one. And now … well, now I know. Now I'm standing in his shoes."

His voice drifted off, leaving them in quiet. Missy didn't offer any words, which suited Thor fine. Having her standing there with him was enough to shake off the sorrow he'd unintentionally revisited. He pulled at her hand, heading toward the back of the truck. "The sun's not going to hold out much longer. As soon as the base of that fireball hits the horizon, it sinks fast. And Big Red and I have a surprise."

She gave him her sweet, soft grin, looking a little melancholy.

That was okay. The woman had a way of getting herself wound up faster than a hot knife sliced butter. Still, in an effort to shift the mood, he shot her a wink as he lowered the tailgate. Then he reached for her and plopped her ass down on it, letting her legs dangle.

The bed of his truck was clean, the way he liked to keep it. His brand-spanking-new Yeti cooler was loaded up with ice, water, beer, Coke, a bottle of Jack, and for the first time ever, white wine. Hoisting himself up, he moved to unfold two beach chairs. "Care for a sunset toast?"

Missy gave a little squeal when she saw the chairs and the open cooler. "A party on Big Red? Absolutely."

"Wine?"

"Wine?" Missy scoffed. "Do badass monster truck drivers drink wine?"

"Jack and Coke it is, then."

"So you planned this? You and Big Red?"

Thor chuckled as he filled a red Solo cup with ice. "I had hoped to get you out here today, yes. What I hadn't planned on was creating a badass monster trucker out of a sweet city girl." He poured two fingers' worth of whiskey in the cup and doused it with Coke. "But desperate times called for desperate measures. I figured if I wanted to shift your attention from all those town slogans you were coming up with, I needed a solid diversion."

Missy took the cup he offered and toasted him with it. "Nice job. Totally did the trick."

"I have my moments." Thor popped the top off his beer. "Speaking of which," he said, giving her a once-over from head to toe. "Pretty Girl, no way are you leaving at the end of lacrosse season. Not after that two-and-a-half-hour brainstorming session I just witnessed. The one where you bested the best of them with your step-by-step, five-year plan for world domination." He leaned back against the cab and crossed one ankle over the other. "I sat there and watched you pull a Pink One over on Pinks, watched you out shine the Golden Boy, saw you high jump over Hale, and then outrun Vance."

The girl didn't even try to disguise the fact that she was eating up his every word. "Jedi mind tricks."

"Come again?"

"My dad, he's a Star Wars fan. He's also built several companies from the ground up. So over eighteen years of dinner conversations, I've picked up a thing or two. He calls them Jedi mind tricks. Most of them are memorization skills. Acronyms. Repetition. Method of loci. Chunking. Rhymes and songs. Trust me, I've learned from a master. He likes it when I call him Yoda."

"Well, Yoda would have been proud of you today, that's for damn sure. The only one remotely capable of keeping up was Scarlett Langford, and that's because she's juiced about Cal Johnson's music career. Which, I have to say, is rather out there, but let's face it, worth a shot in the dark.

"And from what else you've told me about your father, it's plain as day your apple hasn't fallen far from his tree. You like running things, Coach. You *really like* being in charge. And there wasn't anybody sitting at that table listening to you today who doubts that you've got the I.Q, the people skills, and the creative wherewithal to handle running this whole damn show. Which I think is when Vance realized Henderson needs a CEO. Someone to oversee and coordinate all of the components needed to put Henderson on the map.

"And darlin', that's you. You are now the CEO of Henderson. And maybe you were willing to walk away from consulting with E&E, but running the show? Pretty Girl, there is no way you're walking away from that. You know it. I know it. And right now, the Evans family is counting on it."

To her credit, Missy didn't try to deny it. She just stood there, all city girl confident, clamping down hard on a smug smile he knew was bursting to get out.

"You're stuck," he told her as he approached. "You're invested," he said, slipping a palm around her neck. "You're no longer working for Team Henderson. You now *own* the team," he whispered as he brought his forehead to hers. "You're the GM," he said, licking his lips. "You're the coach," he whispered, moving in for a kiss. "You call the plays"—he nuzzled her bottom lip—"right here in your new"— kiss—"home"—kiss—"town."

Then he pulled back and smacked her ass.

"So how about you and I sit down, enjoy this sunset, and then do a little renegotiating on the bullshit you tried to feed me last night?"

"What bullshit?" she scoffed, turning and flouncing her sweet little ass down in the wrong chair.

"Not that one. That's not your chair."

"It *is* my chair," she protested. "It's red."

"Yes, red. Red like my truck. *My* truck, *my* chair. Your chair," he said, pointing. "Patriotic blue. Looks great next to red. Even reminds me of your eyes when you wiggled yourself in between my thighs last night and told me you didn't want to lead me on."

Missy startled with a gasp, whipping her head around from the setting sun. "First of all," she countered, holding her drink out toward him and waving it around, "whoever drove Big Red last sits in the chair of the corresponding color. *Obviously.* And second, after I *wiggled* between your thighs, you said you were *begging* me to lead you on. Which, by the way, was smooth. So smooth, I felt compelled to roll with it. I mean, far be it for me *not* to give the owner of my favorite truck what he wants," she said, supplying him with an impudent grin.

Thor picked up the blue chair, turned it away from the sunset, plopped his ass down, and then turned Melissa's chair so that she was facing him. "Is that what happened last night? You gave me what you think I wanted?"

The red cup halted abruptly at her lips. "Gave you what I think you wanted?"

"Missy. I've been panting at your heels like a damn puppy for weeks. I've made it no secret how I feel about you."

To that, she simply smiled. A big, beautiful, endorsement-quality smile that said she knew damn well she'd been juggling with his heart. And fuck, she was all kinds of cute when she shot back, "No, you haven't made it a secret. And likewise, from the number of times I've jumped into your lap, I'm sure you're aware that you and your big red truck have managed to turn my head. Which—as you may recall—culminated in *me* being the one to drag *you* out of the bar last night and into said truck."

Thor licked his lips. "That's what we need to talk about."

"Are you saying you didn't enjoy what happened in Big Red last night?" she asked primly.

"Of course, I *enjoyed* it, but that's not the point."

"On the contrary. Your enjoyment was *exactly* the point."

"Yes, but it's not *my* point."

"Which is?"

"The motivation behind you willingly wrapping those gorgeous lips of yours around my masterpiece."

At first, he saw her smile. Probably reacting to his terminology. But then her countenance changed. She sat up straight, blinking over wide eyes. "You're concerned about my motivation?"

"More than a little," he told her.

"Because?"

"Because I don't want you going down on me out of sheer gratitude."

Her head jerked back. "Gratitude?"

"For my help during the Spectacular … or any of the times you needed my truck."

He watched her expression tighten up. Watched as she blinked twice before leaning forward, pointing to her cup. "If I didn't think I needed this drink to get through the rest of this conversation, I would throw it in your face. Rest assured there is no chance you'll *ever* need to worry about my *motivation* again."

"Missy, stop. I didn't mean to offend you."

"You've completely offended me."

"No. What I've done is ask for clarification."

Her voice escalated. "What you've done is accuse me of doling out pity sex."

"Because I don't want that," he shouted, reaching out, grabbing Missy's chair and pulling it closer, jamming her knees between his thighs. "Look," he said in earnest. "I fucking loved last night. Every bit of it. *Especially* what happened in the backseat. I've wanted a night like that since the moment I laid eyes on you. Of course"—he threw his hands in the air—"I had no idea I'd have to cool my jets for the next thirty days before I saw you again. Trust me." He got in her face, "I had plenty of time to imagine all sorts of scenarios like last night. So imagine my frustration when finally, there you are—all dressed up like some fairy princess—and *already* in the arms of a fast-handed cowboy," he growled. "*Not* remotely close to any of the scenarios I'd played out in my mind."

"As if any of that were my fault," she retorted.

"You know what the bartender told me that night?" Thor plowed on. "Harry? He said if I wanted you, it was going to take patience and persistence. Told me that unlike the Cowboy, immediate gratification was not in my cards. But after waitin' on you for a full month, I was determined. So I plotted, and I planned, and I made damn sure I was standing right there when you needed a ride home." He moved forward again, lowering his voice. "And once I got your tipsy lips on mine, well, Harry was wrong. Because kissing you *was* immediate gratification." With a self deprecating laugh and a glance toward the sky, Thor shook his head. "Only the next morning, I find myself back to square one—having to endure your infatuation with the Pride of Baltimore. So yeah, turns out Harry was right. Patience and persistence."

"Thor—"

"Not done," he interrupted her. "Because, even though you and I managed to get over the Pinks barrier and go on to have a couple of good dates—*wham*. Friday, Pinks himself informs me you've planned your exit. So now I'm on the clock, patience is out the window, and I've got until the end of lacrosse season to change your mind. About me. About Henderson. About all this land we're sitting on."

"Wait a minute. This … land?" Missy looked around in awe. "This is *your* land? All of this?"

Thor sat back shaking his head, wondering how this could be a surprise. "Where the hell else would I bring you?"

"I don't know," Missy started, still looking around all wide-eyed and slack-jawed. "I pictured a farm. A flat farm. With fields. And corn. Rows and rows of corn. Silos. Barns. Chickens! Not this. Not tree lined … rolling … glorious … *land.*"

Thor hitched his chair closer to Missy's, leaned forward, and clasped his hands around her hips. His thumbs rubbed absently over the slight protrusion of bone as he said, "Okay, so now *this* is the conversation I brought you out here to have."

Thor took a breath in an effort to settle the two of them down.

"Pop always told me that farming was in my blood, but darned if I could feel it. So honestly, I can hardly blame you—a city girl—for being gun-shy about a guy strapped with a legacy of farming. The truth is, I never wanted to be stuck on a farm either. I had absolutely no attachment to the soil I grew up on until the day Pop had his aneurysm. And yeah, I could sell it. E&E would buy it at a fair price. And maybe someday that's what I'll do. But for right now, having my pop die on me like that, I'm tied to this land in a way I've never felt before."

"Thor, I get it. I do. The pain I'd be in if my dad were no longer a phone call away …" She shuddered. "I'd get in bed, pull the covers over my head, and I'd be done."

"Pretty much what I did. I truly envy your daily chats with your pop."

"Most of the time, it's just a quick check-in." She shrugged. "Although, the poor man only got a few brief texts yesterday between the Spectacular and … you know … us."

"Yeah, so this *us*."

"Thor, that wasn't pity sex. You've gotta know I'm into you. I've thrown myself into your lap enough times for any ultra-observant Army Ranger to have figured that out."

"So, me, you're into. My heritage, not so much."

"To be fair, this is the first I'm truly learning about your heritage."

"All right. I guess what I'm asking is, are you into me enough to keep an open mind? Without hanging a damn deadline over my head?"

There it was, that cute little smirk. "I think so."

"Yeah? Last night, you didn't want to lead me on. Today, Vance throws the title of CEO at you, and now you're invested enough to stick around to see if you want to fully invest in me?"

She leaned into him, brushing her head up against the side of his neck. He felt her breath on his skin when she said, "Trust me. I'm plenty invested in you."

He pulled back, holding her face gently between his palms. "Pretty Girl, you were running away."

"Because *everything* was new to me," she insisted, pulling out of his hands. "Henderson was new to me. The job was new to me. You were new to me. And yeah, it's fun running with the A-Team, but you weren't kidding when you warned me about Davis being distracted. From the start, I barely got five minutes at a time with him, and he's my only link to home. And then I find out he's tangled up with Scarlett, and I'm starting to fall for you … Thor," she took a breath. "I got scared. Scared of what was going to happen to Davis when everyone found out about him and Scarlett. Scared of *not* making Opening Day spectacular with Brooks, Vance, *and* Davis breathing down my neck."

"And scared of your feelings for me."

She tilted her head, going soft and easy with her sweet smile, those honey-rich curls cascading around her. "Because everyone needed something from me except you. *You* saw what I needed and did that. How could I not fall for you? So, yeah, I got scared. Because

I grew up in a boardroom. I don't fry chicken and have no interest in living near one. Combine that with all the job stress, and yes, I succumbed to panic and backpedaled."

She leaned in a little closer. "But after the success of the Spectacular and as good as things were between us last night, honestly my first thoughts this morning were about ways I could expand my business. Here, in Henderson. And *then*, well, Scarlett happened. You know, I didn't necessarily want to like her, but I'm telling you, witnessing the way she handled *Cal Johnson*? Scarlett takes girl power to a new stratosphere. Her signing on to Team Henderson is a game changer."

"You do know that being CEO of Henderson is not a paid position, right?"

Missy laughed. "Yeah. I know. But bossing Vance, Brooks, and Davis around is a helluva perk. However, and I'm not sure I mentioned this to the Evanses, for me, playing on the US lacrosse team takes precedence over everything."

"If you're the CEO, Pretty Girl, nobody's setting your schedule."

"Oh, shoot."

"What?"

"We missed the sunset."

CHAPTER EIGHT

Thor growled, tossing off his bed sheets and standing up for a stretch in nothing but the clothes he'd been born in. He scratched his ass and headed toward the shower, grumpy. Edgy. Downright surly, if truth be told. He might be off the clock when it came to Melissa, but that sure as hell didn't mean the damn girl was waking up in his bed. And no way was he spending any more time jerking off. He resorted to that bullshit twice last night in between the times he'd been kicking his own ass.

Pity sex. Really? He had to bring that up? Get all high and mighty over Missy's motivation for giving him an incredible twenty minutes which culminated in the best goddamn orgasm since he could remember?

Fucking hell.

Because sure as shit, he didn't get any pity sex last night, and right about now, pity sex sounded fucking awesome.

Swinging open the shower door and turning on the water, Thor tried not to replay the whole agonizing scene in his head. Missy straddling his lap the way she liked to do. Making out in the blue beach chair and then in the cab of his truck when the night had really set in.

He'd been in no hurry. He was taking his time. Just enjoying the hell out of sucking on her sweet mouth and coasting his hands over her smokin' body. Because he knew it was their night. Knew they'd turned a corner. Knew the time had finally come when he was going to take her home, show her around the place, back her up into his room, toss her onto his bed, and then have her every damn way he'd been picturing in his head for the past two months.

Which meant he was starting it off by going down on her. Not out of pity, but because it was the only recurring dream he'd ever had, and it had recurred plenty.

Only ... that was *so* not how it played out.

At all.

He squirted shampoo into his palm and lathered up as the scene played itself over in his head.

Missy breaking off their kiss with the bright idea of picking up her phone and texting Scarlett. Asking Scarlett to intervene on her behalf and convince Pinks to give her the earlier time slot on the lacrosse field.

Thor had to laugh when Scarlett immediately texted back a big fat "No."

"But she handled Cal Johnson so well," Missy complained, "I just thought ..."

"Scarlett handled Cal Johnson, Pinks, and her father this weekend. There's not a man around Scarlett can't handle."

"Even you?"

"Pfft. Don't be ridiculous."

"But you like her, right?" Missy asked Thor.

"Scarlett? I fucking love Scarlett. She's responsible for taking my stiffest competition out of play." He winked at Missy, who rolled her eyes. "But Pinks is her man. Even with all that girl power, she's not gonna choose you over her man."

"Her man," she scoffed. "*You're* the man," she said snuggling right under his defenses.

"Even when I'm rolling out pastry?"

"Especially then. You playing chef? Sexy." She kissed him, smiling. "But right now, I need you to play the part of sexy monster truck driver. I'm too tired to wrestle with Big Red, and I've got to get home."

"Home? I'm not planning on taking you home. At least not until the sun comes up."

"Thor, I can't," she said, alarmed. "I mean, I wish I could, but I just *can't*."

"You can't?"

"I can't."

"Explain to me how it is you *can't*."

"Well, it's Sunday, and I work tomorrow," she said, as if that had any bearing on the night ahead.

"Not planning to lock you up, Pretty Girl. You'll be free to come and go as you please."

"Yes," she laughed, snuggling against his chest," But right now, I'm exhausted, and I ache all over. I want to soak in Genevra's claw-foot tub, crawl into bed early, and get a good night's sleep. Because now that the Spectacular is over, I need to be up early figuring out how to fix my lacrosse team."

His arms hugged her to him, his hands caressing her back. "So lacrosse team aside, spending the night with me is ranking just below Genevra's tub and a good night's sleep?"

"Of course not," she groaned softly against him. "But trust me, I'll be no good to you until I've hit my personal refresh button."

He tilted her head to the side, leaned in, and sucked on her neck. "Trust me, I plan to hit all your buttons. You will definitely feel refreshed."

"Thor," she begged in a whimper.

"I'll massage out all your kinks."

"My kinks." She gave a soft laugh. "And if my kinks get kinky?" She pulled back from him, smiling.

"All the better," he purred. "You can't end tonight now." His hands slipped under her sweater. "Not when we've just reached an understanding."

"I have to," she said, placing her hands on top of his, stopping his fun. When he cried foul, she extracted herself from his lap telling him the two of them had enough fun for one weekend and crawled over into her own damn seat.

"What do you mean, *enough* fun?"

"I mean …" she said, while buckling up, right before she tossed her hair out of her face. She let out a sweet little sigh, leaned her cheek against the seatback, and looked over at him all soft and sleepy. "Tomorrow's Monday."

Thor started the truck. "Dating the damn CEO is not all it's cracked up to be," he muttered.

"Aww, come on," she teased. "Who gives you the best pity sex?"

He slammed on the brakes. "Is that why I'm not getting any tonight?"

"Maybe," she snickered. "Serves you right."

"Opened my damn mouth," he mumbled, carefully easing Big Red onto the forest path.

And kissing Missy goodnight for all he was worth at Genevra's front door didn't get him an invitation up to her bedroom. Nope, all it got him was another case of blue balls.

Damn.

Thor stood stock still under the water's spray letting suds slip from his hair onto his shoulders and down his body, facing another day he didn't know what to do with.

How the hell had his life become this?

He'd done nothing but take orders and hit the ground running every day for the last six years. Been an integral part of such a tight-knit team the word privacy had fallen out of his vocabulary. Now, he stood alone in a shower big enough for two, inside a quiet house built to accommodate many, surrounded by fallow land stretching out for hundreds of acres. And he didn't have a damn thing to do.

Thor was happy to be done following orders. And he rebuffed Brooks's invitation to join Team Henderson because he was no longer interested in putting time and effort, not to mention his life, on the line for someone else's mission.

So here he was.

His own man.

Yet, hell if he hadn't been waiting on a sign from his dead pop to tell him what to do.

Yeah, that's gotta stop, he thought, grabbing the soap and scrubbing hard at his skin. Not the way he'd pictured it, but freedom was freedom. And it came with a cost. The cost of standing up for what you wanted. The cost of making tough decisions and owning them. The cost of putting your heart out there and convincing *the* girl that what you wanted was going to blend really well with whatever the hell she wanted.

He stepped from the shower, grabbed a towel, and thought about how Missy's eyes lit up when she realized they were sitting on his land. The best he could remember, it was silos and corn and chickens she wasn't interested in. She seemed enamored with the beauty of the land. He needed to get her back out here and take her for a ride on his pop's big, expensive tractor simply because it was *fun*. Show her that owning land was a good thing. Not something he'd simply been stuck with. That this land gave the two of them a world of possibilities. Farming was just one of them.

And if Team Henderson was taking the homestead next to his and starting up a sports academy in order to save the whole damn town of Henderson, surely Thor could think of something to do with all of his property that would contribute to the local area and reel Missy in as well. Or at least not repel her.

Ah—what the hell just happened?

Thor stood eyeing his own reflection in the mirror. Wondering why he'd never been able to expand his view of the plantation from fertile soil and tobacco plants before now.

When the answer came, it hurt his heart.

No expansion from tobacco plants would have happened if his pop was still around.

"Damn," he said aloud.

Stepping out onto his back porch with a steaming mug of coffee, Thor was set to do what he'd done a hundred times before. Only today when he walked the property, he was asking a different question.

What could he create out of all of this that Missy McReady would find wildly intoxicating? But as he stepped off the porch, he heard a skidding sound around the corner of the garage. Curious, he headed in that direction only to be brought up short.

"Marnie?"

A ten-year-old spitfire, wearing navy blue Chuck Taylors, flood-water Levi's and a way-too-big Carolina Panthers football jersey, came around the corner on a full tear, head down, meaning business. She screeched to a halt when she heard her name.

"Oh. Hey. They said you were okay now."

"Okay now?"

"Yeah. That since you've shaved your beard, it was all right to come by."

"They?"

"Mimi and Dadaddy."

"Ah. How are your grandparents?"

"Good." She stood impossibly still, staring at him. "Sorry about your dad."

He nodded. "Sorry about your mom."

She nodded. After a moment, she said, "So are you okay?"

Thor sipped his coffee, loving the frankness of youth. "I'm as okay as you are."

"I'm fine," she shrugged. "Your dad was nice. He liked you. Bet I'd grow a beard too if it was Dadaddy or Mimi who bit it."

"Bit it?"

"Sorry. You know. Died and all."

"Yeah," he chuckled under a sip of coffee. "I know. So Mimi and Dadaddy were worried about me growing the beard?"

"They just didn't think I should bother you while you were wearing it."

"I probably could have used bothering. Whatcha wanna bother me with?'

"You ever kill someone?"

"Whoa—What?"

"In the Army? You ever kill someone?"

"If I did, I'm not gonna brag about it to a ten-year-old."

"Well," she said, flinging her hands out, exasperated. "Do you at least know how to shoot a gun?"

"I do."

"Can you teach me?"

Thor looked at her sideways. "Who needs killin'?"

"I'm not going to kill anyone," she said, starting to move about as she talked. "I just want to learn how to shoot. And play football. Mimi said you played in high school and could teach me the basics."

"She did, did she? What the hell's going on over at your grandparents' place that's got a ten-year-old girl interested in guns and football?"

The little minx folded her arms over her chest and looked him in the eye. "Nothin's going on. I've got my own reasons. And they're personal."

"Is that right? And you aren't in school right now because …?"

"Teachers' professional day. Whatever that means. I've got the day off with nothing to do. Figured it would be the perfect time for you to start teaching me."

"You got the day off, huh? Well," he said, licking his lips. "How 'bout hopping up in Old Man Watson's big rig and going for a ride with me?"

"Sure. Got any more coffee?"

"You don't drink coffee."

"Says who?"

"Come on, Midget." He motioned for her to follow. "Coffee's just gonna stunt your growth so you'll be no good at football, and it'll give you the shakes, causing you to shoot like shit."

She laughed, letting him hoist her up into his pop's big machine. "You said shit."

"Don't tell your Mimi on me. They'll never let you come back. Now, tuck yourself into the window for a moment, and let me get situated."

"You got any idea what you're doin'?"

"Pfft," he scoffed at first, but once he settled himself inside, he looked over and told her, "None at all."

She giggled. "Dadaddy says Ol' Man Watson was a gentleman farmer. Said he had no business owning a piece of machinery like this."

"Your Dadaddy is correct."

"So why'd he buy it?" she asked as they started rumbling along the flat acreage that stretched behind the house.

"Because he could. And it's fun." He grinned at her as he shifted gears, heading them over the ridge and down into the rolling hills.

"I'd rather have a race horse. Race horses are fun."

"Owning a race horse would be fun," Thor agreed. "What else do you think is fun?"

"Dodge ball. My bike. My friend Nancy's trampoline."

Thor nodded. "All fun. What else?"

"Swimmin' with no clothes on." She giggled.

Thor looked over at her and grinned. "Your Mimi and Dadaddy know you like to skinny-dip?"

"No. We do that at Nancy's too."

"Who's this Nancy?"

"My friend. She's rich. Got everything right in her backyard. A pool, a trampoline, a basketball court that we can rollerblade on. But she doesn't have all this land. You know what would be really fun out here?" she said, looking over at a big hill to their right. "A slide. A really long slide that goes all the way from the top of that hill down to the bottom there. I went to a water park once where the slide was so long they gave you a mat to lie on as you went down."

"Water parks are definitely fun."

"You should build a water park."

"Yeah?" He bobbled his head and looked out the other window. "I should definitely build something."

"If you build something fun, I bet all your Army buddies would want to come see you."

"Probably," he laughed.

"Then you wouldn't be lonely."

His head snapped around. "You worried about me being lonely, Midget?"

She slid from her perch on the window ledge and onto his right leg. Putting his arm around her just came natural.

"That beard was not a good look on you."

He laughed at that. "You don't think I rocked it?"

"You definitely didn't rock it." Then she got quiet for a moment before letting out a big sigh. "You and me are orphans."

He cocked his head, not ever having looked at it like that. "Guess we are. Though you got Mimi and Dadaddy. And those two aren't going anywhere for a long time." He downshifted and looked over at her. "You worried about that? About your grandparents dying on you?"

She just stared out the front of the cab and hitched a shoulder at him.

Of course, she was worried.

He gave her a little squeeze. "This got anything to do with you wanting to learn to shoot?"

She shrugged again.

"You need to talk something out, I'm your guy, right? Us orphans need to stick together."

"So if I tell you why I want to learn to shoot and play football, you won't go blabbing to Mimi, right?"

"Right. Unless you're in some kind of trouble I can't handle on my own."

She rolled her eyes dramatically and looked up at him. "Why do you think I'm coming to you? You're an Army Ranger. What kind of trouble are you not going to be able to handle on your own?"

"Nothing you can get into, I hope. However," he stressed, "if you tell me you're gonna shoot somebody, all bets are off. Anything else stays between us."

"Good," she said, nodding her head in a big gesture.

Silence.

"So you gonna spill or what?" Thor might be able to wrap his head around the football idea, because Marnie was an active kid who showed athletic promise. And no way in hell was he pulling the gender card. He'd known too many capable women in the armed forces to be telling a ten-year-old female what she could or couldn't do in her lifetime. But having an interest in learning to shoot a gun at her age was not sitting easy with him.

"I think my dad plays football. And likes to hunt."

Ho-ly hell. He did *not* see that coming.

"Your dad? Do you know ... have you met your dad?"

"No. But I heard talk. At the funeral. My mom's college friends whispering about me like I couldn't hear or understand what they were saying. I'm ten," she exclaimed. "Old enough to know how to Google a name when I hear one."

"You Googled him?"

"Yep. Plays football for a team I hate. Not married. *No kids*," she said dramatically. "Like I don't exist. He's rather scrawny for the NFL," she said, wrinkling her nose. "Not a starter but plays enough."

"Do not tell me his name," Thor said, unsure of what he'd do with that kind of intelligence.

"Don't worry. You haven't heard of him. No one's heard of him."

"You think he's heard of you?"

She shook her head. "Mimi said my mother never told my father about me. Didn't want complications." He saw the eye roll that came after that.

"So because Google says he's a football player and likes to hunt, you think you need to like those things too?"

"What I think is that if Mimi and Dadaddy kick the bucket before I'm old enough to take care of myself, I might need to be able to get on his good side."

"Marnie. Okay, let's just hold it right there." Thor brought the big rig to a halt and turned his full attention to the child at his side. "First of all, it is highly unlikely that what happened to my pop is going to happen to your Mimi or Dadaddy or anybody else you know, ever. It's sort of a freak occurrence. Not something you need to be worried about. Second, if something like that did happen and you needed someone to take care of you, I've got more room in my house than I know what to do with. And like you said, I don't rock that lonely beard look, so you'd be doing me a favor by moving in with me, making sure I remembered to shave. We orphans would figure out how to take care of each other."

"Can you cook?"

"I'm learning."

"What about money?" she asked.

"What about money?"

"I don't have any."

"You don't need any. I've got plenty for the both of us."

"You don't even work," she scoffed. "You can't afford to send a kid to college."

"I can afford to send you to college and buy you a damn race horse."

"You can?"

"Yeah. But don't get your hopes up," he said, putting the tractor in gear. "Your grandfather is so ornery he's going to outlive the both of us."

She giggled at that.

"I'm not telling you not to play football or learn to hunt. But I will tell you not to waste your life trying to please anyone, especially a guy who may-or-may-not be your father. If the day ever comes that you meet your biological father? Trust me. He's going to like you just the way you are."

"Nobody likes anybody the way they are."

That made Thor laugh. "Why do you say that?"

"Mimi wants Dadaddy to stop drinking a beer every night. Which is like, ridiculous. Every night he heads out back, sits in his chair, and drinks a beer looking at the stars. Every night," she stressed. "That's what he does. If he didn't do that, I wouldn't know where to find him."

"I hear that."

"And she wants me to stop sassing her about putting on a dress for church every Sunday, which I feel is the biggest waste of time ever. Because as soon as church is done, she makes me take it off. I don't like to waste time. Getting dressed twice in one day is a huge waste of time."

"Not gonna argue with you."

"Mimi wants to change everybody," Marnie said, going on talking a blue streak, not caring that Thor wasn't chiming in with anything more than an "a-ha," or a half-hearted "is that true." He tuned it out for the most part, turning the tractor toward home. They were almost back to the house when it struck him that Marnie reminded him of Missy, prattling on like she was. Lord knows that girl could talk the ear off a brass monkey.

"Marnie," he interrupted. "I've got a plan. Let's head into the kitchen. I haven't eaten breakfast yet, so that will give me a chance to demonstrate my cooking skills for you, just in case worse comes to worst. Then, I'm sure we'll be able to dig up a football somewhere around the house and get to work on your spiral."

"My spiral?"

"How you throw a football."

"Oh."

"Then this afternoon, I'm going to take you over to the high school to introduce you to somebody I think you'll like."

"Who?"

"It's a surprise."

Later that day, Marnie decided she should know how to use her foot on something called a *foot*ball, so she headed inside to Google "how to kick a football" while Thor dug through his pop's shed searching for supplies to create a makeshift field goal. He and his buddies had constructed two of them back in high school. In fact, they'd had some epic pickup games right here on the turf behind his house.

Supplies in hand, he checked his watch. Only a couple more hours before he and Marnie could slide by Missy's lacrosse game, see if it might be something Marnie wanted to try. He was getting excited about introducing a kid like Marnie to the sport. Wondered if she and Missy would hit it off. Wondered if they'd be able to give Missy a ride home, or if he'd be able to take her to dinner, or better yet, take her to bed.

Of course, he and Marnie would probably be subjected to another earful of Missy's latest fight with Pinks over the damn field they shared—*Whoa.*

Thor looked down at the land beneath his feet.

Missy's team had to share a field with the boys' team. A field that was crap. A field that was, in fact, too small for the women's game.

Holy shit! Missy McReady needed a regulation-size women's lacrosse field that she had access to any time she wanted. And *he* could give it to her.

He looked left toward the horizon, skimmed his gaze across the ground back toward his feet, and then turned to scan the rest of it. Flat. Good drainage. Plenty of land.

He dropped everything he was holding, pulled out his phone, and called his buddy Thatcher. Why this idea hadn't occurred to him the other night at The Sit—

"Thatcher! Thor here. What exactly is it you do in Chapel Hill? Ah-ha. Does that mean you could instruct me on making a rudimentary playing field? Say, a lacrosse field, in my back yard?"

The conversation went on and on. Thor marched into the house while he listened, gave a wave to Marnie, gathered up pen and paper without taking off his boots or coat, and started writing notes. He jotted down the names and numbers he was given. The website.

Asked if Thatcher had any time to give him, telling him he needed this done yesterday. He wouldn't say cost was no object; it was just way down on the list of concerns.

"Okay. Well, do that and check back with me. Listen, I'm willing to pay overtime and string some lights up so we can work at night if that's what it's going to take. All right. I hear ya. Yeah. Get back to me."

He disconnected and went to stare out the sliding glass doors.

What was the one thing Missy McReady really wanted right now?

Her very own lacrosse field.

Damn.

CHAPTER NINE

Marcie Watts walked around Clint Stevens's office, looking at every framed photo, every certificate of merit, every little knick-knack.

"Duke grad?" she asked, pointing to the picture.

"Class of '97."

She nodded, moving on to the next photo, her arms crossed, her perusal measured.

Clint followed along, keeping a few paces behind her. "I'd have thought you'd gone back to your hotel Saturday night and Googled me."

"I did," she said, continuing her expedition.

"And what did you find?"

She stopped and turned, all business. "You were a rising star at Lehman Brothers. Lost your wife on 9/11. Came back home, set up your own financial services business, ran for mayor, and have held the job ever since."

"That's it?"

"That's it."

"Well, hell. My life is even more boring than I feared."

Marcie placed a polished nail over her grin. Something about Clint's one part refined, two parts good ol' boy was getting to her. The idea tickled. "You know, I didn't expect to actually like you."

"Of course, you didn't," he chuckled. "I'm a pariah."

"Because Brooks Bennett is running against you?"

"I didn't win Henderson a championship. I didn't take our state university to the College World Series. I'm not handsome nor am I any good with small talk."

Marcie licked her lips trying to hide her smile. The man was taller than most, held himself proudly like a mayor should, and had a full head of sandy-colored hair. "You're not shabby in the looks department," she told him, closing the distance between them. She had to lift her chin to meet his dark brown eyes. "Saturday night, you had quite the knack for small talk. I'm surprised your fan club isn't much larger."

"I'm old news." He shrugged.

"Yes, but are you a terrible mayor?"

"Well, I haven't been able to squeeze blood from a turnip."

"Meaning?"

He stepped away and moved toward his desk. "Revenue has been falling every year. Businesses close up. People move out. Yet, the ones who are left still want their trash collected. Which costs money. They want their schools safe. Which costs money. They want a full-time fire department, and we can't afford that. I'm a finance guy. I've got zero fat in the budget. This big, old office you are standing in gets no air-conditioning in the summer and very little heat in the winter."

"Is Brooks Bennett a finance guy?" Marcie took the seat Clint indicated.

"Brooks is not. His right-hand man, Vance Evans, is."

"They appear highly motivated."

Clint nodded, his deep brown eyes such a contrast to his fair hair. "They are. And they've got good ideas. Hell, their baseball opener was a huge success."

"You sound like you're handing Brooks your job."

"Just being realistic. Look, Marcie. I don't want Henderson to dry up and die. These are my people. And yeah, maybe I'm being railroaded out of office, but hey, if Brooks can do better, I'm happy to step aside."

"Really?" Marcie's brows lifted. "You're *happy* to step aside?"

"No. Of course, not really. I've got as much ego as the next guy."

Marcie chuckled.

"But like I mentioned, I'm a realist."

"Clint." Marcie sighed. "I'm beginning to think you and I could become very good friends."

From his perch on the corner of his desk, the man cocked his head and tugged the corner of his mouth into a delightfully crooked grin. "Does that mean you're reconsidering my invitation to dinner?"

She crossed one slim leg over the other and clasped her hand around her knee. "I'm definitely thinking about it."

"Really?" His brows rose in actual surprise. "When I asked you out Saturday night, you said this was strictly business."

"It seems I'm changing my mind."

Clint stood and placed his hands on the arms of her chair. His gaze heated as he whispered, "Unfortunately for me, you're on your way out of town. How soon do you plan to return?"

"You seem eager," she whispered back.

"Been a widower a long time."

"Google suggested you have a lady friend."

"Like me, that's old news."

"You sure?"

"Been sure about that for a while now."

"Then, Thursday evening?"

"Will you need a place to stay?"

"I'll find something suitable."

"I'll take you to dinner at the club. Give you a taste of life inside Henderson. Then we'll sit down together Friday. See if you're still interested in helping me develop a game plan."

She reached up and toyed with the knot of his tie. "We can't mix business with pleasure?"

"Not at the club. It wouldn't be wise to strategize my campaign at the club just in case we're overheard."

"But if people see us there together?"

"They'll think I've got very good taste."

CHAPTER TEN

"Marn-eeeee!" The squeal came from behind them.

Thor and Marnie had been waiting just outside the girls' locker room. He'd taken her up to get a glimpse of the boys' game to let her see what lacrosse looked like. But he wanted to introduce her to Missy, so they'd been waiting for the girls' team to make an appearance. The two of them swung around as Ellie Baldecchi, one of the better players on Missy's team, came at Marnie with arms open wide and a lacrosse stick in hand.

"What are you doing here?" Ellie asked as she embraced Marnie enthusiastically. Thor couldn't help but notice that Marnie happily leaned in to Ellie, but didn't throw her arms around her.

"How do you know Marnie?" Thor asked.

"She's my little sister's BFF. Right Marnie-marn?"

Marnie nodded, uncharacteristically quiet, eyes riveted on Ellie, who'd put her hands on her hips. She looked down at Marnie and said, "The real question is how do *you* know the God of Thunder?"

"What?" Marnie looked sharply at Thor.

Ellie looked up at Thor, glee saturating her features. "That what Coach calls him."

"The God of Thunder?" Marnie questioned.

"Thor." When Marnie shook her head, Ellie went on. "Girl, you need to get out more. Come spend the night with Nancy this weekend, and I'll set you two up with the movie and the sequel. You here to watch our game?"

Marnie nodded.

"I want to introduce her to Coach," Thor interjected before Ellie could whisk her up the hill.

"Cool. She'll be right out. I need to go check out the end of the boys' game, so I'll see you up there." Ellie backed away calling, "Cheer for us, Marnie. We need it."

"Aren't they any good?" she asked Thor.

"Just in the learning stages. Pretty much getting their asses handed to them."

"Is that any way to talk about my team?"

Thor turned to find Missy clicking off her phone as she came up beside them.

"Don't tell me. Yoda?"

"Helping me shake up my team," she said.

But Thor was immediately distracted by Missy's hair, which was not all bound up in a clip, but in a ponytail with a big navy bow tied around it. She looked like one of her players. He had to clear his throat and remember where he was. "Missy, this is Marnie Mitchell, my neighbor and partner in crime. Marnie, this is Missy McReady. She's the coach I wanted you to meet."

Marnie stuck out her hand. Missy took it. "Nice to meet you, Marnie. Are you interested in lacrosse?"

"I want to play football."

"Oh." Missy glanced at Thor. "Well, that's ambitious. Good for you."

"Marnie's never seen a lacrosse game. I wanted to bring her over so she could check it out."

"It's fun," Missy warned. "More like basketball because it's fast. Do you like to run?"

"I like to ride my bike."

Missy laughed. "I remember when I used to ride my bike for fun. Come on. How about you stick with me on the sidelines? See what it's gonna take to bring you over to the dark side."

"The dark side?" Marnie asked, stepping out with Missy and heading up the hill.

"Mr. Watson?"

Thor immediately stopped trailing after his girls, recognizing his favorite player on Missy's team by the gentleness of her voice. He'd nicknamed Rett (short for Margaret) Patterson, Ranger Rett, because on the field, the girl was silent and deadly. She worked harder, played smarter, and ran heads and tails around everybody else. If Missy had just one more like her, they'd be dominating the league.

But she didn't.

And really, from the little time Thor had gotten to know Rett, the truth was, there wasn't anyone else like her. Rett was a true sweetheart. Kind to her teammates, generous with her praise. Helpful—the last one off the field, the first one picking up stray equipment or pieces of trash. Sharp as a damn tack, especially about teamwork and playing the game. She had All Star written all over her.

"What can I do ya for?" he asked as she fell in step beside him.

When he felt her hesitate, he stopped and gave her his full attention. "What's up?"

"Sadie Hawkins dance. Girls ask the boys."

"I accept," he said with a big grin.

She grinned back.

"You got your eye on someone?" he asked.

She nodded.

"You nervous about askin'?"

She nodded again.

"Good. Now you know how we men feel." He started heading toward the field.

"Yeah, but I don't want to put him on the spot if he doesn't want to say yes."

"Your name Rett Patterson?"

"Yeah."

"He'll say yes."

"What if he doesn't?"

"Then he's blind or plays for the other team."

"Pretty sure he doesn't play for the other team."

"Does he appear blind?"

"Nope."

"Then stop making the boy wait. Pull on your school-record-holding cleats and get in the game."

"Okay," she said, laughing, nodding her head. Until she looked farther up the hill. Then all the joy melted from her face.

Thor's gaze shifted, following her line of sight. Knew a damn train wreck of epic proportions in the making when he saw it. He wanted to call out—somehow divert the situation. But just like Rett, he was momentarily paralyzed watching the nightmare unfold.

Rett's teammate Ellie had caught up to Hank Ford after calling his name. He'd just started down the hill, covered in sweat after a hard game. But like all pretty-boy athletes, he totally pulled that shit off. He had some height and was built to withstand a hit, but Thor would bet it was the shy smile he was giving Ellie right now that really caught a girl's attention. That and the fact that his hair was a little long, so *the flow* flipped up at his collar.

Girls. Pu-lease.

Those thoughts aside, Thor didn't miss a moment of what happened. What *really* happened. Maybe Ellie was too caught up in the moment of asking Hank to the dance that she didn't notice how Hank hesitated, running a hand through his hair. How he looked down the hill right at Rett and shot her a glare that said FUCK in capital letters before turning his attention back to Ellie and doing what he had to do as a Southern gentleman. He accepted her invitation to the Sadie Hawkins dance.

Thor and Rett stood there. Side by side. Trying to make sense of what just happened. Finally, Thor whispered, "You saw that, right? That look that said he did not want to go with Ellie. That he wanted to go with you?"

Thor heard the heavy sigh. Watched as Rett bent her head toward the ground, leaning on the end of her short stick, collecting herself. "Doesn't matter," she said eventually, moving her body forward up the hill, but at a decidedly right angle in order to steer clear of Ellie and Hank, who were still in conversation. "She's just tagged him."

"She's just what?" Thor asked, stretching his legs to keep up with her.

"Tagged him. Claimed him. I can't date him now. Ever."

"Why?" Thor asked. "Are the two of you best friends or something? Why the hell didn't she know you were going to ask him?"

"We're not best friends. But we are teammates."

Teammates.

Yeah.

The reality of the situation sunk in. "That sucks," Thor said, really feeling for her and for Hank.

"He who hesitates is lost. I hesitated. I lost."

"You got a backup plan?" he asked as she headed onto the field for warm ups.

She turned, jogging backward, "How does a good book and a warm cup of milk sound?" she shouted.

"Horrible," he shouted back. She flashed him a smile before turning to engage in her sport.

"Well, that's ruined my day," Thor mumbled, spinning, his eyes peeled for Marnie. Looked as if the coach had handed her a clipboard and was having her call out the next stretch in the lineup. And that was good, real good, because he needed to find Pinks.

"Pinks," he said, grabbing the guy's arm, pulling him away from the sideline. "How'd your boys do?"

"Pulled it out by the skin of their teeth."

"Nice. Listen, can you keep a secret?"

"Absolutely. It's everyone I tell that can't."

"Okay, here's the—*seriously?*"

Pinks laughed. "An old Abe Lincoln quote. I'm good. Usually. You want to keep something from Missy? Not a problem."

"All right, then. I'm working on a big surprise—hopefully. What I need from you is your advice on a lacrosse stick for me and that little girl over there holding the clipboard."

"Done. I'll email you a link to what you need."

"They'll sell balls, too?"

"Pads, helmets, whatever you want."

"I don't need all that. But I could use a little instruction so I don't look like a moron throwing the ball around."

"I'll teach you the basics. Who's the kid?"

"Neighbor of mine being raised by her grandparents. Active. Interested in playing football, of all things. She reminds me a little of Missy, so I thought lacrosse might be a better fit. Hey, I'm gonna need two lacrosse goals delivered to my place. Can you handle that?"

"When do want them?"

"As soon as you can work it out."

"I'm on it."

"Great. Thanks. And, you know, don't tell Missy. Or anybody else," he threw in as he walked away.

CHAPTER ELEVEN

"I'm celebrating, and you're not here. Davis and I are showering and then going for a drink at the club," Missy said into her cellphone, leaving a message for Thor. "I mean, we're not showering together. We're each going home to shower and then meeting at the club," she clarified. Then she lowered her voice. "This is my first win as a coach, Rambo, and you are MIA. I'm really in the mood to slobber all over you right now. So show up or I'll have no choice but to slobber all over Davis. Just kidding. I'm soooo not into Davis anymore."

Click.

Damn. For weeks, the man is in my face every time I turn around, but my one big shining coach moment? Boom. Gone.

Missy tried not to pout about Thor being MIA since he and Marnie dropped her at home after the lacrosse game on Monday. But she couldn't remember another span of three days where she hadn't laid eyes on Thor.

Not that his texts weren't playing cute with her heart. Or his late-night phone calls weren't making the girly in her crave the manly in him. They were. And he was working that stuff big and in a way he'd never done before. Which meant there was something going on with him.

And not showing up for her game? Unprecedented.

If he was playing a game, trying to coax her into finding her way out to the Watson plantation without an official invitation, it was working. Because if he didn't show up at Henderson Country Club tonight, she was definitely showing up at his place after lights out. She wondered if she typed in "Watson plantation" into Google Maps, it would be able to get her there.

"There's trouble brewing," Davis told Missy the moment she joined him at the doors of the Mixed Grill.

"Perfect," she said. "I'm in the mood for trouble. What's up?"

"See that attractive woman at the bar chatting up Mayor Stevens?" Davis asked.

"Uh-huh."

"Not from Henderson."

"And that's a problem because ..."

"She's Coach Crenshaw's ex."

"Coach Cooper? The Orioles' third base coach?"

"Yes. Cal and I were a little concerned when we spied her at the Spectacular. But having her in Henderson six days later is downright alarming."

"Why? I don't get it."

"All of Baltimore knew Coach Cooper was planning to propose to her at Christmas. But while he was here helping out his grandparents for a few weeks, he fell back in love with his old flame, Christy-Lynn Brilhart. And *she* was the one the Coach proposed to at Christmas."

"Ooooh," Missy gave a strangled guffaw. "Wow."

"I actually met Cal Johnson because *Viper* sent Cal down to Henderson to find out what the hell was going on."

"Viper? They call her Viper?"

"Affectionately."

"So, what? You think she's here to win the Coach back? He's in Florida for spring training."

"I think Hell hath no fury like a woman scorned, and it worries me to see her cozying up to the mayor of Henderson."

"That guy's not going to be mayor for long, right? What harm can she do?"

"Well, let me ask you this," Davis said, taking his eyes off Viper and turning to Missy. "If you were going up against Team Henderson, who would be the first person you'd recruit as your teammate?"

"The guy who wants to stay in office."

"This woman is not stupid. I'm not sure of her goal, but I'm fairly certain of her motivation. So let's walk in there like we know nothing. I'll introduce you to Mayor Stevens, he'll introduce us to his new friend, we'll figure out the three of us are from Baltimore and boom, game on."

Missy shook her head, grinning.

"What?" Davis asked.

"I really am starting to love this town."

Davis chuckled. "I know—right?"

Missy held her wine glass in midair, after taking the first sip from the third glass Mayor Stevens had put on his tab, when Thor walked in shower fresh and dressed up for a business meeting.

Or a wedding.

Missy tilted her head, her wine sloshing just a little, as she watched him saunter over, thinking he might have on exactly what he'd been wearing at the Langford wedding.

She may not have recognized him then because he'd shaved off the beard and ditched the lumberjack attire, but an assortment of hot-tingly sensations indicated her body recognized him now. "You are really, *quite*, spectacular," she told him as he leaned in and kissed her cheek.

"You said you were in the mood to drool all over me," he whispered in her ear. "I wanted to hedge my bets."

"Vegas would give you very good odds."

"Is that right?"

"Mmm-hm," she hummed, taking another sip. "Because you, in that sport coat and tie, are completely droolworthy. But I believe what I actually mentioned earlier was that I wanted to *slobber* all over you."

"We'll get to that," Thor said, giving his attention to Davis as they shook hands and exchanged greetings. Davis introduced Thor to Marcie Watts, a.k.a. Viper, who made no pretense of just how attractive she found Thor. The woman beamed up at him, complimented him on his height, his hair, his jacket, his cologne for God's sake, and asked him barely camouflaged questions to assess his age and his profession. When she found out he was a Ranger she took hold of both his biceps and squeezed, saying something beyond ridiculous about *armed* forces.

Whatever, Missy thought taking another sip of her wine. Who wouldn't find *all that* irresistible? Besides, the woman had to be older than Thor by five years. Although, she was very attractive with that curly hair of hers. A gorgeous golden-brown color, like that tawny port Hale Evans liked to pour at the end of a meal. Hale Evans, her mind wandered. He was darn dreamy too. Henderson was like … loaded with hunky men.

Ding. Ding. Ding.

Missy set down her wine glass, pulling out her phone to text Scarlett.

"Brilliant idea!" She typed. *"A 'Hunky Men of Henderson' calendar. Between Thor, Hale, Vance, Brooks, Harry the bartender, Coach Crenshaw … we can even throw Davis in there and somehow claim Cal Johnson. Let's get on this now, have it available in September. You, Piper, and I can promote the hell out of it across the country."*

Scarlett must have been sitting on her phone.

"Cal and his album go on the cover. Which means I've got my work cut out for me. So the rest of the calendar is on you. But I want a wine bottle featured in every shot."

"Because?"

"Cross promotion for my wine shop."

"What wine shop?"

"The one I'm opening on Main Street. Naming it 'Reds.'"

Missy's eyes widened, loving the name. "Scarlett is fucking awesome," she said to her phone.

"Just how many drinks have you had?" Thor asked abruptly.

"What?" Missy said, looking up into four startled pairs of eyes.

"Pretty Girl," Thor said, picking up Missy's glass of wine and handing it to Harry. "How 'bout we get you some dinner?"

"I'm in the middle of negotiating a really big deal here. And trust me, if I hadn't had those three glasses of wine …" She glanced around Thor and addressed the mayor. "Thank you very much Mayor Stevens. This idea, which is *brilliant,* never would have occurred to me. So, Harry, make sure that wine gets to our table, because I'm on a roll. And when I get on a roll, stand back, there is just no telling where it's going to end."

Davis, damn him, burst out laughing.

"Harry, we need a picture," Davis said, gathering Mayor Stevens and Viper in with him and Thor as they all stood around Missy. "I've known this girl since she was seven. Seen her drunk one time and one time only."

"Ah, that's crap. I've been drunk plenty of times. Plenty!"

"I want to hear about her brilliant idea," Viper said as they all grinned for the picture.

"Top secret," Missy proclaimed, using her hands for emphasis. "*Top* secret. I mean, Thor could probably kiss it out of me because, you know, he's a god of sorts and seriously talented with his lips—"

"Okay. Here we go," Thor said, helping her out of her chair. "Off to dinner."

"What? You are," Missy insisted, as he tugged her off the bar stool, looking around for her phone and purse.

"I've got 'em," Davis said, holding up Missy's accessories. "Marcie? Clint? Please join us. We're celebrating Missy's first win as a coach, so the more the merrier."

"Not sure this one can get any merrier," Thor threw behind him as he helped guide Missy to the dining room.

"We'd be delighted," Viper said, taking Davis's arm.

Missy wasn't exactly clear about why a bread basket was placed in front of her before her bottom hit the chair. Or why Thor was intent on buttering a roll and feeding it to her. She did get that he wanted her to drink a lot of water from the way he kept putting the glass in her hand.

She couldn't remember exactly why she needed to be leery of Marcie Watts or Clint Stevens, because she liked them both. A lot. And Davis was sure pouring on the charm over there on the other side of the table.

"I *love* Henderson," Missy declared.

When they all stopped with some version of their forks halfway to their mouths and stared at her, she shrugged and owned it. "I do. I love Henderson. Because this," she indicated the table by circling her fingers, "wouldn't happen at Baltimore Country Club."

When they all looked at one another, Missy pressed Davis, "Would it?"

Fork at his lips, Davis glanced around before shaking his head. "No. It wouldn't."

"Would it?" Missy asked Marcie.

Marcie's expression softened as she placed her utensil down and dotted the edges of her brightly painted lips with her napkin. "No. In Baltimore, people are more likely to stick to themselves."

"And kids are born with a lacrosse stick in their hand. You don't get the thrill of teaching them this amazing sport when their bodies are really ready to play the game. Most of them are over it by high school or drummed out. Which is such a shame, because who knows how good you can be at anything until you've had a chance to mature? And these girls that I get to coach, they didn't know how to hold a stick when I begged them to try the game last month. And today ... they won." She threw up her hands. "I love Henderson."

Thor chuckled. "And it took you all of five or six weeks?"

"And three glasses of wine," Davis added. "I'm not sure this isn't the wine talking."

"Of course, it's the wine talking," she said. "But I do love Henderson. I love my jobs. All my jobs, especially my coaching job. And I'm happy I'm staying."

Before anyone had a chance to respond, Missy added an enthusiastic, "Oh, and Scarlett. I also *love* Scarlett."

"Girl power," Thor toasted, trying hard to hide his mirth.

"Go ahead and laugh," Missy said, not feeling a care in the world. "I stood on the sidelines today watching a bunch of teenagers come into alignment with a game they've been struggling with for weeks. I watched as they discovered the joy that comes from not giving up, working hard, and finally figuring it out. I'm telling you, it was magic. And maybe that's what I'm feeling. After struggling with being from out of town for weeks, maybe I've finally come into alignment and figured it out. Henderson is magic."

"Pretty Girl, my truck is this way." Thor tugged on Missy's hand out in the parking lot.

"Yeah, but I drove. I'm parked over here."

"No way am I letting you get behind the wheel."

"I'm perfectly sober now," she said, following along in Thor's wake.

"Geez, I hope not," he said, pulling her into his embrace and flattening her up against Big Red. "Because you being tipsy is the start of all our best nights." He placed a palm next to her head and leaned in. "And right now, I have your voice on my phone, talking about you wanting to slobber all over me. Trust me, I don't have the polite vocabulary to describe the dirty images that earful conjured up in my brain. The cold shower I took to get my ass cleaned up and over here had no effect on my anatomy whatsoever. Don't get me started on waltzing in there, finding you all dolled up in this slinky dress, your hair curling around you in a way that tickles my balls, and hearing any form of the F-word drop out of your mouth. Honest to God, if I hadn't been worried about what else was going to spew out of those juicy lips, I would have excused myself to the men's room and listened to your message over and over until I got the job done."

"So," she said, grabbing ahold of his shirt and rubbing up against him. "You gonna toss me in Big Red, drive me out to your plantation, and lock me in the attic?"

"Why would I lock you in the attic?"

"I don't know. Just sort of seems to fit with the flow you've got going on right now."

"No, baby. The flow we've got going is hopping in the backseat of Big Red so I can find out the answer to the mystery, 'Is she wearing any panties under that dress?' Then—"

Missy burst out laughing. "Of course, I'm wearing panties."

"Won't affect my plans one way or the other," he assured her, running his tongue along her neck.

"If I'm ever *not* wearing panties, worry. Because that means I've truly—"

Thor gently cupped a palm over her lips. "I love your mouth," he told her, the neon in his eyes sparking bright. "Putting the kibosh on all that chatter is just another thing about you that turns me on." He replaced his palm with his mouth, preventing any further talk. Although, there was a groan as she melted, letting go of everything except Thor as her arms circled his neck. "There's my soft," he whispered against her lips, gifting her with a smile before slipping his tongue back in for another go.

"Hey, guys," she heard Davis call.

Without moving off her body, Thor tore his mouth from their kiss, turning his head to the side. "I swear to God, Williams, if you cock block me right now, we are gonna have words."

"Sorry," she heard Davis say on a laugh. "Seriously. Sorry. Wasn't thinking. Make sure Missy gets home okay, and we'll circle up in the morning."

"Circle up in the morning," Thor grumbled, stepping back and eyeing her up. "You business types and your lingo. Get in the truck."

The sound of his gruff, take-no-prisoners voice had her following orders fast. "You know, I'm going to need to see a picture of you in your Ranger gear," she told him, crawling up into the driver's seat and then over the console, in a dress. Damn good thing she had underwear on. "Because dressed as you are, you look like a bigger, broader, far-more-handsome Davis. Makes me think I'm dating a member of some executive board. Either that or Tom Brady."

"Comparing me to Tom Brady is not going to hurt my feelings," Thor said, lighting up Big Red.

"You look good dressed up," she told him. "But then you look good in jeans and flannel. How 'bout board shorts? I wouldn't mind seeing you in a pair of board shorts. Are there pictures of you in your uniform out at the plantation? I'd like to see one. Oh, and of you in high school. Ohmygod," she giggled. "And baby Thor. I bet there are pictures of baby Thor. I cannot imagine you as a baby."

"Missy," he whispered.

"Yes?"

"Stop. Talking."

"I'm sorry," she said quietly, cuddling up to him as best she could with the console between them. "I tend to get chatty when I'm excited or nervous. I'll try to work on it."

She felt him brush a kiss on the top of her head. "Pretty Girl, you don't need to change a thing for me."

"Are you taking me to your place?"

"It's Thursday. You work tomorrow."

"Yes, but we're celebrating my big win."

"We're celebrating at Genevra's. It's closer. More to the point," he said, spinning the steering wheel and pulling them to a bumpy stop, "we're celebrating in Genevra's driveway."

"Driveway?" she asked, sitting up straight, looking out at her secluded surroundings.

"You. Backseat. Now."

"Really?" She grinned.

"Really." He grinned back before giving her a quick kiss. "Hit it."

She squealed as she twisted herself between the front seats and fell into the back. "So we're doing this old school," she said. Then, looking around, she called, "Thor?" The back door burst open, and Missy felt her legs pulled from under her and around toward the door with such force that the rest of her fell back against the seat, arms flying over her head. "Whoa."

Thor's handsome face slanted over hers, blue eyes twinkling, lips in a smirk. He still had his sport coat on. The collar of his shirt was clean and crisp. From what she could tell, he was standing outside the truck, leaning in. "That morning, after the wedding, where you smacked me awake? I was in the middle of a dream. This dream," he said, watching her reaction as his hands slid under her dress, palms spread over her thighs, sneaking up and grabbing the sides of her undies. He dipped his chin and placed a kiss on the skin of her chest in the V of her neckline, pulling her underwear down over her bottom, over her thighs, and down past her knees. He backed off her body the same time his hands pushed the skirt of her dress up her thighs.

For all of their lusty make out sessions, for all the longing and midnight fantasies he'd inspired, he'd yet to touch her *there*. Her hips did a reflexive curl just thinking about it as her bare skin was revealed. "Damn, you're fine," he said as he planted a kiss at the top of her sex.

She hummed with the vibration his thumb sent spinning throughout her body. Stroking slowly up and down, coaxing her to blossom. And then, dear God, his tongue—exactly where she needed it—lightly, teasing, tickling, before he kissed her open-mouthed and hummed a tune of his own.

She gripped whatever her hands could find to keep herself from taking hold of his head, not wanting to throw off the skill and finesse of his exquisite slow and delectably steady buildup. There wasn't one thing she'd change about the pleasure she found so easy to surrender to. When Thor backed off, she let out a squeaky groan, desperate for him to keep going and bring her to climax, while at the same time wishing he'd stretch it out and make this last.

Turns out the God of Thunder was president and rock star of Missy's personal Grant-A-Wish Foundation. Because he definitely rocked her world while granting her wish of making it last, and last, and last …

With one thigh lodged over his shoulder, her body trembled, choked, and shuddered with aftershocks bigger and longer than most of her past orgasms. She didn't know how Thor knew what he knew, to do what he did. With his lips and tongue and teeth and full-on mouth, not to mention his, "Oooh," very, "ahhh," talented, "yesss," fingers. What she did know was that if he were willing to write a how-to book on the subject, he'd never have to worry with that land of his again.

"Uuuuggghhhh," she groaned as he extracted himself from the octopus hold she'd created, tangling herself around his body while in the literal throes of passion. Her legs collapsed. Her arms collapsed. She was somewhat certain her lungs had collapsed. She just wanted to lie there, luxuriating in the afterglow. She moaned some more, hearing Thor's chuckle as he fidgeted. What exactly he was doing, she couldn't say. She felt too good, was way too spent to lift her head or worry about what he was doing. She was done.

"Ruined," she said with as much air as her collapsed lungs could muster.

"What's that?" Thor asked. Oh she heard him grinning all right. Fine. Whatever. He deserved to gloat.

"I'm ruined." Seriously. She probably was. Nothing was going to top that. Ever.

She felt Thor crawling into the backseat on top of her, burying his mouth in her neck. "Your reputation might be ruined if you make the mistake of showering in the girls locker room after practice tomorrow. I got a little carried away and left a mark on you."

"You did?" She laughed, not having a clue when that had happened.

"Maybe a couple," he admitted, wrapping his arms around her back and twisting the two of them so he was half underneath her.

"I'll wear them proudly under my clothes," she sighed, hoisting an arm up over his shoulder, her fingers toying with his hair. They were pretty much face-to-face. "Are your feet hanging out of the door?"

He smiled. "A little bit."

"You wanna come upstairs?" she offered quietly.

Thor took his time, holding her gaze as if weighing his answer. Finally, he shook his head. "No."

"Why not?" she asked, still fingering his hair.

"I've got a couple Army buddies staying with me out at Pop's place. Not that I'm worried they'll burn it down while I'm gone, but I've recruited their help with an improvement project, and we want to get back at it as soon as the sun comes up. That's why I missed your game today, Pretty Girl. We were in the middle of some heavy lifting, and it didn't feel right, me skipping out on them."

"Oh," she said on a yawn. "No problem. I just, didn't know. Are you doing a barn raising or something? Because frankly, I'd like to see that."

"No," he said, giving her an enchanting little smiley-kiss, "but I think you're going to like the outcome. So I'm keeping it a secret. But I'm cautiously optimistic it'll be ready to show off at the end of the weekend."

"Is it a gazebo or something?"

"You'll have to wait and see."

"Well, can I meet your buddies? Are they all superhuman big like you?"

"As if," he scoffed. "But, yeah. Why don't we plan to meet up for dinner Saturday night? Guaranteed they'll have worked up an appetite worthy of The Tavern's colossal Big Foot burger, and it'll give me a chance to introduce you to them."

She smiled, liking that he was willing to introduce her to his friends. "I'll look forward to it."

"Me too."

"Thanks, for you know, coming all the way into town tonight."

"Baby," he chuckled, pulling at her hand to bring her fingers to his lips. "After hearing that message, nothing was going to keep me away."

"And yet, I didn't really follow through on that whole slobbering thing I promised."

"I'll happily take a rain check."

"But aren't you, you know, primed?"

"Took care of that when I was taking care of you."

"You what?" She pushed up and stared at him with giddy, horrified shock. When he just nodded, she said, "That is so ... *dirty*."

"Brace yourself, baby, because with the way your eyes are twinkling at me right now, dirty has just become our standard operating procedure."

CHAPTER TWELVE

In Sarasota, Florida, Cal Johnson had had a very good day of spring training. Strike out after strike out after strike out, and his arm didn't even feel warmed up. And since they only let him pitch three innings—because at twenty-three years old they were worried about him throwing it out—*What was that about?*—he was feeling no pain.

So, whatever. Feeling no pain was perfect, since he was fired up and ready for a sweet little Skype session with Miss Great and planning to give his arm another kind of workout.

He crawled into bed, naked, pulled the sheets up to his hips because Miss Great enjoyed looking at his chest, and flipped open his laptop. He was a couple of minutes early, so he checked out the scores and, of course, other pitching stats across the league. He was leading the pack, which felt good but meant nothing. It was too early, even in spring training, for anything to mean anything.

But he wasn't out drinking, so he probably had a good leg up on his competition right now. His little Skype sessions with Natalie for the past four nights had become a new addiction. Seeing her sweet face, laughing at her cute comments, learning more and more about her every day—more and more *he liked* about her every day. And then … he sucked in a deep breath… there was the semi-pseudo cybersex, which had him sleeping like a damn baby. Frankly, it was almost better than real sex in a lot of ways, because he'd fall asleep and stay asleep. No repeat performances needed. Nobody hogging the covers. No awkward goodbyes.

Yeah, Miss Great was making his life much easier. Early to bed and early to rise was helping him get the ball across the plate in a way that felt effortless.

Who knew what staying sober and sleeping alone could do?

His alarm beeped, causing him to rub his hands together, getting ready for the best part of his day. He hit the Skype icon and waited for the magic to happen.

Boom.

There she was.

Her dark brown hair curling just over her shoulders, her stunning brown eyes, her sweet lips, fuck, he really was hooked. Only …

"Wait a minute," he said by way of greeting. "What's going on?"

Natalie just gave him a big-eyed stare.

"Why aren't you in your bedroom? Why are you dressed like that? And why the hell is the Cupcake pacing back and forth in the background?" This was not what he had planned.

"Love you too, Cal." He heard Scarlett drip her sarcasm from the back of the room.

"Didn't mean anything by it, Cupcake. Just need a little alone time with my girl." He leaned in and whispered, "Nat, what's up?"

He watched as she sighed, the irritation in her eyes softening. "It's … nothing."

"Nothing?" Scarlett scoffed. "You've been fighting off guys from every frat house for the last two days. Tell him. He needs to know."

"What?" Cal choked. "You're fighting off what?"

"Frat guys," Scarlett confirmed, leaning in far too close to the computer's camera because he got a shot of the inside of her nose. "*And* the entire baseball team. Natalie is the new *it* girl."

"The what girl?"

"It! She's *it*. She's the new plaything everyone wants to play with."

"What the hell? Cupcake, speak English or get the hell out of the room. Nat? What's going on there?"

Scarlett moved out of the way so he could see his girl. She was dressed in blue, and he could only see her from the breasts up. Usually she wore a sexy little tank top, the one with an Orioles logo. He liked her wearing his team. Most of the time he'd have a real good show of her cleavage. Right now, she was all covered up. Buttons buttoned to her throat, no sleeves, cotton—whatever. He didn't like her being dressed, and he sure as hell didn't like having the Cupcake in on their Skype session.

"Where the hell is Mighty Pinks?" he asked Natalie. "Don't they usually meet up around now, too?"

Natalie nodded. "Your video went viral."

"Which video?" Truth was you could Google his name and all sorts of videos would come up. It used to be fun to check in every night to see if he was trending, but he'd gotten over that.

"The one in Henderson. Where you are singing. To me."

"Okay …"

"So, it's drawn some attention. The fact that I know you."

"Oh. Okay. Sure. I get that. Everybody want to hear our story?"

"Ahh, more than that. It's … ah, gotten out that I'm Nate the Great's daughter."

"Oh."

"Yeah."

"Was that a secret?"

"Up until now," Natalie informed him.

Scarlett stuck her head in next to Natalie's. "And now she's the *it* girl. Apparently being the daughter of a baseball Hall of Famer makes you a hot commodity. Who knew?"

Cal drew his brows together and shot Scarlett a look. Then he turned his attention to Nat. "How were you able to keep this a secret on campus until your last semester?"

Nat shrugged. "The only person who knew was Scarlett, and she didn't have an idea who Nathaniel Houser was until a few weeks ago." Cal noticed she threw an irritated glance behind her toward Scarlett.

"I'm not a sports fan," the Cupcake shouted in defense.

Natalie leaned toward the screen and whispered. "Pinks is in for a surprise when he finds out she can't even spell the word *lacrosse*."

Cal grinned, his voice softening. "So those Rebels of Ole Miss givin' my girl a hard time?"

"A little bit."

"Little?" Scarlett shouted. "We haven't gotten any sleep. They've been at our door night and day."

"I don't like the sound of that," Cal announced, sitting up straighter, like he was going to take care of business through the damn computer. "Fuck."

"Simmer down, Rookie," Natalie soothed. "It's not like I can't handle it."

"Her father had to hire bodyguards," Scarlett added while she paced in and out of the screen.

"Nat? Is it that bad?" Then Cal truly became alarmed. "Did someone hurt you?"

"No," she said, shaking her head. "It's just, I can't get to class on time. Everyone wants to hear either about my dad or about you."

"Oh. I'm sorry, Nat." And he truly was. It was one thing to be harassed because you played well and had made a name for yourself. It was another to be an innocent bystander and not be able to get to class on time. "Is this my fault? I had to sing to you, you know that, right? I had no choice."

"I know," she laughed, her smile lighting up his world. "It's not your fault. And I liked you singing to me."

"You just don't like people knowing about it?"

"Hmm. The truth is, the girls won't stop asking about your anatomy."

"My what?"

"Your dick," Scarlett shouted from outside the viewing area. "They want to know how big your dick is. It's the hot topic on campus."

"Holy shit."

Natalie smirked. "It is. I keep telling them I have no idea, but no one believes me. Clearly, I am the only girl you've sung to who has not immediately fallen into your bed."

"You're the only girl I've sung to period. And the rest will take care of itself." *Hopefully over your Spring Break* he was too afraid to add. "Want me to text you a dick pic? Then you can just flash it around when they ask. That'll shut 'em up."

"Ah, thanks, but no thanks," she laughed.

"I'd do it for you," he teased.

"I appreciate that. If things get worse, I'll let you know."

"You do that. I'm happy to help any way I can." He lowered his voice, rubbing his finger over her image. "I'd be there tonight if I could, you know that, don't you?"

Scarlett's face filled the screen, scaring the shit out of him. "Geez-us," he shouted, throwing himself back against the headboard. "Cupcake, don't you have a date or something?"

"Look. We need to talk a little business before you two get on with your happy ending."

"Seriously?" they both said at the same time.

Scarlett went on undaunted. "My colleague back in Henderson came up with a marketing campaign, and I want to use it to our advantage. Cross-promote your album release."

"Not this again," Cal muttered.

"You said you'd do it. You owe me, and now you owe Nat. Consider this payment to the only two women in the country who are not interested in the size of your dick."

Cal wanted to take exception to that, hoping Natalie was indeed interested in his dick, but Scarlett rolled on.

"I'm working on the album details with Pinks. What I need from you right now are the names of your top twenty bands. The songs you listen to before and after a game. I need details about your music preferences. Your favorite songs. Why you like them, that sort of thing."

"What you got up your sleeve, Cupcake?"

"I'm thinking of contacting those bands. See if they want to collaborate with pitching sensation Cal Johnson, who—oh yeah, by the way—can sing."

"Hmm. Okay. I'll email you."

"You will?"

The Cupcake seemed surprised. "I will if you let Natalie take her computer back to her bedroom and give us some privacy."

"Done." Scarlett started to move off, but then stopped. "Oh. And you won't mind posing for the Henderson calendar, right? Pinks will be in it."

"A calendar?"

"Just say yes. You know I'm going to find a way to squeeze your balls until you do."

"Fine. Yes. Goodnight, Cupcake. But don't think I won't take this up with the Mighty Pinks."

"Whatever," Scarlett said, finally leaving them alone. He could tell because he heard a door slam shut and watched as Natalie looked to make sure Scarlett was gone.

"Sorry about that," she sighed, rolling her eyes.

"You don't need to apologize to me for the Cupcake. I know the difference between you two. And if she ever asks me to do something I'm really not interested in doing, I don't care how hard she squeezes my balls, I won't back down. Count on that."

"Okay. Good to know."

"Now, if you were the one to ask me," he said, giving her his flirty grin, "well, darlin', you know you've got me over a barrel, so then I'd be out of luck."

She smiled at him, looking tired.

"You okay?" he asked.

"I'm fine. I wasn't planning to bother you with my updated campus status, but you know Scarlett. She thought it would be good leverage to get you to work with her on this album."

"The album is just ... fun. I'm not worried about any damn album. What I am worried about is all those guys wanting to date my girl."

Her hair hung to the side as she tilted her head. "You're Cal Johnson," she told him.

"And?"

"Who could possibly turn my head?"

"Hell, I don't know. What I do know is that between me and your father, you're now carrying around a lot of baggage that's making you late to class. I don't want you to decide I'm not worth it and give me my walking papers before I have a chance to woo you over Spring Break."

"Woo me? Mmm. And how does a man who throws a hundred-and-one-mile-an-hour fast ball woo a girl?"

"By winning a game while she's sitting in the stands, taking a shower, and then slowing things ... way ... way ... way down."

"Just nine more days," she said on a breath.

"Yeah," he said, looking into her eyes, knowing he was a goner. "Nine more days."

"So Cal's going to email me a list of his favorite bands and their songs. That was a brilliant idea, by the way."

"I'm just feeding off of your good ideas," Pinks told Scarlett. "When did you talk to him?"

"Just now. He and Nat are Skyping. That's why I'm a little late. How's my Ninja Lover?"

"Missing his Red."

"Good."

"Busy though. Not sure how I'm actually gonna manage with the addition of a social life once you're back in town."

"Uuggg ... my social life is *dead*. Between classes and learning how to produce a record album, I have no time for anything else. And poor Natalie. It's all over campus about her father being Nate the Great. You cannot believe the upheaval it's caused. She's playing it down for Cal, and he's probably better off not knowing, but trust me, every guy on this campus is plotting ways to get a date with Natalie Houser."

"I'll bet," Pinks laughed. "Give it a few weeks. The notoriety will die down."

"She's dating Cal Johnson. I don't think anything's going to die down. The two of us talked and we decided not to tell anybody about changing our plans for Spring Break. Our friends think we'll be in Destin with them as originally planned. They aren't going to be happy when we don't show and then find out we met up with you and Cal Johnson at spring training."

"Why not tell them?"

"Because then they'd all want to come with us."

"Oh. Yeah. We don't need that."

"No."

"Well, as long as you're not leaving them in the lurch with a room bill, just have Cal personalize a few autographed baseballs for your friends. Then they'll forgive you."

"You and your good ideas," she sighed. "That will indeed smooth things over. Thank you."

"No problem."

Silence fell between them.

"What?" Scarlett asked.

"Just taking a minute. Focusing in on how beautiful you are," Pinks told her.

Scarlett blushed.

"Are we okay?" he asked.

She seemed startled by the question. "Why wouldn't we be okay?"

"I just … well I *know* that when Cal and Natalie Skype, their conversations go a little differently than ours. Ours are more like business meetings."

Scarlett blinked.

"Yeah," Pinks chuckled. "They are. Which actually works well for me. I've got so much on my mind lately that putting it out there to you just feels good. And the two of us can brainstorm like crazy. So I like the fact that we've become business partners. But sometimes I get so wrapped up in your business savvy, I forget … us. I don't want to forget us."

Scarlett's eyes narrowed. "Pinks. I love you, but I'm not having cybersex with you."

"Oh, thank God," Pinks said, letting the words fall out on an exaggerated breath.

"Seriously," Scarlett insisted. "We are not that couple. We aren't a phone-sex couple either."

"I know," he laughed. "I just want to make sure you're okay with that."

"You mean, am I okay with you not being a perv like Cal Johnson? Ah-yeah. Now, do I expect you to have trouble keeping your hands off me in eight days, sixteen hours, and however many minutes it is until I see you again? Absolutely."

"Trust me. I know the number of minutes. Every last bit of me knows the number of minutes."

"Business partners by day. Pinks my Ninja Lover at night. Win-win."

"*Big* win-win."

"Besides, I'm counting on you and your sexy business plan for my virtual wine shop. I swear I don't know what I'm still doing in school at this point. I can practically smell the redwood shelves of my beautiful wine cellar now."

"All right. Well, since you brought it up, I do have a couple business items to run by you."

Her eyes lit up. "Good. Let's hear them."

Pinks laughed at that. "You really are the perfect woman," he said.

"I'm the perfect woman for you."

"You are, Red. You really are. Okay, here's what I've been thinking …"

CHAPTER THIRTEEN

"I had a good time last night," Marcie told Clint as he ushered her into his office and shut the door.

"As did I," he said. "Although I woke up this morning wondering how it is possible that I had dinner at Henderson Country Club with three people from Baltimore."

"Two of whom are working for your competition." She began to stroll around the room again, this time studying the artwork, beautiful old baseboards, and chair moldings that made up his office in Henderson's charmingly vintage town hall.

"Technically, Davis Williams and Missy McReady work for E&E Investments."

"They work for Team Henderson," she threw over her shoulder.

"Of which I consider myself an integral part. Brooks has gone out of his way to keep me up to speed on all of Team Henderson's proposals. He generously put my name on the *Henderson Helping Henderson* campaign, which has made a noticeable difference around town. And Brooks was the one to invite me to speak at the baseball opener."

Marcie kept her eyes on the artwork, wandering slowly about. "So you're included in their weekly meetings."

"Well, no."

"You don't think they may be keeping some ideas close to the vest?"

"Look Marcie, Brooks is a stand-up guy. The two of us have been working together for the betterment of the community since he joined the police force. He didn't have to do it, but he came to me first when he decided to run for mayor. He said he wanted to tell me himself. Didn't want me to be blindsided."

"Do you want to stay in office, Clint? Do you want to remain mayor?" she asked without bothering to look in his direction.

"You know I do."

"Are you willing to shake things up? Throw a couple hard balls?"

"You mean play dirty?"

"Play hard ball," she said forcefully as she turned to face him.

"Marcie. Sit down, please. Let's hear what you're thinking."

She nodded, taking the chair opposite his desk and motioning for him to sit as well. "I've come up with a number of ideas to help you defeat Brooks Bennett. Some are subtle, and some are quite the opposite."

"I'm all ears."

"First, I'd like you to consider making your campaign slogan *Keep Henderson Henderson.*"

"Keep Henderson Henderson?"

"Exactly."

"I'm not sure—"

"Think, Clint. What do people hate more than anything? *Anything?*"

"Change?"

"And what is Brooks Bennett trying to do?"

"Bring economic prosperity to Henderson."

Marcie fell back in her chair, crossed her arms over her chest, and squinted her eyes. "And you managed to get into Duke, *how?*"

"Change," Clint sighed with understanding. "Brooks wants change."

"Yes," she agreed. "*Everyone* wants economic prosperity. *No one* wants change. Change is your go-to word. Your entire campaign is based on Brooks Bennett wanting to ram dirty-rotten change down everyone's throat, and you want to keep …"

"Henderson Henderson."

"By George, I think he's got it."

"All right. I like it," he told her.

"I thought you would."

"So, Keep Henderson Henderson."

"Yes. And at precisely the right time, you are going to out the sports academy."

"Out the whose-a-whats-it?"

"The sports academy Evans & Evans and CC Henderson is building."

"They aren't building a sports academy."

"They are."

"Here? In Henderson?"

"You look surprised."

"Because I don't believe you."

Marcie pulled back. "You don't believe me?"

"No."

"Clint." She leaned forward. "That's their big plan. They are using the IMG Academy as their model."

"What? How do you know this?"

Marcie tilted her head and batted her lashes. "Coach Crenshaw spilled the beans back when the two of us were on speaking terms. I've had my ear to the ground, so to speak, ever since."

Clint let out a curse. "You've got to be kidding," he muttered. His head was bent, and he stared at nothing, drumming his fingers on top of the desk. "And here I am, singing the guy's praises. Telling you Brooks is a stand-up guy." Eventually Clint's eyes lifted. "How far along are they with this *sports academy*?" he spit out the words like they were leaving a bad taste in his mouth.

"They are committed. Working hard and fast, as far as I know."

"This doesn't make any sense," Clint argued. "Vance is Henderson High's baseball coach. Brooks is the assistant coach. If they're committed to anything, they're committed to that."

"They want to put Henderson on the map any way they can. Do whatever it takes."

"With a sports academy? I don't like it. For a number of reasons, I just don't like it. And I really don't like being so far out of the loop that this is the first I'm hearing about it."

"So steal their thunder," Marcie told him. "Publicly announce their plan before they're ready to and put your spin on it."

"That Brooks Bennett and Vance Evans have turned their backs on their alma mater?"

"Absolutely."

"That their plan will sabotage the quality of the local high school and overshadow all of its previous sports' achievements?"

"Couldn't have said it better myself."

"That Henderson High will absolutely be downgraded in the eyes of all and become just another also-ran *public* school?"

"While the bright, shiny, new sports academy will be the snobby, entitled, rich-kid-from-the-north, pain in their ass."

"Now that's one helluva rally cry," Clint told her.

"Use it, and you kill two birds with one stone. You take away their momentum on the big project they've got up their sleeve and have the entire town on your side before they can get out a sound bite."

"Fine. Let's do it. When and where?"

"Take a breath," she advised, holding up both hands in an effort to calm him. "Trust me. It will serve you to bide your time and wait until Henderson's baseball team wins their division. As mayor, you'll plan a celebration to honor the team just before they head into the playoffs. It'll draw a big crowd, providing you the perfect opportunity to out Brooks's sports academy when it will do the most damage."

Clint looked at Marcie with a little bit of awe and a little bit of fear. "Who are you?"

"I'm your campaign manager."

CHAPTER FOURTEEN

Coming off the celebration of her team's first win, not to mention the spoils of victory Thor had lavished upon her in the backseat of Big Red last night, Missy was ill-prepared for a day that managed to throw more curve balls than Cal Johnson.

The first one was sweet. Her juniors and the lone senior on her team greeted her that morning at the door of CC Henderson with a decorated basket full of homemade chocolate chip cookies. Apparently, they'd gotten together to celebrate their win last night and didn't want to leave her out. As she hugged each girl in turn, she did her best not only to blink back tears—touched that they would think of her—but also to swallow the reprimand on the tip of her tongue. They'd gone AWOL during school hours in order to bring these to her. If they were caught they could miss valuable playing time.

Geez. When did I become an adult? she wondered as she entered the building. She took the three steps up to the lobby where hardwood floors had been refinished and fresh paint and state-of-the-art lighting fixtures gave the place new life. Unfurnished except for the small reception desk, there was a large Texas flag framed and mounted on the wall. Crain Carraway had given her permission to use his group of offices since his main business was in Dallas and that's where he liked to be. He and his wife, Tansy Langford, both part of Team Henderson, had promised to spend Wednesdays in Henderson. But it was going on week five after their wedding and they'd only returned for the Spectacular last weekend.

Still, Missy never used the first office, the only one furnished out of three. Obviously, that one was Crain's. Used back in the fall when he spent his days in Henderson trying to woo his wife into admitting that she, indeed, was his wife. Instead, Missy had created an L-shaped workspace for herself in the second office by setting up two long folding tables.

Fortunately, the conference room had been tricked out. As in, it was way more cushy and showy than E&E's. Missy wondered if that was Crain's version of my dick is bigger than your dick. Regardless, that was where Missy instructed the Henderson Has-Beens Monday thru Thursday. The generations of Hendersonians who, for the past forty years, had been having too much fun climbing their tiny social ladder to notice the ground beneath it was eroding. But they saw it now, and they were pitching in. Missy was teaching them computer skills, data entry, and how to manipulate the world of social media for the purpose of networking. Their main task: seek contacts Team Henderson could use to benefit the cause. The cause being a thriving, robust economy.

Since today was Friday, Missy had the place all to herself.

However, the front door chimed around ten o'clock, pulling her from her work on the first-ever Henderson electronic newsletter. Venturing into the lobby, she found a well-dressed contingent of forty-somethings—no doubt the daughters and granddaughters of her "Has-Beens."

"May I help you?"

"We hope so," said a beautifully Southern blonde who handed Missy a pink to-go cup that matched the ones all of the women were holding. "You are Missy McReady?"

"I am, and thank you." She held up the coffee, liking these women already.

"My name is Sandra Wilcox. This is my good friend, Jan Boyce, and my cousin, Sarah Fortune. We understand you're a party planner."

"Well, at present I'm the event planner for Evans & Evans Investments across the street."

"Exclusively?" Sandra asked.

"No, I suppose not."

"Good. Our daughters will be making their debut this fall in Raleigh. The three of us are planning a combined local celebration this summer. In Oxford."

"Oxford?"

"Oxford," Sandra confirmed.

Missy quirked her brow. "How did you get my name?"

"Yesterday, Sarah had lunch with Maddie Gentry, whose daughter is a cheerleader at Oxford High. The new statistics teacher over there is from Henderson, Vivi DuVal?"

"Vivi?" Missy shook her head.

"Well, Miss DuVal is also the new cheerleading coach who, back when the JV squad got themselves into a little bit of trouble on social media, called in Henderson's well-known Keeper of the Debutantes to set the girls straight. Maddie's daughter has been following Annabelle on Twitter ever since. Being a careful momma, Maddie takes sneak peeks at her daughter's phone from time to time and read Annabelle's tweet last Sunday about a something, something spectacular and you being the ultimate party planner by getting Cal Johnson to show up and sing."

"Ah." Missy held up her hands to stop them right there. "I'm sorry, ladies. I did plan the Spectacular, but I had absolutely nothing to do with Cal Johnson showing up or singing."

"But you planned the event."

"Yes."

"And you're new to Henderson."

"I am."

"Well, are you interested in expanding your business?"

Missy smiled, remembering her first thoughts last Sunday. "As a matter of fact, I have recently considered doing just that."

"And I'm sure you'd want to do your best for your first non-corporate clients, so word of mouth could serve as advertising?"

"Sandra, I have to say, I like the way you are reeling me in."

"Good, because to be honest, the three of us are standing in enemy territory," she said, circling her finger at her friends.

"I don't understand."

"Henderson's debutantes are lauded as hosting the ultimate parties of the season. We're tired of hearing it, and we'd like you to help us change it."

"You ... want me ...to help you, *top* Henderson?"

Sandra folded her hands in front of her and smiled gently. "We want you ... to help us ... *up* Oxford's game."

"Oh," Missy said. "I suppose I can do that."

Sandra grinned.

After spending some time discussing the scope of their project, Missy scheduled a future meeting with the Oxford belles. She wanted time to do some research on North Carolina's debut process which definitely needed to include a sit-down with Annabelle Devine.

So, between the impromptu debutante meeting, trying unsuccessfully to track down Annabelle, and the black hole she fell into conducting research online, Missy was in no mood to deal with the "emergency" Team Henderson meeting Davis had whipped out of his back pocket and thrown into her schedule.

"Meet without me," she yelled from her desk after managing to finally get back to work on the newsletter.

"Can't," Davis said, standing in her doorway. "Need our CEO. That's you. Come on."

"You know, a good CEO delegates," she said, pushing out of her chair and following him to the door.

"Yep. But you gotta know what needs to be done before you know what to delegate."

"All right. But are these emergency meetings a regular thing?"

"This is the first one. I want to fill everyone in on Viper and Mayor Stevens before something comes up over the weekend and we forget about it."

"Oh. Yeah. I already forgot about it."

"And they call you the female Pinks," he scoffed, holding the front door open for her.

Once everyone was present—Vance, Hale, Brooks, Duncan James (fraternity brother of Vance and Brooks, new corporate lawyer for E&E and Team Henderson, *and* Annabelle Devine's fiancé), the Big Em, and Josh McCourt (Henderson High's computer guru and assistant football coach)—Davis took over the meeting by first announcing that Henderson High's girls' lacrosse team had managed its first win. That was greeted with a round of applause and a couple cheers, which Missy truly appreciated.

Then Davis explained about Coach Cooper's relationship with Marcie Watts, a.k.a. Viper. He went on to voice his concern over Viper attending the Spectacular last weekend, and being seen almost a week later cozying up to Henderson's lame duck mayor, Clint Stevens.

The silence that greeted this news was thick, and it was telling.

After a few heartbeats, Missy held up her hands. "Let me say that having met Marcie at the club last night, she seems to be a very agreeable woman. Davis and I wormed our way into their conversation, and she couldn't have been more pleasant. In fact, if I wasn't concerned about her motives, I'd really like her."

"But it does seem fishy," Vance said.

"Yes," Missy agreed. "Fishy for sure. But the woman flat out admitted that she was a friend of the Coach's and of Cal Johnson's, which was why she attended the Spectacular, where she happened to meet Mayor Stevens. She went on to say the two of them hit it off, and he'd talked her into returning to Henderson. I'm assuming Mayor Stevens is single?"

"A widower," Hale said. "Lost his wife on 9/11. The two of them were very young at the time. He eventually moved back from New York, saw a need, and ran for office."

"Won on a sympathy vote," Vance added. "Been running the place since then. But he's been known to see a woman over in Oxford, on and off."

"So, this could be legit," Davis offered. "Still, I did some snooping on the Web last night. Found out Watts is with a large advertising firm located outside D.C. Her breakup with the Coach was definitely fodder for local gossip hounds. It had a sharp hit for a few weeks on social media, but it has since died down. I spoke to Cal on the phone last night. According to him, Coach had no idea Viper was anywhere near Henderson on Opening Day."

"See, I don't trust that," Vance said. "Why was Viper—and yes, I'm totally calling her Viper because it is an *awesome* nickname—

here in the first place? If she didn't confront the Coach or Christy-Lynn, either she got cold feet …"

"Or she's plotting something entirely different," Brooks finished. "As much as I'd like to believe she just happened to meet and fall for Clint, I share Pinks's concern." He stood. "I think I'll walk over to City Hall and pay Clint a visit. This could be nothing. Probably is nothing. But we're working too hard not to keep the two of them on our radar."

Nobody disagreed.

"Before you go, Brooks," Missy said, hedging, wondering if she should tackle this debacle now or later. "Last night, while working on my third glass of wine," she admitted, "it struck me that Henderson is full of really gorgeous men. Many of whom are sitting here at this table."

There were some chuckles. Josh actually turned red. But Vance, being Vance, said, "You just coming to this now?"

"Sort of," she said. "I mean, no. Of course not. Vance, you and your father top the list of hot businessmen for sure. But between Brooks and Josh and Duncan and *even Davis*—"

"What do you mean, *even Davis*?" Davis argued, insulted.

"I mean, I knew you when … so keep your gym shorts on. Now," she eyed them all, watching as Brooks reseated himself at the table. "Before I say anything else, you should know that *Scarlett* is already in on this. She's going to be roping Cal Johnson into it too, so you're in good company."

"We are in good company for what?" Brooks asked.

"For participating in the 'Hunks of Henderson' calendar."

"A 'Hunks of Henderson' calendar," Brooks repeated slowly, like he was having trouble picturing the concept.

"Scarlett will put Cal Johnson and his new album on the cover of the calendar, meaning he's the lead-in and, more importantly, Henderson is claiming him. Which, you know, is a big deal for the town's status and our national appeal."

"We want national appeal?" Brooks asked.

"Of course, we want national appeal. But we'll settle for regional appeal or any appeal we can get. Trust me, you're going to want far-reaching appeal when you're ready to fill up the sports academy with actual students."

"True that," he gave her.

"Hold on," Hale said. "Are you talking about a beefcake calendar? Like the ones with muscle-bound firemen or gearheads?"

"I am."

"Ah—that's a big, fat no," Vance said.

"Nuh-uh. Ain't gonna happen," Brooks chimed in.

"Yeah, that's a little—"

"Shove it, Williams," Missy said to Davis. "I did say I've got Scarlett onboard, right? *You* have absolutely no choice." Then she looked at Hale, knowing exactly how to reel the rest of them in. "Hale, of course, you have a choice. But being Team Henderson's patriarch and being as you are physically … gifted, I would appreciate it if you'd give this some thought. I was picturing you in your very GQ business attire, photographed at the desk in your study at home. I assure you, it will be tasteful, elegant, and will only enhance your business appeal."

"I'm in," Hale said with a big grin.

"Are you crazy?" Vance asked, looking at his father like he'd lost his mind.

"I'm fifty-two. And thanks to you, I'm going to be a grandfather soon. As excited as I am about that, I do not relish thinking of myself as a grandpa. So if a couple of beautiful young ladies think *I'm worthy of a beefcake calendar*, I'm going to enjoy every moment of it. So yeah, I'm in. And you should be too. Because you are no longer the playboy you used to be, and in two short months, you aren't going to be known as anything but Vance, Jr.'s father."

"That's the picture," Missy said. "You, the *hot* grandfather. Oooh and you can be holding your new child and Vance's son." Her eyes got huge. "This is brilliant!"

"That's pretty good," Davis admitted. "Show off the population at all ages. Maybe get one of the high school kids in on it. Someone who not only looks the part physically, but is a scholar as well."

"I like it," Missy told him.

"And I suppose it will be one of your lacrosse players?" Brooks spat.

"Hey, you got a baller who can show up better than any of my guys, he's got the spot."

"Brooks, you could represent the police department, or be in pitching coach mode. Either one will work," Missy said.

"I'll represent the police. One of the boys on the team will take care of baseball."

"What the hell?" Vance argued. "I'm the damn baseball coach."

"Vance," Missy soothed. "I was thinking of you, shirtless after a run, all hot and sweaty, in front of your Tender Foot Boutique."

"Now you're talking," Vance said. "Marketing more than my hot body is a great idea."

"Oh, and Scarlett will be placing a bottle of wine in every photo. She wants to promote the fantasy wine shop she plans to open on Main Street after she graduates."

"She's opening a wine shop?" Hale asked.

"She's calling it *Reds*. Isn't that brilliant?" Missy beamed, just loving the name and loving her new best friend, who was dating her old best friend. Whatever.

"Wine in every photo?" Brooks asked. "Not sure that's going to fly with the high school layouts."

"Knowing Scarlett, she'll figure it out. Maybe just a *Reds* shopping bag will be fine. I'll make a note to have Scarlett come up with a logo."

"My head is literally spinning," Duncan piped in. "The way you people cross market everything." He started laughing.

"No kidding," Brooks agreed. "And don't think you're exempt from this embarrassment. All for one and one for all. You can stand under that brand new sign, DUNCAN JAMES, ATTORNEY AT LAW, Pinks had made. Get a good shot of Main Street in there."

"Of course, I'm going to make Thor join in the fun." Missy gave them all a self-deprecating smile. "And as hypocritical as this is, I'm totally playing up the farmer aspect with him. I mean, the guy makes farming look hot. With all the farmland around here, we need him to represent."

"Or put him in his Ranger uniform," Emelina suggested.

"Yeah … right … wow," Missy stammered, imaging Thor bare chested, dog tags hanging from his neck, in nothing but a pair of

Army fatigues. She licked her lips and did her best to ignore all the knowing smiles and snickering aimed her way. "Josh, can I twist your arm for this? Assistant football coach or the tech guru. Either one will work."

"I have to say, I'm with Hale. Being reclassified from nerd to beefcake will not offend me at all." He winked at Missy.

"Good. Thank you. All of you. I'll get back to you with details. I'm planning to get us enough exposure that the Today Show picks it up. If we can get the Hunks of Henderson calendar on national TV in time for the gift-giving season, well, who knows where it will take us?"

Vance was shaking his head, chuckling. "How do you come up with this stuff?"

Missy blushed, remembering how ogling Thor in his blazer got her hormones running. "Magic," she told him.

"So back to Cal's album," Brooks prodded.

"Just need to make sure his baseball team signs off. Shit. I better get on that," Davis said as he picked up his notebook and left the room.

"Is that the meeting?" Vance asked. "Viper and Hunks of Henderson?"

"Yes. Well … I've been working on the digital newsletter we're sending to everyone who signed up at the Spectacular. I want to get the inaugural edition out to keep the momentum from last weekend rolling."

"Okay. What do you need from us?" Hale asked.

"Permission."

"Permission?"

"Yes. Permission. Because where I understand gossip is part of the problem in Henderson, it is also what's going to grab people's attention and get them to read subsequent newsletters."

"Gossip," Vance deadpanned.

"Not hurtful gossip, although you know, some people will love having their names in the newsletter or blog and others—"

"Blog?" Brooks asked.

"Yes, a blog." Missy arched a brow. "On the new and improved Henderson website. We need to give people a reason to keep checking in with Henderson. I figure writing about the social scene would be a good pull. Event details, who attended, and anything interesting that may have happened."

"Like who hooked up with whom? Damn, I'm glad I'm married. I feel like I've just dodged a bullet," Vance said.

"True that." Brooks laughed.

"I'd really like to put a picture of Davis and Scarlett in this newsletter, along with Cal and Natalie, because truly, next to the baseball team winning, the four of them were the big news. Definitely a little … titillating. What do y'all think?"

"I think if you're the one writing this column, you'll be the one getting the backlash," Hale said. "You ready to handle that?"

"Actually, my idea is to pull together a group of journalists who would go by one name. A made-up name."

"What's going to be sacred?" Brooks asked.

"Sacred?"

"The line that will not be crossed. I don't want friendships and marriages torn apart. That's not the Henderson we're trying to revive."

"My vision is harmless fun. The stuff people can laugh at themselves for." She stopped. Thinking. "Or am I nuts?"

"Listen, we need people engaged with Henderson," Hale said. "From near and far, we want them engaged. So this is a good idea. Let's just make sure it doesn't backfire."

"Understood." Missy nodded. "I'll write up the first column, run it by all of you and Davis this one time, get your opinions, and make a decision from there."

"Sounds good. Meeting adjourned."

CHAPTER FIFTEEN

Friday evening, cuddled into a plump, cushioned chair on Genevra's screened-in porch, warmed by a handmade quilt soft with age and a red wine suggested by Scarlett, Missy enjoyed a lengthy telephone chat with her father.

Which was rare.

Their daily conversations were short and sweet. Just connecting and sharing the highlights of their day.

Tonight, they mostly talked lacrosse. Missy shared her deepest feelings about what it was like to start a team from scratch. To plant the seeds and watch her players sprout into fledgling little seedlings. Then nourish them while they grew in skill and enthusiasm, incorporated the idea of teamwork, and finally blossomed into a single unit with one purpose.

Missy laughed at her imagery. Cultivating seeds reminded her of Thor and his land. She hadn't bothered to mention Thor to her dad before now. Mostly because throughout the course of their conversations it seemed fairly obvious that Jack McReady still held out hope. Hope that with Missy in Henderson, at the end of lacrosse season Davis Williams would come to his senses, return to Baltimore, and take up the position with Loftus-McAllen he'd been offered. Or that Missy and Davis would develop more than a friendship while working together in Henderson, eventually returning to Baltimore as a couple. Either scenario would make the man happy. Very happy.

Since Missy originally shared some of her father's hopes and dreams where Davis was concerned, she hadn't mentioned the help

Thor had been to her early on. She certainly hadn't divulged how much she enjoyed sucking face with Thor the first night she was in town. Or that he'd woken up in her bed the next day.

Yeah, no.

And when she'd found out about Davis and Scarlett, well ... how was she going to explain that to her father? She'd barely understood it and all of the pending ramifications, herself. On top of which, the Spectacular kept getting bigger and bigger. So with the pressure mounting, their conversations had mostly been him counseling her on how to get the job done and done well.

And lacrosse.

Always lacrosse.

But now, the Spectacular was a success and things with heroically handsome, Thurgood Watson III had changed.

Drastically changed.

And she'd changed. Her mind. About him. About Henderson. About her job. She was staying. Indefinitely. Something she now needed to tell her father.

Not that she didn't think he'd understand. Because, really, all of it was good news. It just wasn't the good news her father was expecting.

So when he asked about Davis's lacrosse team and how their work for Henderson was coming along, she told him about their continuing battle over sharing the one stupid, not-even-regulation-sized lacrosse field, and then got caught up relaying Davis's suspicions about Marcie Watts in great detail. After all, her father always did appreciate a good suspense.

Saturday night there was a ruckus so loud and abrupt, Missy worried something horrible was happening to her neighbors. With cellphone in hand and her fingers poised to dial 911, she peered out of Genevra's bay window and had to let her mind catch up to what her eyes were seeing.

Big Red—with lights flashing and horn honking—had men leaning out of windows, climbing around in the bed of the truck, banging on the sides, and hollering what she hoped for the neighbors' sake were not obscenities. When she realized the noise had drifted into some semblance of a chant, and that chant sounded suspiciously like her name, it hit her. Thor's Rangers had arrived.

Yeah. She was going to need backup.

She dialed Davis.

"Thor's Army buddies are in town, and they are *all* taking me to dinner. I need you, Vance, and Em on the phone now, steering as many eligible women this town has to offer over to The Tavern, pronto. I don't know how many there are, but from the noise they are making out in Genevra's driveway, I'd say it's a full battalion. I've got to go. Over and out."

"Missy. Missy. Missy ..." The chant grew louder.

"Oh, Lord," she said, grabbing up her tiny handbag, not taking time to put on her sweater, hoping she could end the madness outside before her neighbors were the ones calling the police.

As she stepped out into the porchlight, a boisterous cheer went up, followed by a rousing ovation. Missy laughed, dipping into a curtsy before turning her back on them so she could lock up. It was then one long wolf whistle pierced the night air.

Doors slammed, gravel rustled, a "holy shit" was uttered, and by the time Missy turned back around, she witnessed the tail end of a lot of pushing and shoving as six of her country's finest stood at ease, grinning up from the bottom of the porch steps.

"Great dress," the really cute stocky one uttered. He had dark hair, brown eyes, and a truly contagious grin.

"You like?" She grinned back, showing off the tiny lilac print.

"Not sure," the tall blond next to him said. "I think it'd be good if you'd spin around one more time."

"Like this," she teased, falling into their game. She turned slowly, holding her sweater and clutch away from her sides. She'd pulled her hair into a high ponytail done up with a big bow in keeping with the retro style of the dress Lolly had made just for her. She glanced back over her shoulder—her bare shoulder—exposed along with her back in the halter-styled dress.

"Yeah," the blond acknowledged. "Really great dress."

"Well, Thurgood did not tell me y'all were so fashion conscious." She started down the steps slowly.

"Thurgood's a chump."

Honk. Honk. "Y'all wanna take a step back and give my girl a little breathing room?" Thor yelled from the window of Big Red.

"Don't mind him," the cute one told her, offering his hand as she made her way to the ground. "He's seen the writing on the wall."

"Oh?"

"He knows he's toast now that you have real men to compare him to."

"And you are?"

"Anyone you want me to be."

"Jesus, call him Pickle." The blond stepped in, pushing Pickle out of the way. "He deserves it. I'm Rhodes. Taller, smarter, faster than the rest."

The fellow closest to Rhodes wore a ball cap and immediately coughed *"bullshit"* into his fist. Missy shot him a grin and noticed Mr. Ball Cap had a lot of sexy scruff going on. "Bill Hook," he said, shaking her hand. Friends call me Hooker, and I'm the only one who wasn't born in a barn."

"Jeremy Cox," the next one volunteered. He looked young with his fair skin and freckles. "This here's Ryland Balls." He pointed to a gorgeous black man whose shirt could not contain his muscles. "Together, we're known as Cock and Balls," Jeremy said proudly. "And then we've got Tinker whose real name is Randy English. When the three of us are together, you've got yourself a Randy Cock and Balls."

"Seriously," Missy said, wondering if they'd made it all up.

"I know. We're thinking about taking it on the road."

"Speaking of," Thor hollered, "those burgers are not going to eat themselves. Hop in."

Randy opened the passenger door. "Happy to have you sit on my lap, darlin'."

Thor jerked his thumb. "In the back, asshole."

"Spoilsport," Randy muttered while being a true gentleman and helping her into the truck. He then launched himself into the bed of Big Red with several others.

"Sorry about all that," Thor said as she pulled on her seatbelt.

"Don't be silly."

"All right," Thor said, speaking to the group. "Now that y'all've had your fun, let's try taking it under the radar. Don't want to attract the attention of the local authorities, being as they're friends of mine."

"We hear that."

Thor shook his head, putting the truck in drive. "Been pounding beers since noon. Starting to think I should have kept the animals on the farm."

Pickle, who'd been shoved into the middle of the backseat between Cox and Balls, leaned forward. "So, Missy. What were the other two wishes Thor asked for when he let that genie out of the bottle?"

She twisted in her seat and smiled. "Pardon?"

"Obviously, his first wish was for a gorgeous woman."

"Aww," Missy sat back, startled. "You're gonna make me blush."

Pickle shined his mega-watt smile at her as Thor reached for her hand and gave it a squeeze. "I told them about you being a coach."

"Congratulations on your first win," Balls said. "We heard you're starting from scratch way out in the backwoods here."

"Lacrosse is new to the area," she said. "Where are you all from?"

"I'm from Charleston," Balls supplied. "Wrestler. Picks is from California."

"I played soccer," Pickle supplied.

"Michigan," Cox said. "Wrestled some. Love to sail."

Balls picked it up from there. "Then, in the back, Hooker is from Annapolis. He's played lacrosse. Rhodes is from Memphis and I think he lettered in half a dozen sports if you're willing to believe the crap that comes out of his mouth. Tinker is a diehard Alabama fan." Balls lowered his voice. "Please do not say the words *roll* or *tide*."

"God, no," Cox agreed.

Thor chuckled.

"Where did you all meet?" Missy wondered.

"Ranger Regiment, Ft. Benning, Georgia," Pickles supplied.

"So what is it that separates a Ranger Regiment from other regiments?"

Pickles shrugged. "Generally a lot of direct action behind enemy lines."

"How do you get behind enemy lines?"

"Parachute or chopper."

"And direct action means?"

"Combat. Missions for personnel recovery, airfield seizure, HVT raids, that sort of thing."

"HVT?"

"High-value targets. Could be a person, place, or thing. We'd be sent in to destroy, contain, or extract."

"Wow." Suddenly this all became very real to Missy. She put her hand on Thor's forearm. "How long were you in?"

"Six years."

"How many deployments?"

"Close to a dozen. We'd deploy to Iraq or Afghanistan for three months and then go back to the States for three to six months for a little R&R and more training."

"Oh." She was dying to ask specifics, and their success record, but she wasn't sure of the protocol. "Have you all left the Army?"

The three in the back nodded. "Rhodes is the only one still in," Balls answered. "Actually, he's on leave for a while. When he goes back, he'll be overseeing operations and logistics. More of a desk job."

"So what are you doing now?"

"Picks and I work for government contractors," Balls said.

"What's that mean?"

"It means," Jeremy said, "they do the same thing they've been doing, only they get paid the big bucks now."

"Coxie is going back to school," Picks supplied.

"Really?" she asked, twisting around some more so she could look at Jeremy. "What are you studying?"

"Technology. I like gadgets."

"He's going to MIT," Picks said.

Missy's eyes went wide. "Wow."

"I'm pretty geeked."

"You mean you are a geek," Picks insisted.

Missy smiled and turned around to face front as the truck pulled into The Tavern's parking lot. The place looked busy.

"Did you tell them we were coming?" she asked Thor.

"Yep. Warned them that they'd be hungry and should be seated as far away from respectable diners as possible."

Missy grinned, unlatching her seatbelt. "I'm sure it'll be fine."

While the owner's wife welcomed Thor's buddies warmly, thanked them for their service to their country, and then led them toward the back of the rustic burger joint, Missy checked her text messages. She waited with Thor while he went out of his way to shake hands with The Tavern's owner. Apparently, the man had been a good friend of Thor's father, and it gratified Missy the way Thor handed him his credit card up front, telling him that the evening was on him and he wanted it to be memorable. He explained his buddies had given up their weekend to help him with a project.

Then he introduced Missy as his girlfriend.

She wasn't sure why that surprised her. But when he said the word girlfriend, she'd felt an immediate jolt within her body. Like a whoa and a wow mixed up together. Searching for clarification on the whoa-wow jolt, she realized that even with all her girl-power sensitivities, it gave her a certain thrill to have Thor claim her in public.

She just didn't expect to be … turned on by it.

She felt a little giddy and—truth be told—twinkly. Yes, twinkly. Like she was lit up on the inside, flitting about on her tippy-toes, loving her new dress, loving The Tavern, loving every branch of the military. She even loved the text message from Davis and couldn't wait to see how that played out. She was delighted to learn pitchers of beer had been placed on their table in anticipation of their arrival, and she'd never hungered for an enormous, juicy burger more.

Clearly, being Thor Watson's girlfriend was sitting well with her. Which is why, she supposed, when they joined the others at the table, she had the overwhelming urge to sit herself right in his lap.

The barrage of PG-13 comments that action set off were as embarrassing as they were flattering. She just went right ahead and owned it. Threw an arm around Thor's shoulders and … twinkled.

With an arm wrapped around her, Thor used one hand to pour the two of them beers, paying no attention to the fuss. But she felt it when he gave her waist a squeeze, and when she looked up, she noticed that he too … twinkled.

CHAPTER SIXTEEN

All of a sudden, things got easy.

Thor didn't know how it happened. Everything had been hard for so long. Hell, he wasn't sure what to make of this.

Missy on his lap.

Being … his.

In front of everybody.

For a moment, he didn't breathe. Didn't want to shake loose whatever just fell into place. Didn't trust that *easy* and *Missy* could go together. Because he'd been diligently working to turn her head for a long couple of months. And it was an uphill battle for the better part of those two months. And until, well, *this moment*, he didn't have all that much to show for it.

But now, before her first taste of beer, she'd brought on the soft and was looking at him like he was something special. Like he was her first choice instead of a consolation prize. So, yeah, breathing right now—pretty damn risky.

"You okay?" she asked him.

"Never better." It was honest, and hell, due to lack of air, those were about all the words he could muster.

"I'm not embarrassing you, am I?" she whispered.

What?

Thor let go of his beer and sat back, rubbing her leg and looking at her full in the face. So many thoughts drifted through his mind. So many hopes and plans for their future. He took his first, full breath. "Means the world to me, you being here. Like this."

She ducked her chin, hiding a shy smile and toying with a button on his shirt. After a moment, she met his eyes. "I liked being introduced as your girlfriend."

Swear to God, all he could think about was laying her down and … *Jesus.*

The yearning gripped him, his body responding to the need. All his sensations heightened with the locomotive that was his mind barreling down one track. His mouth was dry, his jaw was clenched, and every muscle group from his quads to his forearms twitched in anticipation. And she was right there, on his lap, giving him a green light as clear as day.

Goddamnit. What the hell happened to easy?

"Baby," he breathed. "When I get you alone."

She gave him her profile and then snuggled her head against his shoulder, laying some of her weight against his chest. Sweet. Soft.

His.

A broad spectrum of appetizers were delivered by two servers who then replaced the empty pitchers. The waitress took their burger orders, Missy moved to her seat, and Thor's body unwound itself slowly, his head finding its way back into the party.

They were finishing their main courses when Thor heard the seductive intonations of Emelina Flores's Spanish accent. "My dear boy," she said, placing a hand on his shoulder, leaning down to whisper in his ear. "Forgive me for interrupting."

"Em." Thurgood rose to greet Vance's grandmother, prompting every one of his buddies to do likewise. "Please, I'd be honored if you'd meet my friends." He put an arm around her, proudly making the introduction. "Boys, this gorgeous woman is Emelina Flores. She and her family made the mistake of inviting me to dinner one night, and like the stray dog I am, I continue to find my way back to her home for more. They've yet to kick me to the curb. Em, these ugly bastards are the closest thing I have to brothers. Nothin' I wouldn't do for them. They won't answer to anything but their nicknames, so indulge them. This is Hooker, Picks, Rhodes, Coxie, Balls, and Tinker."

"Gentlemen, so very good to meet you. Please, sit. Finish your meal," she begged. "I'll see who else may be able to help me."

"What? No," their voices rose in unison.

"Em, anything you need," Thor told her. "You know it."

"It's not actually for me," she said, speaking to the table at large. "There's a group of young women whose car broke down just a block from here. None of them are wearing sensible shoes, so this is as far as they managed to walk. I want to help, but I can't fit them all in my little two-seater. So when I saw Thor's truck parked outside, I wondered if he wouldn't mind tossing them in the back and ..." she paused, spreading her hands, "do what you Rangers do. Save the day."

"Further, faster, harder," Rhodes told her. "Are any of these young women old enough to drink?"

"In their twenties. Single. Attractive," she assured him.

"Send them in. We'll buy them a round. Once we finish our meals, we'll do exactly as you suggested. Toss 'em in the truck and"— Rhodes cocked his head and offered a sly grin—"do what we do."

Missy burst out laughing.

Em's dazzling smile and flirtatious wink was aimed directly at Rhodes. "I'll see if I can twist their arms."

"Happy to assist," Picks exclaimed, breaking rank and providing escort to Em as she made her way back to the front of the restaurant.

"Got your back," Balls called out, following behind.

The rest of them sat to resume eating as Hooker said, "Never seen a grandma who looked like that."

With his mouth full, Thor noted, "Cusses like a truck driver."

"No way," Rhodes said, amazed. "For real?"

"For real."

Missy confirmed it with a nod. "But her accent makes everything sound so refined, I'm constantly wanting to hit a rewind button. Never exactly sure what I've just heard come out of her mouth."

"Missy and Em work together. Part of Team Henderson."

"Holy—" Hooker stood up slowly while wiping his hands. "Sergeant Hook reporting for duty," he whispered.

Thor turned to watch a parade of Henderson's debutantes—all dolled up for a night out clubbing—wind their way toward them. Balls had the lead while Picks brought up the rear, chatting a blue streak with a strawberry blonde fit for an Irish jig.

"Okay, then," Thor said under his breath, standing. "Fellas. I will remind you that I live in this town. If an angry father comes gunning for me, I *will* give him your contact information."

"Chill, bro." Rhodes shot Thor a cocky grin and a wink. "We're just gonna do what we do."

Jesus.

The girls gathered themselves in a bunch at the head of the table. Thor might have recognized a couple, but they were younger than him by enough years that he wouldn't have known their names. Emelina was in her element, though. So while Hooker and Balls gathered extra chairs to squeeze in around the table, Em took over the introductions.

"My dear and most gallant gentleman. Allow me to introduce Henderson's loveliest daughters. This darling girl is Madeline Casanova."

"I go by Baby," the dark-haired angel clarified.

"And," Emelina went on, "since everyone dies famous in a small town, I will tell you that Miss Casanova was captain of the fencing team at Carolina and is now the athletic director at Vance-Granville community college. She's a legend at the country club for introducing vanilla vodka to the traditional gimlet, and though her parents would like to forget it, the rest of the town loves that she had a two-year stint as a Dallas Cowboys cheerleader."

A short, piercing whistle brought Madeline's (and everyone else's) attention toward the far end of the table where Coxie gave her a simple chin lift. Baby practically floated her way over to him.

Missy chuckled, and Thor responded by whispering in her ear, "This has trouble written all over it."

Emelina brought forth a second tantalizing morsel. This one was a looker with long brown hair, a tight navy sweater, and a flowy polka dot skirt. "This is Courtney Currier, my dear friend Eliza's granddaughter, who is famously known by her nickname, Dirty Girl. Like you gentlemen, her job as an environmental scientist takes her to remote areas where she's required to carry all her belongings on her back. We're happy to have her home and shower fresh for a few weeks before she's next off to Uruguay."

"Hell, Hooker and I specialize in dirty. Dirty Girl, why don't you grab your best dirty-girl friend and the two of you come sit by us?" Randy encouraged.

"All right," she agreed, looking behind her to pull forward a statuesque brunette. "This my cousin, Kayla Tinsley."

"Well, hello-o Kayla," Hooker greeted her enthusiastically. "I'm just itching to know what you're famous for."

"Oh. Well …" Kayla took a tentative glance back at Em.

"Darling," Em said in her Spanish accent. "It isn't as if I haven't seen you in action. Although tonight you might find yourself surrounded by stiff competition."

"Competition?" Hooker asked.

Kayla shrugged a shoulder. "I hold the record for shot-gunning beer."

"What? There's a record?"

"Well, you know, during college. Here in Henderson."

"So what does that mean exactly?" Hooker inquired. "You're the fastest on record? Done the most consecutive shotguns in a row? What?"

Kayla struck a haughty pose. "Are you … challenging me?"

"Just want a little clarification on what I'm up against," he said while pulling out her chair. Thor had never seen Hooker so mesmerized.

Em proceeded with the introductions. "And these two lovely ladies happen to be sisters. Lauren is, shall we say, the more demanding of the two. Kristin was on the basketball team at Cornell and actually coaches here in town.

"Great. Bossy one sits by me. Basketball queen can probably teach Balls a thing or two," Rhodes said.

"And then we have …"

All eyes turned toward Picks and Shannon, who were standing in the middle of The Tavern in animated conversation. "Well," Emelina said. "My work here is done. I trust you will enjoy yourselves."

"Miss Emelina. You can't possibly leave," Rhodes implored, pulling out an empty chair. "At least not until the boys and I wheedle out of you what *you'll* die famous for."

Em blushed like a teenager, for God's sake. Thor was thinking about how to recount this story to Vance, when surprise, surprise, Piper, Vance, and Pinks showed up on the scene.

"Piper?" Thor asked, shocked. "Aren't you on bedrest?"

"Thank goodness the contractions haven't started up for a full week, so I've been cut loose."

"Not happy about how fast she got herself fixed up after the Big Em called reporting on all the muscle sitting at your table," Vance muttered.

"Why wouldn't I want to meet Thor's friends?" Piper shot him a teasing grin while moving toward an empty chair.

"I see you salivating over all those tats," he accused his wife. "Missy?" Vance asked, turning his attention to her. "You found one you like better than Thurgood yet?"

"Not yet."

"You sure?" Pinks teased. "Big as Thor is, he is clearly not the only game in town tonight."

"He's the only game I'm playing," Missy said in an offhanded fashion before taking a sip of her beer.

Pinks and Vance patted Thor on the back in a way-too-obvious "attaboy" for his taste. Christ, when did his mission become a team event?

"Y'all should do something fun tonight," Piper announced to the table. "The weather is perfect for a bonfire."

"Ah …" Thor hedged. A bonfire wasn't a bad idea. Get these hoodlums back out on private property before all hell broke loose. But he really didn't want Missy to see what they were working on until it was done. Frankly, he'd hoped they'd come in, eat burgers, and then head to bed early. Looking around the table at all the flirting going on, he figured he'd better just throw in the towel and join the party. By the looks of things, they weren't hitting the hay until close to sunrise.

"Come on out to the Evans place," Pinks suggested. "The weather's been so good lately I've taken the liberty of heating up the pool. And if that's still too cold, we always have the hot tub. Plus, we've got that old oil drum in the shed we can use as a makeshift fire pit."

"And way too much pie," Vance added. "Piper's done nothing but bake since the moment she was allowed out of bed. Honestly, you'd be doing me a favor bringing this crowd over for dessert. Besides," Vance said to Thor, "no way you're shaking Piper and Em off any time soon. Look at the two of them drooling over all that testosterone." He pointed at his grandmother and his wife who had charmed their way into conversations around the table.

"Hard to resist a Ranger," Missy told the three of them, hugging Thor's arm.

Mission—freaking—accomplished.

Picks, who had introduced himself as Bryce McNally to the sweet piece of sass by his side, was starting to kick himself.

He'd just signed on for a job on the other side of the country, playing bodyguard for a pain-in-the-ass celebrity. A young guy who liked to visit the seedier nightclubs in LA. He'd been looking forward to a month off after his extended overseas assignment. The firm had promised him that. Even so, it hadn't dawned on him to say no. He'd been mission-oriented for so long it hadn't occurred to him that he had a choice about putting his life at risk for a glorified babysitting job no matter how much it paid.

But now that he was in Henderson?

Bryce hadn't seen Thor since before his father died. And although they'd managed a couple phone conversations, neither one of them found cellphones conducive to a lengthy conversation. Especially with the piss-poor cell service out Thor's way. But man, Bryce loved that plantation of his. The moment he set foot on it two days ago, he envied his closest friend. Having been raised in the inner city, and suffered one too many bleak desert deployments, Bryce knew if he owned land like that, he wouldn't go anywhere. He'd stay put.

Adding to that harsh pang of want, he was now talking to a pretty young thing who must be some kind of master at mixed martial arts because she'd knocked him out with a one-two punch the moment he laid eyes on her.

Bryce wasn't tall. Not that five foot ten was short, but standing next to Thor, he always came off looking like the little brother. It never bothered him. Never. But there sure was something gratifying about this tiny bit of femininity having to tilt her head back to look at him. Except for a few interesting curves, Shannon was as petit as she could be from head to toe. She totally rocked those corkscrew curls, was gifted with sexy bedroom eyes, and her strawberry-colored lips were bringing life to his johnson even as he and Shannon stood apart, chatting it up in the middle of a burger joint.

There was an instant chemistry flaring up within their chatter because, like him, this girl had a hard-on for sports. In the first five minutes, they'd bonded over their preference for Manning over Brady, their intolerance for Nick Saban in general, and the fact that baseball was excruciatingly boring unless you were actually at the stadium on a temperate night with a beer in your hand. Still, they both thought the season should be shortened by a month on each end.

And don't get them started on golf. Yeah, they both admitted to watching the Masters and thought the young guys coming up were good for the game, but neither were interested in whacking a ball around for over four hours. She was a fan of the WNBA, which Bryce could easily forgive because, like him, her first love was soccer.

And right now, damned if he wasn't interested in being her second love.

And the fact that this girl lived in the town near Thor's plantation just made Bryce want to extend his stay indefinitely.

"So what is it you do?" he asked Shannon.

"I could tell you, but then I'd have to kill you."

"Yeah?" he laughed. "Good one."

"Seriously. I've *always* wanted to meet a Navy Seal."

Shit. And he'd been liking her so well.

It was the twinkle in her eye that clued him in. He pressed his lips together, trying not to grin. "Cute."

"I know y'all are Army Rangers. Everyone in Henderson knows you're Army Rangers. Which, you know, is way impressive if it's anything like we see in the movies or read about in novels."

"We, you know, do what needs to be done," he offered. "Sometimes it's cool and lights you on fire. Other times, it's boring.

And I'm not gonna lie—sometimes it just plain scares the shit out of you."

"Yeah?" she questioned. "Once I heard a military guy speak who actually disabled bombs underwater. That was his job. I was sitting there as he was telling his story, and I could see in his eyes, he just wasn't normal. And that's when I understood. The men and women who take on those crazy, high-risk missions, they aren't right in the head."

Bryce nodded, smacking his lips. "When you're right, you're right. More times than not, highly trained special ops definitely have a screw loose."

"So which screw of yours is loose?" she asked.

He feigned surprise. "You can't tell?"

She shook her head, her smile cute as could be. "Far as I can tell, you're a little too normal to be deadly."

"I suppose you're just going to have to stick with me all night then. Maybe by morning you'll have figured it out."

The impromptu pool party at the Evans estate was loud and rambunctious and packed with people. Vance had called Brooks and Lolly out of Raleigh and made them jump in the car to come meet Thor's friends. "Networking," he cited. "You never know when Henderson may need the courage, skill, or weapons assistance of a pack of Rangers.

"Weapons assistance?" Brooks wondered. "I doubt Oxford is planning to attack us any time soon."

"Never can be too sure. We've got things heating up here, and you can be sure Oxford's going to catch wind and try to horn the fuck in on something. Not enough for them to have a damn football team we haven't beaten in a dozen years, they want in on whatever good we've got. And with the way things are moving—finally— there's going to be plenty of good they'll want to wrap their greedy little fingers around."

Missy, having overheard the conversation, scooted away from Thor and inserted herself between Brooks and Vance. "Talk to me about Oxford," she requested, sounding more like Henderson's CEO than she had all evening.

"Bigger than us. Jealous of everything we do," Vance offered.

"Like what?"

"I don't know. It's just a rivalry. Mostly between the high schools. But you know, that's the kind of thing you never outgrow."

"Hmm."

"Hmm?"

Missy sighed. "I'm considering taking an event-planning job in Oxford."

"Why?" Vance cried. "We've got plenty for you to do right here."

"Why not?" she countered. "If I'm going to be in business, it only makes sense to offer my services to Oxford. We certainly won't mind them sending their children to the sports academy or buying Henderson's Big Pie Plates. We're definitely going to want to lure them over to enjoy whatever new shops and restaurants we open, especially if we get that brew pub."

"She's right about all that," Brooks said. "Oxford's money is as green as everyone else's. Hell, we should consider a campaign enticing them to want to move over here."

"Who wants them over here?" Vance winced.

"Careful. Your Henderson High roots are showing."

"Damn right. But, okay, I get it. Sports rivalry aside, both towns need a thriving economy. If we can cross-promote the area by including Oxford in things, so be it."

"So you don't think this is a problem for me, do you?" Missy asked. "It wouldn't be a conflict of interest?"

"You're just throwing parties, right? What could be the fallout?" Vance asked.

"As I understand it, Henderson has a reputation for their parties."

"Our deb parties," Brooks specified. "They kick ass and then some because of Annabelle's influence."

"What makes them so kick-ass?" Missy asked, wanting to know specifics.

Brooks shrugged. "The band, the food, the people."

"So that's it?" Missy wondered. "No special magic Henderson wields to make their deb parties unforgettable?"

"No. They're just … fun. Well, usually there's a theme."

"A theme?"

"Yeah. Something catchy. Something that wraps in decorations and the food and the attire. A theme."

"Cool."

"Yeah. Henderson's had some good ones over the years."

"That's what I hear," Missy said before walking away and joining back up with Thor.

"Hey, Pretty Girl," he said when she slipped her hand into his. He leaned down and kissed her temple.

"You're not interested in the hot tub?" she asked, pulling him away from the crowd and into a dark, grassy area just off the patio.

Even in the dark, she saw the blue of his eyes spark into that neon hue that could still unnerve her. It reminded her there was a time when she could scarcely look him in the eye at all. Like right now, when the intensity of his eyes bore into her own.

"What?" she snapped defensively.

"A hot tub any other night would be killer. But seeing as the girls have stripped down to their undies to indulge, you and I are staying as far from that nightmare as we can get."

Missy gave a brief laugh. "Why are you afraid of girls in their underwear?"

"The nightmare I'm referring to is the one that would occur if *you* were stripped down to your underwear."

"Me?"

"Baby, I love my boys, but they are horny, disgusting pigs. I'm not interested in them seeing my girl in her underwear. There is a damn good reason Piper is not out here in that hot tub."

"Yeah. She's pregnant."

"Pregnant or no, Vance would go apeshit if Piper pranced around in her altogether letting a bunch of crazy-ass yahoos ogle her."

"Yes, he would. Because it is a well-known fact that when it comes to Piper, Vance is overprotective. You, Thurgood Watson, are not."

"I'm not what?" he asked cautiously.

"Overprotective."

There was silence.

Missy tilted her head.

"I might be a little possessive," he claimed.

"Really?"

"I think so, yeah."

"Hmm."

"Hmm, what? And I'm not getting a warm, fuzzy feeling from that look in your eye."

"Davis," she yelled over her shoulder. "Is there a way to turn off the lights in the pool?"

"Why'd ya wanna do that?" Pinks yelled back.

"Thor wants to go skinny-dipping." She smirked up at Thor.

"You're messing with me," he told her. "Pinks," he hollered. "The pool lights stay on."

Missy shrugged. "I'm not modest. Skinny-dipping with lights on or off makes no difference to me."

"Good. Happy to hear it. But just so you know, skinny-dipping in a pool is bullshit. When the two of us go dipping, it will be in the lake."

"I'm talking about tonight," she whispered, leaning in.

He leaned in double. "Not happening. Not tonight."

"You sure?" she asked. She handed him her Solo cup, took the hem of her dress in her hands, and slowly pulled it up over her head.

Missy's back was toward the party behind her. She and Thor were off in the shadows. If anyone bothered looking in their direction, and she was betting heavily they would not, they'd only see her white bikini undies standing out in the dark.

But Thor, he could see ... everything. Her wedge sandals, her bare legs, her modest satin panties, and her bare ... chest. Which is where his eyes rested.

Between the angry lock of his jaw and the lust shooting out of his eyes, Missy was surprised his head didn't explode. She watched him pull his eyes off her breasts and direct them over her head. He stepped in close, surveying the scene behind her. "Is this a test or somethin'? Because I'm pretty sure I'm gonna fail."

"I wouldn't say, test," she teased.

His eyes glanced down briefly and then flicked back to the party. "What would you say?"

"I'd say it's more like a dare."

"Ohhhhh," he drawled out. "A dare. Understood." He snapped the dress out of her hand, bent low, and wrapped the top half of her body around his shoulders, slinging her into a fireman's carry. He spun and took three steps down the grassy slope into the night before Missy's brain caught up with what was happening.

"Thor," she spit out, half laughing, half wincing in pain. "Stop." She started laughing for real. "Put me down," she squeaked out, laughing harder with every jostle.

"A dare," he mocked, shaking his head as he took them farther into the darkness.

"Ouch." Her eyes were tearing up. Because as hard as she was finding it to breathe with his shoulder jammed between her smushed breasts, the shock of being so easily tossed over his shoulder (she definitely hadn't seen that coming), the absurdity of being mostly naked, and the sheer happiness she felt at being able to mess with him like this just blew out of her in an unadulterated fit of laughter.

"Oww," she managed through her guffaws. "Seriously," she sputtered in between snorts. "You're squishing me."

"Baby, you do not *dare* a member of the 75th."

It wasn't until she started cackling, "I'm sorry, I'm sorry, I'm sorry," that Thor slowed and eventually bent to put her down.

To say she wasn't steady on her feet was an understatement. Still laughing, trying to wipe tears from her eyes, and wearing wedged sandals in the lush grass, she teetered backward and was grateful for Thor's quick reflexes. "Hold on there, Pretty Girl."

"Oh," she stammered, grabbing at her stomach, which hurt from all the laughing. "That was"—she sniffed—"so good. I"—she wiped more tears from her eyes—"haven't had a laugh … like that … in years." Her eyes locked with his once she finally managed to get her mirth under control. "Thank you."

Which made him laugh. "You're welcome," he said, handing her back her dress. She promptly began putting it back on.

Missy couldn't stop grinning. "I don't know what came over me." She stopped and went still. "You know I was totally teasing, right?"

"You saying we wouldn't have had war if I'd have called your bluff?"

She shook her head, going back to fixing her dress. "I don't know. I don't know what I would have done." She moved forward and laid her hands on his chest. "What I do know is that I really enjoy myself when I'm with you."

He wrapped his arms around her shoulders and pulled her in tight, saying into her hair, "Every last one of my boys has found a way to tell me how much they approve."

"Approve?"

"How much they like you. And they like that I like you."

"That's good, right?"

"Makes my life easy."

"Hey, Tinker isn't single is he?"

"No, he is not."

"I've noticed he's the only one keeping his hands to himself."

"He's got a great girl. Stuck by him a long time now."

"And the rest of them?"

"Acting like fools but not breaking any hearts tonight."

"Oh, I don't know about that. It's gonna be a long time before Henderson has another battalion of hot-looking war heroes drop by unannounced. Unless you've got another bunch up your sleeve."

"Only the one."

"Well, they make me laugh. I like them."

"You think you can manage to keep your clothes on the rest of the night?"

"No one saw that."

He wrapped a hand around her ponytail and pulled her face directly under his. "I saw it," he said, his eyes sparking with desire. "Hottest thing that's ever happened to me. Hot because you had the balls to do it in the middle of a party. Hot because you managed not to cause a scene. Hot because between the curve of your waist and your gorgeous tit—" He bit his lip, stopping the flow of words. "Damn hot."

Then he kissed her, right before he threw down his Rambo card.

"Do not *ever* do it again."

CHAPTER SEVENTEEN

"So she's the one, huh?"

Monday morning after the rest of the guys had left, Thor and Bryce marched over the ground wearing rucksacks loaded with forty-five pounds of equipment, doing twelve-minute miles just to remind themselves they could.

"If she'll have me," Thor said.

"Things looked good from where I was standing Saturday night."

"Since you were locked inside that pixie's personal space, fairly certain all you saw was curly hair and freckles."

"I saw plenty. Trust me."

They marched on for a while in silence. Then Bryce voiced what Thor figured took some guts. "Shannon—that's the pixie's name, by the way—asked me a lot of questions about our time overseas."

"Huh."

"You tell Missy anything about that? Specifics?"

"She hasn't asked. I don't think she wants to know."

"Do you want to tell her?"

Thor shrugged.

"Have you told anybody?"

"My dad. He was great. Told me he was eager to hear anything I was interested in sharing. Mostly, I just wanted to share stuff about you guys."

After a brief silence, Bryce asked, "You suffering any of that PTSD shit?"

"Are you?"

Bryce shook his head. "I don't think I've sat still long enough for it to surface yet."

"Sitting still will bring it on," Thor acknowledged. "For me, it started about a month after my pop died. After the shock wore off and there was just … numbness. And guilt. I went to The Situation seeking company and experienced my first panic attack. It was the third of July, so a lot of people were back in town and the place was mobbed. I was hyper-aware of the place becoming more and more crowded. Paid close attention to where the exits were. Somebody lit off a firecracker in the parking lot, and I was done. I hadn't experienced a sense of terror like that in all my days in the Army.

"After that, I had some nightmares and another couple panic attacks, but they were mild by comparison. Nothing too frequent, but it kept me away from crowds for a long time. I didn't eat. Was probably depressed."

"And now?"

"Feelin' pretty good now," Thor told the truth. "Miss my pop every damn day. Miss you. Miss Coxie and Tinker. Hell, I miss the missions. Not the intensity, but the teamwork and the sense of accomplishment. I get why soldiers stay in for life. It's hard acclimating to the civilian world. You're an outcast. Nobody knows what you know or has done what you've done. Everyone's just doing their own thing, living their own lives. There's no sense of community."

"Really? Even in a small town like this? No community?"

Thor thought about that. "After last weekend, in a much broader sense maybe. This Team Henderson thing Missy's involved with is catching on. I guess that's strengthening the sense of community around here. Bringing people together for the good of the town. Giving them a common purpose." Thor smiled over at Picks as they marched. "Hadn't looked at it like that."

"Fresh air, green grass, and building a lacrosse field is not a mission we're used to, but damn if we didn't get it done. And it felt good not having to watch my back. Doubt there's one of us who couldn't use a few more civilian missions like that. It was good you made the call. Got us here and on it, working together again."

"You think Rhodes and Tinker are gonna make it back to center?"

"I think Rhodes and Tinker are fucked. Delta Force is who they are, and they ain't comin' back from that shit. Tinker takes all the riskiest jobs and practically ties one arm behind his back to level the playing field. Still, he eased up all right when the civilians joined the fun the other night."

"And Coxie?"

"Well, he damn sure isn't going to MIT to be a computer tech."

"He tell you that?"

"Not in so many words."

"So he's not out?"

"He's out as far as you and I and everybody else are concerned. But no, man, he ain't out. He doesn't want out."

"How about you? You happy you're out? Working private?"

"Was until I saw this place. Seriously. You may have to throw me off your property. Rolling hills. Grass, trees, sky. Water, for God's sake. If I didn't have to leave, I'd pitch a tent and stay."

"No tent necessary. Your ass is welcome to the garage."

"That is not a deterrent. Damn sight better than a containerized housing unit."

Thor's eyes scanned the landscape around them. "You got any ideas what I should do with all of this?"

"I know what I'd do with it."

"Yeah? What's that?"

"Train kids."

"Train kids?"

"For the outdoors. Camping. Survival. Adventure."

"Like Boy Scouts?"

"Yeah. Only, cooler. Something like Boy Scouts mashed up with the X Games."

"X Games?"

"Dirt bikes, mountain bikes, skateboards, and something like that America Ninja Warrior course would be totally badass. Maybe a mud run."

"Marnie said if I built something fun, all my Army buddies would come visit me. Sounds like she was right."

"Marnie? Missy know about this Marnie?"

"Marnie is *ten*. Marnie is my neighbor. Marnie is a bundle of tomboy wrapped up in her own hurt and angst who wants me to teach her how to shoot a gun and play football. I dare say Marnie would be all over your Scouts/X Games mashup."

"See, my Scouts/X Games mashup is a gold mine."

Thor grinned. "You could be right. If I were a kid, *I'd* be all over it."

"Hell …"

"What?" Thor asked.

"I'm just thinking. I mean, why let the kids have all the fun? Why not do it for adults?"

"A Scouts/X Games mashup for adults?"

"Absolutely. It could be like a dude ranch, only instead of playing cowboy, people will get to play Ranger."

"Ranger?"

"Fuck, yes. This is brilliant."

"You think people are going to want to 'play Ranger?'"

"Are you serious? Look at Call of Duty. Look at Battlefield and all the military video games. Look at paintball, for God's sake. Do you have any idea what kind of kick-ass Capture the Flag game we could create on this land? I'm talking the whole nine yards with strategic battle plans, high-tech communication, air support—"

"Air support?"

"Go big or go home, man."

Thor laughed.

"Come on. This is a great idea," Bryce encouraged.

"It's an idea, all right. Not sure how great it is."

"Okay, forget the air support. What I'm talking about is taking the best parts of Ranger School and—"

"Best parts of Ranger School? Are you insane? Ranger School sucked ass."

"Yeah, so we make it *fantasy* Ranger School without the extreme exhaustion, the brutal discomfort, and the nonstop shouting. Because you know if they had actually fed us or let us sleep, Ranger School would've been awesome."

"True that."

"Team building. It's a thing, man. And it's a thing we specialize in. We could do it and make it fun. Take the best parts of being a Ranger and share that. Share the thrill of a mission with people who sit at a desk all day. Dude. I would so want to be a part of that."

"Sounds to me like you're the one who should be running it."

"Hey. It's your land."

"And your vision."

Bryce stopped marching. "You want to do this?"

"I definitely want to explore it," Thor told him.

"All right."

"All right."

"Further. Faster. Harder."

"Hooah."

CHAPTER EIGHTEEN

That afternoon, Thor burst into CC Henderson and came to a screeching halt. There were people, good-looking, polished business people. People he'd never laid eyes on before and quite obviously people who were not from around here. They seemed as shell-shocked as he was by the look of things.

"Let me understand this," one lanky dude in a suit was saying to his Melissa. "The local Starbucks is …"

"Nonexistent," Missy replied.

It was like she was speaking Chinese for all the suits understood. "I know," she went on with her charming, soft smile of understanding. "It's a bit of culture shock coming from Dallas. But Henderson has its charms. You'll see. The best coffee I've found is at the Gas & Go. Or The Situation, but that's really a bar and doesn't officially open until eleven. However, I do have a Keurig machine here you are welcome to use, and perhaps you can persuade Mr. Carraway of the necessity of a fancier coffee maker to outfit the office. That, or see if he'll gather funding for a gourmet coffee franchise."

"Write that down," the tall one ordered. And damn if the tiny little secretary standing behind him didn't do just that.

"And you are?"

It took Thor a minute to drag his gaze off the tiny, little mouse who busily wrote notes to realize the suit was talking to him.

"Thurgood Watson," he said, sticking out his hand. "Friend of Miss McReady's." He nodded toward Missy.

"Charles Douglas Higginbotham," the suit said, shaking his hand. "In charge of PR and management of CC Henderson."

"Is that so? Now see, I thought CC Henderson was just a shingle."

"It took Mr. Carraway some time to sort out who he wanted representing him in Henderson, but the five of us have been hand-selected. We are here to nurture CC Dallas's interests in North Carolina."

"Well, welcome," Thor said all friendly-like though he definitely did not like the way the suit's associates were eyeing up his woman. "If I can borrow Melissa for a moment, I'll get out of your hair and let y'all get settled in."

Missy moved through the throng of tight asses and followed him out the door. "I'll be right back," she told them as she closed them all inside.

"What's going on?" Thor asked.

"I'm not exactly sure." Missy started bubbling with laughter. "I thought I was bad, moving to Henderson and getting used to the lack of fancy coffee at my fingertips. This crowd is not going to cut it. From the looks on their faces and the questions they're asking, it's like they've been dropped into a Third World country."

"Did you know they were coming?"

"No idea at all. I was getting used to having the building to myself. Then, all of a sudden, I've got the next generation of Dallas's elite standing around, looking lost, and acting as if I'm their personal secretary."

"Whoa. Personal secretary? How do you mean?"

"They started asking me to arrange office furniture and phone service and TVs ..."

"Did you set them straight?"

"I didn't get a chance, because the drama queen among them started moaning about a caffeine fix and the rest of them fell into agreement. Then we got on to the coffee shop situation—as in there aren't any—and after that they simply couldn't speak. That's when you walked in."

Thor's smile grew big and broad. "I'm sticking around. This is damn good stuff. Come on." He started to open the door and pull her inside, but she halted him.

"Wait a minute. What did you come into town for?"

His smile grew even bigger. "The project the boys and I were working on is complete. I want to show it to you before lacrosse practice."

"All right. Is it still a surprise?"

His eyes lit up. "A big surprise. For you."

"Oh, God."

Thor started to laugh. "You should see your face. Really," he insisted. "The guy you're swapping spit with tells you he has a big surprise and you panic? What the hell, *Melissa*? I promise I'm not getting down on one knee and making you a farmer's wife for God's sake."

"You better hadn't be," came the voice of the suit

Thor looked up, and yep, the lanky one's head stuck out the front door, eyes staring back at the two of them.

"And what if I was?" Thor asked, scooting his Melissa behind him. "What's it to you, Slick?"

Slick shrugged. "No skin off my nose. But CC's brother told me, told Brass, and told Dan that we were to keep our hands off this one." He pointed to Missy. "He didn't claim her in so many words, but his point did not escape us."

"Yeah? Well, you tell *the Cowboy* time has marched on here in Henderson, and the bell has been rung on his wedding escapades."

Missy cut Thor off. "Tell Cash I send him my best."

The suit threw Thor a smug grin and ducked back inside.

"What the hell?"

"I just did that to get rid of him. You're not starting a pissing contest with a guy twelve hundred miles away."

"I will if he thinks he has a hold on you."

"Mmm, Army Ranger Watson. You're kind of yummy when you go all Rambo."

"I'm yummy?"

"Yep. Jealousy makes you tantalizingly yummy. You stiffen up all ramrod straight, toss your shoulders back, and thrust out your chest. Kinda hot."

"All right. Good. Frankly, with that look you're throwing me right now, I'm thinking of flying Cash in here myself. You want yummy, I'll give you yummy." He reached his arms out to drag her against him, but she squealed and ducked under, spinning away.

"Hey. What happened to yummy?"

"I don't want to *do* yummy in front of the Dallas contingent."

Thor turned to look, and yeah, all of the tightasses had their noses plastered up against the window. He sent them a finger wave and then marched Melissa down the street and out of their line of sight.

"Are you in charge of these aliens?" he asked.

"Aliens?"

"Outlanders."

"Really?"

"Well, they sure as hell aren't locals, and that's not the damn point. What's your responsibility to all of that?"

"I honestly don't know. I'm going to head across the street and talk to Hale or Vance and see if they know anything about what's going on."

It was then that Pinks, who was actually wearing a lavender dress shirt tucked into a pair of light gray slacks, came out of E&E and strode across the street straight into CC Henderson. The man was obviously on a mission because he didn't notice or acknowledge the two of them standing a half a block away.

"All right. Well, it looks as though that's going to be handled. How 'bout you take an early lunch and come with me? I've got something to show you. Something you need to see before three o'clock this afternoon."

"I've got practice at three."

"Actually, Pinks's team has practice at three. Which means you get to babysit until they're done. *Then* you've got practice." Thor couldn't help but smile at her disgruntled expression.

"Cheer up, Pretty Girl." He leaned down close and whispered in her ear. "I have a surprise."

Missy chatted nervously about the Dallas contingent all the way out to Thor's plantation. Since they'd had their heart-to-heart over a week ago, she'd enjoyed the way Thor had continued to seduce her into being a couple with his sweet end-of-the-day phone calls and his cute innuendo-filled texts. The way he'd introduced her as his girlfriend to one of his father's friends was still making her inner girly-girl swoon.

Just like the season of spring, things between them were fresh, new, and budding, and there'd been no further discussion on the issue he was having—the issue she was having—since that evening after the Evans's crazy brunch. In fact, with all that had happened over the last week, she hadn't had time to worry about falling for an Army Ranger with a plantation strapped to his back.

So she was rambling on and on about the personnel lineup for CC Henderson. In her head, she knew it was driving him crazy, and she should just hush up as these Southerners would say. But she couldn't seem to stop herself from talking. She told him about Charles Douglas, and then she told him about Daniel, and then Poppy, and Brass, and Adelaide. When she started all over again, Thor's hand darted from the steering wheel and over to her leg.

"Pretty Girl," he whispered. "It's okay. Truly. I'm not going to propose. I'm not even going to lock you up in the attic or tie you to my bedpost."

"Yes, but I have no idea what you are going to do."

"Relax. I'm just showing you an idea I had. Hoping that you'll like it."

"Can I guess?"

"Sure. Go ahead."

"A gazebo."

"Why a gazebo?"

"To watch the sunset. Not that the back of Big Red wasn't romantic. It's just a gazebo is very romantic."

"It's not a gazebo, but if you'd like to help me choose the best place to put one, that will be my next project. Certainly don't want to be classified as unromantic and, to be honest, I think I remember my mom talking about wanting one."

"That would be a nice way to honor your mom," she said softly. "But please don't keep me in suspense by making that a surprise too. Even though I had plenty of work to keep me busy, I still missed seeing you every day," she admitted.

Thor tweaked her knee between his thumb and forefinger, which made her squeal.

"Missed you, too," he said in his low, sexy timbre. "How 'bout I stretch my culinary skills tonight and fix you dinner? Make up for a little lost time."

"I'd like that. I've got a lot I want to tell you."

He glanced in her direction before he rolled his eyes.

"Not about the Dallas group, I promise. That was just … you know—"

"Nervous rambling?"

"Yeah. Sorry."

"Well, I'm about to put an end to your misery," he said, pulling into the long, white-graveled drive.

It was the first glimpse Missy had of Thor's home, and the charming, rural picture it made took her breath away. The big, proud farmhouse stood up to the word "plantation" featuring six white columns rising a full two stories, creating both a covered porch and a second-story balcony. White with black shutters, the house also boasted three dormer windows at the third-floor level, protruding from a sloped gray roof.

The structure was majestic and beautifully suited to the landscape. It was also far younger than Missy had imagined, being aware the land had been in Thor's family for generations. She adored the patriotic touch of the American flag hanging from the left column flanking the main entrance, along with North Carolina's flag on the right. The two flags added color, character, and pride.

"Thor," she breathed, so ashamed of the prejudice she'd created in her mind. "This is … *glorious*."

"Really?" He drew back in disbelief.

She succumbed to her own horrid mortification with a bit of choked-up laughter. "I'm such a snob," she confessed. "Your home, this … setting, is so much grander than what I come from."

"In what *possible* way?" he scoffed.

"Oh," she breathed, shaking her head, taking in every detail as he drove them farther up the drive. "I don't know," she lied. Because she did know. Exactly. She just didn't know how to put it into words.

She didn't know how to tell Thurgood Watson III that her heart broke open at the sight of his familial home. That the feeling it evoked was the equivalent to the opened arms of a loved one, a beckoning oasis. There was a gentleness in the picturesque setting. A graciousness.

"It's a sanctuary," she finally said. "And I thought ... well, I don't know what I thought, but I definitely didn't expect this.

"A sanctuary, huh?" Thor snorted. He drove the truck around to the right. Then swung left and pulled up perpendicular to the house with the truck's nose almost touching the door of the attached two-car garage. "Not sure about the sanctuary part, but it's the only home I've ever known."

He looked over at Missy, and in that moment, it occurred to her that *he* was a sanctuary. He'd been her sanctuary since the day she arrived in Henderson.

So often he'd be the one to show up and offer relief when she felt overwhelmed. And the night of the Spectacular, after she'd completed her job—when she realized the day was a success and she'd allowed herself to ease against his body as he sat on that barstool—that was the same feeling she'd had when she saw his beautiful property.

She felt compelled to tell him. To tell Thor what he was to her. But before she could, he turned off the engine and began to speak.

"I've got a lot of acreage I haven't figured out what to do with, but there's one piece of land in back of the house and off to the right—a really fine piece—that practically slapped me upside the head with an idea so obvious I'm sorry I didn't think of it sooner." The grin he tossed her was compelling. "Come on."

CHAPTER NINETEEN

Pinks might have noticed the heads gathered in the window as he headed into CC Henderson. He certainly noticed how they all stood up straight when he entered the building, like they'd been caught with their hands in the cookie jar.

"What?" he asked the startled group of faces.

"We were just …" the tall one stammered.

"Spying on Cash's girlfriend and that big dude," another one shared.

"Cash's *girlfriend*?" Pinks wondered aloud.

"The looker who works here."

"Missy?"

"Right. That's her name. Missy."

"She's not Cash's girlfriend," Pinks told them. "Tell Cash he needs to get that idea out of his head. Unless he's moving to Henderson and bringing his roping skills with him, Missy McReady is tied up with our local war hero, and I don't see Cash or anybody else challenging him for the privilege." Pinks looked the men over. "That was a warning, if I didn't make myself clear."

"You Pinks?"

"I am. And you are?"

"Charles Douglas Higginbotham."

Pinks reached in to shake the guy's hand. "You go by Charles, Charlie?"

"Charles Douglas."

"Quite the mouthful."

"My mother's idea."

Pinks figured Vance would be calling Mr. Higginbotham, Chuck by the end of the day.

"And this is Brass Castillo," Chuck pointed out the Hispanic guy whose eyes quietly said savvy but whose suit yelled flash.

"Nice suit," Pinks commented, shaking Brass's hand.

"This is Dan Mellin," Chuck went on introducing a Prince Harry look-alike complete with red hair, hazel eyes, and a grin he was sure the ladies would go for.

"Dan," Pinks nodded, shaking the man's hand.

"This is Dan's twin sister, Poppy."

Whoa. Prince Harry looked damn good as a girl. And the name fit. With the color of her hair and her complexion, she indeed reminded Pinks of a Poppy.

"And the one we can't live without, Adelaide Bartholomew."

"Wow," Pinks said, shaking Poppy's hand but addressing Adelaide. "That's a big name for a tiny, little girl. Shit. That sounded ... sexist, maybe. I didn't mean anything by it," Pinks backpedaled. "It's just, you're, you know, petite."

And nervous, Pinks noticed. She stood there wringing her hands and blinking her dark eyes up at him from under even darker curls. "You okay?" he finally asked.

"Aww, she's just dazzled," the flashy suit—Brass—said.

I really ought to have studied these names, Pinks thought. "Dazzled?"

"We've heard the talk," Chuck said.

"Make that the legend," Dan added.

"Legend?"

"Of Pinks. The Pink One," Chuck used air quotes. "In fact, Mr. Carraway told us he's looking for *his* Pinks. He's trusting that one of us is going to step up and do the job like you do. Be CC Henderson's Git 'r Done guy or gal."

"Well, I'm no legend, but I've managed to figure out what I'm good at. So why don't you tell me a little bit about what you're good at?"

No surprise, Chuck started in. "I'm Crain's PR agent and consultant in Henderson. I'm the face of CC Henderson when CC is not in town."

"All right," Pinks said, thinking that was not a bad call for Crain to make. Charles Douglas might be a mouthful, but he was confident, dressed like he worked on Wall Street, and had the take-charge attitude Crain would want representing him. He was clearly the leader of this brigade.

Brass, the Hispanic guy with short-cropped hair and gray eyes, brought on the flash by the accessories he wore. Like the brightly colored tie and matching pocket square tucked into his blue blazer. "I'm the finance guy. I assume you and I will be working together."

"You, me, and Vance. Vance is the real money guy when it comes to the overall sports academy project. The nitty gritty. I'm more big picture and the one who sets up the sponsorship meetings. Basically, I'm the advance man across the street. For everything."

"Okay, well, maybe you and I will be working together then," Dan said. "I'm marketing."

"And I'm the sports liaison," Poppy spoke up.

"And you?" Pinks asked the nervous little mouse in the corner.

"Writer and Orders," she said, her voice not as quiet as Pinks anticipated. Nor did she sound nervous or unsure as she went on. "Mr. Carraway has asked me to come work for both him and Team Henderson. I write speeches—sound bites for marketing or publicity—but I'm also well versed in business proposals."

Pinks felt his own eyes light up. "Really? We need you and a couple more like you. Right now our lone lawyer, Duncan James, is having a hard time keeping up. I'd really like to introduce the two of you as soon as possible and see if you can give him some help."

Pinks looked at the group at large. "So are you all moved into the houses Crain rented?"

Chuck shook his head. "We came straight here from the airport."

"All right, well, let me give you a quick tour of the office. Won't take long, but we'll make a list of what you'll need to get settled. Then Vance and I will take you to lunch at the club and introduce you to Harry."

"Oh, we've heard all about Harry," Dan said.

"I'll bet. Crain does get a kick out of Harry. Then, after lunch we'll make our way over to your homes away from home."

"Is there really not a Starbucks in town?" Poppy asked.

"Don't worry," Pinks said, leading them down the hallway. "Y'all are gonna love it here."

CHAPTER TWENTY

Thor took Missy's hand as they exited his truck, directing her around to the back of the house and into the backyard.

He stood there a moment, not wanting to walk her toward the patio but waiting for her to notice the field, the painted lines ... something. But she seemed content to hold his hand and simply glance from the back of the house to his face now and again. Finally, he tugged her around so that her back was to him and her gaze was directed down the field.

Nothing happened for a moment. Then he saw her posture straighten and her head turn this way and that. She reached down and slid off her heels, dropping them where she stood before venturing out in her bare feet onto the beautiful green carpet of sod.

At first, she tiptoed, like she wasn't sure what she was stepping on and didn't want to damage anything. He found that surprising and damn adorable, and he would have paid good money to know what was going through her head at that moment. He grinned as she picked up her pace, walking a few steps before breaking into a jog in that camel-colored wraparound dress that had caught his eye the first time he'd seen her. The dress's hem fluttered in the breeze as he watched her kick up her heels in an all-out run to the opposite end of the field. There she stopped and traversed from side to side, came back to the center, and then paced it off all the way back to his end. She sprinted across the width of the field twice more before she stopped dead, turned toward him, and burst with laughter.

"A lacrosse field?" she hollered. "You built a lacrosse field?"

"A *women's* lacrosse field," he yelled back. He heard her shriek with glee as she ran toward the painted circle waiting for a goal and dodged a few unseen defensemen before pantomiming a shot.

"The nets are being delivered around three, so you and your lady players are in business."

"Thor," she said, strolling toward him but studying the chalk lines, taking in the entire field, her body turning a complete circle as she walked. When she caught him in her sights, she ran and jumped into his arms, circling her legs around his waist and her arms around his neck. "You are *so* getting laid tonight," she told him through a happy, happy grin right before she planted one on him.

"I didn't do it for that," he said. "Not that I'm not interested," he assured her, hiking her up and putting his arms under her butt to support her body. "But I didn't do it for that. I did it because I could, Pretty Girl. I had the land. You needed a field. Once I stopped thinking about what I didn't want to do, the idea of what I could do popped into my head. The fact that it was going to make you happy—hell, killed two birds with one stone."

"Yeah? How's that?"

"Well, if I can get you out here to indulge in your lacrosse passion, I figure you might get a little more comfortable being on the Watson plantation."

She grinned at him.

"And if the two of us start thinking outside the box a little bit, we may find some mutual ground—literally—to build something on."

"I like it. All of it. But you're still getting laid."

He pulled his arm from underneath her ass and checked his watch. "We've got an hour," he said. "Give or take."

"Later," she said, grinning into his face before she kissed him. "Tonight," she promised against his lips. "After we figure out how to get my team out here, after they get the feel of their *new home turf*," she said proudly, "and definitely after we rub Davis's nose in this, then …"

"I get laid?" He grinned against her lips.

"Big time."

"I might like to get that in writing." He kissed her thoroughly.

"Trust me." She scrambled down his body, leaving him feeling energized and excited. She turned back to the field. "I just wish I had my stick."

"Hold that thought." Thor turned away and headed to the back door of the garage. He came out with two sticks, saying, "I had Pinks set me up." He handed her a defensemen's stick while he kept the shorter version for himself. "He showed me a few things. Mostly how to throw the ball against the side of the garage and catch it. Damn sport isn't as easy as it looks," he said. "Come on."

The two of them headed onto the virgin field, playing catch. When Missy thought about what was happening—that she was tossing the ball around with *Thor*, on a field he'd built *for her*—all she could do was shake her head and dissolve into a fit of giggles. "I can't believe you did this for me," she said, stopping everything, dropping her arms to simply stare at him, seeing so much good, and kindness, and ingenuity, and sweetness wrapped up into one big bundle of hunky farm boy. "Thor," she breathed, stumbling to him and throwing herself into his arms, feeling too overcome to hold herself up any longer. "This is amazing. Thank you."

"You sure are welcome," he breathed into the top of her head as he smoothed a hand down her hair.

"The girls are going to love this. Ohmygoodness." She pulled back and threw him a look. "They are already crushing on you. This is going to send them over the edge."

"Crushing on me?"

"They think you're hot."

"Me? They think a twenty-nine-year-old is hot?"

"They have no idea how old you are. But they do have excellent taste."

"Does that mean you think I'm hot?" He moved in tight with all sorts of Southern swagger, placing his hands on her waist.

She leaned her head to one side and gave him a get-real look. "Pfft. As if you don't already know your brand of L.L. Bean really works for me." She couldn't help but run her hands over his biceps. "I'm tellin' ya. This outdoor stuff looks good on you."

He smirked. "I'll bet you say that to all the guys."

"Only the ones who build me lacrosse fields."

He leaned in and touched his forehead to hers. "You like?"

"I do," she said, sincerely. "I am"— she looked around and drew in a deep breath, expelling it on the word—"overwhelmed."

"You think you can get practice moved over here?"

"I will certainly do my best."

"The field is available weekends and nights," he told her. "In fact, I was looking into a way to light it up for y'all."

"How did you even do this? In a week?"

"I had a lot of help. Not only from the guys you met but also from Thatcher and a bunch of fellas he knew who were interested in overtime pay."

"Wow."

"Missy?"

She blinked at him and then glanced around the field. "So this was bigger than laying some grass and figuring out where to chalk the lines."

"A little bit. It needed to be sloped to accommodate the issue of drainage. Thatcher does this sort of thing for a living, so he knew what corners to cut. He helped me get it done as quickly and as budget friendly as possible."

Oh, God. She wanted to ask him—how much did he spend? On a field. For her! But she knew he wasn't going to tell her how much this had cost, and she didn't want to appear ungrateful and ask or worry about it. Even though she sort of was.

Of course, using his hyper-aware Ranger skills, he read her mind.

"Stop," he insisted. "Stop right now. This is *my* property, this is *my* field, and I'm naming it for my *mother*. *You* are just the custodian. I'd like you and your team to enjoy the field in exchange for agreeing to include Marnie as an honorary member. And just so you know, the main reason I built the damn thing was to stop the drama over field time between you and Pinks. I just can't listen to it any longer."

"That is not why you did this."

"Hell, if it isn't. That is exactly what inspired the idea. So yeah, enjoy it, use the hell out of it, but do not waste a moment worrying about it, Pretty Girl. I did this for *me*."

"Yeah? Well, you're still getting laid. In fact …" She dropped her stick and started untying her dress.

"Missy," he warned. "Don't mess with me."

"You said we have an hour."

Thor checked his watch as she slid the dress off her shoulders and let it fall to the ground.

"We're down to forty-five minutes, and what the hell is with your underwear?" His features were drawn up in distaste.

"My underwear?" Missy looked down to check out her white-and-black Nike sports bra and matching Nike boy shorts.

"You've just ruined the little-bitty-lace fantasy I've been having since seeing you in that dress."

"You don't approve?" she asked haughtily, using her fingers to indicate the state of her undress.

Thor quirked a brow. "Of your smokin' hot body, yes. Of what you've got covering it up, hell no. Wear that shit under your coaching clothes—no, not even then. Wear it under your uniform when you're on the field being a warrior. When you're off the field, keep it hidden in a drawer. Because when you're off the field, you're not a warrior," he said, pulling her to him, "you're my sweet"—kiss—"soft"—kiss—"very … pretty … girl."

"Thor," Missy said through his kisses.

"Yeah," he said back, not taking his lips off hers.

"I happen to be standing on a field right now."

"You know what I mean," he said, slipping his hand into the waistband of her Nike boy shorts and cupping her left cheek. He gave her ass a squeeze as he deepened the kiss, making Missy forget everything.

Car doors slammed.

Usually this would cause Thor to go into full alert mode, as he didn't get many visitors out there. But under the circumstances, with his hands on Missy's ass, his tongue down her throat, and his mind in the damn gutter, it took a familiar sounding "Yoo-hoo," to jolt his brain into painful awareness.

Fuck.

They were not alone. At least they were not going to be alone for long.

"That's Em," he told Missy.

"Wha? What? No. What?"

"Pull it together. That's Em, and she's gonna be on us in less than ten seconds. Damnit."

He turned and took off running, hoping to distract Emelina, Garland Langford, and Evie Jackson as they made their way around the side of the garage. He didn't call their names, just let them head to his back door, hoping that with all their prattling they wouldn't notice Missy, practically nude, standing in the middle of a brand new lacrosse field.

"Ladies," he said as he came upon them from the side.

"Thor," Emelina gasped as if he'd startled her.

"Sorry. Heard y'all, so I came running. What's up?" *Shit, that probably sounded pushy. Like he was in the middle of something. Which he damn well was, so ... fuck it.*

"We were hoping to speak with you about a Garden Club project," Evie Jackson said, sounding so pushy it made his pushy sound hardly pushy at all.

Whatever happened to pleasantries?

Thor had never had a run-in with Evie Jackson. He, like the rest of Henderson, knew her by sight and was terrified of her reputation. With the small stature of an elderly matron, Evie ruled the town as much as Brooks did. When she asked to speak with you, you stopped what you were doing and listened.

At least he sure as hell had to stop what he'd been doing. The thought made him rub his forehead and let out a little chuckle and then a big sigh. He wasn't convinced he was ever gonna have the pleasure of knowing Missy McReady in the biblical sense.

"Ladies." He motioned toward his back porch, deciding to reinstate pleasantries. "Why don't y'all have a seat ,and I'll pour us some sweet tea."

Evie's eyes lit up. "Your mother and father would be proud," she told him.

For having sweet tea on hand, yeah. For thinking it was a good idea to make love to Missy in the middle of the field in broad daylight, not so much. He had to smile at that as he glanced over to see if Missy had managed to get her dress back on. When he didn't see her where he'd left her, his eyes scanned the horizon.

"Well, if it isn't my favorite Henderson Has-Beens," came Missy's voice from behind them. "What are you bothering the handsomest man in Henderson about now?"

"Why, Missy," they all cooed at once. "Come join us. Help us convince Thor that donating a wee, little piece of his hundred-acre woods will be to the benefit of all."

"You ladies, sit. I'll get the tea." Thor left them to it. He knew he was in for it. Knew that whatever Emelina asked him to do, he'd do, because she was the Big Em and he owed her and her whole clan. He also knew he'd do whatever Evie asked of him because if he didn't, she'd deem him an outcast or worse. So as he retrieved the big pitcher of tea he and Marnie had made, he resigned himself to the word "yes" and prayed whatever it was, it wasn't going to be too painful.

"It's a sound idea," Thor told Pinks that afternoon when he caught him at the high school. "Fruit and vegetables. Not me. Them."

"Them who? Evie, Garland, and Em?"

"The Garden Club. I'm just donating a few acres. They'd like to expand from 'old, boring flowers'—those were Em's words—in the hope of attracting younger members. Maybe even families. They're considering organic farming but admitted they are clueless and need to do some research. I'm happy to donate the land to the cause. Frankly, I'm happy to have them take it over. Only ... "

"Only what?'

"Well, they sort of gave me another idea for enticing Missy."

"What's that?"

"A rose garden. And a hothouse to grow long-stemmed roses all year. The Garden Club is looking at it as a fund-raiser. Selfishly, I'm thinking I'd be able to deliver roses to Missy at her home or office regularly."

Pinks gave him a sideways look. "Girls love that shit. I mean, sometimes I totally forget Missy's a woman. Which is why it's a good thing she's got you. You remember her softer side."

"That's the side I'm cultivating."

"You do that. What else ya got?"

"My buddy Picks has a couple ideas for the rest of the land we'd like to run by you."

"Why me?"

"Why not you?"

"Hale and Vance are the investors."

"I don't need investors. I just need some sound business advice. And being as my property butts up against this school for jocks y'all are so hyped up on, I figured we're gonna have to get along. And if Picks's idea is going to negatively affect your school for future Olympians, I need to know now, so I can head in a different direction."

"Thor. That property is yours to do with as you see fit."

"Yes, but a shooting range within walking distance of campus might not sit well with all those rich parents paying the big bucks to send their little jock-itch-laden, snotty-nose brats down here."

"You're installing a shooting range?"

"Not necessarily. We've got a couple ideas, but that's what I need to talk with you about. I'm not interested in stepping on any toes."

"Okay. Let's set up a meeting. Get something on the calendar."

"Thanks."

"And just for the record," Pinks said, jogging away from him backward. "You happen to be *dating* one of those snotty-nosed brats."

CHAPTER TWENTY-ONE

Thor was in his kitchen when Missy arrived back at his place. She hadn't been able to move lacrosse practice out to the plantation that afternoon, but she had gone to the principal and explained the opportunity. Then started calling all of her team's parents.

"The girls were all a-twitter," she said as she entered the kitchen by way of the back door, without so much as a knock. She came in and started talking, moving straight to him like they'd done this before. Like it wasn't the first time she was setting foot in his home.

Putting down a wooden spoon and turning off the flame under the pot he'd been stirring, Thor's well-built physique turned in her direction. He was shower fresh, wearing worn jeans, an Old Dominion T-shirt, and flip-flops, making him look relaxed and mighty yummy. That yummy thing intensified when he looked her up and down and then whispered, "Come here," reaching out to pull her the rest of the way to him. She felt his hand caressing her back while he slid fingers through her hair, cupping the side of her head.

Missy's body, jacked from the energy and excitement of the day, responded by softening. The low timbre of his voice eased all the tumbling thoughts from her mind. The soft caress of his thumb on her cheek combined with the possessive feel of his embrace gave her body permission to relax against his strength. And the seriousness in the way he kissed her lips and then opened her up so he could give her a little more, felt so right and yet was so new.

They'd been fooling around since she'd moved to town but *this*, this was different, and boy did she feel it. Ranger Thor had shown up fully. More confident, or maybe simply more sure about her. Whatever it was, it was noticeable. It was … intense and certainly more than Missy had anticipated as she'd driven over with her thoughts solely on the new field.

Right now, after answering his kiss with a soft sigh, her thoughts had nothing whatsoever to do with lacrosse.

Thor tasted of wine maybe, smooth and delicious. His broad shoulders and firm chest were immovable, rock-solid, and steady. She held on to that, needing the foundation to tether her as she let herself enjoy all of the giddy, tingling sensations swamping her body.

This was good, her brain acknowledged. Thor was *good*. At all of this. His hands, his lips, his mouth, and his body melded with her own, her mind reeling and then going blank as the beauty that was Thor moved over and through her.

"Hey."

It took a little bit for her to resurface into reality. To open her eyes and come back from where she'd gone. To come back from the place he'd taken her with a few serious kisses and a lot of body against body. Were they really still standing in his kitchen? Missy blinked.

"You want wine?"

Thor was standing there, clearly unaffected by the kiss. Or at least, not as affected as she'd been. She rubbed her lips together and tilted her head, looking at Thurgood Watson a little differently.

"Sure," she whispered, feeling confused. *What is happening here?*

"You okay?" he asked, his fingertips chasing a few stray hairs from her face while he looked her over.

"I think you kissed the sense out of me," she said on a light laugh. "I was … gone for a moment."

"Yeah?" he asked on a grin, kissing her lips like he now owned them. Like he was entitled to kiss them any time he wanted.

That was it.

That was the difference, she thought, her head physically shifting, tilting in the other direction. Thurgood Watson wasn't panting at her heels anymore. He was now firmly in the driver's seat.

Hmm.

She let her palms slide up his chest, her hands on their way to locking behind his neck. "Thank you," she said, leaning her body against him. "For the field. For … this."

"This?" His brow quirked.

"Yeah. This." She kissed him again. Because she wanted to. Because it felt darn good, and she felt no resistance to what was happening between them any longer.

Thor squeezed her ass and tugged her against him. Her pelvis and tummy right against the hard length she deemed a masterpiece over a week ago. She felt that masterpiece hardening with desire, felt her own nipples tighten up in response.

She really wasn't interested in dinner.

Apparently Thor was changing his plans as well, because he spoke while kissing her, while backing her up. "I'd like to show you around the place properly, but I'm feeling the urge to start in the bedroom."

"Bedroom's good," she mumbled against his lips.

Then he swung her up "Officer and a Gentleman" style and took her up the stairs.

Missy was not tiny, definitely not a featherweight. She was five-seven with a lot of muscle and some soft places thanks to fewer workouts since college and more cocktails since she'd turned twenty-one. But she felt secure in Thor's arms. And this was a whole lot more comfortable than when he'd tossed her over his shoulder. In fact, she was loving this treatment, and she was eager for what was coming. Snuggling her lips against his neck as Thor climbed the stairs, she heard his breath grow heavier.

"I'm crazy about you." The words came out without thought or pretense. She just said them because it was the truth. Because he was taking charge and she was letting him. That had never happened before. Maybe because Thor was older, and more man, than any of her previous boyfriends. He certainly could squash the lot of them like bugs. Not only physically, but in every other way. Certainly in this way, she thought as they reached a bedroom and he set her on her feet.

"You showered," he said into her hair, turning her around to unzip her dress. "And put on a dress."

"Were you expecting me to show up in sweaty lacrosse attire?"

"Pretty much."

She spun around. "Is that all I am?" She hadn't put a lot of thought into it, but it turned out to be a serious question.

"What do you mean?" he asked, pushing the fabric down past her shoulders.

She shrugged the garment to the floor and stepped out. "An athlete? Is that what you expected? Is that who I am?"

Thor took a step back, looked her up and down, and then smirked. He didn't say a word. He simply reached behind his head and pulled off his shirt.

Holy-moly.

Missy couldn't drag her gaze from his chest and abs. She just stood there in awe, realizing it was the first time she'd seen this hunk of incredibly bulky, sculpted flesh in the light of day. Whatever she'd been asking flew from her head. "Take off your pants," she whispered. Breathless.

Biting his grin, his wicked-blue eyes held her gaze while he flicked off his flip-flops and undid the snap and zipper of his jeans. He took a moment to pull a black packet out of his pocket and toss it toward the bed. Then he pushed his jeans down over massive thighs and shook them from his feet to stand before her in nothing but hot, tight, skimpy drawers.

Hail Mary, Full of Grace.

She didn't know what caused her to do it, but suddenly Missy looked down her own body, finding herself clad in another Nike sports bra and matching underwear set. "Oh. I get it. This is the kind of thing women in the military wear, right?" She asked, still looking at her very sporty, very utilitarian, and completely not-sexy underwear.

"Nope," Thor stated emphatically. "Never seen any woman wear underwear like that."

"What did they wear?"

He shrugged.

"Seriously. You've commented on my underwear before. You don't like it."

"I like *you* in your underwear. So ... you know. I'm good."

"But ..."

"You're an athlete. That's what you wear."

"Yeah, but I also want to be a girl. And maybe even a little … sexy." As soon as she said it, she realized how foreign the word felt.

Thor cupped her bicep, pulling her to him. "You're sexy. Damn sexy. Your underwear sucks," he said as he kissed her. "But I'm getting used to it."

"Uh."

"Besides, as long as it's coming off real soon, I don't care."

"I *am* an athlete," she grumbled. "I thought I was becoming more than that," she moaned in defeat. "But obviously *underneath it all*, I'm just a lacrosse player pretending to be a professional something else."

"Darlin', I have no issue with whatever you are or whatever you want to be. Because right now, all I'm thinking about is that you're mine."

Those sweet words sent a shiver from one piece of utilitarian underwear to the other. "Take it off me," she whispered even as she wrapped her arms around his waist. She kissed him between the muscles of his chest. "Take it off me."

"Gladly."

Unceremoniously pulling her bra over her head—because that's how you put it on and took it off. No clasps to worry with—Thor pushed her backward toward the bed.

"You ready for this?" he asked. It wasn't a serious question. Well, maybe it was, but Thor didn't *look* serious. He looked like he'd known all along this was exactly where the two of them would end up.

She laughed. "You look like you're finally getting what you want."

"Nike undies aside … pretty much, yeah."

"You look smug."

He pushed her back flat on the bed and stepped between her dangling legs. "Feelin' a little smug, truth be told."

"I'm on the pill."

That stopped him and his smug-a-thon. With fists propped on his hips, he thrust it into All-Ranger mode, growling, "And why the hell is that?"

She popped up on her elbows. "Same reason you've got a condom in your pocket."

His head tilted while he stood down, looking over her mostly naked body. "You think we're good without both?"

"I'm good. You good?"

"Oh, I'm good," he assured her. "I'm damn good."

The way he said it, the way his mouth and his body just spouted intent and confidence had her falling back and giggling. She'd never giggled during sex before. At least not the first time with a new partner. It was usually awkward for the most part, unless it was tipsy and then it was … *that*. But right now—with Thor—it was fun and easy, and she was really ready to get on with this.

"Miss?" he asked, dropping to his knees.

"Yeah," she answered, her head sliding to the side. He was so tall she didn't have to lift her head off the bed to see him.

"You know how I feel about you, right?" he asked while soothing her, his large hands gently sliding up and down her legs.

"I do."

"Good. And you know I'm not interested in sharing you with the Pride of Baltimore, or the Cowboy, or anyone else here or abroad."

"Abroad?" she wondered.

He shrugged. "And if things work out for us, and you don't like it in Henderson, I'd move. For you."

Man.

If that didn't bring everything to a slow beat. She sighed, finding his expression so humble and honest.

She reached out and grabbed his hand. "If things work out for us, we'd decide that together. I'm not leaving, Thor. I don't have a date circled on my calendar. I'm no longer trying to protect myself from … this. From you."

"You're certain?"

"Am I all in? Yeah. Am I certain we're gonna make it? Not after the way you looked at my underwear." That got a smile out of him.

"Some things are easier to change than others."

She wasn't sure if he was talking about leaving Henderson or her undergarments.

Thor stood up slowly, moving over her, caging her with his arms. "You know I'm in this for the long haul, right? I've worked damn hard to get you in this bed, and I'm not about to mess any of that up now. So." He stopped talking so he could kiss her. "Are we good to go?" he whispered over her lips. "Ready for a little direct action?"

"Yeah," she told him softly, running her fingers through his thick, rust-colored hair. "We're good to go. Just … you know, lead me to what you like and—"

"I *like* you," he whispered, sliding his hands over her shoulders and down her body, taking care to miss her breasts before taking hold of the sides of her Nike undies. "So relax. Don't think." He looked down at her girl boxers and then grinned back at her. "Just do it."

She laughed that off and looked toward the ceiling as he slid the fabric down her legs, knowing that as groomed as she tried to keep herself down there, she hadn't been to a professional waxer in close to two months. She hadn't given it a thought the other night, but now things seemed different. More important. From the appreciative way Thor was mumbling unintelligible sounds, she didn't think it was bothering him one bit. She heard him take a deep breath before coming back up and kissing her mouth.

She clasped his face above hers and searched his eyes. With a voice steeped in passion, she told him, "I want you. I have for a while."

Thor's pupils dilated, and his nostrils flared. He leaned down and kissed her with a slow and sultry hunger that revved her engines and expanded her desire. One hand possessively gripped the back of her neck, holding her mouth where he wanted it as he feasted. Her body, slick and eager, began to move under him. Her arms wrapped around his back to pull his full weight down upon her. But Thor resisted, moving to kiss her neck, and she allowed it, luxuriating in the sensation. She felt his mouth suck in tender flesh, felt the scrape of his tongue playing there. Wondered if he'd leave a mark. Sort of hoped that he would. She tried to spread her legs, but Thor's thighs blocked her efforts.

"Relax," he breathed, his mouth moving from her neck to her breast. "Be still for a minute. Let me love you."

Callused fingers found purchase with one breast while his lips fell to the other. Thor's mouth and touch created sensations foreign to Missy. Vastly different from any of her previous experiences. There were moments where she felt scorched. Where the pressure between her thighs became too intense, forcing her hips from the bed, eager to feel his weight pressed against her there. "Oh," she whispered, giddy with longing and overcome by physical delights.

Overwhelmed, she gave into Thor's suggestion. To relax and let her mind go. To stop worrying about being a good lover and what she could do to please him. He seemed pleased enough for the moment, and the sensations created with his hands and mouth were something she truly wanted to bask in. So she laid her head back, closed her eyes, put her fingertips in his hair, and stroked through the russet strands slowly while his mouth worked her flesh.

It became a beautiful meditation. Focusing on the play of his fingers, the dampness of his tongue, and the painful pleasure of his teeth as he explored, nipped, then soothed, then sucked. The sensations appeared as graphics behind her lids, flashing in reds, pyramids expanding into the beyond as she fully experienced every measured touch, every tantalizing breath, every slow lick, every appreciative squeeze, and every soft tickle.

Desire flowed through her body, rolling forward with anticipation. She felt ripe … juicy. One foot crossed the other and slid against Thor's calf. She started to hum in low, needy tones as part of the meditation. A meditation on the beauty of the physical. Of the awareness of her own body. Of the pleasure found in his.

She seemed to drift backward, then realized she'd been resettled further up the bed. When the weight of Thor's torso retreated, leaving her breasts exposed to the cool air, spontaneous twinges erupted deep down in her core. She refocused on his hot breath and wet mouth now teasing her belly button, nipping at the soft flesh of her tummy. She felt his thumbs press against her hip bones just as his mouth laid claim to the essence of her desire.

He'd hardly begun, yet it felt too good. She reminded herself to concentrate, to keep meditating on the details. Focus not only on his mouth, but on his palms pressing her thighs open and how his fingers dug into her flesh. Her body became greedy. Wanting more than tenderness. Wanting more than his teasing lips and tongue. She wanted pressure, and force, and … every bit of Thor he could offer.

"I've got you," his voice came low and rough.

Had she spoken? Whimpered? Cried out?

She kept her eyes closed, wanting to remain focused on every sensation. Especially the delicious craving. The eager readiness of her body willing to expand. Wanting him in. Allowing him in. Easing him in.

And in.

And in.

His body settled against hers. One arm wrapping around her back, pressing flesh to flesh. She could feel the coarse texture of his hair by her ear, his scratchy jaw against her cheek. She heard his breath. Felt him turn and place a kiss to her temple.

Then came his oh-so-quiet whisper. "Damn."

Yes, she thought with her eyes tightly shut. *Damn.*

There was a shift. Then, "Miss, look at me."

It took a moment to open her eyes, to focus on Thor's gorgeous face above hers. The planes were pulled taut, his eyes tense as he looked her features over. She heard him draw in air, felt his chest expand with it.

Then … he started to move.

"Eyes on me," he whispered.

Not a simple request to fill. Her eyes wanted to roll back into her head. Her chin wanted to reach toward the ceiling. Her body wanted to bow into him.

"Easy," he soothed. "We're just getting started."

She whimpered at that, unsure how much she could take. Her body ached with need. So primed, just a little stimulus was all it would take. After that, she'd be content to focus on what Thor was giving her.

Her hand snaked between them, intent on satisfaction. But Thor reached for her hand and pushed it over her head.

"Try this," he whispered. His Ranger-ready body shifted forward, crouching over her with his feet shifting up the mattress to the outside of her thighs. "Bend one knee." She followed his instructions, feeling the back of his thigh against the front of hers. His arms pressed straight into the mattress on either side of her chest. "Now lift up on the ball of your foot," he directed, his face over hers, their eyes connected.

The contact was immediate and exquisite, and she jolted at the pleasure of his pelvis scraping over her need. His penetration slid deeper, the stimulation inside and out, perfection. Seeing his arms flexing and taut in her peripheral vision as he moved over her was downright erotic.

"Tonight we do this together," he said. "Body to body. Eye to eye."

Soul to soul, she thought as she got lost in his eyes. Lost in his motion. Lost in his body.

Lost to all but Thor.

CHAPTER TWENTY-TWO

The next morning, a blissful state of euphoria encompassed Missy as she walked into town. Although as she drew closer and closer to her office, she began to hope her eyes were deceiving her. Because there on the sidewalk, leaning up against CC Henderson's window, were both of her folding tables. Adjacent to them were two cardboard boxes filled with her personal office supplies and a file box, all sitting out on Main Street where anyone—*anyone at all*—could cart them off.

What the hell?

Going from euphoria to outraged confusion, Missy stood on the street staring at her office, which had been relocated to the sidewalk. She glanced across the street to E&E Investments and then back to CC Henderson.

Apparently she was now truly out on her own.

Well, crap, she thought. I *have work to get done. Where the hell am I supposed to do it? And beyond that,* her brain shouted, *who the hell puts someone out on the street like this? They couldn't even wait until I got here?*

She was not happy. Not happy at all. Actually, *beside* herself was what she was. And ... she wanted to cry.

Really.

She *really* wanted to cry.

Because she'd been going full steam ahead since she entered this town and had more work on her docket at the moment than she'd ever imagined possible. And now, with lacrosse practice, her own workouts that she really needed to get back into, the digital newsletter (which should have already gone out), recruiting gossip journalists, the Hunks of Henderson calendar (which she just remembered she hadn't mentioned to Thor yet), and the Oxford belles and their debutante party (she totally needed to call Annabelle about that), she apparently didn't have an office in which to perform any of it.

Her first instinct was to turn around in hopes of finding Thor and Big Red ready, willing, and able to make everything all right.

So she did. She turned around.

No Thor.

She could call him. She knew he'd drop everything and come running. She knew it. Especially after last night.

And now she sorta wanted to cry about that. Because she'd held Thor off for so long and, dear Lord, did the man know how to use that hunkalicious body of his to blow her mind.

She swayed slightly, recalling the first orgasm, feeling the memory of it light up her body.

Her phone rang, distracting her back to the present.

Please be him, please be him, please … *shit,* she thought. She'd certainly come a long way from dodging the God of Thunder's gaze. Now she absolutely *depended* on him. *Expected* him to be her hero at every turn.

When she pulled her phone out, she saw that it wasn't *him,* but her other hero.

"Hey, Dad," she sighed.

"How's my girl doing today?" he asked, his ever-cheerful demeanor shining through.

"Oh …" she thought briefly about telling him she'd been evicted from her office but … "I'm good. Just a little tired. Got a lot on my plate."

"Well, that's good, sweetheart. The busier you are, the more efficient you become. What can I help you with?"

That made her smile. His offer to help. Because it was exactly what Thor would do.

She hadn't really connected the dots before. Hadn't really noticed how much Thor and her father were alike. At least in how they related to her.

Always there to help.

Always checking in.

Always making sure she was okay.

More importantly, they both made her feel seen, heard, and appreciated.

Okay, maybe Thor didn't necessarily make her feel heard, as he made no bones about her talking too much. But he sure did make her feel seen, and last night especially, she'd felt *very* appreciated.

"You've already helped by calling," she told her father honestly. "Thank you for that. Is there something specific on your mind?"

"There is. Your mother can't make your lacrosse tournament in Orlando, but I'll be there, and I'm planning to take you and Davis to dinner Saturday night."

With the door to CC Henderson opening, Missy became distracted. "Sure, Dad. That sounds good. I'll look forward to it."

"How are things going with Davis?" he asked.

She looked from the sheepish expression of Charles Douglas's face to all her crap that needed to be moved somewhere. "Things with Davis are good, Dad. Real good. Listen, I've got someone here at the moment. How about I give you a call this evening?"

"Fine, sweetheart. Have a good day, and I'll talk to you later."

She clicked off her phone and shot a scathing look at Charles Douglas.

"I'm sorry," he said, coming out of the door, holding both palms up. "The Pink One worked faster than we imagined, and the furniture delivery came early this morning. He said he tried to contact you but couldn't reach ya. We tried our best to be respectful, especially with your files. And we are happy to help you move all this to your new location."

She stared him down simply because she felt like it. Oh yeah, and because she didn't *have* a new location.

But then she sighed. "I suppose I should have seen this coming. There are five of you. It's just, I had a big day yesterday and …."

"You've been blindsided."

"Feels like that," she mumbled.

"I get it. So, okay, where do we move you to?" he asked.

She thought about setting up shop at Genevra's. The weather was really turning now, and she wouldn't mind working on the porch. But damn. She liked having access to E&E. She liked being on Main Street. She had really liked having the whole building to herself at times, and being inundated with the entirety of the Henderson Has Been at others.

Then she saw Duncan James pull up and park right in front of his brand new office just a few buildings down.

"Come with me. And bring those tables," she ordered. She figured if Charles Douglas put the tables out on the street, he could damn well carry the suckers.

Duncan must have seen her coming. He stood on the sidewalk in his expensive lawyer suit, with his expensive lawyer haircut, and his darling not-so-lawyer smile, holding his elegant lawyer briefcase, and Missy saw the picture she wanted for the Hunks of Henderson calendar take shape in her mind.

"You happen to have office space for rent?" she asked as she got close. Whether he did or didn't, she was determined to move in.

"You need a new place to hang your shingle?" He smiled, clearly amused by her situation.

"Apparently," she grumbled. "Think we can work out a deal? I received a bonus check from Hale for the Spectacular if you need first and last month's rent."

"We'll work something out," he said, holding his hand out to gather her toward the door. "It's not as shiny and new on the inside as CC Henderson, but at least you'll have a roof over your head."

"Thanks," she said, meaning it.

"Happy for the company," he said, holding the door open for Charles Douglas and her folding tables.

CHAPTER TWENTY-THREE

When Marcie walked into Clint's office Tuesday morning, she was greeted with a kiss and a bow tie. She stepped back to assess both.

"I'm not generally a bow-tie girl. But I have to say, Mayor Stevens, you certainly pull this Southern gentleman thing off rather well."

"I'm glad you approve."

"I really do."

He laughed at the surprise in her voice. "I may not be a professional baseball coach, but for the moment, I am still mayor."

Marcie waved off mention of her old flame as she walked by him to sit down. "You've got more brains than the entire Baltimore organization put together. And as for staying mayor ..." She turned and offered him her most dazzling grin. "Right now, you have a real opportunity. You are flying under the radar. Everyone in this town believes Brooks Bennett has already won the election. Nobody is paying any attention to you. Which is why laying the groundwork is going to be so easy. Nobody will see it coming."

"No one will see what coming?"

"All the reasons your *Keep Henderson Henderson* slogan will immediately turn into a rally cry."

"All right. Fill me in. What sort of groundwork are we laying?"

"I've managed to join Henderson Country Club as a corporate member."

"Really? Since when do we take corporate members?"

"Clint? How far out of the loop are you?"

"Apparently a lot farther than I've thought."

"I'm guessing it's a relatively new thing, but it will serve our purposes beautifully. I plan to persuade the most obnoxious business people I know to join."

"I'm not sure I like the sound of that."

"No one is going to like the sound of that. That's the point. I'm stirring the pot," she claimed with a sneaky grin. "Creating compelling reasons for your constituents to want to *Keep Henderson Henderson*. Reducing their place of sanctuary to a tension-filled mess of *newfangled* interlopers will give you that."

Clint chuckled. "Messing with the country club will definitely get results."

"And the baseball team."

"The baseball team?" Clint balked.

"Yes. Because the baseball team is where your opponent got his start. The baseball team is the foundation of who Brooks is to this town. The reason he's so wildly popular. And it will be a problem for him when we expose how he's turning his back on his own team and legacy to build the sports academy. It will look like he's selling out."

"Right. Absolutely. That's our plan."

"That's the *basis* of our plan. Once we put it in play, the focus on Brooks and the team will be magnified. You'll want to capitalize on that."

"Marcie, baseball in Henderson is hallowed ground. How are you planning to mess with the baseball team?"

"I haven't decided. But whatever scandal develops will be connected to Brooks personally and immediately."

"Scandal? These are good kids. Great athletes. Vance has a tight leash on each and every one of them. They haven't even lost a game."

"I'm not above bribing umpires."

Clint flinched.

"That too much for you?" She put on a teasing grin, coming back to play with his bow tie. "Maybe you'd rather not know about my plans for the baseball team."

"Marcie," he breathed. "Please don't mess with the team."

"Are you getting squeamish on me?"

"Maybe Google forgot to mention I was on that team. Ten years before Brooks, but I was on that team. I graduated from that school. Nobody was happier than I when they won the state championship."

"Then you will be as outraged as the rest of this town when the baseball team starts derailing. *You* will rally the troops and lead the charge."

"And be completely guilt-ridden if I'm aware that you're behind it."

"Fine, then. If you don't ask, I won't tell. It's probably better that way."

As she began to step away, Clint pulled her to him and wrapped her up in his arms. "For whatever reason, I find myself captivated by your criminally creative mind. Yet, I can't help but wonder if you are using your powers for good or evil."

Whoa. The way Clint was looking at her, the way he was holding her, made Marcie believe that the Southern gentleman actually had some moves. She licked her lips and did her best to gather her scattered thoughts. "I'm using them to get you reelected."

"Because you're angry with Brooks."

"I've never made that a secret."

"No. But *I* kept your secret when Brooks waltzed in here and not so casually asked about our relationship."

"So, you told Brooks …?"

"That I'm interested in you romantically."

"Oh? Well? Are you?"

"Have I not been clear?"

"You've been … sweet." She smiled. "And charming. And a perfect gentleman."

A sly grin appeared, setting off a sexy twinkle in those deep brown eyes. "Ms. Watts. I don't know how things are done up north, but down here, when it comes to the really important stuff, we Southern boys like to take our time." His deep Southern drawl had her tongue going limp in her mouth.

And then he abruptly set her aside. "Now, how 'bout I take you to lunch? Do my job as residing mayor and see if I can sell you on the idea of extending your stay in our beautiful town."

Marcie patted her hair and tugged at her skirt. "Mr. Mayor. By all means, please lead the way."

CHAPTER TWENTY-FOUR

"Where did you get your furniture?" Missy stood just outside Duncan's office admiring his desk chair. "I'm assuming Annabelle helped you pick all of this out? I need to chat with her anyway. Do you think she'd mind helping me?"

"Annabelle is out of town for a few days. Some sorority check-in up and down the East Coast. But, you're in luck, because Annabelle had nothing to do with setting up this office. That was all Pinks."

"Davis?"

"Yep."

"Does he take care of everything?"

"Ah …" Duncan looked up from his desk. "Yes. I think he literally does take care of everything."

Missy laughed in spite of herself. Then gave a heavy sigh. "All right. I'll call Davis."

"What's going on with you two?" Duncan asked. "I mean, you, Davis, Scarlett, and Thor?"

"He's with Scarlett, I'm with Thor. He and I are good buddies." She sighed. "But I'm still getting used to him … running everything."

"Not what you expected?"

"Not at all what I expected. I mean, he's always been smart. But now it's like he's developed a sixth sense or something. Although, if he truly did have superpowers, he would have already ordered me a desk and chair—a matching ensemble to yours."

Her phone rang, so she pulled it out and spoke while leaning against Duncan's doorjamb. "Just talking about you," she said to Davis. "Wondered with your knack for getting things done so efficiently why I'm stuck with two folding tables and cardboard boxes for an office."

"Open the door, smart ass," Davis said.

"Door? What door?" Missy looked down the hallway and through the picture window. A short moving van was parked outside. "You have got to be kidding."

"Thank me later," Davis said before hanging up.

Missy turned to Duncan. "He really has developed superpowers," she said in utter disbelief. She heard Duncan chuckle behind her as she raced toward the door.

An hour later, she had Duncan on a step stool hanging the framed picture of Team USA Davis had surprised her with. The furniture delivery guys had found it wrapped in brown paper and left by the front door as they headed out. The attached envelope was addressed to Missy. She opened the note, and on handsome stationary with the name Davis Williams engraved at the top was a simple, handwritten message. "Thank you for staying in Henderson. Go Team USA."

It created a bit of a stir when she ran down the sidewalk to Davis's office, crashed into the conference room and flung herself into his arms in front of Hale and Vance.

"I love you," she said.

"Oh, shit," growled Vance.

"Not what you think," stated Davis while he embraced Missy, rubbed her back, and told her she deserved it.

"What now?" Brooks barked as he came in and caught Davis and Missy in a clinch. "Honestly, I do not understand what every female in this town sees in that one," he said to Hale and Vance while throwing a thumb at Davis.

"It's not what you think," Vance and Hale said together.

"No, it's not," Missy scolded, pulling away from Davis and wiping a tear from her eye. "He had my team picture framed for my new office."

"There you have it," Hale told Brooks. "The man knows women."

"Thank God, he sucked with Lolly," Brooks muttered, taking a seat at the table.

"Did you all hear about my lacrosse field?" Missy asked the men.

"No," said Hale.

"Pinks finally relent to being pussy-whipped and give you the earlier practice?" asked Vance.

Davis scoffed. "Don't be ridiculous. My team actually has a chance at the play-offs."

"Well, *my team* has their very own lacrosse field located out on the *Watson plantation*. It is perfect and pristine, and we will be christening the field this afternoon with our first practice at three fifteen. Why don't you all come by and see it for yourselves?"

"Missy?" Vance asked. "No disrespect. But can you teach Piper whatever the hell you know how to do that got Thurgood to build you a damn field?"

"It wasn't anything I did. Army Ranger Watson is way too good to me. I'm just hoping to play a little catch up before he figures that out."

"Before I figure what out?"

Missy turned to find the man of her dreams looking crazy dreamy in athletic shorts and that Go Army sweatshirt she'd finally returned to him.

"Nothing," she said, going over to give him a kiss on the cheek. "Come see my new office when you get a chance."

"Will do," he said for her ears only.

Yep, that's all it took for her to go weak in the knees. Her ability to speak had been erased as well, so she simply waved a hand at the rest of the men and made her exit. She did, however, manage a laugh as Brooks started giving Thor hell for making the rest of them look bad.

She wondered if she could put that in the next newsletter.

The newsletter! She'd put a picture of her team on Thor's lacrosse field in the next newsletter. She'd let everybody know just who Thurgood Watson was, and at the same time show off Henderson's latest sports craze.

She may as well use the newsletter for her own propaganda before she turned it over to someone else. Maybe she and Thor could even throw a party out at his place. Use that as an opportunity to show off her event-planning skills. She'd put the pictures in the newsletter, hoping to drum up business. After all, once the website, the newsletter, and the blog got rolling, she'd have the time to branch out.

Still, she needed to confide in someone about the Oxford debutante party. Make sure she wasn't going to be seen as jumping ship if she upped their game.

Competition is what makes this country great, she told herself as she walked back to her fully furnished office. And she was fine being in competition with herself, making each event she was hired to coordinate better than the last. Suddenly, her future in party planning looked brighter. She checked her watch and decided to call her dad back early, wanting to run the Oxford-Henderson debutante thing by him.

"You aren't planning to kick me out of here any time soon are you?" she asked Duncan as he was coming out the door.

"Nope."

"Do I have conference room privileges?"

"Of course."

"May I run my event-planning business out of here as well as my Team Henderson stuff?"

"Missy. I'm happy to have you sharing office space with me. I'm used to a big law firm filled with people. Isolation isn't something I relish. So, really, trust me when I say you aren't going to show up one day and find all of your furniture out on the street."

She gave him a broad smile. "I guess that's really what I wanted to know. Thanks."

At three thirty that afternoon, Thurgood Watson's backyard was inundated with girls, parents, a few dogs on leashes, some younger brothers and sisters and several nosy neighbors. Word had gotten out about the new lacrosse field and speculation had spread like wildfire.

Speculation about him and Missy.

Thor figured he better set the record straight. Or as straight as he thought appropriate.

He borrowed Missy's coach's whistle and blew it loud and long, using his arms to gather the growing crowd around him as he headed to the center of the field.

"I'm excited y'all are here today. It certainly seems not much has changed since I was a high schooler. Good news still circulates quicker than Grant took Richmond."

Yes, that was the spin he was putting on this. Good news for everyone.

"In an effort to honor my beloved mother who passed away twelve years ago and my dear pop who was taken from me so abruptly last spring, I looked around for a need to fill. And seeing as I've had my eye on this pretty newcomer over here, Coach McReady, I figured a regulation-size women's lacrosse field might be a welcome addition. The high school didn't have the land required to fill the need, but I did. So, thank you for stopping by and cheering the girls on in their first remote practice. I know Missy appreciates the parents' efforts to get the girls out to their new field. So, without further ado, I'd like to christen the Phyllis and Thurgood Watson, Jr. Memorial Field."

There was a smattering of applause as he turned the field over to Missy. He walked off the field surrounded by parents who introduced themselves as they offered up gratitude on the girls' behalf.

When he met Rob Patterson, he smiled in surprise and pulled him aside. "Your daughter Rett is an all-star. She's quick, has great ball-handling skills, and knows where everyone is on the field at all times."

Rett's father beamed. "I used to play," he said. "It never occurred to me to share the sport with Rett. And now she's hooked."

A good-looking brunette with an engaging smile pushed her sunglasses to the top of her head as she entered their conversation. "Hey, Rob. Thurgood, I'm Merv Baldecchi. Ellie's mom." She held out her hand for Thor to shake.

"Your girl has some moves," Thor told her. "Ellie's the best defenseman Missy's got."

"She's really becoming enamored with lacrosse. She and Rett. In fact, they've conspired to watch Missy play. Team USA has a tournament in Orlando, Florida next weekend."

"Is that right?" Thor wondered. *Why the hell didn't I know about this?*

"Saturday and Sunday," Rob said.

"My husband's company owns a travel van, so I've committed to taking some of the girls to see it. We're keeping it a secret from Coach McReady because the girls want to surprise her."

"Missy will love that." Thor chuckled. "Hell, I'd love to be in on that."

"Good, because I was wondering what kind of a bribe I'd have to offer to get you to join us. My husband's going to be in Myrtle Beach playing golf with college buddies, and I'm a little nervous driving that big ol' van. I sure wouldn't mind having a Ranger with us in case there's a flat tire or something."

"Well," Thor smiled at Merv as he took two seconds to think it over. "You got room for Marnie?" Thor pointed to the ten-year-old, stuck to Missy like glue and holding a clipboard. "I've heard all about your daughter, Nancy, her BFF."

"Oh," Merv exclaimed. "Actually, that would tickle my Nancy. We can toss those two in the back to entertain each other, and you and I can share the driving."

"No offense, Merv, but since I'm not the least bit nervous about driving a big ol' van, I'll be doing the driving."

"Works for me. I'm happy to sit in back with the girls and be chauffeured."

"That'll work." Thor smiled.

He very much liked how well it would work.

After practice, Thor was the center of attention. Fifteen teenage girls gushing about their new field and how awesome it was, how totally cool he was to build it, and how they hoped to get their games moved out there too. He couldn't wipe the smile off his face. Especially when their coach came over and kissed him in front of everybody.

Damn, if that didn't feel right.

He shook hands, walked people to their cars, even invited the neighbors to his back porch while Missy went to greet the Pride of Baltimore, who showed up wearing his own coaching gear. He stood a moment, watching the two of them move onto the field together, Pinks talking lacrosse the way Thor couldn't give it to her.

Thor brought out sweet tea for Marnie's grandmother and her best friend, leaving Marnie inside playing video games. His eyes kept straying over to the dynamic duo on the field. Finally, he thought fuck it and took a seat where he could both entertain his guests and watch what was happening with his girl.

He told himself he wasn't jealous. He knew darn well where Pinks's affections lay. He also knew he and Missy had turned a corner. Still, lacrosse was *their* thing. He had a minor moment of regret seeing the two of them out there together. Banging away at each other. Laughing. Arguing. Being real. He shook it off quick, reminding himself that, thank God, they were no longer engaged in a battle of wills over field time. That the tension between those two was lessening because of it. He just …

Wanted her.

After Pinks had complimented him on a job well done and taken his leave, Thor asked Missy, "You coming back?"

"Due to being ousted from my office, I have a lot of work to catch up on. I'd hoped I could make that up to you by inviting you to dinner at my place tomorrow," she said, leaning her face in for a kiss, but keeping her body away from him.

"You worried about getting me sweaty?"

"Just want to smell better before I get too close."

"You work tonight. Tomorrow evening, I'll come to you. Want me to cook?"

"You cooked last night."

"I cooked, but we never ate."

"I know." She gave him a little grin. "I didn't miss it. Did you?"

"Not at all."

"Any chance I can bum some leftovers to take with me?"

He laughed. "Of course. Come on in," he said, starting toward the back door.

"I'll wait here. I'm too sweaty, and it'll give me a chance to return a few texts."

Thor stopped short. "You really *are* going to work tonight."

"Did you think I was blowing you off?"

"Maybe."

"Thor …" she exaggerated. "No. I'm not blowing you off. I *need* to work. I *need* to catch up. So that *tomorrow* I can spend the evening with you and not be distracted."

"Well, I definitely don't want you distracted." He leaned in for another kiss. "Text away. I'll go pack up the leftovers."

"Thank you," she told him as he moved off.

He tried not to feel the disappointment hanging in his gut. They'd shared last night together, he told himself. He couldn't expect to see her every night, could he? At least she was thinking ahead to tomorrow and had him on the calendar. If things went well, he thought as he pulled out the gallon-sized plastic bag filled with spaghetti noodles, he'd talk to her about spending more time together. See where her head was.

Because his was in the damn gutter all the stupid time.

He dished out a healthy serving of meat sauce and put it in his momma's old Tupperware. Then he cut off a large section of the Italian loaf that was now a day old and wrapped that in plastic. He wondered what the hell he was going to do with himself, realizing he had absolutely expected to be spending his evenings with Coach McReady from now on.

And then a thought occurred to him.

Google Team USA. Get the scoop on what was happening in Florida next weekend. Dial up Ellie's mom to firm up plans. He probably needed to make some overnight reservations and see if Merv had talked to Marnie's grandmother about her joining the trip.

So when he rambled outside with a grocery bag full of protein and carbs to help sustain the athlete in his life, he wasn't feeling grouchy or needy at all. He was energized.

"Bye, Dad," he heard her say as she hung up the phone.

"Yoda?" he asked. The woman talked to her father more than anyone he'd ever met.

"Yeah. I had called him earlier for some business advice. He called me back."

"Everything okay with your new office?"

"Duncan has assured me I won't be finding my personal belongings on the sidewalk any time soon."

He chuckled. "Good to hear. Here's your dinner, Coach."

She grinned up at him greedily, smacking her lips. "I do remember how delicious it smelled when I walked into your kitchen last night. I've had a hankering for spaghetti all day."

"I put plenty in there." Thor tucked his hands into his back pockets. "How 'bout you call me before you close your eyes?"

And there it was. His girl went soft. "I'd like that. Thank you."

He leaned in. "Call me," he whispered against her lips. "I'll be waiting."

Thor ate some spaghetti and then called Merv and found out she and her husband were putting the girls up overnight at Universal Studios. Thor said he'd take care of his own room and be happy to pay Marnie's way for whatever Merv had planned. He was happy to be giving Marnie a break from her grandparents and vice versa. Although what he was really looking forward to was seeing his girl do what she did.

When the phone rang at twelve-thirty that night, Thor was sound asleep. He cleared his throat and said hello a couple of times before picking up. The last thing he wanted was for Missy to think she was waking him.

"Oh, good," she said on a sigh of relief. "I was so worried you'd be asleep by now, I almost didn't call."

"I wouldn't have liked that," he told her. "Been waiting to hear from you. How'd it go tonight?"

"Well, after I enjoyed a delicious spaghetti dinner—whose recipe was that by the way? Your mom's or Genevra's?"

"Mom's. I dug it out of her recipe box and tried it. Easy."

"Delicious," she countered. "Anyway, I need to hit the hay, but I did want to hear your voice and thank you again for making my dream and my team's dream come true."

"The field?"

"Yes, the field. All evening, I kept finding myself grinning as I worked. I still can't believe you did that. And what was really fun about today was that the girls got to show off for their parents. So that was a win-win."

"It was. I sure didn't expect onlookers, but in the name of expanding your lacrosse brand, I think it worked out well."

"Now *you* sound like the marketing guy. Oh—that reminds me. Can I throw a party at your place?"

"Sure."

"Sure?" She laughed. "Just like that?"

"I'm gonna tell you no when my chief objective is to get you to spend more time out here?"

"Oh. Well. Okay." He could hear her grin.

"This party for any particular reason?" he asked.

"Well, hopefully the party will be fun for our guests, but yes, I have an ulterior motive."

"Hmm. And that would be?"

"I want to advertise my event-planning skills without actually advertising them."

"Makes perfect sense." He laughed.

"Since I'm presently in charge of the newsletter and entertainment blog, I thought I might use it to my advantage. While I need pictures and stories that make Henderson look like it's the new happening place to be on weekends, I wouldn't mind getting some business out of the deal either. Since, you know, I'm staying in Henderson."

Hearing those powerful words ... Thor almost couldn't speak.

"Thor?"

"Anything you want, Pretty Girl. Anything you want."

CHAPTER TWENTY-FIVE

Walking into Genevra's old cottage the next evening, Thor smelled plenty of evidence of take-out food. He'd had one too many of his favorite pizzas from The Situation not to recognize it by scent. Plus the garlic salad dressing from The Tavern was a dead giveaway. He smiled, thinking Missy was never gonna be Genevra when it came to cooking. But now that he was surviving okay on his own culinary merits, he wasn't stuck on marrying a woman who majored in home economics.

"Anybody home?" he called.

The word "Kitchen," floated back to him. Damn if her voice didn't soothe him better than Piper's Big Apple Pie anyway.

Noticing the flicker of light as he made his way toward that voice, he discovered candlelight permeating the small kitchen. Most of it was cast from a collection of candles clustered in the center of the tiny round table where a linen tablecloth, matching napkins, delicate china, and polished silverware showed off his sweet Melissa's roots.

"Wine?" she asked. Thor's gaze slid from the surprising touch of elegance to the woman standing beside the refrigerator.

"Miss?" The name dropped from his mouth in a breath. A whisper. Because his lungs had collapsed when his heart went into hyperdrive.

One look at her changed … *everything.*

He fell in love so hard it hurt.

Fell in love with the skimpy white dress she wore, so sheer and delicate it looked more like a handkerchief. Fell in love with how the dress showed off Missy's sculpted shoulders along with the rounded cleavage of her magnificent breasts. And he really loved the way it stopped at her upper thigh, just short of being proper. The dress was as provocative as an article of clothing could be. Innocent in its color, yet obscene with what it revealed. There was no way—in hell—black-and-white Nike underwear could hide under there.

His nuts ached, eager for her to walk around the kitchen and show off that dress. Show off just how much of her inner thigh would be exposed. His thoughts drifted to what would be revealed when she bent over to open the oven and retrieve the pizza. His masterpiece was hanging hard and growing long, definitely interested in a front row seat.

Eyes stuck at the hem of her dress where sweet thigh met sweet thigh, a seductive glass of red wine slipped into his line of sight, right at the tantalizing spot he'd been dreaming about since he'd kissed it goodbye Tuesday morning. And damn, if that wasn't crazy erotic. Red wine offered between her thighs.

Yep. His chin was hanging down, and he was salivating. He knew that because he had to bring a hand up to wipe his mouth.

When he finally gathered enough sense to lift his gaze, he was immediately confronted with far more than he was able to handle.

Missy's hair.

Left down and curled, it called to him like warm whiskey on a cold winter's night. It was full and bouncy, accenting her breasts, her neck, and her beautiful face in a way it never had before.

And then—God help him—his gaze fell on her lips, painted only the palest of pink but left shiny and slick. He swallowed hard, remembering what she'd done with those lips.

"I borrowed it from Lolly."

He barely heard her speak with the sound of lust boiling up in his ears. He forced himself to tune in as she approached, holding out that red wine. "I haven't had the chance to get to Raleigh and shop since last time, so I made a deal with Lolly, and she set me up."

"Set you up?" he questioned, taking the wine from her hand. No way was he drawing attention to his dick by moving his package around while she was standing within an arm's reach.

She twirled on her bare feet showing off the dress. The barely there, I-want-to-take-her-right-fucking-now dress.

"Lolly lent this to me."

"Not gonna stay on long," he said before drinking a healthy gulp.

She lifted a brow. "You've got to be hungry."

"Oh, I'm hungry," he said, setting the glass on the nearest surface he could reach. Right before he reached for her.

He pulled her to him, his hands feeling everything through the tissue-thin material. He hadn't planned to undress her, but the hint of what she had on underneath the veil was too compelling to resist. So he gave in to temptation and stripped the dress up over her head, going easy at the last moment when he realized she held a glass of wine of her own.

"Sorry," he said, not meaning it at all. And then … "God help me."

Because there she stood in wedding night *come-and-get-me* lingerie. It was lacy, like a bridal gown, yet so damn dirty.

Fuck him, he had to take a step back.

With hand at his mouth, he took in the swell of soft, plump skin overflowing that maddening itty-bitty bra. His fingers itched to feel the texture of that lace. His mouth yearned to feast on those curves. His teeth ached to sink into soft and leave their mark.

His gaze drifted along her creamy torso. That span of flesh was so enticing because it encompassed the sculpted indentation of her waist—the first part of her body he'd had the pleasure to touch. The first part he'd fallen in love with. Then his eyes focused on that half-innie, half-outie belly button he'd gotten familiar with recently, not to mention the soft—God, the part he really loved to press up against—flesh between her belly button and her fucking—yes, *fucking*—lace panties.

Jesus, she was trying to kill him.

"By your reaction, I'm guessing this is more of what you had in mind."

"What?" he croaked, startled from his reverie.

"You aren't wild about my inner lacrosse player and her choice of underwear."

His tongue slid around his mouth, trying to work up some moisture at the same time he was working on getting his dick and balls to shut the fuck up so he could concentrate on forming words that were appropriate for mixed company.

"Fuck it."

Yeah, those were *not* the words.

Still, he heard them come out of his mouth again.

"Fuck it."

And then it just got worse as the strung-out, horny Neanderthal in him continued with, "I mean. Fuck. As in. I wanna. Right here," he said, moving in and putting both hands on that soft, mind-bending tuck of her waist.

He backed her up, took Missy's wine out of her hand, and felt no regret replacing the glass with his dick. Yep, he did it. He put her hand right where he wanted it. On him. Held her palm against his jeans on top of his overgrown masterpiece and worked it up and down guiding her while his other arm wrapped around her waist.

She'd put on a dress, curled her hair, and finally gave him sexy lingerie. Missy knew what she was in for, his brain decided. She also knew how to say no, so he was going to do his thing until that word came out of those hot, tempting lips. Not that he was taking any chances, he thought as he drowned out whatever the hell her busy mouth was fixin' to say.

"Busy hands," he said, still helping her work the one over his dick. He pulled her other hand around to his ass. "Quiet mouth," he whispered before doing his job and kissing the two of them senseless.

He was going to kiss every inch of her, he promised himself. He wasn't going to take the lingerie off her sexy body until the last possible minute, too afraid he wasn't ever going to get her to put it on again. He was determined to make this fantasy last.

At least as long as he could.

Lord, it felt damn good being this horny.

"Your hair like this," he whispered into their kiss. His free hand bunching up the curls, his nose plunging into the center, needing to get a trail on her scent from top to bottom. He tightened his fist in those fragrant, blond tresses and kissed her temple. "Gorgeous."

He felt her hand move up to unbuckle his belt. Fine, he'd gladly help that along. They fumbled together, but as soon as the zipper went down, he stuffed her hand inside his shorts and moaned into her mouth.

"Sweet Jesus, that feels so good."

With both hands in her hair, he held her steady, kissing her, relishing the feel of her hand gripping his cock. He really, really had to choke himself back from asking her to marry him. Because this moment—right now—exceeded all of his expectations, and the only thing he was interested in was making it last.

He kept up the kissing while she worked him over, grabbing her flesh when he wanted, tickling her skin when it suited, anything to keep what was happening happening. Finally, the pleasure caught up to him, and he needed to shift things up or he was gonna erupt in her hand.

His woman was that good at being bad.

He plopped her cute lace-clad ass on the only bit of cleared countertop he could find, grabbed the closest glass of wine, fed himself, and then fed her. He took another sip before reengaging her mouth. Sucking on her bottom lip before invading the lush inner flesh with his tongue.

Her hands were under his shirt, squeezing his nipples and directing shockwaves to his balls. "Take it off me," he demanded, pulling the wine glass to his mouth again. He watched and drank as Missy's fingers unbuttoned his shirt from the bottom up. She was engrossed in her mission, quiet and focused.

That was a first.

"Miss?"

Her sea-colored eyes glanced up at him, all heated and eager. It made him grin. "Cat got your tongue?"

She shook her head. "You told me not to talk," she said, going back to watch her hands ease his shirt from his shoulders.

"You usually have trouble following a direct order," he teased. "Especially when it comes to talking."

"Mmm, and yet you've always found an effective way of shutting me up." With her hands in his hair, she pulled his face down for a kiss. Then she took the wine from his hand and finished it off.

Thor peered out the window over the sink. "It's almost dark. You got a problem taking this out to the porch?"

In answer, Missy wrapped her legs around his waist. Thor grunted as he lifted her, moving the two of them onto the enormous screened-in porch. The wicker couch would give them plenty of room, but Thor wanted something different. So he sat in the roomy armchair, sitting forward so her legs could stay wrapped around his back. "Warm enough?"

"Grab the quilt," she suggested.

He reached over and took it from the ottoman, wrapping it around Missy's back. She grabbed the ends in both hands and placed her fists on top of his shoulders. Thor's arms slid inside the tent she'd created. He lifted his hips and pushed at his jeans, releasing the masterpiece. Using his arms, he situated her body right where he wanted it.

"That's it, baby," he said, looking between them, pushing that sweet bit of lace aside, and guiding himself into her. "Damn, that's it," he said tightly as her body absorbed him. He half hummed, half grunted, relishing the exquisite feel of being inside her.

His hands settled on those lacy cups, his thumbs running back and forth across the fabric as he tried to concentrate on the smell of her skin, the way her body looked in this lingerie, and the heavenly feel of her breasts as he freed them so he could lean in to kiss them, lick them, whatever-the-hell-he-wanted them.

His mind floated back to the time he'd watched her undress, but hadn't the right to touch. Emotion swamped him, so grateful he could finally have her like this. He looked up into her face and smiled, enjoying the way she was gently rocking against his cock.

"Kiss me," he said, loving that she actually leaned down and did it. Loving that he had her mouth on his, his hands on her fabulous tits, his cock where it constantly wanted to be.

Together they rocked real easy. Slow and sweet. Taking the time to savor the feel of body connected to body now that their immediate needs had been granted sweet relief. It was hot, and it was good, and

...

Suddenly, he pulled her in tighter, holding her firmer while he pumped and then pumped again, starting a new rhythm.

"A-huh," he said. Liking it. Liking where this was going. Loving her body on his. The scent of lavender spiking as she started to sweat, the smell of her sex mingling with the rest of it. He breathed in deep, committing it all to memory. Stuck his nose into her neck, licked at the soft spot there, increased the drive of his hips, and dropped his hands to her backside.

"Damn, this is good," he said into the quiet night. Into the squeaking of the chair. Into the soft sounds coming from his sweet Melissa. "Baby?"

"Hmm," she said, like she was lost in some distant world.

"You good?"

"Mmmm," she hummed above him. Her body answering by kicking their pace up a notch.

"Mmm-right," he said, starting to focus as his balls got tight. He shifted by spreading his legs and sliding down just a little, until Missy gasped.

"Ah-ha," he thought out loud, tucking his hand inside the lace on her hip, and scooting it around to the front where her undies had been tugged to the side. He'd planned to use his fingers to make sure she came, but he decided to give her a reason to *want* to wear little, bitty lace undies. He positioned the fabric where she could feel the roughness on her most sensitive nerve endings and then pulled it taut. He rested a finger right over the spot, letting their movement do the work. When her pelvis started a bigger grind and she was holding the end motion for a split second longer, he knew it was working.

"You feel good?"

"Mmm."

"'Cause you're getting me off so good, right now. And I want you with me." He jacked his hips higher and harder. Began a faster pace as he watched her face for clues, wanting so much to do it for her like she was doing it for him.

"That's it, Pretty Girl," he whispered. "We're doing our thing. You and me. And it is so ... fucking ... hot."

Missy came long, hard, and quiet, grinding down and keeping it all contained. Watching that happen, feeling that vortex of energy, Thor did the exact opposite. He grunted and groaned and rocked the shit out of the old wicker chair, as he rolled with an orgasm, or two or three, like he wasn't gonna get the chance to ever do it again.

"Okay. So, I know this could be construed as hitting you when you're down, but I need you to pose for a photo in your Army Ranger fatigues. Well, just the bottom half of your uniform will do."

"For what?" Thor asked with his mouth full of pizza.

The two of them sat in their underwear at the fancy table Missy had set earlier. The candles burned down significantly.

"The 'Hunks of Henderson' calendar."

The look Thor threw at Missy let her know she had an uphill battle.

"You've got to do it," she insisted.

"I do not have to do it. And what the hell is it, anyway?"

"A marketing ploy. And frankly, it's all your fault."

"My fault?"

"Yeah," she laughed. "When I was a little bit tipsy at the club and you came strutting in with your hot-looking self all cleaned-up handsome and sporting a blue blazer."

"And?"

"And … well, you know how my mind works. I start thinking about ways to use that to Henderson's advantage. Thus the calendar idea. I texted Scarlett right away. She's going to get Cal Johnson to be on the cover, showing off his album."

"You girls are working overtime, you know that?" he told her, pointing his fork in her direction. "Not every man you meet has to be on Team Henderson."

"Which begs the question, why are you *not* on Team Henderson?"

"We've been over this."

"We've been over this a while ago. Now, you and I are … together."

Thor smirked. "Still hard for you to say?"

"No," she defended.

"That's all right, Pretty Girl. As long as you know it and I know it, I don't really care who else knows it."

"Well, everyone important knows it."

"Then I'm satisfied."

"Anyway, since we are *together*, it would help me out if you'd agree to pose for the calendar."

"All right, Pretty Girl. For you, just about anything."

She smiled. "Are you saying you wouldn't do it for Henderson?"

"I'm saying I'm no model, and my buddies will tear me up one side and down the other if they ever see this. So, I'm doing it for you. I want to be clear on that."

"Thank you," she said shyly.

He reached over and stroked her cheek. "Any time."

Missy went back to eating. "We'll want the calendar to show off the surrounding farmland. Maybe your buddy Thatcher could be talked into representing."

"He'd probably rather be photographed standing on your lacrosse field. That's his business. That's what he does."

"Well, do you know any true farmers in the area who fit the bill?"

"The bill?"

"This is a beefcake calendar, so you know, handsome, muscular, sexy."

A laugh burst from Thor. "You better have one hell of a photographer on hand, because there is not an awful lot of sexy rolling around Henderson."

Missy looked down at her lace bra and undies and then over to his bare chest. "I beg to differ. I'd say right now there's definitely a whole lot of sexy happening in Henderson."

"True that," he said around another mouthful.

"That's what we should try to capture with our party theme."

"Our party has a theme?"

"It will. And since sex sells—cue the Hunks of Henderson idea—maybe we should think up a sexy theme for our party out at the plantation." She stopped herself. "Although I really kinda like the title of that. *Party at the Plantation*."

"Old South costume ball," Thor suggested.

"I would love to put on a hoop skirt."

"And I'd love to get you out of it."

They shared a smile.

"Be easier to do a *Green Acres* theme," Thor said. "Remember that old sitcom where the wealthy couple from New York moved to a farm? Sort of a reverse of the Beverly Hillbillies? We could invite everyone to come as *their* version of a farmer. Farming is not traditionally sexy, but farmers' daughters sure are."

"I like it. I'm just wondering how overalls can be sexy."

"Hell, did you see those girls at the Spectacular? The ones trying to catch Cal Johnson's eye? They all had on some kind of baseball attire, but man did they know how to sex up a jersey and wear a ball cap. Trust me. The women of Henderson are perfectly capable of thinking up sexy farmer attire."

Missy threw her fork down on her plate and took a swing at him.

"Ouch," Thor said, grabbing his bicep. "What'd I do?"

"You're doing my job better than I can. This is a *great* idea for a party."

"It is?"

"Hay bales, checkered table cloths, picnic baskets, rope swings, toy tractors—"

"Real tractors," Thor insisted.

"Okay, real tractors. Oooh. Let's do a hayride. We'll pipe in country and bluegrass music, pile ice and drinks in huge galvanized tubs, and cook up everything on a big barbecue."

"Definitely sounds like a party. But, ah, Miss? You aren't planning to do all the cooking for this shindig, are you?"

She gave him a deadpan stare.

He chuckled. "I'm only thinking I don't want my date stuck in the kitchen all night."

"No," she spat. "Of course, I'm not going to be cooking. We'll have it catered. That's next on my jam-packed agenda. Locate caterers and other party resources." She sighed.

"What?"

"I've got a lot of good ideas but not a lot of resources to help me implement them. I may need an assistant."

"Have you forgotten about me and Big Red?"

"No." She grinned, leaning over for a kiss. "But where you and Big Red might be really good at picking up and hauling a huge grill and other party supplies to your place, I doubt your truck is going to give you much help in the way of cooking for a large crowd."

"Harry."

"What?"

"Talk to Harry. He's in the service business and knows way more than he should about everybody and everything."

"Harry," she breathed. "I like Harry."

"Everybody likes Harry."

"Harry would actually be a great source for my gossip column."

"Your what?"

"Henderson's digital newsletter and blog. I'm planning to recruit locals who are in the know and willing to write about what they know so I can hand off the job. I'll set up an appointment with Harry. Tomorrow. Plus"—she looked over at Thor sheepishly—"I want him in the 'Hunks of Henderson' calendar too."

CHAPTER TWENTY-SIX

"You said you'd do what?" Annabelle Devine shrieked at Missy.

Neither woman noticed Duncan quietly get up and slink out of his own conference room.

"Well, I've wanted to talk to you about it for a while now, but you've been out of town for weeks—"

"Ten days. I've been out of town for ten days, and I have a cell phone. You could have reached me at any time."

"I'm sorry. I've had so much going on that this item kept moving down my list of priorities. But now that my second meeting with these Oxford moms is impending, I knew I needed to talk to you."

"I can't believe you're doing this," Annabelle said, clearly distraught.

"Okay," Missy said, quieting her voice and slowing herself down. "Nothing is written in stone. Let's you and I have a calm conversation and together come up with a solution."

Missy wasn't giving up the party in Oxford. No way. But she needed Annabelle on her side, especially after that outburst. The always impeccable and well-mannered redhead had essentially just flipped out. That did not bode well for Missy's business expansion.

"Why don't you give me a little background on the subject," Missy went on. "I understand you've been deemed the Keeper of the Debutantes here in Henderson. But you may be curious to know that *even the Oxford moms* call you that. In fact, that's why I'm coming to you," she soothed. "Apparently, you're the reason they've approached me in the first place."

"Me?"

"Yes. You did a little attitude coaching over at their high school? Met with the cheerleaders who were letting their reputations run amok?"

"Oh. Yes." Missy saw realization dawn in Annabelle's eyes.

"Well, apparently you've made an impression. They are all following you on Twitter. So when you tweeted about my event-planning skills for the Spectacular, Oxford took notice. Frankly," Missy said, taking the opportunity to throw it back at Annabelle, "this is all your fault."

"They are following me on Twitter?" Annabelle said a little dreamily.

Hmm. There was no mistaking things had just taken a turn for the better.

"Apparently," Missy acknowledged. "It sounds to me like you've really made a name for yourself over there. You know, those Oxford debutantes need gowns just like they do over here."

"They do, don't they?" Annabelle said, sitting up straighter.

"I mean," Missy went on, "it's not like you and Lolly aren't going to sell your beautiful House of DuVal designs to the women of Oxford. So, really, it shouldn't be any different with my business."

Annabelle sighed. "I see your point. And you're right. It's just that I've worked so hard on our debutantes, and I really like this town being number one in *something*. I would hate to see Oxford take over what has been Henderson's defining status."

"Other than baseball."

"Right," Annabelle conceded. "Other than baseball."

"I understand. But competition makes this country great. And it's what's going to make me a great event planner. Because I'm going to want each party I have my name on to be better than the last. Just as you and Lolly are going to want next year's line to surpass this year's. So, help me. And let's give Oxford, and all the money they are willing to spend on Henderson's goods and services, a chance to make *us* great."

"Well, when you put it like that. Okay. But I want to be in on that meeting. I want to meet the moms and get the House of DuVal a chance to show off our gowns before they all head to Raleigh to shop."

"See," Missy said. "Win-win. Duncan," she called. "It's safe to come back in the water now."

Duncan stuck his head in the door. "Thank God. I was worried my officemate and my fiancée were going to be at odds. If that were the case, I'd be the one moving out."

The girls chuckled.

"No," Annabelle assured him. "I just needed a push to get out of my own stubborn way to see how Missy is bringing progress not only to Henderson but to my business as well."

"Change is never easy," Duncan cajoled, before leaving them alone again.

Annabelle sighed after him. "He's really gorgeous isn't he?"

Missy had to laugh. "He is. And it's fun for me to see how madly in love with him you are."

"Oh, I am. I'm wild for the prim and proper lawyer from Richmond."

"How are wedding plans going?"

Annabelle's eyes shot wide. "You want to help me? With my wedding?"

"As a friend? Or are you hiring me? I'm good either way. I just don't want to step on any more of your toes."

"As much as I look forward to us becoming true friends, I would like to formally hire you to work beside me."

"Annabelle, I'd be honored. And, I know I'll learn a lot from you in the process. So why don't we collaborate on your wedding as business associates. We'll trade expertise instead of money."

"Sounds ideal," Annabelle said. "I, you know, want control of the event. After all, I'm me and this is my wedding. But, because I'm me …"

"Everyone is expecting perfection."

Annabelle nodded as tears sprung to her eyes.

Missy felt emotion roll forth in her own chest. It was darn hard meeting everyone's expectations all the time. She reached over and grabbed Annabelle's hand. "Trust me. I understand … perfectly."

Later that afternoon, Missy greeted Sandra Wilcox and her sidekicks as she showed them back to Duncan's conference room. "So good to see you ladies again. This is my business associate, Annabelle Devine. I think you may know her as the Keeper of the Debutantes."

No one said a word.

Not a word. There was dead silence.

Poor Annabelle stood there, looking radiant with her white spring suit, and her beautiful red curls, in her kick-ass lime green stilettos, and simply blinked rapidly, as it was obvious the Oxford belles were not at all enthused by her presence.

"Is there a problem?" Missy ventured.

"We've hired you to beat Henderson at the party game," Sandra said out of the side of her mouth, staring at Annabelle and somehow smiling all the while. "A game created by Miss Devine."

"Ah," Missy understood. "If y'all would like to help yourself to the Big Pie Plate Apple Pie and some tea before taking a seat, I think I can quiet everyone's concerns."

Clearly they did not share Missy's certainty. The women didn't take their eyes off Annabelle as they moved to help themselves to Piper's pie. But when they sat and took a bite, tensions eased.

"Is this your recipe?" Jan asked Missy.

"No. No. The owner of *that* recipe will be opening a shop in town next fall. I believe she will be *giving* that recipe away during the Grand Opening." Coming up with the idea out of the blue, Missy pushed her legal pad and pen toward the women. "If you'd like to be included on the very exclusive invitation list, write down your contact information. I'll personally make sure you receive invitations."

They signed up and added three of their friends.

"Okay." Missy looked at Annabelle who had remained standing. She'd heard the rumors. The Keeper of the Debutantes could handle any social situation at any time, no matter how awkward. Well, this was clearly awkward, so she was going to see if the rumors held up. "Annabelle, why don't you explain to Sandra, Jan, and Sarah why it's to their benefit that I've invited you to this meeting."

Annabelle's eyes flashed panic for a moment—just a brief flutter of a moment—before Missy watched the very savvy, highly professional Queen of Etiquette do her thing.

"Ladies," Annabelle started, ingratiating herself with a brilliant smile. "When I caught wind that you'd hired our Missy for your debutante party, I knew you were the ones I needed to meet. Obviously, the three of you are Oxford's movers and shakers. The women who are setting the trends over in our sister town. Therefore, *you* are the ones I want attending the very first showing of the House of DuVal Debutante collection.

"My colleague Lolly DuVal and I would like you and your daughters to be not only our first guests from Oxford to see the line, but our first guests *period*. What we are inviting you to is our *premiere* viewing. No one has seen these gowns. And you know how this works. Once a gown is chosen, that is *your* gown. We do not sell that particular gown to anyone else attending the Debutante Ball in Raleigh this season. This is an exclusive offer to the three of you and your daughters from the House of DuVal."

"Why?" Sandra asked.

"I want trendsetters wearing our gowns. And let me say right here, you are under no obligation to purchase. However, if you and your daughters are looking for next-generation designs, things you will not see in those tired, matronly Raleigh shops, then I suggest you give my partner and me a shot."

"Well," Sandra breathed. "I don't know."

"I do," Jan piped in. "I'm all about full service and one-of-a-kinds. Count me in, Annabelle. And if I like what I see, well, I don't want to brag, but I am the president of the Daughters of the American Revolution, Raleigh Chapter. And I have the ear of the most prominent households in Oxford."

"I appreciate the opportunity to dazzle you," Annabelle said. "Shall I leave now, or would you mind me sitting in on the rest of the meeting?"

"By all means, sit," Sarah said, licking her fingers. "My goodness, if Henderson can make pies like this, I'm looking forward to seeing the gowns. Now, Missy, why don't you *dazzle* us with your ideas."

Taking over the floor, that's exactly what Missy did.

CHAPTER TWENTY-SEVEN

Thursday evening, wild and raucous laughter filtered out of the Mixed Grill as Davis entered the club. He'd been the one to answer Harry's call since both Hale and Vance were busy tending to their very pregnant wives.

With Genevra now a few days past her due date, the entire Evans household was on pins and needles. Genevra was all smiles and said she was feeling fine, but Hale was noticeably sweating bullets as the countdown hit zero and kept on going.

Pinks chuckled to himself. He was definitely not ready to exchange places with either Hale or Vance. As much as he loved Genevra and Piper, he too felt the pressure mounting. And if Hale was biting bullets, Pinks didn't want to think about how Vance was going to handle Piper's due date if that came and went as well.

"Harry," he said, coming to the bar but getting distracted by the unusually large crowd. "It is Thursday, right?"

"Yep," Harry said. "It's Thursday, and we are packed."

"What's doing?"

"Lots of potential new members."

"New members?" Pinks took another look around. He noticed the Dallas contingent mingling about, drinks in hand. Since CC Dallas and CC Henderson held corporate memberships to HCC, all five of them were welcome to use the club. He supposed they liked eating here while they got their new housing situation figured out. He also noticed that the leader of the gang, Charles Douglas, was engaged in conversation with Viper. "I see Ms. Watts is still in town. Who's she here with?"

"I understand she's a new member. A corporate member."

"*She's* a corporate member?"

"Yes. And she's brought in a lot of … well, boisterous guests who I have overheard are considering corporate membership as well."

Pinks squinted his eyes as he looked back at Harry. "What corporations?"

"I have no idea. But I called Hale because he was the one to suggest corporate memberships to the board. And I can tell you right now, there has been a lot of grumbling tonight among the active members. They want to be able to walk in and sit at their usual table. That has not been the case over the last week. Hale's gonna want to get on top of this fast."

"Hale is about to become a father for the first time in thirty years. What can you and I do to keep him out of this?"

Harry shrugged. "Find out what's going on. You infiltrate the crowd, and I'll tend bar. Pick up what we can, and then we'll piece it together at the end of the night."

"Deal," Pinks said, taking a beer from Harry and moving into the crowd.

Over the course of the next ninety minutes, Pinks got a good sense of what was happening. Marcie Watts was holding court, selling Henderson Country Club to people who had no business being members. As far as he could tell, no one lived in or was doing any business in Henderson. Finally, he pulled Viper aside and asked her point blank what she was trying to do.

"Market Henderson," she told him, like this was obvious.

"Why?" Pinks asked.

"Why?" Marcie laughed. "Isn't that what you want? Isn't that what Team Henderson wants? People to actually *come* to Henderson?"

"No. Not if they aren't planning to live here, work here, or shop here. No. Henderson Country Club is a *club*. A members-*only* club. It's not a place for outsiders to gather."

"You and I are outsiders," she countered.

"I live here. This is my home," he defended. "What sort of roots do you plan to put down?"

"Well, since you've asked, I'm looking for something to rent. I like your mayor and have decided to help him with his campaign. So, I imagine I'll be coming and going through September—at least until the campaign is successfully complete."

"Successful as in … how exactly?"

"Mayor Stevens being elected for another term, of course."

"Marcie, you know that's not going to happen."

"I think it will, *Pinks*." She gave his nickname a good bit of scorn.

Pinks's grin came slow and was full of satisfaction. "Careful, *Viper*, your true colors are starting to show."

Marcie gave him a magnificently wicked grin in return. "Trust me. When my true colors make an appearance, you'll know it." She winked before turning away, joining a tall, loud, brute of a man who barely passed the dress code.

"What's doing, Pinks?" Brass asked.

The handsome, Hispanic financier from CC Henderson looked like he was feeling no pain. "Carraway said this place was gonna feel dead after coming from our country club in Dallas. But this is quite a lively crowd for a Thursday night."

"Yeah. I think we are under siege."

Brass's eyes widened. "Really? How?"

See that woman over there?" Pinks pointed out a laughing Marcie Watts. "That's Viper, and I'm fairly confident she's set out to undermine everything E&E and CC Dallas are planning for Henderson. I need you to point her out to the rest of your gang and make sure no one talks to her about anything that you are working on. Better yet, just avoid her completely. I don't trust her. I'm certain she's up to no good."

"All right. Well, you're the Pink One, so I'll take the warning to heart and make sure the others do as well."

"I appreciate it. How about starting over there with Poppy. Looks like Viper is about to get her fangs into her."

"I'm on it."

Pinks smiled. "Right answer," he mumbled as Brass headed toward the women.

Pinks made it home in time for the eleven o'clock Skype session with Red. Although this particular session was proving a bit of a fiasco. Pinks could see Scarlett *and* Natalie looking at him through his computer screen, while from Natalie's lap he could also see Cal's mug being broadcasted through her laptop.

"Did you not tell *Missy* that Natalie was being inundated with marriage proposals down here?" Red scolded.

"Wait. What?" Pinks heard Cal ask.

Pinks watched Natalie turn her laptop so that Cal's head faced her and heard her soothing him with words like, "You know Scarlett … exaggerating … nothing to worry about."

While that went on, Pinks tried to explain to Red, "Missy is crazy busy. She wanted me to review the newsletter, but I didn't have time. She ended up reading it to me over the phone, but I was only listening with one ear because Brooks was shouting in the other. So I approved it without thinking too much about Natalie."

"Big mistake," Red said, pushing Natalie out of the way and leaning into the screen. "We are not getting any sleep." Then she started to laugh. "You should have see—" Red stopped herself, turned toward Nat, and slammed the laptop she held closed.

"Why did you do that?" Natalie cried. "Cal wants to be a part of this."

"I know. But I want to tell Pinks what happened last night, and there is no way you want Cal finding out. So … just … stall his Skype revival while I tell Pinks."

Natalie's head shoved into view. "You can't tell Cal about this," she warned. "He's a little on the jealous side, so I'm trying to play all this down."

"Understood," Pinks said. When Red's face came back front and center, he asked, "So what happened?"

"We had just gone to bed when there was a big sound outside. Like a bass guitar gone haywire. Turns out it was one of the well-known bands on campus. All five of the guys completely set up for a show right outside our front door. I don't know how they did it," she said. "But when we opened the door, there was the lead singer with an armful of roses, I mean *really* beautiful red roses, a bottle of champagne, and a song he had written just for Nat."

Natalie's face leaned in. "It was awesome. Don't tell Cal," she ordered fiercely before backing away and giving the stage back to Red.

Scarlett's eyebrows lifted up and down a couple of times over a sexy smirk. "It *was* awesome," she confirmed. "This guy is hot. And he was smooth. He took Natalie by the hand and led her to a couple of beach chairs they had set up—there was one for me, so I got to go too—and he told her that he had admired her for several years now after being in her English class and a couple others back when they were freshman. He said he didn't care that Nate the Great was her father, but since the entire male population of Ole Miss was vying for her hand, he didn't see any reason he shouldn't declare his long-silent infatuation. Then he took the lead and sang a song that was *beautiful*. I mean it, you and I need to sign him after we sign Cal."

"Red, we aren't a record label."

"Not yet. But things are looking like that might be the direction to go. This kid is from Mississippi, and I made Natalie be nice to him so we could keep him on the hook until I can figure something out."

"Red," Pinks sighed with a laugh. "What are you doing?"

"I don't know," she cried, laughing out loud. "I'm sort of going crazy with this record business thing. But it's not my fault. These amazing artists just keep falling into my lap."

"You mean Natalie's lap."

"Well, you don't want me to be the one keeping them on the hook, do you?"

"No, but I'm sure Cal doesn't want Natalie hanging out there as bait for *your* record label."

"I know. I know. I'll get a grip on myself. I promise. It's just now that I'm learning the basics, I figure why stop with Cal if I have talent coming at me?"

"I can't blame you. Just use your business savvy instead of your roommate to keep the talent hooked."

"Pot calling the kettle black?" she accused.

"How so?"

"Cal's back online by the way, so mum's the word about the new talent. Anyway, the newsletter. *Henderson's* newsletter. You've allowed

Missy to use the four of us as the hook to drum up interest in 'What's Happening in Henderson.'"

"Yeah. But I don't see how that's affecting life down there at Ole Miss."

Red swung back, rolling her eyes, before shifting forward and coming way too close to the screen. "Are you not on any form of social media? Someone from Henderson reads the newsletter and then they tweet about it or blog about it or Instagram the photos, all with #CalJohnson, #OleMiss, # OleMissHottyToddy, and on and on. It gets around, I'm telling you. Anybody who didn't know that Natalie was carrying the genes of one All Star while dating another sure knows it now."

Pinks chuckled underneath his hand.

"What?" she demanded.

"I'm sorry you girls are inundated with unwanted attention, but come on, Red. This news couldn't be better for Henderson."

"Somehow, I doubt Henderson is being overrun with zealot baseball fans since Natalie is here and Cal is in Florida. This is not helping or hurting Henderson at all."

"Sure it is. People will check out the next newsletter for more information about Natalie."

"*And us,*" she stressed. "I could have lived a long time without my sorority sisters knowing you slept with my sister."

"What?" Pinks shouted. "How the hell did *that* get out?"

"Oh," Scarlett chided, "*now* you have a problem with the newsletter? The newsletter you approved with one ear?"

"That was not written in the damn newsletter."

"Oh, but it was implied. Anyone reading between the lines got it. And do I have to remind you that Tansy went to school here? And my mother? Trust me, #OleMiss&Henderson is trending."

"I need to see a copy of this newsletter."

"You need to have a chat with Missy. I don't want to be the bad guy on this because I like her texting me in a drunken stupor with really good ideas. I don't want to shut down that channel."

"Okay. I'll speak to Missy, but the damage has been done, so … whatever."

"Says the man sitting in Henderson."

There was a loud banging on the door just then. Scarlett's head whipped around toward the sound. "Here. You and Cal chat while we find out what that's about." Scarlett situated Natalie's laptop in front of hers so that Pinks could see Cal. He could also see what was happening behind Cal with Natalie and Scarlett at the front door.

"Mighty Pinks," Cal said in greeting.

"Hey, Cal. You doing okay?" Pinks asked as he tried not to make it too obvious that he was watching the action behind Cal.

"Never been better. Only a few days to go until you, the Cupcake, and Nat get your asses down here for some more Red and Pinks fun and games.

"Yeah," Pinks smiled. "I think it's safe to say all of us are looking forward to the reunion. Oh, shit!" Pinks cupped a hand over his mouth as he stared wide-eyed at what was happening at the front door.

Scarlett was standing to the side of Natalie, who was framed front and center in the opened door. Beyond them was a group of guys, maybe five or so. There was music, and swear to God, it looked like they were doing a coordinated striptease. Yep, there went the shirts. All tossed over Natalie's head and into their living room.

"Pinks, buddy, what's going on?" he heard Cal ask.

"Oh, man," Pinks said, glancing back at Cal while keeping one eye on the action. "Harmless fun, I'm sure, but right behind you, Scarlett and Natalie are being serenaded."

"Man, everybody is trying to steal my thunder. I'm the only one who should be singing to Nat."

"No, man. They aren't singing. They are dancing. Magic Mike style. Dancing, and … ah … taking off their clothes."

"Fuck, no."

"Sorry, man," Pinks said through his laughter. "And they aren't half bad, if I'm being honest."

"Why isn't Natalie shutting the door in their faces? Tell her to slam the damn door."

Pinks felt a white lie was appropriate. "Scarlett is holding the door open. Natalie is being forced to watch."

The truth was slightly less comforting. Natalie and Scarlett were now outside dancing on the front porch with all five guys who had dropped their shorts and were down to boxers. He wasn't alarmed because his Red kept waving to him, very aware that he was watching the whole thing, or that he could at least see part of it. Still, his girl and her roommate were taking full advantage of the situation. So Pinks decided this whole holier-than-thou business about the newsletter wasn't something he had to take too seriously.

If Missy got hashtags going that engrossed an entire campus seven hundred miles away, she was doing her job, and she was doing it damn well. As long as Natalie didn't dump Cal for some Ole Miss Rebel and Red came home to him after graduation, he could live with this. For Henderson's sake.

"Pinks. Pinks. PINKS!" Cal shouted.

"Yeah, man. Sorry. Just watching the show."

"You think I need to get over there? Throw a little professional athlete mojo around campus so everybody will back off my girl?"

"Nope. I think that would only get you fined for going AWOL and attract more attention to Natalie. Trust me. These guys are just goofing off. Seniors being seniors. By the time Spring Break is over, Natalie will be old news."

"From your lips."

"Yeah. She's okay," Pinks said, watching the antics. "Not interested in anyone but you. The secret of keeping that status quo is letting the girls have their fun."

"You mean not go all possessive caveman on her ass."

"Exactly. Dating an MLB player like you will no doubt have its ups and downs. You need to make life easier for Natalie where you can. Show her you're secure in your relationship, no matter who's dropping trou in front of her. Then she'll be able to do the same when some fanatical fangirl walks up and hands you a room key or a pair of panties with her number embroidered on them."

"Seriously. I've hired a bodyguard during Nat's visit. I do not want that shit happening while she's here. I've been a fucking monk since I met Nat, and I don't want any crazy hootchie mommas messing things up for me."

Pinks leaned in closer to his screen and lowered his voice. "Cal? Buddy? This is me you're talking to. I have seen you in action."

"Hand to God, Mighty Pinks. A fucking monk."

"Why?"

"You're telling me you'd step out on Red?"

"No. Never. But I'm not Rookie of the Year or Major League Baseball's latest sex symbol either. You have to be inundated with temptation."

"Which is why I stay in and Skype with Nat every night. Natalie is all the temptation I need."

CHAPTER TWENTY-EIGHT

"Harry," Missy called out as soon as she entered the Mixed Grill Friday just as the club opened for lunch.

"What can I do you for, Miss McReady?"

"I need your help. Who can cater a BBQ on short notice?"

"Already done. Mr. Watson called me early this morning. Trust that between the two of us, your food and drink needs for the Party at the Plantation next weekend are all taken care of."

Missy's mouth hung open in shock.

"What's next?" Harry asked.

She snapped her mouth shut, grateful that one huge item was now checked off her list. "I need your advice. Tell me who would be really good at taking over Henderson's digital newsletter."

"You mean," Harry said, leaning in and lowering his voice, "who is ready, willing, and able to dish juicy gossip?"

"Harry, I love how you get me." Missy's eyes shone with delight. "Now, who can I count on? I've got ten minutes before I need to pack for the weekend and head off to practice."

"Well, obviously Vance's grandmother, Mrs. Flores, is dying to be involved."

"What?"

Harry gave her a disappointed glare. "Come on, city girl. Keep up." He bent over and placed his elbows on the bar. "Emelina Flores has got the goods on the older crowd but wheedles her way in with the young ones as well. She knew Davis was dating Scarlett Langford before Davis did. And she's got a lovely way of divulging gossip without upsetting the primary players."

"I agree. She's perfect for the job. But you know what? *You* are too. Would you consider it?"

Harry gave her a grin before he pushed himself back from the bar and winked. "I'm going to have to get back to you on that."

"Your number, please." Missy handed Harry her phone, not about to take no for an answer. "I hear you're magical," she commented, watching him.

"Who says that?" Harry inquired.

"Vance."

"Vance," Harry scoffed. "Vance just wants it to be true. That's why he says that stuff. Vance is a full-grown man enjoying the childhood he never had."

"Now that he has Piper?"

Harry handed her phone back. "Yeah, Piper and this new baby. Vance is having fun."

Over the past several days, Thor's intent had been to work sporadically on a small plot of land close to the farmhouse, cultivating it for a rose garden. He'd spoken with members of the Garden Club, done some online research, and put a call into his buddy Thatcher's father to get information on where to buy the best plants locally. The man may grow sod, but he was a wealth of knowledge when it came to growing just about anything else. It shouldn't have surprised Thor, but he'd forgotten that Thatcher's dad actually farmed his own land for his own table. And, as it turned out, Thatcher's mother had grown State Fair prize-winning roses three separate times over the years.

So now he had the information he needed, and he set out to plant a rose garden surrounding a path that could eventually lead to the greenhouse or gazebo he was considering. Either way, he'd have roses to give to Missy throughout the summer.

But the surprise came as Thor realized he actually enjoyed working the land. Man, he wished his dad were here to see this, he thought absently as he dug up a side bed with one of his pop's favorite shovels. That familiar anguish bubbled to the surface, so profound it caused him to stop and take a few deep breaths. Resting both gloved hands on the end of the shovel, Thor looked out toward the horizon. His own voice startled him when he spoke.

"Pop," he said into the wind. "Pop, are you seeing me out here working your land?" And then Thor started to laugh, the pain lifting from his chest. From his heart. "I feel you, Pop. I do. Frankly, I think I hear you laughing at me. Telling me, 'I told you so.'"

Thor went back to work, continuing the conversation in his head.

"She's a great girl," he told his dad. "Wish you'd stayed around long enough to meet her. I don't know what it is, but the moment I saw her, I knew she'd be good for me. Or, maybe I'd be good for her. Don't know. Hell, you probably know more about it than I do."

And then Thor stopped mid-shovel.

He knew, with a certainty the likes of which he'd never felt before, that his dad was aware of Melissa. That his dad had somehow had a hand in bringing a woman from Baltimore here to fix his life.

Minutes drifted by as Thor gathered his wits enough to start working again. "Whatever," he grumbled into the wind. "You had anything to do with that, Pop, I'll just say thank you."

After a few more shovels, he added, "And I miss you."

Then, "Tell Mom hi."

And then, "Shit." He scowled, tossing away the shovel. "I'm losing my freaking mind."

Vance Evans did not like Viper showing up at his baseball games. And after the shit she pulled last night, he sure didn't like her lurking around his ball club.

"Viper's here again," he said, turning to his buddy. "I'm thinking we need to take care of business."

"Yep," Brooks agreed, looking directly at Viper, rubbing the hell out of a baseball.

"After the game?" Vance asked.

"Yep."

"You got anything to say other than 'yep?'"

"Nope."

"All right, then. After the game." Vance patted Brooks on the back. "Good talk."

The Henderson Bulldogs won handily, as they had most of their games this season. There were a couple teams in their division they had to watch out for, but overall, they were head and shoulders above their competition. Brooks was already scouting the regional and state teams they were likely to meet in the playoffs.

After the players headed to the locker room, Brooks and Vance made their way through the crowd of parents and fans, getting lots of high-fives and praise as they headed in Marcie Watts's direction.

"Ms. Watts," Brooks called out.

With her back to them, she took a moment to react to Brooks's shout-out. Probably not real interested in having a conversation with Henderson's Golden Boy, the man next in line for Clint Stevens's job. But when she turned their way, she presented them with a dazzling smile.

"Mr. Bennett," Viper cooed. "Congratulations on another decisive victory."

"Thanks. What are you doing here?"

Vance might have been a little surprised by Brooks's abrupt interrogation, but truth be told, Viper was becoming a pain in Henderson's collective ass. The quicker she knew they weren't going to let her get away with much, the better off all of them would be.

"What am I doing here?" she repeated as if the question were spoken in a foreign language.

"Yes, ma'am," Brooks asked. "I'd like to know what you're doing here."

"Well … I'm a fan, of course."

"A fan?"

"Yes. Is that so outrageous? I'm sure you're aware that your own Coach Crenshaw and I have a history. The two of us bonded over baseball."

"Major League Baseball," Brooks pointed out.

"If there was a major league team in Henderson, I'd be at their games," Viper assured him. "As it is, I have to make do. Although, this high school team appears talented enough to take on a Triple-A farm team and win. So, being a fan of the Bulldogs is not a hardship. Rather the opposite."

"Kind of you to say, but under the circumstances, I'd just as soon you steer clear of my team."

"Your team?" Her brows rose up as if in shock. "I wasn't aware the Henderson Police Department had a team."

"I think you know what I'm saying," Brooks insisted. "You want to help Clint run his campaign, I can't stop you."

"Oh, but you'd like to."

"Damn right. You're an outsider stirring up trouble."

"I've done no such thing."

"I beg to differ. Bringing in your rabble-rousing cronies to try to join our club—not cool."

"You don't want to expand the membership and bring new business to Henderson? Fine by me. I'm only trying to help."

"None of those folks had any interest in setting up shop in Henderson. I'm not exactly sure why you're interested in pissing off the members, but I'm absolutely convinced that was your intent. You're too smart and wily for it not to have been a calculated move."

"You're too kind." She batted her lashes.

"Not my intention, I assure you. You're messing with my town, my people. So I'm standing here telling you that's gotta stop. You've got a problem with me, then you deal with me. Leave the country club alone. Leave the baseball team alone. Leave *Henderson* alone."

"Is that how you plan to greet all your new residents?"

"Only the ones who have a cross to burn."

"No cross. I come in peace," she claimed.

"Bullshit. You blame me for Coach Crenshaw dumping your ass."

By the look on Viper's face, Brooks concluded that he'd hit upon the truth. And if that wasn't obvious enough, her leaning in to Brooks and growling her next words certainly were.

"You're going down, Brooks Bennett. You and your juvenile pie-in-the-sky Team Henderson will not be winning this next election."

"I know you're gonna give it your best shot. But I'm telling you right now. Play fair. You hurt my club, my town, or any one of my constituents, I'm coming after you. Not Clint. I'm coming after *you*."

Viper backed off, smoothing her skirt and replacing her anger with that same beautiful smile. "I've got six months to prove Clint Stevens is the better man for the job. You might want to get used to me at a few baseball games." With that, she turned on her heels and left.

Vance clapped Brooks on the back as the two watched her go. "I don't think that went so well."

"Sure it did," Brooks responded deadpan, watching to make sure Viper found her way off school property. "No more need to speculate. We now know exactly where she stands."

Thor felt the mattress give as Missy climbed in quietly, shifting toward him under the covers. Her fingertips on his back felt tentative, which made him grin. How could she possibly think he was still asleep?

He rolled from his side, careful as he situated himself on top of her naked body. "I fucking love my life," he said, thinking out loud.

"You're awake."

"'Course I'm awake. You don't think a provocative text from the girl I'm crazy about is gonna keep me up?"

"But you didn't text back."

"Worried a little bit about you coming all this way in the dead of night. Didn't feel it was right to give you the green light, but didn't have the strength to tell you no, either." He sighed. "Truly love that you're here, Pretty Girl. Makes me happy," he trailed off, kissing her lips. "Consider my bed yours any time you want. No invitation needed. Just rather have you here, wrapped up and safe a little earlier, for my peace of mind."

"I needed to see you."

He pulled back. "Yeah? You need to talk?"

She shook her head.

That answer really made him grin. "I think it's safe to say that this is a first."

She nodded, biting her lip, sliding her arms around his back as she raised her upper body toward him to steal a kiss. "I'm just … gonna miss you," she whispered.

Damn, he liked that.

"I'd have come to your place." In a fucking New York minute.

"I know," she said. Smiling. Soothing him with her fingertips. "I kinda wanted to surprise you. Only then I worried you'd think someone was breaking in. So I got nervous and texted from the car."

"I'd have known it was you, even without a text."

"How?"

"Sound of your car. Pace of your walk. The way you opened the slider."

"Your Ranger spidey senses?"

"Can certainly detect when you're in the area."

"I'm gonna drive to the airport from here. I really should have flown to Orlando this afternoon, but like I told you this morning, this tournament snuck up on me. I could have sworn I had another full week."

"What time is your first game?" he asked, pretending he didn't know.

"Not until eleven. Then we play again at three. I should be fine. I'm actually meeting up with a couple of teammates who are flying in tomorrow too. The three of us will take a cab to the stadium and meet the rest of the team there."

"That mean I need to let you sleep?" he asked, kissing her neck.

She licked her lips. "I was sort of hoping you'd help me with one final workout before game time."

"Anything for you," he said, right before he flipped her over onto her belly.

Missy laughed. "You've got something specific in mind?"

"Yep," he said, sliding his hand between her legs. "It's called a passionate push-up."

"What?" She tried to flip back over, but he halted her on her side.

"You said you wanted a final workout. I'm just trying to help."

"With a passionate push-up?"

"Sorta sounds like it will fit the bill, right?"

"What exactly is a passionate push-up?"

He pushed her shoulder so she was face down again. "I'll show you."

She started to laugh into his pillow until he pulled it out from under her. "Put your arms like you're getting ready to do a push-up."

"You're serious?"

"Baby, this is the perfect time to try this."

"Try what?"

"A passionate push-up. Come on, work with me."

"Oh my gosh," she grumbled, arranging her upper body into push-up position. "I'm afraid to ask how you even know about this push-up thing."

"Vance gave me a book," he said as he placed his arms outside of hers.

Missy whipped her head to the side, aghast. "Vance Evans gave you a book on sexual positions?"

"No. Vance gave me a bullshit book that he claimed made him irresistible to women. I took one look at the cover, tossed the thing back at him, and found my own damn book."

"What was Vance's book?"

"Something about His Wicked Ways."

"Huh?"

Thor shook his head. "Trust me. I would not be caught dead holding that thing."

"Well, what's your book?"

"365 Sex Moves."

"Are you serious?"

"As serious as a passionate push-up. We doing this?"

"Is that how you knew—wait. What are you doing?"

"What do you mean, what am I doing?" Thor repeated as he started to laugh. "I'm trying to connect my masterpiece to your masterpiece."

Missy started to laugh with him. "And then we're supposed to do push-ups?"

"In concert. Together. That's the plan."

Missy held still a moment, as if she were thinking. "All right. I'm intrigued. I mean if you and I can't figure this one out … but why don't we just"—she got up on her knees giving him much easier access to her masterpiece—"start out the old-fashioned way and see if we can work into a push-up position."

"Kinda like the old-fashioned way," Thor claimed as he slid his masterpiece home.

"Yeah," Missy whispered, lifting her chin. "Something to be said for the basics."

"Mmm," he agreed, giving her the basics one slow stroke at a time.

"Mmm, yeah."

Around the time his bed really started to dance, Thor was pulled out of his head with Missy's, "Okay-okay-okay-okay."

"What?"

"Push-ups. Remember?"

"Nah. Good with the basics." He kept on going.

"Nooooo. This could be cool. We'll come back to the basics if we need to. Let's just try it," Missy pleaded.

Thor blew out a breath, trying to rein himself in. "Me and my big mouth," he mumbled. "Okay, fine. Just ... all right. Slowly, so you don't shake me loose. Just, together, slide our legs out straight ... yeah, like that ... okay, on our toes. Can you, ah, spread your feet out a little more? Yeah, good." He pushed himself farther into her body, hoping to secure their connection. "Damn," he said, starting to love this game. "You gonna be okay like that?"

When she didn't respond, Thor asked, "Baby?"

"I gotta tell you," she said, sounding like she was beginning to breathe heavy. "That feels ... amazing."

"Yeah?" He positioned his shoulders a little higher over hers and levered his hands farther to the outside. "Let's do this, okay? Down ... up."

"Ha!" Missy burst out with a laugh at their success. They did it again.

"That's two," she said, halting him as he started their third push-up. "I've never thought about making a sex tape before. But I'm just thinking your body has got to look really hot doing naked push-ups."

"Hold that thought, babe," he grunted. "Let's see how many we can do."

"That's the Ranger talking."

"To the girl who wears Nike underwear. On three. Till you can't go anymore. One. Two. Three."

They found a slow rhythm, went to ten, and kept on going.

"This working for you?" he grunted as they hit twenty.

"So good. Don't wanna stop," she told him.

At the count of thirty-seven, he said, "You got a game tomorrow."

"Still don't wanna … Ooooh—yesss—okay—that's—hmmm." Her arms folded and Thor took over in a modified "basic," pushing her to ecstasy and then pushed on through to his own.

As his chest collapsed onto the back of his favorite girl athlete, his body was exhausted but his brain was still in competitive mode. Because in his head, he was congratulating the two of them. He was darn confident they had just set the world record for passionate push-ups.

CHAPTER TWENTY-NINE

Thor approached the sideline of the field behind the bouncing, spinning youth he'd driven all the way to Orlando. The five juniors, one senior, and two elementary schoolers had more energy than a bag of cats as they darted ahead of him eager to surprise Missy with their presence.

In truth, he was just as eager. Though it was his heart that was doing all of the bouncing and spinning.

Missy was as surprised and excited by their turnout as Thor had imagined she'd be. Letting out a shout of delight and hugging first Ellie, then Rett, and then the entire mob of high schoolers. She saved the biggest hug for Marnie. Every one of them was speaking at once, with Missy asking how they'd managed to come so far. The girls pointed out Ellie's mom, who waited back by the stands, and then had Missy glancing around, astounded, after someone mentioned his name. When her eyes locked on his, she gave him the prettiest grin he'd ever seen.

Yeah, that was worth enduring the drive to Florida with eight squawking girls. Everything about Missy the Competitor softened when she smiled at him. Just like when he used his mouth to shut her up. He didn't venture into the fray, just stood back grinning at her as the girls took over, gaining her attention once again. They carried on about how well she played, about how fast her team moved the ball down the field, about how many goals were scored, on and on about everything they'd witnessed.

Thor's chest puffed up seeing Missy like this. Easy. Happy. Sweaty, even. She loved this game, and it sure showed when she was on the field. Loved it even when she'd been standing on the sideline. And now, she was just as engaged with her team. Listening to their every word. Hugging them to her over and over, elated that they were here.

He couldn't have given her a better gift, he thought. And he had to admit, it was fun sharing this experience with those girls. Because they sure had one thing in common. They were all big fans of Missy.

A handsome man dressed in casual business attire moved into the crowd, and Missy shrieked as he grabbed her up into a great big bear hug.

Her father.

Had to be.

Finally, Thor was going to meet the infamous Yoda—Jack McReady—the man Missy thought so much of and was so very close to.

After a few brief words, Missy turned to the girls and started introducing them one by one to her pop. She beamed like a proud momma duck showing off her ducklings. She went on and on about them coming all this way to surprise her. Then she mentioned which position each of them played, and from what Thor could hear, it sounded like she gave her father a little anecdote about each girl. Something unique so that he could easily remember who was who, even if he didn't manage to capture all of their names.

She was good like that, Thor thought. Sizing things up to the good and then singling that out. She was doing it for Henderson, she was doing it for E&E, and clearly she'd been doing it for her players all along.

When she'd finished introducing the girls, she reached out a hand toward Thor, coaxing him closer. The girls all bounced back, making room for him.

"Dad, this is Thurgood Watson the Third. He helped drive my players down here to surprise me." She beamed.

Thor held out his hand in greeting.

Mr. McReady took it and gave him a hearty handshake, looking him right in the eye with a grateful smile. "That's awful kind of you."

"Happy to do it, sir. We all wanted to see Coach McReady in action. Your daughter sure knows how to wield a mean lacrosse stick."

"That she does," he agreed, smiling directly at Thor before lines formed over his forehead, and he appeared to look around. "Where's Davis?"

Davis?

"Ah ... he's in Sarasota at spring training," Missy told him. "He said to tell you hello."

"Spring training? Why isn't he here? With you. I planned to take the two of you to dinner."

"Yeah, I know, but he's crazy busy and has his own things going on."

"Well, that's a shame. I was looking forward to seeing the boy."

"I know, Dad. He'd have liked to catch up with you too. His thing just fell on the same weekend. Couldn't be changed."

As Thor stood there, watching the exchange, a sinking feeling crept over him. He tried hard to argue with it, but there was no denying that Mr. McReady was surprised that Pinks wasn't there. And more than that, he seemed disappointed. As in *severely* disappointed.

And with the glances Missy was throwing between him, her father, and the goddamn ground, it was pretty clear that her father had no idea who he was to Missy.

No. Idea.

How the hell could that be? She talked to the man every day and twice on Sunday. About *everything*. About lacrosse, about business, about the town she was living in and the people she was working with. But apparently, she'd never mentioned the guy she happened to be *sleeping* with.

Go figure.

Thor took a step back. And his face must have shown his newly found understanding because Missy reached out to him and interrupted her father.

"Dad, Thurgood's the one who built the lacrosse field for me."

"What's that?" her dad asked. His head swung around to get another look at Thor. "A lacrosse field?"

"Yeah," Missy went on kind of desperately as all the blood from Thor's head drained toward his feet. Honest to God, he felt like he was listing sideways, stuck inside his own nightmare.

"He built me, well the whole team, our own lacrosse field so the girls and I could practice and play whenever we wanted. So we wouldn't have to wait for the boys to finish up."

"You built a lacrosse field?" Her father asked him. "Where?"

Thor was too—Stunned? Numb?—to answer that.

"He owns a lot of property outside of Henderson proper," Missy offered.

"Is that your business?" Mr. McReady asked.

"No, sir," Thor said. "That was the first field I've ever been involved in creating. Didn't quite realize what all it took. We cut a few corners to get it done quickly, but it's a level, regulation-size women's lacrosse field, so it serves its purpose."

That wasn't at all true, Thor thought. It clearly had not served its purpose if Missy's father was just hearing about it now.

"Well, hell. Looks like I better take *all* of you to dinner. I dare say Missy owes you more than that for building her and the girls a field."

"No, sir. Missy owes me nothing." *Did that come out harsh?* Thor wondered. *I bet it came out harsh.* "In fact, the last thing I want to do is wedge my way between a father and his daughter. So you two go on and enjoy yourselves. I'll round up the crazy train over here and take them to Universal Studios. Let them burn off some energy before we head on back to North Carolina."

"You're heading back? Already?" Missy gasped.

"Hadn't planned on it, but seeing as the rug has been pulled out from under me, I'm going with my instincts here. Mr. McReady." He held out his hand to Missy's father and shook it. "Truly an eye-opening experience finally meeting the man I've heard so much about. Have a good evening and safe travels home."

"Thank you, son. And thanks for bring the team down to watch my Melissa play. I can tell it pleased the punch right out of her."

"Yeah. I saw that too." He shot Missy a quick stare. Nodded a final farewell to her father and turned away.

"Thor," she called, but he ignored that and rounded the girls up, telling them to say their goodbyes and meet him at the main stadium gate in twenty minutes. Then, with a final glare at Mr. McReady's Melissa, he started marching.

He wasn't going to look back.

That was for damn sure.

Brain-dead numb was how Thor would describe his state when he and his posse hit Universal Studios early that evening. Nothing but a hollow-sounding echo in his head since he'd realized Missy's father had never heard his name.

Oh, he'd done all right responding to Merv and all the high-pitched, excited questions tossed at him as he drove away from the stadium. And he was acutely aware that Rett, who'd taken over the shotgun seat, was noticeably quiet. He even managed to stick around while Ellie's mom herded the girls together for some strict dos and don'ts before they synchronized watches and established the first checkpoint. It was there he waved them off, choosing a quiet table on the deck of the Margaritaville restaurant where he ordered a shot of whiskey and a cold beer.

"Melissa? Your order?" Missy's father prompted.

"Oh. Sorry," she apologized to the waiter. "I just ... sorry." Missy studied the menu in front of her, still unable to decipher a thing on it. "Protein," she said. "Steak?" she asked, shaking her head.

"She'll have the filet, a baked potato, the Caprese salad to start, and we'll enjoy the chocolate soufflé for dessert," Jack McReady said, taking over.

"Very good, sir."

The ambience at Shula's was the kind of thing Missy generally enjoyed. But with the sinking feeling she'd experienced the moment Thor and her father shook hands, Missy was unable to appreciate any of it.

That sensation had proved to be right on the money, since her multiple texts to Thor had gone unanswered. She was staring at her place setting when she heard her father's throat clear. "All right. What's going on?"

The tone he'd used wasn't one she could shrug off. It was his president-of-the-company tone. The one he used when he was prepared to hear, and deal with, bad news.

She looked up, fighting back the panic she felt. "I have screwed up. Royally," she admitted. She closed her eyes and let the weight of it all sink down deep. She felt her father's hand on top of hers while he waited for her to proceed.

"I …" She shook her head. "I don't know where to start. Honestly. I guess I've been lying to you through omission. Only, I didn't see it that way. I just—"

"What's going on?" her father pressed. Only this time, his voice was full of worry.

"The man you met back at the field? The one who brought all the girls down to watch my game?"

"Thurgood. Built you a lacrosse field."

"I'm sleeping with him."

Her father's brows shot up to his hairline as he fell back in his chair. "Excuse me?"

"It's not casual. I'm crazy about him."

"What about Davis?"

"Davis is in love with someone else. Has been since before I moved to Henderson. I was simply unaware—for a while—which is a long story and not necessarily his fault."

"Melissa," he said sharply.

"I know. I should have kept you in the loop. More than that, I should have mentioned Thor."

"Thor?"

"Thurgood. He …" She shook her head, looking back down at her place setting. "He rescued me the very first night I was in town. He helped me locate and move lacrosse goals and set up the field for my first practice because Davis was too busy with work. He's watched out for me, he's supported me, he's done nothing but help me throughout my tenure in Henderson, and now I've hurt his feelings more than I ever wanted to."

"I'm not quite following."

"He's no dummy. It was more than obvious when I introduced the two of you that you've never heard his name."

"Because you didn't want me to know you were sleeping with someone?"

"Because I didn't know how to ease you off of the hope of Davis."

"My hope of Davis?"

"You know. Of Davis and me. Of Davis moving back to Baltimore with me. Of Davis coming to work for you someday. Being part of the family."

"I had no such hope."

"Daddy," she scolded. "Of course, you did."

"No way. I was glad to see you two spending time together, sure. But I knew the boy wasn't coming back. Hell, I knew that when Arthur and Sabina went down to try to drag his butt home. They'd told me all about the Evans family and what they're trying to accomplish. Told me about what Davis was doing for them. I did a little research into Hale Evans, and I was pleased the boy had found his place, at least for the time being. I just wanted what was best for him, and if I could have given him a leg up, I was happy to do it."

"But what you said about the two of us coaching together?"

"Sweetheart. What did I say?"

Missy tried to think back on it. *What had he said?* "I'm not sure. But it seemed to me you encouraged me to pursue Davis. Romantically."

"Maybe I did. But ... if it didn't work out ..." He shrugged.

Missy sipped her water, trying to understand where it had all gotten so off track.

"Were you worried I'd be disappointed?" her father asked.

She nodded. "A little bit. I was more worried you'd hold it against Davis. Because truthfully, at first, I was hoping he and I would have a chance to become more than we've always been. More than friends. Maybe I was transferring my feelings onto you."

"Maybe?"

The waiter delivered their salads and poured more of the cabernet they'd let air. Missy's head was spinning, trying to work all of this out in her own mind. Wondering how she'd explain this to Thor when she couldn't really sort it out herself.

"So, this Thurgood?" her father pried.

Missy sighed through a pitiful smile as she took up her fork. "Thor," she said, cutting into her salad. "And I'm sorry I told you that we've been intimate, Dad. I'm aware going from no information to too much information wasn't the right move on my part."

Her father cleared his throat. "It does explain the lacrosse field."

Missy laughed in spite of herself. "He sort of fell for me the moment he laid eyes on me. I wasn't aware, because I was blinded by my hope for Davis. But Thor found a lot of ways to be helpful, and I cannot explain to you just how much I needed his help. Especially in the early days. I mean, Davis was already handling as much as he could when I got there, so he didn't have the time he thought he would to ease me into things. Plus, he was having some personal issues of his own. Which I was not aware of."

"He okay?"

"Yeah." She smiled at her father. "Davis is just fine. He's good, too," she admitted. "I mean in the business world. Well, at everything," she conceded. "So when it hit my ears that they were calling me Davis's twin? Hell, I took it as a compliment. Your company lost a good one in Davis. But you certainly don't need him like Henderson does. And he's staying put. He's growing roots there."

"Don't tell his mother that."

"I know. Believe me."

"What about your mother?" Jack asked.

"What about her?"

"She's curious if you're growing roots."

"I am," she admitted. "I'm crazy about Thor. I'm crazy about my job. I'm crazy about the insane gossip that goes on there. I mean, this small-town stuff is awkward and hilarious and so simple and yet so darn complicated." She laughed. "I'm falling in love with it."

"So," her dad said, leaning in, "why haven't you told me any of this?"

"I don't know. Maybe I didn't want it to be true. Or I was worried you'd be disappointed."

"How could you possibly disappoint me?"

"Dad, Thor is not Davis. He's not a corporate business executive, not even close. And frankly, thank God for that. Only it took me a while to figure that out. I thought I wanted a *Davis*. Someone like *you*. Turns out that even before I became CEO—"

"CEO?"

"Yep." She grinned. "That's my title. CEO of Henderson. Not a bit of money behind it, and maybe it was just a trick to get me to stay, but I fell for it. Just like I fell for Thor. And his truck. Because Thor's exactly the kind of guy every businesswoman *needs* to fall for. He loves me in spite of my faults, my city-girl prejudices, and my hectic schedule. On top of that he's always ready, willing, and able to swoop in with his big red truck and play the hero. I thought I didn't want a farmer or a military man. I thought he was Mr. Wrong. But as it turns out, I was the one who was wrong. About a lot of things."

"Thor's a farmer?"

"I just told you, he's my personal hero." She smiled. "He's also a retired Army Ranger who has recently inherited a tobacco plantation. Since his mother died from lung cancer, he refuses to continue with tobacco. He never really wanted to be a farmer, but since his daddy died suddenly, he's now guilt-ridden about not taking up the Watson family mantle. I think he'd like to honor his ancestors by figuring out something productive to do with the land."

"Like what?"

"Well, that's the question he's been wrestling with." She smiled. "For the moment, there's a lacrosse field." She bit into her salad, her heart twisting at the thought of all Thor had done for her and that he hadn't texted her back.

"Go call him," her father suggested. "Don't worry about me. You go find a quiet spot and call the man. Straighten this out. Now. Before you lose any sleep."

"Thank you," she breathed, getting up and moving to kiss his cheek. "I'll be back—"

"When you're back. I'll tell the waiter to hold off on your steak. I'll be fine. Not the first time I've sat at a table alone."

CHAPTER THIRTY

Cal Johnson lived on the mound. It was where he felt most at home. Didn't matter in what city that mound was situated or how big the ballpark. Standing out there, he was home. He could breathe. He could think. He could control the game from the mound.

Except for right now.

Right now, he'd caught a glimpse of Pinks, the Cupcake, and the smoke show he'd come to favor calling Miss Great taking the seats he'd reserved for them in back of home plate.

Now, why the hell did I do that? he wondered. He'd set the whole thing up. He *wanted* to be pitching for Natalie today. The day he'd finally get to see her after two weeks of phone calls, texts, a few sexts, and a whole lot of Skype-a-thons. He wanted to show off his stuff for his girl, and now … well, shit.

He held up his hand, asking for a timeout. His catcher and close personal friend, Tazer Randall, jogged out to him with a smile on his face. "Dude. You look like you swallowed that worm at the bottom of a tequila bottle. I'm guessing Nate Houser's offspring is in the house?"

"You know it. I look down that mound at you, I see a gorgeous brunette with my name on her. Freaking me the fuck out."

Taze chuckled. "She's just a chick, man. Got nothing to do with baseball."

Cal took a deep breath. "Right. You're right. Just doing my job here. Spring training and whatnot."

"Yeah, except that she's Nate the Great's daughter. So she's measuring you up against dear, old Daddy, and dude, you're good, but he's …"

"I know, I know. He's Nate."

"The fucking Great."

"Fuck off, man. Get back there so I can shoot this fastball at your damn head."

"Now we're talking."

Taze went back to work, and so did Cal. His fastball, aimed right for his buddy's head, clocked in at one hundred two MPH. He actually heard Natalie's "holy shit," when the number was posted on the scoreboard.

Yeah, his girl for sure.

This time when he stood on the mound with the ball, he looked over at Nat and winked before he went into his pitching windup and threw another fastball, just because he could.

Because he was Cal Fucking Johnson and Nate the Great could eat his shorts.

Natalie felt like she wanted to jump out of her skin. Cal Johnson was one crazy hotty-toddy and so good at throwing that baseball that she'd practically convulsed, thrown up, and at one point, fainted right there in her seat. The looks he was shooting her as he walked to and from the mound between innings did things to her no Skype session could conjure. Maybe it was being in a ballpark. Seeing him in action. Realizing that he was indeed the *actual* Cal Johnson that all of America knew and loved. Because meeting him in Henderson, he'd just seemed so … normal.

But now. Now he was *Cal Johnson* for real, and Natalie was feeling all kinds of nervous about being able to measure up to *Cal Johnson's* expectations.

She was just a regular girl after all. And he'd probably sampled so many exotic varieties of female that a regular girl was just not going to cut it.

"What the hell?" Scarlett nudged her. "Are you? Are you hyperventilating?"

"Oh, God. Maybe. You got a paper bag? I might need to breathe into a paper bag. Pinks," she shouted to him on the other side of Scarlett, "I need a paper bag."

"A paper what?" Pinks responded.

"She's hyperventilating," Scarlett supplied with a roll-her-eyes sort of intonation.

"Why?" Pinks asked. "Cal's doing great. Might be pitching his best game ever."

"Ah-duh." Scarlett said. "I'm guessing that's the reason for the hyperventilating."

"I don't understand," Pinks said.

Scarlett turned back to Natalie and pushed her head between her knees. "Breathe," Scarlett ordered. "He's just a ballplayer. Albeit a hot one."

Natalie breathed in through her nose and out through her mouth, wondering why she ever decided to come to spring training. Why she ever thought she could handle Cal Johnson.

"Call your mother," Scarlett suggested, reaching into Natalie's bag and digging around for her phone. "I'll call her. You just stay down there and keep breathing."

"Why are you calling my mother?" Natalie gasped with her head between her knees.

"I'm guessing she might have done a little hyperventilating over your father back in their day. Maybe she can talk you through this."

"Oh." Natalie nodded her head, never really thinking of her parents like that. Did her mother at one time feel like she did? Like she couldn't handle being with Nate the Great because he was so great?

She grabbed the phone out of Scarlett's hand when Scarlett started to speak.

"Mom?"

"Natalie?"

"Yeah, yeah. Mom, it's me. I'm … ah, well, I'm sort of having a panic attack."

"I thought final exams didn't start for a while yet."

"Not about exams. About Cal. I'm with Scarlett in Sarasota, and we're at the game and Cal's pitching like a no-hitter or something, and he's so good, Mom, and I'm just me, and I don't think I can handle this. I mean, what am I gonna say when he comes off the field? Good game? The guy is throwing lights out, and I'm falling madly in love with a major league player, and I know he's going to break my heart, and I'm just going to be miserable for the rest of my life and—"

"Natalie!" her mother shouted trying to interrupt Nat's tirade for the third time. "Snap out of it!"

"What?"

"Hand the phone back to Scarlett."

"What? Mom, no. I need to talk to you." Natalie felt like she was going to cry. Her hands were shaking, and her body was sweating bullets. "Tell me you were like this with Daddy. Tell me how you handled the pressure."

"Sweetheart," her mother's voice softened. "He's just a man who is good at what he does. He's not immortal."

"Mom, seriously. He's looking pretty damn immortal right now. In fact, you need to tell Dad to get his hands on tapes of this game. I'm sure there's going to be a highlight reel on ESPN, but Daddy is not going to want to miss this."

"Tell me more."

"Well," Natalie sat up straight and looked out to the mound. "He's hit one hundred three MPH with two of his fastballs. No one has connected for a base hit yet. In fact, they've hardly touched the ball. He's killing it, Mom. I'm so proud of him. Daddy would be too."

"There's my girl."

"What?"

"You know baseball, baby. You're your father's girl. That's why Cal's smitten with you. You appreciate what he can do with a ball. So show up for him, okay? Get out of your head, and show up for him. Sounds like he's putting on a hell of a show for you. Don't think this isn't that. Your father always pitched better when I was in the stands. I equated it to the cavemen bringing home the wooly mammoth. He's showing off and getting it done for you. So make sure Natalie Houser, Miss Great, is the one who shows up for *him*."

"I can do that," she assured her mother. "I just … lost it for a minute. I mean, Mom, he's … that good."

"Fine. But you are *that good*, as well. And don't you forget it. Every man needs someone special to perform for. If Cal's lucky to have you as his someone special, own it. Enjoyyyy it," her mother dragged out. "Before you know it, Cal will be taking his final bows as he retires and heads into the Hall of Fame."

"Oh good Lord, Mom. This is his second year in the league."

"Darling, it flies by. Trust me. Watch every pitch. Enjoy every game, win or lose. Nothing lasts forever, especially a career in baseball."

"Wow. You sound melancholy."

"No. I just wish someone had told me how fast it all goes back when I was standing in your shoes. I'd have savored the moments a little bit more."

"I love you, Mom."

"I love you too, Nat."

"Thanks."

"Any time, sweet baby girl."

The game at Ed Smith Stadium ended, and all Cal wanted to do was walk over to Natalie and her gang. But his teammates had other plans for him. First came the Gatorade as he spoke to the press about his no-hitter. Damn stuff was sticky as all get out, and now he was a freaking mess from his right shoulder all down his back. Still, he managed to look over in Nat's direction. She was standing close to the dugout with the Cupcake and Mighty Pinks, all of them clapping and laughing at the insanity being displayed. He took off his cap and smoothed his hair back from his face before replacing it, trying his best to answer the reporter's questions without looking like he'd lost his train of thought.

Finally, he was released, and after a high-five from his mentor, Cooper Crenshaw, he hightailed it over to the edge of the protective netting behind home plate, directly to his girl.

"Nat," he said, smiling, walking over, and trying not to lose his cool. Because she was beaming at him, and damn that felt good.

Swear to God, he could have pitched another nine innings knowing she was here to see it.

"Cal," she called, clapping her hands together. "You're amazing."

Nah, he thought. He just was good with a baseball. Natalie Houser was the one who was amazing. "Come here," he said, waving her through the crowd who had gathered hoping for autographs. He didn't have to ask; the crowd just parted. He stuck his hand into the swarm, and she took hold. The next thing he knew, she somehow fell out of the stands and into his arms.

He turned them around so that his back was to the crowd, not wanting to be distracted from her sweet face when he said, "Hi."

She kept beaming. At him. So he kissed her. It might have been a stupid-ass thing to do with the reporter standing right there and who knew how many cameras taking in the scene. But Natalie Houser felt good in his arms, was good for his game, and man, she really had a grip on his heart. And right at that moment, he didn't care who knew it.

In fact, he was quite simply happy to tell the whole damn world.

"We're gonna be trending, you know that don't you?" he said after their kiss.

"Well, the good news is, I'm kinda getting used to it."

"I'm glad you're here," he said.

"That was quite the pitching demonstration you put on."

"I was nervous as hell the moment I caught a glimpse of you in your seat."

She laughed at that. "Nervous? Stop."

"Seriously. Did you see me call Taze out to the mound? We were not talking about which bar I was planning to take you to. He had to talk me down, get my head on straight. I nearly lost it out there, thinking about pitching in front of Nate the Great's daughter."

"And I had to call my mother to figure out how to stop hyperventilating when you threw the hundred and three mile per hour fastball. Who does that?"

"Me. With you in the stands. Not sure I'm gonna be able to let you go back and finish up at Ole Miss. Might have to keep you down here with me permanently."

"Okay, you two. Enough lovey-dovey stuff."

Cal turned to find Mighty Pinks and his redheaded marketing guru walking in their direction.

"Usher let us on the field," Pinks said. "Said you gave him our names."

Cal waved to the usher. "That I did." He grabbed Pinks's hand in greeting, and glanced over at Scarlett. "Cupcake, you like the game?"

"I did," Scarlett boasted, holding up an honest-to-goodness score card. "Natalie taught me a thing or two, and I have to say, baseball is far more interesting than I originally thought. *And* I like sitting in the front row."

"Of course, you do. Hey, come on down into the dugout and let me introduce y'all around."

"Perfect," Scarlett said. "Since the Orioles organization is being a little stingy with you, I need a meeting with the GM and whoever is in charge of PR. It'll be good to get the business part of this trip out of the way." Scarlett's stance was a little bit like she was rolling up her sleeves for a good fight.

"Lions isn't going to know what hit him. Come on," Cal said, directing them into the inner sanctum.

CHAPTER THIRTY-ONE

Thor's long drive home Sunday with the girls was poignantly painful.

Not one of them questioned why he turned off his phone and shoved it in the van's glove compartment. Or why he didn't come in to watch Missy's game when he dropped them off at the stadium the next morning. Although Rett had certainly given him a stare. He obviously couldn't punish the girls for the hell Missy was putting him through, but he couldn't very well sit in the stands and watch her play either. That would just be ...what did she call it? Emotional suicide.

Yeah. That was about right.

Merv and the girls were all fed and Rett was still riding shotgun when he hit the main highway heading north just before noon. Thor was hoping they'd all fall asleep quickly, but the knife kept twisting with all the excited chirping about how Team USA dominated the tournament. He had to bite his tongue to keep from spelling out to the van full of Coach McReady worshipers that Team USA was made up of the best college graduates, so they were far more experienced and talent laden than the poor college teams trying to compete with them. But things got even worse when the talk in the backseat focused on Ellie and her upcoming date with Hank Ford.

Thor watched as Rett sat ramrod straight and stared directly out the windshield. She didn't have her earbuds in though, so apparently, like him, she was a glutton for punishment.

"He's okay," Ellie said in response to one of the other girl's question. "I mean, he's cute and all. I'm just not sure I'm that into him."

"So why'd you ask him to the Sadie Hawkins dance?"

"Because he's going to look good in a tuxedo at prom, and I wanted to get that locked down now."

"Why, if you don't really like him?" another inquired.

"It's not that I don't like him," Ellie said. "I like him. I just wish he were more talkative. I mean, I'm always having to track him down or suggest we go watch the baseball game together."

Thor turned his head, wanting to give Rett a good, hard look to indicate she needed to have a serious conversation with this Hank Ford. Clearly, the poor guy was having a hard time getting himself untangled from the web known as Ellie.

She gave him a quick glance and a sad shrug before looking out the window to her right.

Fine. The girl didn't want his advice, he'd respect that. After all, who the hell did he think he was trying to give any sort of advice on this subject? He sucked at this subject.

In fact. The subject sucked. Love sucked. And if little Rett Patterson could sit here and suck it up like an All-Star, well, then maybe she ought to be the one giving him advice.

And sure enough, not an hour later, he caught her looking over her shoulder, getting ready to deliver her own brand of advice.

"They're all asleep with their earbuds in," she said quietly.

Thor glanced over at her. She was looking straight ahead. Pretending they weren't talking. "What happened?" she asked him quietly.

"Nothing," he said, shrugging it off like a godamn jackass.

"Something definitely happened. I saw it happen," she insisted. "Coach McReady's father didn't know about you."

"No. No, he didn't. And yeah. That happened."

"You're mad at Coach?"

He didn't answer. Didn't know how to answer without a lot of expletives not fit for Rett or anybody else's ears. Finally, he gave her something, because she'd been sweet enough to ask and had definitely put herself out there the day he stood witness to her pain. "You ever felt sucker punched?"

That got her head turned toward him. "You were there when it happened," she said.

He nodded. "Yeah, well I guess we're kindred spirits like that. Because you were standing there when it happened to me."

She nodded.

"We banned from your field now? I know you built that for Coach."

"No. You and your friends are welcome on that field. Any time."

"But you're gonna ban Coach McReady?"

Thor thought about that. It had gone through his mind that he'd like to take a damn plow to the lacrosse field and dig it the hell up. Tonight. He might have done it, too, if Rett hadn't called him on it.

"No. Not gonna hurt you and the team like that. As far as lacrosse practice goes, your games included, everything is status quo. I just ..." He stopped, sucked in a breath, and then spit it out. "I just might not be watching from the sidelines anymore."

"I understand," she said.

"Nothin' on you or the girls. You got that?"

"Yeah. I got it."

They traveled the rest of the way in silence.

After Thor dropped off the females and saddled up Big Red, he sat in the quiet cab for a while not quite ready to go home. He needed a distraction. So he turned Big Red in the direction of the country club.

"Well, look what the cat dragged in," Harry said, setting up a cocktail napkin in front of Thor as he took a seat at the bar. "Don't mind me saying so, but you look like you could use a drink."

"That bad, huh?"

"Seen you a little less Ranger-fied and a little more ... ah, personable, shall we say? Looks like you're out to kill someone."

Grunt. "If it would do me any good, I might consider it. But spending the rest of my days locked in a cell sounds only slightly less appealing than the situation I have suddenly found myself in."

Harry was already pouring Thor's Guinness. "I'm a bartender, and I'm not all that busy at the moment, so lay it on me."

"Right," Thor said, rubbing a hand over his mouth and stretching his shoulders as if he'd been stuck in a damn cell all day. "I'm moving on," he declared.

"On to what?"

"To … somebody new," he declared, deciding right then and there that he was done with Missy.

"And how does Miss McReady feel about that?"

"Wouldn't know. Don't care," Thor shot back. Then he took up his glass and chugged a good half of the dark liquid down.

"Hmm," Harry said. "Seems I recall you were sitting in that exact seat just a few months ago, wondering how you were going to get her and her lavender dress out of the Cowboy's arms and into your own. Thought you'd gone ahead and had pretty good success with that."

"You and I, both," Thor informed him. "Turns out, while I'm digging for roses and planting a lacrosse field, thanking the good Lord on a daily basis that something soft had entered my life, there was nothing but a piece of ice cold marble underneath all that lavender."

"Ice cold marble?"

"Fooled you too, huh?"

"What happened?"

"Nothin'."

"Nothin'?"

"Yep. Nothin'. *Exactly nothin'.* The girl speaks to her father every day. *Every day,*" he stressed. "For the past two months, Melissa McReady has talked to her father at length about her life in Henderson. And I hear all about their conversations. All about him. I know what the man does. I know his hobbies. I know his particular likes in the food department. I know the sports he plays and the records he's set. I know the guy's freaking middle name. After knowing Missy for two months, I knew more about a man I'd never met than I did about my own pop."

Harry's eyes narrowed, and he took a step back.

"You see where this is going, don'tcha?" Thor accused.

Harry only blinked.

"You would have thought when I was finally introduced to the guy, he'd have some clue as to who I am, right? Because I did mention that Missy and her father talk *every fucking day*," he growled. "So how is it at all possible that she had never once—not one damn time—mentioned my name?"

"It's not possible. And I'm fairly sure you are mistaken."

"No, sir." Thor shook his head. "I did not read this wrong. I'm telling you the man was pleasant. Looked me right in the eye and shook my hand. But there was absolutely no recognition. And he's a smart guy. If Missy had ever mentioned me, he would have remembered. I'm telling you, he was as caught off guard as I was. Which, of course led to the twisting of the knife in my heart, when he immediately let go of my hand and started looking around for Pinks."

"Ahh—" Harry popped a hand over his mouth.

"And here I thought nothing could shock you, Harry. Being as you're a bartender and some sort of Houdini on top of it."

"I don't know what to say. I can read people pretty good, and I'm telling you, Miss McReady is smitten with our resident Ranger. So, this turn of events is, indeed, unexpected. What did she say about it all?"

"Pfft. Like my pride hasn't been handed to me on a silver platter. No way am I giving her the satisfaction. She and I are *done*. We are *through*. As a matter of fact, I am here tonight to get a list of all the eligible ladies left in this town from the guy who apparently knows what's going on with everybody."

"Who?"

"You, that's who."

"Me?" Harry asked. "I serve tequila shots and hand out unsolicited advice. All part of the job."

"With the stories I've heard about you"—Thor shook his head—"I'm not buying it. So bring it on. The tequila *and* the advice. And a name," he said, holding up his hand. "The name of the future Mrs. Watson. A fair damsel who is soft and pretty all the way through. Not one hiding a core of hard and ugly."

Harry squinted his eyes, looking back at Thor as if he was having a hard time believing Melissa was the one he described.

"Honest to God, I didn't believe it either," Thor admitted. "Took me most of the drive home from Florida to figure it out. But you see … I finally did figure it out."

"Well, then, please. Lay it on me."

"Her father likes Pinks—No. Her father loves Pinks. Her father had offered Pinks a job in his fancy-ass firm before Pinks had even graduated college. Pinks blows him off. Stays down here. Missy heads down here, and I'm pretty sure father and daughter had conspired about winning Pinks back into the fold. Whether it was about a marriage contract or a business agreement, I can't say. What I can say is that the man was shocked that Pinks was nowhere in sight at Missy's game. Clearly, he expected them to be closer than they are. Considering."

"Considering?"

"Considering Pinks is in love with Scarlett Langford. I think that's a bit of information Missy has been omitting from those conversations with her father, right along with my name."

Harry pulled out a shot glass and his best whiskey.

"That's not tequila," Thor protested.

"Trust me. You don't want tequila right now."

"Whatever."

"So, if your speculation is correct," Harry asked as he poured the shot, "why do you suppose Miss McReady did all of that? Leave you and Scarlett out of the conversation with her father."

"She wants Pinks," Thor offered as if it was a given. "Or she wants her father to think that things are going well between her and Pinks."

"Because …" Harry egged him on.

"How the fuck do I know? Because she didn't want to disappoint dear, old dad."

Harry gave a brief nod and stared at Thor.

"What? Like I'm supposed to be cool with that?"

"You can be however you want to be with that."

"I'm not cool with it. I don't care what was behind it or the reasons for it. Everyone has their relationships with their parents, and I get that, probably more than anybody. But that *girl* meant the world to me. *The world*. Yet, I wasn't worthy of even a mention to the person she's closest to."

"It looks bad," Harry said.

"I built her a lacrosse field, Harry. Her own damn lacrosse field."

"Real bad," Harry agreed.

"Yeah, well." The rage seeped out of Thor as his tirade came to an end. "Hurts real bad too," he said quietly.

He sat for a moment and then took hold of the shot glass and downed the whiskey. He chased it with the rest of his beer. When he spoke again, it was in a quiet, subdued tone. "You know I'm having a big party next weekend." Thor's eyes glanced up from the counter to Harry. "I need a date. Someone who won't mind being a fill-in for Missy, as I'm sure word of our demise will spread rather quickly."

"You're the host. You don't need a date."

"I need a date." Thor wasn't interested in laying out the details. The fact was, he did not trust Missy to have the good sense not to show up at his place during the event or trust himself not to throw her ass off his property, drawing far more attention to this breakup than he wanted.

"A blonde or brunette?"

"As different from Miss McReady as you can get."

"Oh, okay. So, intelligence isn't a priority."

"Well, she doesn't have to be a rocket scientist."

"And clever and witty isn't a prerequisite?"

"What are you getting at, Harry?"

"I'll show you. You buy the two who just walked in the door a drink, and if you can spend an hour in their presence, their drinks are on me."

Thor looked behind him. Women, hell. They were girls. Dolled-up, fancy girls who had the good sense to smile when their eyes fell on him.

He stood as they approached.

"To what do Harry and I owe this pleasure?" he asked, helping each of them onto a stool.

And that's when he saw her standing at the threshold. Missy McReady, in the flesh. Looking as soft as ever, yet the sight of her stopped him cold and plummeted his mood further into the ice age. He growled like a damn mammoth, deep in his throat.

"Can we talk?" she whispered quietly from the doorway, yet he heard it plain as day. He'd given this moment a lot of thought, and he had come to the same conclusion time and time again. There was nothing Missy McReady could say to him that would excuse, or make up for, the breach he'd discovered was between them. And on top of that, he wasn't sure he could stomach hearing it.

So he chose to ignore her request, turning his back on her and his attention to the two dolled-up females who were already giving Harry their drink order.

Still, he felt the moment she retreated.

Knew how many minutes passed between that moment and the moment he was finally able to extricate himself from the crowd that had gathered around the bar.

Knew the miles he drove out to his pop's farm. Knew how tired he was and yet understood how elusive a good night's sleep would prove to be.

Knew that war was hell.

And now, so was heartbreak.

CHAPTER THIRTY-TWO

Missy waited until ten o'clock that night before driving out to Thor's home. It was probably good he refused to speak to her at the club. They needed privacy to work this out.

Because she'd hurt him. Bad.

She'd seen it on his face. Knew it when he hadn't answered her phone calls or texts. And that hurt had obviously translated into anger, because this was not him.

Thor had forgiven her so much early on. He'd continued giving her the benefit of the doubt, trusting that their relationship would work itself out eventually. And it had.

It really had.

Not mentioning Thor to her dad was so much more about the crazy schedule she'd been keeping and not having the time or the energy when they did talk to give her father the details he'd need to understand why she was staying in Henderson. It wasn't at all a reflection on how much Thor meant to her.

But she understood why Thor might see it that way. And it broke her heart that she'd done this to him and to them.

So, she was wasting no more time. She was heading to the plantation, determined to see him. Determined to explain exactly how this managed to come about. Determined to beg his forgiveness.

There weren't a whole lot of lights on as she pulled into the drive. She decided to use the front door, hoping there would be a bell to ring, instead of going around to the back door, which she'd used exclusively. She didn't want to face the fact that he might have locked her out.

Locating the doorbell, she prayed it actually worked and rapidly pressed it twice. Then she stood back and waited.

Impatiently.

With her heart in her throat.

When she heard the door being unlocked, she felt a bit of relief that he was at home and she was finally, finally going to get to talk to him.

"Thor," she said when he opened the door.

He simply stared. His piercing neon-blue eyes boring into her, conveying his contempt.

"I'm so sorry," she started. "I know you're upset with me, but I can explain."

"Explain what?" he asked. "Why the one person in the entire world you are closest to has never heard my name?"

"Yes. That. Exactly that."

"All right." Thor folded his arms over his chest, barring entry to the house. "Try."

"Here?" she wondered, ill-prepared to lay it all out while standing in the night air.

"Forgive me if I don't feel like inviting you in."

"Thor, please," she begged. "Can't we sit down? Open a bottle of wine. Talk this out?"

He stepped back, and thinking she was invited in, she stepped forward, looking down to step onto the threshold. The loud bang startled her almost as much as looking up to find her face mere millimeters from the closed door.

"What?" It took her a moment to understand what had happened. That he'd literally just slammed the door in her face. "Thor," she yelled, banging repeatedly on the great wood barrier.

When her pleas went unanswered, she pulled out her phone and called him.

He didn't pick up.

"Thor," she yelled again. "Please open up so I can talk to you."

Nothing.

"Thor!" She rang the bell repeatedly. Pounded on the door. "Thor!"

"Are you kidding me?" she finally yelled, stepping back and looking up at the second-story windows as if he'd be standing there watching her lose her shit. She could see no evidence that he was there, but she started yelling up at them just the same.

"I told him I love you," she cried. "Right after the game. Right at dinner. I told him about you. All about you. I told him how much you mean to me and how wonderful you are. And I told him that I'd hurt you bad, and that I hoped you were going to forgive me, because I can't imagine what I'd do if you didn't."

Silence.

"I told him!" she shouted.

She felt it then.

The fallout.

The overwhelming feeling of fear. The kind of dread that squeezed your lungs and shook up your insides. How was it possible that her God of Thunder, her hero without a cape, wasn't letting her explain? She started to shake.

This is bad, she thought. She needed to get inside. To make him understand how crazy she was about him. How much he truly meant to her.

She stepped forward and rang the bell a dozen times. Too impatient to wait any longer, she stole around the side of the house to the garage and pulled the thing open, very grateful it wasn't locked or that he hadn't bothered to install an electric door opener. She tripped her way past Big Red and to the house door, only to find it—oh, thank God—unlocked.

Moving through the mudroom and into the dimly lit kitchen, she passed into the family room and headed for the stairs to the second floor. As soon as she put her foot on the bottom step, she was greeted with a growl from the top.

"Do. Not," he ordered. "Not one more step. Do you understand?"

Missy blinked back a tide of tears, her head immediately emptying of everything except fear. She couldn't move. Just stared up at him.

"You talk to your father every day. Every day I hear about your conversations with him. Big things. Little things. I *know* that man. At least the version of him you know. He's in your heart so strong that there isn't a moment of your life that isn't somehow tied to him."

"He's my"—her breath hitched—"father."

Thor nodded. "I know you have feelings for me, but baby, meeting your dad was one helluva wake-up call. You tell him about lacrosse. You tell him about your work. But I am so far down your list of priorities that I haven't yet been a footnote to one of your conversations."

"That's because he wasn't expecting … this. You. I wasn't expecting this. Us."

"Oh, believe me, I know. You and Daddy were expecting Pinks. And Pinks didn't deliver. And you weren't willing to tell him that, obviously, because he assumed Pinks was going to be with you at the game."

"Please listen to me," she begged. "I was going to explain about Davis and Scarlett and you and me when I saw him this weekend. I just thought it would be easier to give him the whole story—starting with you and me meeting up on my first night in town—if it were over dinner instead of over the phone."

"Understood."

Thor didn't say anything else. Just continued to look down on her with contempt.

She licked her lips, searching her brain for words to soothe him, but he put an abrupt halt to that with a harsh, "Get out."

"Thor," she cried, starting up the steps.

"Out!" he shouted. "I don't want you here. Your team can use my field whenever they want, and because it would hurt them to ban you completely, you may use that field when they are here. But I don't want you in this house. I don't want you to talk to me. I don't want you to approach me in any way. Do you understand?"

"No." She burst into tears. "I don't understand."

"Missy. I'm not a toy or a hobby or a pastime. I may be big and tough, but I'm human. Being your second string is as much as I'm willing to endure. I may love you. Hard. But I gotta find a way to get over that. Because you have made it clear—perfectly clear—that I don't matter."

"You *do* matter," she cried through falling tears. "Of course, you matter."

"Go," he ordered. "I mean it. Don't come back. Don't try to call me. We are done."

"Thor," she sobbed.

"Done," he declared.

Then he turned his back on her and walked away.

Missy didn't go. Didn't leave as he'd ordered. Thor could hear her sobbing at the foot of the stairs as he paced back and forth in his father's bedroom. He'd forced himself all the way down the hall and into the room as far from Missy as he could get, not trusting himself not to cave in to those tears.

He sat down at the edge of his parents' old canopy bed and listened to her sobs. Picturing her collapsed and grieving.

He could go to her.

He could go to her and pick her up, put her in her damn car, and leave her there overnight. Or, he could go to her, pick her up ... and give her comfort.

He wanted to.

He wanted to find a way around this that would work. Because he truly loved her. And he wanted her. But having been down this road, he now knew it was a dead end.

Missy liked him a lot. And she sure was fun. But "fool me once" was the old saying, and he had *never* known it not to be true. He was way too invested. There was no way he could take her back tonight and chance living through another breakup further down the road. To eventually watch her hand in her resignation to Henderson and head back home to Daddy and his big business world. It's what she knew. It's who she was.

He'd been kidding himself thinking they'd make a life together in Henderson. There was no way he and Missy were going to work out. That was a fact written in stone. So, yeah, he thought as he heard her call out for him, this was going to be painful. He and Missy living in the same town until she gave up the ghost. But he wouldn't survive her burning him twice.

So he really didn't have a choice.

After thirty minutes of listening to the woman he loved endure this torture on her own, his body made the decision his head kept protesting. He headed down the stairs.

Gathering a weeping Melissa into his arms, Thor pulled her onto his lap, urged her to lean her head against him, and held on tight. There was no stopping his innate response to kiss her hair or to try to soothe her with his hands or his words. So he just let it happen. Maybe he had to fight to maintain his will when she put her arms around him. But he rocked her until she quieted. Until she had let all of it out.

Then he carried her to her car, placing her in the passenger seat.

Her keys were in the ignition, so he started the hatchback up and headed toward Genevra's without a word. Once there, he came around and carried a sleeping Melissa into the dark house and up the dark stairs. He laid her on the bed, kissed her forehead and then stared down at *the* girl for a long, long time before he finally turned and left.

CHAPTER THIRTY-THREE

Missy woke up Monday morning with Thor's voice in her head saying, "It's all going to be okay," over and over.

That's what he'd promised when he picked her up off the steps last night. When he comforted her with his arms and his body. He promised her that they would survive this. That life would go on.

And that he was sorry, too.

Too.

At first, she'd hoped that him coming down that staircase meant he'd changed his mind. That he'd give her the chance to explain. But the words he whispered weren't those of forgiveness but of shared pain.

Thor didn't want this breakup. For whatever reason, without knowing one little thing about her, Thurgood Watson had fallen in love with Missy McReady the moment he'd laid eyes on her. For real. And then he worked his ass off trying to turn her head and get them to where they'd been before the incident with her father.

Thor didn't want this.

She didn't want this.

But she was definitely the one who needed to fix it. He was done. He'd told her that, and she believed him. He'd been the one who'd worked at their relationship. He was the one who'd laid their foundation brick by brick. And now, hurt and angry, he was done, and yeah—frankly—she couldn't blame him.

But that didn't mean she couldn't pick up where Thor had left off. It didn't mean she couldn't be *his* superhero without a cape. She wouldn't be able to live with herself if she didn't at least try.

"I need to call Davis," she said aloud, remembering that even though he was scheduled to be in Sarasota with Scarlett all week, Crain Carraway had sent AirDallas for him, bringing him in for a four-hour meeting in Henderson today and then flying him back to Red this afternoon. "I need to tell Davis what happened." Getting out of bed, she wondered if maybe he already knew. Wondered if Thor had called him. Told him and the Evans family how badly she'd hurt him. Wondered what the response had been if he had. Wondered if Davis would be willing to plead her case and get Thor to reconsider casting her from his life.

It was worth a shot.

She sighed, moving slowly into the bathroom, her head pounding from the crying jag.

Lord, what a mess she'd been. The poor guy couldn't get rid of her. Had to come down and physically remove her from his home.

Wow.

This falling in love thing sucked.

She typed out, *I need to speak to you ASAP* in a text to Davis before she got in the shower.

His text was waiting for her when she got out, *Before Team Henderson meeting or after?*

Before, if possible. And then she added, *Thor broke up with me.*

Within thirty seconds, the phone rang.

"I checked the calendar. April Fool's Day isn't until tomorrow, so I don't get the joke," Davis said, sounding like his highly energetic, nothing-I-can't-take-care-of self. Man, for the first time ever did Missy hope that was indeed the case.

"No joke. He broke up with me." And then she proceeded to tell Davis the whole, horrible story.

Pinks found Thor mowing the lacrosse field, which he thought was … telling.

Telling him what, he wasn't exactly sure.

He stood on the sidelines waiting for Thor to spot him, imagining how Thor must have felt Saturday after Missy's game.

Pissed off?

Hurt?

Defeated?

He knew better than anyone that the father thing was tricky. He'd had plenty of personal experience since Rye Langford had led the charge to have him run out of town not once, but on two separate occasions.

Pinks wasn't under any delusions that he was probably the last person Thor wanted to see right now since—yeah—he was part of the problem. He'd inadvertently been a thorn in the big guy's side since the moment they'd met. But they'd managed to reach an understanding about Missy a good while back. So Pinks figured coming out here this morning and giving Thor a chance to blow off some steam about this mess might be worthwhile.

Personal feelings aside, as in, his life would suck if Thor and Missy couldn't find their way through this, Thor and Missy were good together.

And together, they were good for Henderson.

Regardless, Missy was hurting. So there was no way he wasn't going to stick his nose into this.

But after standing there ten long minutes, the son of a bitch still hadn't given him the time of day. Pinks looked pointedly at his watch, feeling his valuable time being eaten up by Thor's bullshit maneuver. The man had seen him. No way he could have missed Pinks standing there on that first, second, or third turn of the tractor. But he didn't seem at all interested in coming this way.

Fine. The mountain will go to Muhammad.

Pinks made a beeline for the John Deere, determined not to be further ignored. When he closed in, heading straight for the son of a bitch, Thor stopped the tractor and cut the engine.

"I know I'm not the guy you're itching to see right now," Pinks hollered as he got close.

"You got that right," Thor growled. Pinks immediately slowed up, realizing he was confronting the equivalent of a bear with a thorn stuck in his paw.

"Man, I know you're hurting," Pinks gave him. "I know that shit stung. But it was nothing more than an unfortunate series of events. As soon as the dust settles, you're going to see that."

"Move aside."

"What? Come on. Talk to me."

"I've got nothing to say to you."

"Who else you gonna say it to?" Pinks moved a few steps closer. "I'm right in the middle of this bullshit. I know Missy, I know Jack, and I know you. I know the whole story. I know how it started, and I sure as hell know you're not going to let it end this way. Because when it comes right down to it, this was nothing more than poor communication between Missy and her father. Which has now been completely cleared up."

"Says the Pride of Baltimore."

"Come on, man. I'm on your side here. I have been all along."

Thor shook his head and then turned to look far afield. "Look, I know you're trying to help. But even you can't fix everything."

"She loves you."

"I don't care," Thor said, his face snapping back to Pinks.

"Of course, you care," Pinks argued. "You've done nothing but care since she set foot in Henderson. Don't tell me you don't care."

"I don't care that she loves me. I don't care that she's sorry. I don't care. I *can't* care."

"That's just more bullshit," Pinks spat.

"Really? Is it? You, with your mom and your dad and your grandparents all still alive, think it's bullshit? You with Vance and Hale and all those lovely ladies who've embraced you as family here in Henderson are telling me it's bullshit? You, facing a future with hot little Scarlett Langford, want to tell me that I'm full of bullshit? I … have … no one."

Like a wave, Pinks felt the anger and the sorrow rolling out of Thurgood. It swamped him. Rendered him speechless. All he could do was bear witness to the suffering.

"I have hundreds of acres and no one to share them with," Thor yelled. "You know what I saw the very first time I saw Melissa? I saw the two of us, here. Literally saw the pictures in my head of the two of us, with children, living here. It was as real to me as anything has ever been. More than that, it was compelling. So compelling that I believed in it. I trusted it. Fought for it. I put everything I had left into it."

"That dream isn't dead," Pinks said softly. "That dream is still alive. Missy wants that dream."

"Not like I do."

The two men stared at each other, facing that truth.

Every step Thor had taken since the moment he saw Missy, he'd taken with her in mind. Putting her first. He was as committed as a man could be.

Missy's path to Thor was far less direct. And it was hard for Pinks to argue that if she'd gotten to where Thor stood, to where Thor thought they stood, Thor wouldn't have been a surprise to Jack McReady.

"I'd have given this up for her," Thor said. "Do you know that? If she really wanted to move back to Baltimore, I was prepared to sell it all to Hale. So this little incident in Orlando has been one hell of a wake-up call. I was prepared to sell off what meant the *world* to my father. Sell off my *family's history*. My *heritage*.

"Her father had never once heard my name," he told Davis. "I gave her everything. She couldn't even give me that."

When Davis started to speak, Thor interrupted him again. "I understand Missy'd get around to mentioning my name eventually. I've just come to the conclusion that eventually isn't good enough." He took a deep breath. "So," he said, looking around a bit before coming back to Davis. "I appreciate you coming out here today. We've become friends, and that's not going to change. But I will ask you to leave this be. I'm happy to talk to you about anything else, but not this.

"Not our girl.

"Not anymore."

CHAPTER THIRTY-FOUR

Thor watched Pinks leave. Watched him get in Hale's One-77, back up, turn around, and gingerly drive that low-riding machine down his gravel drive.

Then he looked around him, at all the land, at all the elements, at all the space … at all the loneliness.

It wasn't his imagination. The colors were gone. Just like the day he buried his pop, the colors had simply vanished, somehow hidden from his view. A deep-seated fear settled in his gut, registering a serious wake-up call.

Because the last time this happened, it signified his stumble into the bog of depression.

And then he stopped eating and shaving.

And that's when the PTSD symptoms emerged.

In desperation, Thor swung his gaze back toward Pinks just in time to see the sleek sports car drive out of view. There was no denying he needed people in his life. He'd learned that when his mother had passed. Learned it again—the hard way—when his pop died. And now that his busted-up heart was dealing with another loss, he knew he needed to protect the only thing he had left.

His mind.

He needed to protect his mind.

Thor sat on the John Deere contemplating that.

The one thing that had become crystal clear during that endless ride home from Florida? He was not throwing his heritage away for Missy or anybody else. This land was his, and he was going to respect it, live on it, and make his living from it. So even if he had nothing else right now, he had that.

But he knew he needed more.

So ... fuck it. He'd commit.

He'd join Team Henderson. Because his land wasn't going to be worth much if the town beside it folded. And for as much as he protested not wanting to be on a team anymore, hell, he was a great team player. In fact, he didn't know how to be anything but. Sitting out here by his lonesome would be a slow form of suicide, and hell, even Missy wasn't worth that.

He got off his tractor. Left it in the middle of the lacrosse field. Left the keys in it so the coach could move the damn thing herself if she wanted to. Then he took himself inside for a shower. He was starting a new chapter.

Day One on Team Henderson.

When Davis stuck his head inside the conference room, Missy stopped Josh in mid-sentence and begged his forgiveness.

"Just one second, Josh, if you don't mind." She didn't wait for Josh to answer, too anxious to hear what happened when Davis went out to see Thor. She followed Davis and then preceded him into his private office, where he closed the two of them inside.

"What happened?" she asked, spinning around. But the miserable look on Davis's face told her everything.

She took a deep breath, rose to her full height, and crossed her arms over her stomach, making an effort to stem a new flow of tears.

"He needs time," Davis said.

"Did he say that?" she asked hopefully.

"No. That's me giving you the best advice I can at the moment."

"So, he's done." It's what he'd told her. She shouldn't be surprised.

"That's what he said. Today."

"Okay," she said, not meaning it at all. "Okay. So?"

"He's hurting," Davis went on.

"I know that."

"Bad," he told her.

"You're not helping."

"Because I don't know how," he said honestly, staring her straight in the eye. "He asked me not to speak to him about you again."

She nodded.

"I'm going to respect that for the time being."

She nodded again.

"But I'm here for you in any other way," he swore. "My goal is to get the two of you back together, if that's what you truly want."

"Of course, that's what I want. How could you think that's not what I want?"

"Miss. You can't monkey around with him. Thor's serious. He's lost a lot of people in his life. Losing you on top of that ..." Davis shook his head. "He's protecting himself. He wants a wife, he wants a family, and he wants it on his plantation. So, if that's not what you want, you need to walk away. You need to leave the man alone."

"How can I do that?" she whispered, trying really hard not to cry. "I'm crazy about him. But marriage and kids? How can I know he's truly the one after only a couple months?"

Davis just stared at her, wiggling change around in his pocket. Licking his lips.

"What?" she pleaded.

"He knew. The day he met you. The day he first laid eyes on you. He knew you were the one he wanted, for all of that."

Missy's shoulders fell.

"That's what you're dealing with," Davis stated.

She shook her head. She'd known that. She'd known that was exactly what she was dealing with. She just didn't think she'd have to deal with it all so soon.

"What are you going to do?" Davis asked.

Her head sprung up. "What do you mean?"

"Are you gonna stay in Henderson?"

The question threw Missy. "What?" But by the skeptical look he was giving her, she understood. "I'm not leaving Henderson," she said defiantly. "I'm in love with Thor," she told Davis. "I have work to do here. My team is here," she said, angry now that he would think she'd jump ship and leave everybody and everything she'd grown to care about.

"Okay. Whew," he sighed. "I just ..."

"You just what?" she snapped. She'd had enough. Pinks was just ... Davis. He was not a superhero. He was definitely not her hero in any way, shape, or form. "Get out of my way," she said, busting by him, making sure to check him with an elbow to his rib as she went.

"Uooph," Davis exclaimed, grabbing his stomach. "You're welcome," he shouted after her.

Thanks for nothing, she thought, storming back to the conference room. She stopped short when she realized Vance, Hale, and the rest of Team Henderson had already gathered for the weekly ten o'clock.

"Okay," she said, settling herself down, gathering her nerves as she gathered their attention. "Thor has broken up with me," she blurted. "It's my fault. Although unintentional, I managed to severely hurt his feelings." She sucked in a long breath, her bravado fading quickly under the heavy silence in the room and the many stunned expressions directed at her. Davis gave her shoulder a reassuring squeeze as he snuck by with his notebook in hand and took his seat at the table.

"You needed to know," she said, swallowing. "Obviously." She hesitated, wondering what more there was to say.

"What happened?" Hale asked, his voice holding nothing but warmth and concern.

"I ... he ..." She sighed. "He met my father in Florida this past weekend. I hadn't told my father about Thurgood. That didn't sit well with Thor."

"Noooo," Vance dragged out. "I don't imagine it would."

"Yeah. My bad," she said, owning it.

She was going to say more, wanted to say more, but heck, these men were here for a business meeting, not a sob story. "We'll start the meeting with Josh's update on the website so he can get back to school. Then we'll bring in the CC Henderson group before we get into the updates on the sports academy. Today's the day everybody starts working together. Josh." She indicated he should take her spot at the head of the table as she moved to take her seat.

Forcing herself to take copious notes on everything that was being said kept her mind from wandering too far into God of Thunder territory. Although when an idea did occur to her about how she might begin to soften Thor, she wrote it down in the margin of her notebook. She was reading the list over while everyone was reseating themselves after a short break when Thor himself came through the door.

Her heart stopped, her mouth fell open, and hope sprung eternal.

His big, burly body was dressed in casual business wear, not the flannel and denim she was used to seeing him in. He was fresh from the shower, and his gorgeous, thick hair had been styled. He had a little scruff going along his jaw, but it was obvious he'd shaved around it, so it must have been left intentionally. His bright blue eyes darted around the room and landed directly on her for a split second before he pulled them off and stood inside the door.

"Got room for one more?"

"You in?" Brooks asked with surprised enthusiasm.

"I'm in," he said directly to Brooks. "I know your CEO and I are on the outs, but hell, that's a small town for ya. The two of us will learn to work around it," he promised, speaking like what was happening between the two of them was no big deal. "And considering the circumstances, I'm sure y'all will forgive me for canceling the Party at the Plantation next weekend." His gaze slid to Missy, sending her a very clear message before he went back to addressing everyone else. "I've decided to keep my land, and I'm looking forward to building my future there. I figure if Team Henderson is putting a lot of hope on a hoity-toity academy being built right next to my place, I'd better get my ass on that team. Y'all okay with that?"

"Absolutely," Brooks said.

"Great. Because as of today, I'm dedicating myself to the cause. And I've got some ideas on how to use my land to contribute. Gonna need your input to figure out what's what."

"Take a seat," Brooks urged.

Chairs had been lined up along the wall for the Dallas contingency who were all gaping at what was going down now. The only available seat was directly behind Missy.

Thor strode over to it without casting her a glance.

Missy slapped her notebook shut.

The moment he'd come through the door, she was certain he'd come for her. Instead, he publicly stomped all over her broken heart while bulldozing his way on to Team Henderson. Apparently, he really was moving on and thought she should have a ringside seat to watch him do it.

She started to sweat as panic threatened to engulf her once again. She seriously contemplated what it would look like if she got up and left the room. It was hard not to notice Davis, Hale, and Vance continually glancing in her direction, clearly worried she was falling apart.

Lord knew she had no idea how she managed to hold it together until they broke for lunch. At that point, she didn't care that she was the first one out of her seat, out of the room, and out of the building. She hustled down Main Street as fast as she could to hide—yes, literally hide—in her office.

A few minutes later, cute, sweet, Duncan-the-lawyer pushed open her door to find her standing in the corner of the room.

"Hey. You okay?" he inquired.

She shook her head no.

"Everyone's heading to The Tavern for lunch. Let's you and I go to the club."

She nodded.

"I'll get Annabelle to join us. Give Harry a heads up. When it comes to romantic blowups, Henderson has seen worse than this, trust me. Just ask Brooks and Vance," he said. "I don't know how it works, but between Annabelle and Harry ... I wouldn't count out a miracle."

CHAPTER THIRTY-FIVE

Missy, Duncan, and Annabelle were led to a secluded table where a bottle of tequila replaced the traditional floral centerpiece. At each place setting sat a small crystal saltshaker, a large shot glass, and saucer of lime wedges. Missy had never had a two-martini lunch before, but this looked like it would prove to be the equivalent.

After Duncan—gentleman that he was—helped seat both Missy and his fiancée, he took no time pouring each of them a shot.

It worked for me and Annabelle," he told Missy. "Saved Brooks, Lolly, and Vance and who knows who else. We may as well give it a try for you and Thor."

Missy figured why not? She'd try anything at this point. She followed along with Annabelle, who had clearly done this a time or two.

"So," Annabelle said, delicately dabbing her lips with her napkin. "I think Thor needs a little reminder."

"A reminder?"

"About why he loves you. Why he'd be foolish to let you go."

"Yes. That would be helpful. I'm afraid right now he's only thinking about why he's sorry he ever met me."

"I have an idea. But first, Duncan mentioned your Party at the Plantation has been canceled." Annabelle's look was the perfect blend of business and empathy. "Would you like to hold it at my parents' place? They're in Florida and would truly not object to me hosting a party there. Big back yard. It's not a plantation, but we could still pull it off and get you pictures for the newsletter."

"No, Annabelle, but thank you. I'm happy to put the party on the back burner for now." Missy didn't want Thor to think he or his plantation were replaceable in her eyes. And the last thing she was worried about at the moment was publicity for her business ventures.

"Okay, then, back to the issue at hand." Annabelle waited while overflowing Cobb salads were set in front of them. While Missy was in no mood to eat, Duncan dug in with zeal.

"Lolly and I have wanted to post pictures of you in that lavender dress on our website ever since the Langford wedding. I know you caught Thurgood's eye while wearing that dress here at the club. Duncan will make sure he happens to be here while that photo shoot takes place, say this Thursday night?"

"You're hoping he sees me in the dress and falls at my feet?" Missy couldn't help but scoff at the idea.

"No. I'm hoping he'll remember what he's given up. I want to remind him of everything the two of you've shared up until last weekend when things …"

"Went to shit," Missy finished for Annabelle.

"When things *derailed*," Annabelle corrected.

"Right. Derailed. Sorry, that's the uncouth athlete in me sneaking in."

"No apology necessary," Annabelle said. "I'm quite used to Lolly."

Later that afternoon, after it had taken every bit of courage she had, plus another shot of tequila, to walk back into the Team Henderson meeting and feel Thor's presence at her back, Missy was happy Thor remained absent from lacrosse practice.

Needing to shake things up, she put her team through a new set of drills, several of them done by her USA team in Orlando. She participated in every one of them, desperate to burn off the angst, the heartache, and any remaining alcohol. Then when practice was over, she ran laps around the field, pushing herself physically in hopes of releasing what was jammed up emotionally.

Thor did not come home.

She cut the rest of the lacrosse field with his John Deere, and when finished, tucked it safely inside the shed. Deciding to give up waiting on him, or whatever the hell she was doing by all this procrastinating, she absently gave the sliding glass door a quick tug as she walked by.

And … wow. Unlocked.

In she went, wishing she had a token to leave him. Something, as Annabelle suggested, that would remind Thor of what they had. Of what she wasn't willing to let go.

She searched for pen and paper, writing out a quick note, thanking him for allowing her to use the field, telling him that both she and the girls missed him on the sidelines. Then she stood there, wanting to add so much more.

Figuring he probably wouldn't read it anyhow, she hedged her bets, and left the note unfolded, big as life, right there on the countertop, facing the back door where he was most likely to see it.

When she snuck back inside after practice on Tuesday, the crumbled note was in the trash. In its place was another one written in big red letters.

STAY OUT OF MY HOUSE.

Crap.

CHAPTER THIRTY-SIX

Wednesday, April 3 turned out to be a big, big day in Henderson. Missy's phone buzzed at five-thirty that morning.

"It's a Boy!" the text read.

Beau Evans, grandson to Emelina Flores, son to Genevra Evans, second son to Hale Evans, and brother to Vance Evans, had been born shortly before four a.m. Davis's text insisted Missy head over to the hospital as soon as she was able to represent him since he was back in Sarasota with Red.

Weeks ago, she and Davis had put their heads together to create the perfect gift basket. It contained two plush toys for the new baby. The Oriole Bird, mascot of the Baltimore Orioles and Poe, the mascot of the Baltimore Ravens. There were also various adult treats from their hometown such as Old Bay-flavored Lay's potato chips, fudge-topped Berger cookies, and a six-pack of National Bohemian. It was Davis's and Missy's intention to cultivate Beau Evans's allegiance to the right teams early. They decided to save the toddler-sized lacrosse stick for his first birthday.

Missy was extremely curious to see just what an hours-old member of the incredibly gorgeous Evans family would look like. And she was greatly relieved that, at Genevra's slightly risky child-bearing age, all had gone well. Eight pounds, ten ounces, ten fingers, ten toes, and a full head of hair is what Lolly fired back when Missy texted her for details.

With camera in hand—because she was thinking ahead for the newsletter—Missy walked into a full-blown birthday party complete with cake and balloons and standing room only at seven o'clock that morning. With babe in arms, Genevra's warm smile welcomed Missy into the celebration. Just as she was presenting her and Davis's basket of goodies, Thor walked in.

"You and Pinks put your heads together and thought that up, did you?"

Missy turned, stunned to find Thor behind her in the lobby of the hospital as she made her way out.

"Baltimore thing," she stammered. "Wanted to represent."

He scoffed and continued walking right on by.

"Thor," she pleaded, turning to follow him. "Please talk to me."

He spun around so fast she bumped into him. "Look. Why don't you just go ahead and pack your bags? Head on home to your Ravens and your Orioles. Get your big-city life back on track. Because you don't need to be here. Not anymore. You've given Henderson a good run. You've introduced lacrosse and given the town an uptick in digital marketing. But there's no need for you to stick around any longer. Because I've decided to stick around. I'm in. I'm committed. And I'm not going anywhere, ever. In fact, I'm so in, I'm going to become the damn *president* of Team Henderson and invest everything I've got into the place."

"*You're* going to be president of Team Henderson?" she asked, outraged.

"I am," he snarled, putting them nose to nose.

"Then maybe you ought to be aware that you're *talking* to the C … E … O."

"Hey, y'all," Piper called, derailing their heated exchange. "Would anybody mind helping a pregnant woman to her car?"

Both she and Thor turned to help Piper, Thor taking the load of gifts she was wobbling out the door with, and Missy relieving her of her large yellow tote.

"Thank you," Piper breathed. "I think I bit off more than I could chew."

"No problem," Thor grunted, leading the way over to Piper's car like he couldn't wait to get out of Missy's presence. In fact, he didn't speak another word, just opened her trunk, set everything inside, and then turned and walked away, getting in Big Red and peeling out of the drive as fast as he could.

"Wow," Piper said, blinking in disbelief as she watched him go. "Things are as awkward as Vance claimed."

"Oh. Yes. They are indeed." Missy had to take a few deep breaths to reestablish her equilibrium.

"He's hurt. So, whatever he was saying to you, he didn't really mean."

"So you don't think he really wants me to pack up and move back to Baltimore because Henderson doesn't need me anymore?"

"I think he probably means just the opposite."

"Piper, I hope that's true."

"Trust me. When Vance and I started dating, we had this huge argument. Right in the middle of the road. In the middle of the night. And he left me there, on my own, to deal with it."

"Really? Vance left you standing alone on the side of the road in the middle of the night?"

"Oh, I had my car. But, yeah."

"He seems way too protective to have done that," Missy surmised.

"He is. But I'd hurt him bad. He was doing what he could to protect himself."

Missy tilted her head, now very curious. "So what did you do to get the two of you over that?"

"I took a good hard look at myself. Apologized. Baked him dessert."

"Really?" Missy laughed. And then she sighed. "You think you could teach me how to bake a pie?"

"Except for giving birth right now, there's nothing I'd rather do this afternoon. You free?"

"According to the self-proclaimed president of Team Henderson, I am no longer needed. So, yes," she said. "Lead the way to your kitchen."

That evening after practice, Missy let herself into Thor's home and placed the first Big Pie Plate Apple Pie she'd ever made on his kitchen counter. The beautiful stationery Piper had swiped from Genevra's stash read, "I made this for you with Piper's help. She'll attest that it's not laced with arsenic."

∽⁂∽

Thor must have stared at that pie for ten long minutes without moving. He was hungry. Hadn't eaten since lunch. Since he was making a point to stay away from his lacrosse field during the afternoons and evenings, he'd been out in his pop's tractor with a map of his own land in hand.

So, yeah. Homemade pie looked tasty.

The fact that Missy made it for him, not so much.

He stood there straddling the fence, undecided whether to eat the damn thing or to toss it, pie plate and all, into the garbage. Because the CEO of Henderson needed a big message, and leaving his trashcan in the center of his kitchen with that pie in it might finally make it clear that he wasn't interested in anything she had to say.

Still undecided, he licked his lips and took himself off to the shower.

It was two o'clock in the morning, after tossing and turning and not one wink of sleep, when Thor ventured back down into the kitchen, took out a fork, and set about eating the best pie he'd ever tasted in his life.

Damnit all to hell.

The next afternoon, just as Thor was getting ready to vacate the premises before lacrosse practice, his home phone rang.

The sound was rather jolting. He wondered if he'd heard the darn thing ring since before his father passed. Everyone he knew called his cell. He'd practically forgotten there was a home phone.

"Hello?" he answered, curious.

"Thurgood Watson?" came the businesslike baritone.

"Speaking."

"Thurgood. This is Jack McReady. We met last Saturday—"

"I know who you are," Thor interrupted.

"Good. All right. Then I hope you'll forgive this breach of privacy. I … ah, well, my daughter Melissa has not been taking my calls." Thor's brows lifted at that. "I'm aware there's a rift between the two of you, though I'd hoped it would have been resolved by now. I suspect Melissa not answering her phone means the opposite."

"Actually, things are quite resolved," Thor stated firmly.

"May I ask, in what way?"

"Missy's going her way, and I'm going mine."

There was silence.

"Look, Mr. McReady. Melissa—Missy and I have talked this through, and although it's not easy for either one of us, we've decided the best thing to do is part ways."

"The two of you decided?"

"It was my suggestion," Thor conceded.

"Thurgood, I know I'm overstepping here. And maybe one day, if you're blessed with a daughter, you'll understand where I'm coming from. If there is anything in my power that I can do to restore her happiness, I'm going to do it."

"I understand. You're a good father."

"Then you'll hear me out? Give me five minutes of your valuable time to share with you a little of what she told me after we met last Saturday?"

Thor sighed, his stomach turning over on itself. Seeing Missy Monday at the Team Henderson meeting, and then again at the hospital when baby Beau was born, was about all he could take for the time being. Now with her notes and her damned apple pie, no, he didn't think he could listen to what Mr. McReady wanted to tell him.

But he didn't have it in him not to listen to it, either.

"Five minutes," he agreed, and then he closed his eyes and prayed for strength.

CHAPTER THIRTY-SEVEN

Oh, he'd definitely been set up.

Thor knew it the moment he walked into Henderson Country Club Thursday night.

Fucking Brooks.

And fucking Duncan too.

Like he wasn't going to notice what was happening in the foyer of the damn place. All those photography lights set up? A tiny woman dressed in black slacks and a white button-down holding that big round screen at just the right angle so no reflection would be created by the camera's flash? Missy, with her hair down and curled, looking like a fairy princess in his favorite dress?

He would have walked right back out the door too, if he hadn't been thunder-struck for the second time in his life.

He would kill Brooks and Duncan, just as soon as he had the chance. Because it was obvious that the two of them were not on his side. How the hell was he supposed to stop thinking about Missy every time he closed his eyes if they'd arranged to put *this* image back in his head?

She probably had on Nike underwear under that dress, he told himself as he watched her wet her lips with her tongue.

Did she look a little pale under those bright lights? A little thinner, maybe?

She looks hot, Jackass. Keep walking. Just walk right on by.

But his feet didn't move.

Thor stood there mesmerized, feeling like he did the first time he'd seen her. Reenvisioning their life together. He could be mad at her all he wanted, but there was no getting away from the fact that he still had it bad for his Melissa. No, for Missy. Just … Missy.

Damn.

He was there to play cards in the Men's Grill. But he waited until the photo shoot was over. Waited until Missy couldn't help but notice he stood there. Waited for her to approach him. And when she did, all he said was, "Pick up when your father calls. This wasn't his fault."

Then he went and played cards.

Poorly.

CHAPTER THIRTY-EIGHT

On Friday, Missy opened her notebook to look over the ideas she'd written in the margin on Monday. All the ideas she'd come up with to try to soften Thor.

She remained resolved. Determined to somehow be his hero without a cape. Show him she wasn't going anywhere and was willing to wait for as long as it took for him to come around.

Only she hadn't counted on it taking this long.

Or having to endure this much pain.

It may have only been a week since the last time he touched her. Since the last time he offered her a smile. But it felt like a whole lot longer. Like a month maybe. Or right smack dab on the edge of eternity.

But last night, as she laid awake, once again unable to sleep, she reminded herself that the God of Thunder had put in weeks of effort to turn her head. So she was going to offer him weeks as well. Months, if need be. Maybe a full year.

Yeah, because after a full year, somebody, probably Annabelle, would sit her down and gently urge her to move on.

That was bound to be embarrassing.

Still, until somebody did that—somebody other than the God of Thunder himself, who had no trouble finding a plethora of ways to suggest she move on—she was resolute when it came to Thurgood Watson the Third.

Res-o-lute.

So after her various meetings, Missy took the rest of the day off to scour the Internet for ideas to reengage Thor.

She found an obscure little website and took her time crafting an old-school scoreboard for Thor's lacrosse field. The look was in keeping with his farmhouse. Charming, white, simple. But the black lettering at the top was the real reason for the gift. The Phyllis & Thurgood Watson, Jr. Memorial Field.

She hoped he'd like that. Thought that he would. Spent a lot of additional money to get it made quickly, calling the lone artisan and pleading her case over the phone. He said he'd do his best because he was a sucker for a good love story.

She hoped that's what she was creating. A good love story. One with a happy ending.

Piper stopped by Friday evening, gifting Missy with her own Big Pie Plate, a handful of her easiest recipes, and a bag of ingredients. She directed Missy while sitting in a kitchen chair, instructing her in the how-tos of baking, while keeping her up-to-date on Genevra and baby Beau, and how Hale and Vance fought over whose turn it was to hold him. That *and* the baby's name. Vance continually called him Brody.

Missy laughed at that. "Sounds like it's a good thing you're having one of your own."

"Can't come soon enough," Piper moaned, rubbing a hand over her protruding belly.

"How much longer?"

"A month. Give or take."

"Maybe he'll come earlier."

"My daily prayer," Piper stated.

"And your blood pressure?"

"A teensy bit high, but nothing the doctor is worried about."

"I'm glad that worked out," Missy said. "And thank you for being so kind to me."

"We're all rooting for you."

"No one's taking Thor's side on this?"

"Why would we do that? Being right isn't making him happy. We want him to be happy. We want you to be happy."

"*Genevra* is on my side?"

"Of course. In fact, *Genevra* called Thor on her way to the hospital, while in the throes of labor, and told him he needed to forgive you."

"What? Why then?"

"She'd just found out. Hale didn't want to upset her and send her into labor, so he hadn't mentioned it and asked the rest of us not to. Of course, when Lolly called to check on her mother, she spilled the beans, and that really did set off labor."

"No. You don't think the news of Thor and me breaking up could have sent her into labor, do you?"

"Of course not. She was a whole week overdue. But when she heard the news, she jolted upright from a lounging position, and that's when her water broke. She was thrilled—that her water broke. *But*, she used it as leverage with Thor, telling him that the shock of your breakup sent her right into labor. It didn't sound like she felt bad at all about dumping that into his lap. In fact, she told me to tell you that if he doesn't come around before she's fully back on her feet, she'll teach you how to make fried chicken. Thor loves her fried chicken."

"He does, that," Missy chuckled, imagining herself frying a chicken. She shrugged. "I'm willing to do anything. Tell Genevra I'll take her up on her offer as soon as she's up to it."

And although Missy's mood lightened while Piper was teaching her to bake, and the feeling stuck around afterwards while she soaked her muscles in Genevra's claw-footed tub, once she set her book down and turned out the light, she was right back inside the grip of despair.

Lonely.

Sad.

Anxious.

She talked herself down for one solid hour before she got up, got dressed, and drove the dessert she'd made out to the Watson plantation.

It was past midnight, or maybe even past one, by the time she got there. She didn't look at the time. It didn't matter. She was so miserable she was looking for relief in any form she could get it. So if Thor was still up watching TV and gave her hell for sneaking into his house with a delicious dessert, she'd take it. Any attention from Thor at this point was better than nothing.

The house was dark, the slider slid unlocked. Missy took her Big Pie Plate with the Butterfinger Fudge Cookie Bars and carefully placed them in the same spot she'd previously left her notes and apple pie. Then she stood perfectly still and listened.

Nothing.

No Ranger-ready sounds coming down the steps, intent on reaming her out for yet again disobeying his order to stay out of his house.

Crazy as it seemed, Missy was disappointed.

She cast her gaze on the back door. Imagined herself walking through it and getting back in her car. She imagined the ride home through the dark countryside, then through the empty streets and back to Genevra's dark house and empty bed.

She couldn't do it.

Couldn't face another night like the last six.

So she turned toward the steps instead. Tugged her shirt out of the waistband of her jeans and drew it over her head as she climbed the stairs.

His bedroom door was open. The lights were off. There was no sound at all. Maybe he was holding his breath. Just like she was.

Because there was no way he wasn't awake. Wasn't aware that she was there. And as she quietly unzipped her jeans and slid them off at the foot of his bed, for the first time in a week, she had a glimmer of hope. If he hadn't stopped her yet, he wasn't going to.

She hadn't slipped under the comforter fully before his hands were on her, tugging her toward the center of the bed, tucking her body underneath his.

His voice was low and rough when he said, "This doesn't change anything," as he went about divesting her of her bra and stripping her of her underwear.

"It'll change tonight," she told him, pushing his boxers down as far as she could reach.

His massive body rolled and shifted, getting rid of clothes. He positioned her limbs and his own before he came to rest on top of her, his weight levered over his forearms, one of his thighs stuffed between both of hers. He didn't hesitate to dip his chin and kiss her neck. And as much as she liked that, she wasn't letting him get away with it either. She caught his head, tilted his face up, and pressed her lips to his.

He didn't avoid kissing her then. No, he let his hurt and anger pour over her. His kiss was hard and aggressive, messy and raw. Then he wrapped his muscular arms underneath her, holding her against his torso before rolling them both. "You want to take charge? Fine," he said, pushing at her shoulders, moving her chest off his, and then clasping her thighs and spreading her legs across his pelvis. He rolled his hips up forcefully, leaving no question about what he wanted. "Have at it."

Missy pressed her palms against his chest as she tried to stabilize herself on top of him. When he clasped his hands behind his head, like he wasn't going to participate, she decided she was having none of that. She tugged at his wrists, breaking the connection, pulling his hands to her breasts.

He may be angry with her. He may be hurt. But his hands still enjoyed her breasts, and it didn't take long before his mouth remembered it liked them too. He jackknifed into a sitting position, wrapped one arm around her lower back, and pulled her body up higher and closer. His mouth closed over a breast, sucking the flesh in hard, and then he used his teeth to scrape her skin as he pulled away until he'd caught her nipple between them.

His tongue and his teeth worked her over while his free hand reached around and directed his masterpiece to ground zero.

Their subsequent connection was sublime.

He had her hair bunched up in his hands, his lips moving up to lock on hers as her body adjusted around him. They kissed with a passion that contained the heat of their discord, the fierceness of their longing, and their frustration at being denied. It was all there. Rage. Lust. Obsession. Agony.

Love.

She loved him. She loved Thor. And she wanted to do right by him. Wanted to put him first and forsake all others. Sex might not be the answer, but it was bringing forth clarity. He hadn't written her off, not entirely. He was straddling that fine line between love and hate. She was committed to pulling him back to her side—to love—however long that would take.

When the kiss fell apart because their bodies had found another way to play out their clamoring emotions, she gave him what he'd originally wanted. Pressing him back into the mattress, she took it upon herself to push his hands up toward the back of his head. Then she pressed her own hands against his massive chest until she was sitting upright, circling her hips, grinding herself against him, bringing them both to the place where nothing else mattered but what pleasure their bodies working together could provide.

She didn't think about putting on a show. Didn't worry about if he was watching her, or if he had his eyes closed. She fought for her own gratification, completely aware that being with Thor like this ever again was no guarantee. So she made it good for herself, felt him making it good for himself, took it slow, came hard …

And then was flipped onto her back so he could pound his way home.

CHAPTER THIRTY-NINE

Missy woke when Thor rolled from her. Over to his side of the bed. Facing away.

She should probably go, she thought. It was his bed. She hadn't been invited. As much as she resolved to be persistent, she didn't want to undo any progress by being pushy and making him face her and their shared nightmare first thing in the morning. She waited another minute, hoping he'd fallen asleep before she quietly shifted, making moves to get out of bed.

Thor's arm reached behind him, stopping her. "Not 'til daylight," he said, still facing away. "Don't want you on the roads 'til daylight."

Then he pulled his arm back, leaving her alone on the far side of his bed.

O-kay.

He still didn't like her much, but she'd take the breadcrumbs and be glad he didn't want her falling asleep at the wheel either.

And staying put until daylight sounded just fine to her. So she turned onto her side, facing away from Thor, and snuggled down for the first decent night's sleep she'd had since the incident.

Some might call pressing her foot back against his calf pushy.

She preferred to think of it as persistent.

Every trace of Melissa was gone when Thor dragged himself out of bed the next morning. He'd tossed her underwear into dead spots in his room, but she'd managed to find them—without waking him—and had flown the coop.

Just as well, he assured himself. He had nothing to say to her, except maybe thank you for a good night's sleep. He sure had needed it, and his body felt better for it.

The sleep.

Not the sex.

Whatever.

He shut his mind down, got in the shower, and spent a full morning out in the rose garden. Until he *realized* he was in the rose garden. The one Missy had inspired, and the one he'd abandoned a week ago.

Goddamnit.

He wasn't taking her back.

He *couldn't* take her back.

Yeah, he still loved her. But he loved a comfortable bed, air-conditioning, and clean water, and had managed to live chunks of his life without those too.

Still, his resolve was slipping, no doubt about that. And that dessert she left wasn't helping things either. Because he was hungry. And thirsty. And lonely. *And really liked her in his bed.* And he was standing in a rose garden inspired by her, for Lord's sake. With a fucking lacrosse field a dozen steps from his house.

"Man," he sighed out loud, realizing he was into Missy so deep that no ladder was long enough to help him climb out.

And honest to God, he didn't know how he was going to live with himself, one way or the other. He was damned if he did and damned if he didn't. Because he could take her back, and yeah, all the colors would return, and his life would be a whole lot easier. Except he'd never fully trust her. Always hold a piece of himself back. Never fully commit. Always be wobbling on the tightrope of "will she stay or will she go?" trying to protect himself from another round of heartbreak.

He stood still, leaning on his shovel, looking around the grounds, the house, his life. *This was a damn mess.*

He glanced down at the shovel in his hands and then chucked the thing toward the dormant rosebushes still waiting to be planted.

He stomped the mud off his boots and pulled the work gloves from his hands as he headed to the garage. He changed into his Army boots, laced them up good and tight, and then hoisted the forty-five pound, locked-and-loaded rucksack onto his back, setting the timer on his watch for three hours.

Desperate for relief from his own thoughts, he vowed to go fifteen miles. Physical exertion was the only way he knew how to shut 'r down.

CHAPTER FORTY

"Bigger, stronger, faster."

"Pardon me?"

Viper cocked her head, eyeing the lone starting sophomore on Henderson High's baseball team. Henry DuVal had a natural athletic ability. He could play any sport in high school and stand out in all of them. But if he wanted to play baseball in college, he needed to be ... "Bigger, stronger, faster. That's what the college recruiters are looking for."

When the sandy-haired, brown-eyed, all-American boy simply stared, she decided to introduce herself. "I'm Marcie Watts," she said, pushing off the rear of her car and holding out her hand. "I used to be with the Orioles organization. You've heard of Cooper Crenshaw?"

"The Coach?" Henry responded, shaking her hand. "Sure."

"He and I met while I was working on an advertising campaign for the Os." Not exactly true, but close enough if the kid had the wherewithal to Google her. "Spending time with him and spending time deep inside a major league organization gave me a lot of insight."

"What kind of insight?"

"Insight on how the best players are ... made. Look," she said quickly as Henry started to rock between both feet. "I don't mean to pry. I've just noticed that you're one of the team's top players. I was wondering what kind of weight training regime Coach Evans has suggested. As an outfielder, you need to be fast and agile. As a top hitter, you need to have more muscle and weight behind your swing."

"Coach Evans has us lifting some, stretching a lot, but during the off-season, he likes to see us doing circuit training. Gets the cardio and weight training in all at one time."

"Sure. That's great. At this level. But, my advice to you? Given that college scouts are now attending your games?" She held up three business cards, all from Southern schools, as if she'd just collected them today. "Hit the gym and focus on weight training. Don't be afraid to bulk up a bit. You've got a good eye and a fair swing. Putting a little muscle behind the bat will improve your RBIs and turn your doubles into home runs. And it won't take long, trust me." She handed him the cards.

"That'd be cool." Henry's eyes lit up when he saw the card from Duke's assistant coach. "Wow. Okay," he said, more engaged. "I'll see about doing that."

"Here," she said, handing him a different card. "It's a website that'll give you some pointers. Plus suggestions on what to eat before and after a training session to help your body build muscle."

"You mean like protein powder?"

"Right. Protein powder, supplements, shakes. The whole deal. I mean, you certainly don't need any of that stuff. But if you're interested in maximizing your efforts and seeing results sooner rather than later, it'd be good to take a look."

"Couldn't hurt," he agreed, rubbing a finger over the card and studying her.

"I'll be watching you. I think you've got a real shot at getting a look from some of the better baseball schools," she said as she turned and walked to the door of her car. "You need anything, just let me know," she threw over her shoulder without giving him another look.

"Sure thing. Thanks," Henry said, pocketing all of the cards and heading farther down the parking lot.

Viper watched him from her rearview mirror, adjusting it as he went. She had a backup plan if Henry didn't take the bait. But her research suggested that the name DuVal was prominent in this Podunk town and would make a better headline. The fact that Brooks Bennett was dating Henry's cousin, Lolly, just made Henry all the more appetizing.

CHAPTER FORTY-ONE

"You do realize that she tells me everything, right?"

Thor's head whipped around at that little bit of information.

"It's been *three weeks*," the Pride of Baltimore stressed. As if Thor had no idea how long he and Missy had been engaged in this struggle.

"Your point?" Thor asked, taking a menacing step toward Pinks.

Pinks didn't back down. The two men faced off in the middle of Main Street, just after their latest Team Henderson meeting broke up.

"Look, man, I know you asked me not to speak to you about *our girl*," Pinks sneered. "So I've turned a blind eye to a helluva lot of your bullshit over the past several weeks. But letting her sneak into your bed three separate times and not making sure she stayed for breakfast the next morning? Not cool, man. Not cool."

Yeah? Tell me something I don't know.

When Thor refused to defend himself, Pinks went on. "I see you looking at her," he practically shouted. "Nothing's changed. You still love her. So put yourself out of your misery, man. Put *her* out of her misery. What the hell are you waiting for?"

Thor shook his head. He didn't know. He didn't know what he was waiting for. Frankly, he thought he'd be having this conversation with Missy. Thought she'd be the one to finally get in his face and read him the riot act. Thought he'd figure his shit out then. Right when push came to shove.

Because yeah, he'd eaten her fried chicken. Enjoyed every damn morsel of it. Then sat there in silence and watched her clean up his kitchen only to leave him with dessert, coffee, and a late-night snack before she headed home.

And when that scoreboard was delivered, he watched from long range as Missy saw to its installation. Then made sure she was long gone before venturing over to take a closer look. Saw that big yellow ribbon and his momma and pop's names and almost folded right then. He read the card attached to the ribbon. A thank you from the Henderson girls' lacrosse team. When he called Rett, she confirmed what he suspected. The team didn't know anything about the scoreboard. It was all Missy.

Though he still wasn't speaking to her, he couldn't stop himself from finishing the rose garden. Even found himself pacing the sidelines during her last two games. Left Big Red in her driveway, keys inside and lacrosse goals loaded on the day she had to cart them thirty miles away for a weekend tournament. One she'd arranged so her girls would get more game-playing opportunities. Hell, he wondered why she didn't just host the tournament at his place until he realized she hadn't asked him for a damn thing since the night of their breakup.

She just gave.

Even when he didn't say thank you.

And continued to give.

Even when he didn't acknowledge the little things she was doing. Like leaving him research on ideas he was running by Team Henderson for use of his land. Like the desserts she'd baked and the notes she'd left.

Like the lingerie.

Yeah, he couldn't get the words *Adore Me* or the robin's-egg-colored box they were printed on out of his mind. Delivered by UPS to his front porch, inside was the softest, sexiest, Caribbean-blue nightie Thor had ever had the pleasure to handle. The note said she'd signed him up for a monthly delivery. One she'd be willing to model for him any time he asked.

All he had to do was ask.

The girl was *killing* him.

And the Ranger in him was no match.

She found a way to get around, leap over, or tunnel under all of the defenses he kept hammering into place. His Ranger training was no help in extracting his own heart from this hostage situation.

So yeah, what the hell *was* he waiting for?

"The other shoe to drop." The words fell out of Thor's mouth, startling him and Pinks at the same time. *Really?*

"*What* other shoe?" Pinks yelled, clearly fed up.

Thor yelled back because he was just as frustrated. "I don't know. A coaching job offer from a school that actually knows how to play the game? Her father swooping in offering up an event-planning position in his world-wide company? Another old boyfriend stealing her affection? I just don't know."

"Oh, come on. That's all crap."

"Maybe," Thor conceded. "But after being severely shell-shocked, I can't help but keep a lookout for every other possible negative scenario. That's what I'm trained to do."

"This is not war, man."

"Seems a little bit like it, dude. Believe me. The stakes are just as high."

"You gotta trust her," Pinks insisted. "Missy's not putting herself out there for you over and over just to shut you down again. I told her on day one she couldn't monkey with you. That either she needed to be all in or she needed to stay out. The way she's been going at this? What she's put up with? She's definitely all in. Now, what's it gonna take for you, my friend? What's it gonna take for you to realize you're doing nothing but wasting valuable time?"

"I don't know, man." Thor shrugged. "I really don't know. Something."

The two of them faced off in silence, Pinks clearly not happy with Thor's indecisive conclusion.

"You're stringing her along," he accused, putting a finger in Thor's face. "Making her pay tenfold for one lapse in judgment. I swear to God, if there is not a positive outcome for Missy at the end of all this bullshit, I'm gonna kick your ass. You may be twice my size and have access to military-grade weaponry, but they don't call me the Ninja for nothing," he assured him before he turned and walked away. "Just ask Vance," he yelled over his shoulder.

Shit.

CHAPTER FORTY-TWO

Like a damn leopard in a cage, Thor thought as he paced his bedroom. It was one thirty in the morning, and he couldn't get that conversation with Pinks out of his mind for nothing.

It was never his intention to make Missy *pay* for what had gone down. His intention was to end things and get on with his life. Figure out a way to live it without her in it. Only, thanks to Missy's attempts at reconciliation, that was proving downright impossible.

So now, *he's* the asshole.

Because he didn't have the conviction to stiff-arm her when she crawled into his bed. To not indulge in what she dangled in front of him. He didn't have the fortitude not to take a step out of his anguish and find relief, if only for a few brief moments.

Maybe he couldn't put the brakes on what was hurtling down the track. Hell, if his woman showed up here tonight, no chance he'd turn her away. He'd welcome her with open arms. And it had never once occurred to him to lock the back door.

So, yeah. What the hell *was* he waiting for? If he couldn't say no, he needed to suck it up and say yes. Put the two of them out of this misery. He knew better than most that life held no guarantees. And history showed he had managed to survive brutal heartache before. Chances were, he'd most likely be able to do it again. But building back his dream of a life with Missy, knowing he could lose her all over again? He just didn't think he was there yet.

But he loved her.

There was no denying it.

So there was bound to be something that pushed him over the edge. Made him give into the dream. Because ultimately, he knew deep down inside that for him, there were no other options.

Just before four thirty, Thor's eyes opened to the sound of a large SUV rolling up his graveled drive. His jeans were zipped and fastened before he heard two car doors slam shut. Too loud for a home invasion, still a visit at this hour had bad news written all over it. He took the time to pull on a long sleeved T-shirt. Even got his socks on and his work boots laced up before the doorbell rang.

Opening the door, Thor found Vance as grim as he'd ever seen him. But it was Pinks who encapsulated deadly calm when he told him, "Time to man up."

CHAPTER FORTY-THREE

"Missy's dad?" Thor didn't know how he knew. He just did.

Pinks nodded as Vance said, "Get your phone. You may have connections."

All right. So not a car accident.

Thor grabbed his wallet, his phone, a jean jacket, and following his gut, he grabbed his rucksack.

The three men walked in silence, Pinks slipping into the backseat of Vance's Land Rover with Thor. He started talking the moment Vance put the SUV in reverse.

"Jack's been kidnapped," Pinks said.

"Where?"

"South Africa. Jack's CFO, Gus Hoenke, was contacted at two a.m. Kidnappers are demanding five million dollars."

"Any proof they actually have Jack?"

"It was a video call. Showed Jack sitting on the floor, his back to the wall. Didn't appear to be tied up, but looked ... shaken."

"Shaken?"

"Gus said he looked a little roughed up. No apparent blood. Definitely conscious. In fact, Jack did the talking, repeating what they were telling him off camera. The thing is, the CFO says Jack's got a tracking device. Literally, like in his hip. So somebody should be able to figure out exactly where he is."

"Who?"

"The GPS company who monitors the chip."

"Which is?"

"They are figuring that out now."

"How do you know all this?" Thor asked.

"Mrs. McReady phoned my father, asking if he'd alert me to the situation so I could go be with Missy. She didn't want Missy hearing the news alone."

So Missy didn't know yet. Yeah, he couldn't get sidetracked thinking about that right now.

"What the hell is Jack doing conducting business in South Africa? Africa's a freaking shit-show. No border patrols. No nothing."

"Not there on business. He's down there swimming with the sharks."

"What?"

"Yeah. He and his diver buddy. Getting in a cage and swimming with the Great Whites has been on their bucket list."

"The man needs a better list," Thor muttered.

"True that," Pinks said.

They sat in silence, Thor now stuck thinking about all kinds of things he didn't want to think about it.

"How bad is this?" Pinks asked.

Thor looked in his direction. "Depends who we're dealing with. But if they're already asking for ransom, I'd say he's got a good chance of getting out alive. Better than fifty-fifty."

Vance spoke for the first time. "You know anybody with skills sitting in South Africa?"

Thor's body rocked back and forth while his ego fought with good ol' common sense. It didn't come easy, but while coasting his palms over his thighs, he accepted the logistics of getting him on the ground as part of the direct action. As much as he wanted to gather his team, it was a good seventeen-hour flight once the six of them were assembled. Vance's idea was better. Way better. Especially considering Thor had an emotional stake in this one. He sighed, leaned back, and gave up control.

"You remember meeting Rhodes and Tinker? Both Delta Force. They're gonna have connections," he said, thinking aloud. "Connections who know how to get things done quickly and under the grid. We may also have somebody in intelligence. Picks knows for sure. I'm out of that loop."

"Odds go up or down if they get involved?"

"Up. Way up. Especially if they know where McReady is. Not gonna cost five million, but it won't be cheap."

"I think it's safe to say money is no object," Pinks advised.

Thor didn't have big money to bargain with, but he was willing to promise whatever to whomever in order to bring about a positive outcome. He pulled out his phone and called Picks because he still had his foot in the game and he'd have quick access to Rhodes and Tinker. Best to hand it off to the one he trusted implicitly.

He relayed the facts and then told Picks he was handing his phone over to Davis Williams. "Code name: Pride of Baltimore. He's the one who is gonna connect you to whomever they've got handling the details in Baltimore. Hopefully, they'll have a location soon. Do whatever you can to set this up in South Africa, but if we need to suit up and go, we go. Until it comes to that, you two are running this op. I'm out."

Thor cut the call and handed his phone to Davis.

"He'll get 'r done?" Pinks asked.

"He salivates over this shit. Think you can get him in with Baltimore?"

"Absolutely. Where are you going to be?"

"Holding Missy's hand."

Pinks nodded. "Good call."

CHAPTER FORTY-FOUR

Way before dawn, Missy heard car doors slamming and then low murmured voices below her bedroom window. When she heard the sturdy rap against Genevra's screen door, she was out of bed, looking out the window. She couldn't see who was below, but she thought she recognized Vance's Land Rover in the drive.

Wondering if Piper was okay, or if she'd overlooked an email about an out-of-town sports academy meeting, she pulled on yoga pants and a long T-shirt, then stuffed her feet into clog-like slippers and pulled on her favorite hoodie. She was winding her hair up into a knot as she opened the door, expecting Vance, but finding Davis standing in front of him.

"Everything okay?" she said as her gaze landed on Thor. "What's going on?" she wondered, her confusion mounting.

"Can we come in?" Davis asked.

"Sure. Of course." She stepped back, making way for all three of the men saying, "What's up?" to Davis, "Piper okay?" to Vance, and "You all headed out of town?" to Thor.

"Missy," Davis started. But she wasn't focused on Davis. Her eyes were locked on the God of Thunder. Because for the first time in weeks, he wasn't dodging her gaze. He was returning it.

"Yeah?" She pulled her gaze from Thor's and tracked over to Davis, wondering what was happening.

"Your father," Davis said. "He's … " With Missy's mind on Thor and what it meant that he had willingly come to her home, it took her a moment to realize Davis had stumbled. A heavy foreboding settled in, stirring up more confusion. To combat it, she finished Davis's sentence for him.

"He's in South Africa, swimming with sharks." And then she understood. "Oh, God. Did the cage break? Did he get attacked? By sharks?"

"No," Davis said, at the same time Thor moved to her back. She turned her head to look up, over her shoulder at Thor, while Davis kept speaking, bringing her attention back to him. "No problem with the sharks. But after that. He was at dinner. Went to the men's room. Miss," Davis faltered. "He's been kidnapped."

"What?" Missy said, her mental self drifting apart from her physical self.

"Gus Hoenke spoke to him," Davis went on. "He's being held for ransom."

Missy shook her head, truly not understanding. "Gus spoke to him? So he's okay?"

"No," Davis started, but Thor turned her around gently.

"Your father is alive. He's being held for ransom. The kidnappers made a video call to Gus. Gus spoke to your father. Told your mother he looked shaken but not hurt."

"Why? Why would anyone kidnap him?"

"Because he's the CEO of a profitable company," Thor said as he placed a hand on her shoulder and bent down to engage her eye to eye. "This sort of thing happens more often than you hear about. The company pays, the hostage is released."

Missy believed what Thor was saying. She did. But this was her father, so fear tore through her, some of it in the form of tears she tried to blink back. Thor leaned his forehead against hers, speaking softly but firmly. "I've got you. My boys are already on this. Working it from every angle. Your job is to be strong for your mother. We're gonna get you two hooked up by phone. She's gonna need to hear your voice."

Missy's head popped up. "He's got that chip thing they put in dogs," she said. "Only it's a tracking device of some sort."

"Gus is working on getting in contact with that company. If the tracking chip pans out, and my guys have contacts on the ground in South Africa, they move in quick."

"Is that safe? Moving in quick?"

"For your dad, yeah. For the assholes, no."

"But Dad could be shot by mistake?"

"Not gonna happen, Pretty Girl."

"How do you know?" she argued.

"Nobody does this stuff better."

"Who?"

"C.A.G. Well, former Combat Applications Groups. These guys aren't just anybody. They're ex-Delta Force and Navy Seals now working as government contractors providing security in hostile environments. They are the best of the best. And are paid royally to do what they do."

"This is ridiculous," Missy said, feeling her body start to shake. "He wasn't conducting business. He just went to swim with sharks. They should have left him alone."

"Miss," Thor shook her shoulder sharply. "Your mother, babe. You got it in you to call your mother? She knows Davis is breaking the news to you right now, and she is going to want to hear your voice. But not if you're losing it. Deep breaths. For now. Just for now. Let's talk to your mom, see if she's got any more information, then …"

"Then what?" she sniffed.

"You can lose it all you want. I got you," he promised.

Thor watched Missy head up the stairs after pleading she needed a minute before phoning her mother. She claimed to want to use the bathroom, brush her teeth, and muster some courage so she wouldn't dissolve into tears the moment she heard her mother's voice. He told her she had five minutes before he was coming up after her. When she disappeared from view, he turned to Davis.

"Can you charter a plane or something? Get her mother down here? I don't want Missy packing up and driving home right now. But they should be together. Just tell her mom that they'll have more privacy here if this is leaked to the press."

"You worried Missy won't come back?"

Thor nodded. "This goes south, I'm very worried she won't come back."

Davis lifted a brow. "Our little talk get to ya?"

As Thor fumbled for an answer, Vance piled on with, "You and Pinks have a little talk, did ya?"

"We're in crisis mode, assholes. How 'bout you pitching in by making some coffee?" he ordered Vance. "And you make the call to get Missy's mother down here. I'll go up and see that Miss phones home."

Vance gave him a chin lift. "We'll handle things down here. You just go on up and take care of your woman."

Thor grunted his thanks, taking the steps two at a time, his insides churning when he heard her sobs.

He found her curled up on her bed in the fetal position, phone to her ear, crying like her worst fears had already come to pass. He sat down with his back to the headboard and pulled her body up against his chest, easing the phone from her hand.

"Mrs. McReady?" he said into the phone. "This is Thurgood Watson, ma'am. I've got your girl. I'm not gonna leave her side until we get word that your husband is safe."

"Oh, *Thurgood*," the melodious voice drifting through the phone was pleasant, despite the obvious sniffles. "I'm so relieved you're there. Missy and her father are so close, you know. I can't imagine there's anyone who'd bring her more comfort than you right now."

"Except her momma," Thor said. He couldn't help feeling a small degree of relief realizing the woman had heard his name. "Ma'am, have you been informed I have contacts who can help?"

"Yes. I believe the security company we're working with here has spoken to a friend of yours. Ah, Bryce McNally. He mentioned he goes by Picks? Do I have that right?"

"Yes, ma'am. I'd trust him with my life."

"As I understand it, they are negotiating the available options. Thurgood, my Jack trusts this security company. He hand-selected them. I'm going to have to trust their decision on how to handle this."

"Absolutely. Like I said, I'm sticking by Missy's side. I just wanted to offer up whatever help I could."

"I appreciate it. More than I can say."

"I'd like you to come down here once you're able. I think it would do the two of you good, being together. Davis is working the details out, but I implore you to give it some thought."

"I will. Of course. If you'll just stay with Missy until I'm able to get there."

"Count on it."

"Thank you, Thurgood. For everything. Tell Missy I'll see her soon."

"Ma'am."

Thor hung up Missy's phone and placed it on the bedside table. Missy started rubbing at her eyes and reached over to grab a tissue, mopping her face. He eased her head back to his chest, not caring a bit about the tears or snot or whatever his T-shirt was soaked in.

"Your momma's holding up well," he told her quietly. "She's a strong woman. Probably in shock. But she's hanging in there. Staying present. Being a help rather than a hindrance."

Missy simply nodded, trying to get her breath under control while her body shuddered against him.

"I've got you, Miss," he whispered.

She moved her arms from beneath her chest and wrapped them around his waist as best she could. He stroked her hair absently, wondering if Picks had managed to dig up contacts on the ground. Wondering what Jack was facing at that moment. He rerouted his thinking by looking down at *the* girl. When he stroked the hair back off her forehead, she started to speak through her tears.

"Thank you," she sobbed, trying so hard to pull herself together. "Just. If you could just, you know, get me through this," she said, sniffing and crying. "I'll … back off. Thor, I promise. I'll back off."

"You'll what?" he questioned.

"Leave you"—sniff—"alone. Just, stick with me though this. And I'll …"

"Miss. Baby. Pretty Girl. I love you. I'm not … I don't want … Damn."

"It's okay," she told him, wiping her eyes. "I know."

"I don't think you do." He picked her head up with both of his hands and tilted it so he could see her eyes. "I'm done being an ass. I'm not leaving you. Not now. Not ever."

Missy started to cry all over again. Her body shook, her sobs got louder, and she started talking a blue streak, though he couldn't understand any of it. Though he caught the words *you* and *my father* and *sorry* and *miserable*, so he got the point.

"Baby, shh. Shh. Calm down now, yeah?" He wrapped her up in his arms and hugged her tight. "We're okay. I'm okay. I just needed time. And you gave me plenty. I love what you did for me, even when I was too stuck in my own stupidity to express it properly. I ate it up. All of it. Your desserts, that scoreboard, your fried chicken, the notes, the research—love the farm-to-table idea by the way—"

"That wasn't me, that was Davis," she sniffled. "Well, his idea. My research."

"See, I've finally seen the light," he told her. "You and Davis are a team. Team Baltimore. A really good team. I get that now. You and your dad—another team—Team Melissa. One that's got a lot of years to go yet, I promise. We just need to have a little talk with Yoda about his extra-curricular activities. Maybe edit his bucket list." That got a nod out of Missy. "And my boys and I were a solid team. But you? You and I? We're a new team. And we're getting the hang of it."

For some reason, that made her cry harder.

"Pretty Girl, I'm sorry for putting you through all that. I was hurt and scared. There's no denying it. I just needed a little time to figure out that life is made up of highs and lows. And if I don't learn how to pull on my high-water boots or glue my heart back together from time to time, the rest isn't going to be worth wading through. So, I've mended my heart, knowing it's likely gonna break another time or two before it stops beating. But the thing my past has taught me? I'm a survivor. My heart breaks, but it also heals."

"I love you," came her muffled declaration, buried into the fabric across his chest.

"I love you, too, Pretty Girl. We're gonna get through this thing with your daddy together. And the next time I see the man, I'm taking him up on his offer and joining the two of you for dinner. You can be sure of that."

She nodded her head against his chest. "He's gonna come home, right?" she asked.

"Yes, Pretty Girl. You said it yourself. The man knows Jedi mind tricks. And between you and your mother, he's got plenty to live for. I have no doubt that he's coming home."

CHAPTER FORTY-FIVE

It took forty-eight hours for the news of Jack McReady's rescue to hit Henderson. It came in the form of a phone call to Mrs. McReady's cell while she sat on the screened porch of Genevra's cottage, sipping a strong mug of coffee after being up most of the night. The gasp that hit Missy's ears had her racing to the kitchen doorway, watching as her mother picked up the phone with shaking hands and said, "Jack?"

And that's when the flood of grateful tears started.

Thor was there. Davis was there. In less than an hour, the entire Evans household joined them, descending on Missy and her mother in celebration with food, beverages, and baby Beau sound asleep, swaddled tightly in a lightweight blanket.

Word was Jack planned to fly right to them, asking his wife and daughter to stay put so that he could properly meet and thank all those who'd taken care of his family while he had stupidly been kidnapped.

"He said that?" Hale asked while cradling Beau in his arms "That he'd been stupidly kidnapped?"

There wasn't a person there who hadn't taken it upon themselves to speak to Hale about protecting himself from a similar fate. Whether they wanted him to have a chip implanted, take a class on surviving terrorism, or hire one of Thor's Ranger buddies whenever he left of the country, the McReady crisis had definitely made an impression, forcing the town of Henderson to sit up and take notice.

"He blames himself," Mrs. McReady said. "Figures swimming with Great Whites wasn't a particularly smart decision, and maybe he deserved a wake-up call."

Hale looked over at his wife and then at Vance, who had his arm around Piper. "My wake-up call came a year ago," he said. "So I appreciate everyone's concern about me getting a chip like Jack's and everything else. But I love my life. I'm not planning to put myself in harm's way, be it sharks, polar bears, or a toddler's playdate."

"Here, here," Davis said, waving the champagne bottle and pouring it in every type of glass he could find.

Even Piper took a glass of champagne. While rubbing her pregnant belly, she announced that she'd given her son nine full months of alcohol-free development. But a celebration was a celebration, and since he was being born into the Evans clan, he better get used to celebrating. "One sip will not hurt," she declared.

With that one tiny sip, Vance, Jr. responded by creating a celebration of his own. Missy saw it happen. Saw the look on Piper's face as the first contraction hit her. "Whoa," Piper said, handing Vance her glass. "Either I have jumped into full-blown labor, or Vance, Jr.'s determined to be a teetotaler.

"Highly unlikely," claimed Brooks as he and Lolly entered the crowded dining room. They hugged Missy and her mother while Piper, Vance, and Genevra tried to figure out if Vance, Jr. was truly planning to be born today.

"Ah-yeah," Piper squeaked. "I'm thinking he's not happy that he's missing all of the action out here," she said while holding her breath, finishing with a squeaky little "oooh-ee."

"Baby Doll," Vance said, moving her toward the door. "Take a breath, that's it, let's get you to the truck and—"

And that's when it happened. While every eye was on Piper, that's when her water broke. All over Genevra's front porch.

"Okay, yeah, so we're in labor," Vance said, standing there, staring at the mess at his wife's feet. "Pinks! Gonna need you on this."

"Be right there," Davis said, quickly organizing the makeshift bar he'd created on the dining room table. He looked over at Brooks who was all smiles. "Take over for me?"

"Gladly. You're gonna have your hands full," he told Davis. "Vance looks like he's gonna lose it."

"Yeah," Davis laughed. "I hope Piper's all right with me in the labor and delivery suite, because Vance is going to need some hand holding through this."

Davis kissed Missy's cheek on his way out the door. "Let me know when you hear from your father, and I'll text you the headlines from the hospital."

"Good. Thanks. I'd like to be there when things get close."

"We'd all like to be there when things get close," Hale said.

"I'm on it," Davis said, wrapping an arm around Piper's waist and helping her descend the wood steps while Vance held the door, staring down at the wet spot, looking like he was going into shock.

"Come on, Big Daddy," Davis called. "We gotta get your baby momma to the hospital."

Lolly shoved a bunch of bath towels into Vance's hands, which pulled him out of his stupor. "I'm not planning on delivering Vance, Jr. myself," he told her, trying to give them back.

"Have Piper sit on those so she doesn't mess up the seats of your Land Rover."

"Oh. Ah. Okay. Ha!" he laughed. "Yeah. Thanks, better ah … go and … Piper, wait up a second."

The rest of the crowd watched Davis and Vance pile up the towels and then hoist Piper on top.

"Princess and the Pea," Emelina commented. Turning from the window, she asked, "Care to wager on the length of labor?" She sat down, nabbed a paper cocktail napkin and pulled a pen from her handbag. "Five dollars a bet. Winner takes all."

Brunch was served, and this time Missy worked side by side with Genevra preparing it in the kitchen they both knew so well. Brooks did a stellar job at taking over the bar. No one wanted for a traditional Bloody Mary or a very untraditional Bourbon and Ginger. The party was buoyantly high-spirited in anticipation of the arrivals of both Jack McReady and Vance Evans, Jr.

When word came in from Davis that Piper was indeed in labor, but not very far along with the dilation process, they felt at ease continuing the merriment. Hours later, the women went into nesting mode, together cleaning everything and leaving Missy's home spotless and organized.

"I'm going to lie down," Missy's mother said once everyone had gone. "I think I'll finally be able to sleep, knowing your father is now safe." The two women embraced while Missy mentioned she and Thor were headed out to check on his place. She promised they would return for her mother before heading to the hospital.

"You sure you don't want to catch up on some sleep?" Thor asked Missy once her mother was upstairs.

"Pretty sure you're what I want to catch up on," she said, launching herself at Thor, wrapping him up in her arms and legs.

"Big Red is waiting right outside, Pretty Girl," he said, grabbing up his jean jacket and putting his phone in his back pocket without setting her down.

Missy did her best to distract Thor all the way out to his place. Her hands grazing over the spots she knew drove him crazy and a few extras just to be certain. He groaned as he unseated himself from Big Red, but moved well enough to chase her through the back door and up the stairs. Missy squealed as she leapt onto the bed.

"That was honest to God torture," he accused as he toed off his boots. "You are so getting my revenge."

"Promise?" she teased, standing up and bouncing lightly on his bed.

"Damn right. Come here," he said, grabbing her around her thighs and picking her up just to lay her down. He crawled over her body and kissed her like she'd been craving for weeks. Easy and sweet, then hard and fast, and then really slow and definitely steady, all …

the way …

to her…

toes.

"Vance," Piper said calmly, in that sweet girl-that-I-love voice.

"Yes, Baby Doll?"

"Go get Pinks."

"What? No. We're good. I've got this. Honest."

"Vance?"

He mopped his brow again with the washcloth he swiped from the bathroom. "Yes?"

"I need you to sit down. Over there. But before you do, I want Pinks."

"What? Seriously. I'm fine now. Must have been something I ate."

"Vance! You've thrown up twice. I'm worried you're going to pass out, and I can't give birth worried you're gonna hit your head and make me a widow."

"I'm not that bad."

"You are. You are *that* bad. And holding your hand is like holding a mealy, dead fish. I need Pinks. Get him. Now!"

"All right. Okay. I'm … I'm getting the Ninja. Be … right back."

"Hurry," she squeaked as a contraction took over.

Pinks must have been standing outside the door because he was taking up Piper's hand before the contraction started to ease.

"Make him sit down," she said through clenched teeth. "Where I can keep an eye on him."

Vance didn't have to be told by Pinks. He sat down and took a deep breath. He knew he was losing it, and he didn't want to be that guy. That husband. That dad who couldn't handle the birth of his own child. But when the lady doc told Piper she'd give her one more hour and then she was giving her a C-section, well, that's when panic set in.

"Piper," Pinks was saying in a low tone. "You've done your best by Vance, Jr. But right now, trying to keep this going any longer and not listening to the medical professionals, it's not in your best interest or his. Plenty of brilliant children have been delivered by C-section."

"You think?" Piper started to cry. "I really wanted to do this naturally."

It was hearing his wife break down that brought back the man in him. Vance rubbed his face, sucked in air, opened a bottle of water, and downed half of it before moving Pinks out of the way. "I've got this," he told Pinks. "If you'll go out and tell the doctor we've changed our minds, I'd appreciate it."

Then Vance leaned down and kissed the one he cherished. "I'm right here, Baby Doll. You go ahead and cry. I can handle whatever's coming next, so you don't have to."

He felt her squeeze his hand, and he gave her a squeeze back just as a delivery team descended on the room.

Vance walked into the waiting room at the end of the corridor and held his hands up in triumph. Twenty-seven hours after he'd left Genevra's cottage, he finally had the news all of these friends and family members had been waiting for.

"Ten pounds, two ounces and twenty-three inches long," he announced proudly. "Obviously headed for the Hall of Fame."

There was a lot of happy chatter coming at him at once, but it was Genevra's soft voice saying, "So he's good? Everything's good?" that quieted the crowd down.

"Well, I wouldn't say that exactly," Vance hedged. "I mean, he was perfectly calm being born with all the doctors and nurses pulling at him and poking him with stuff. His Apgar score was topnotch. But when they finally bring him over and he gets one good look at me and Piper, he starts screaming like a banshee. I kid you not."

"What?" Brooks said on a laugh.

"Yeah. Not sure who he was expecting, but he's clearly not pleased with the parents he's been stuck with. Piper and I discussed it, and we've decided to keep him anyway. We figure it's our job as parents to make his life a living hell, and obviously we've got a leg up on that."

Hale came over and clasped his arms around Vance. "Welcome to fatherhood."

"How's Piper?" Genevra asked.

"Perfect," Vance said. "You know, she's just …" And that's when the emotion washed over him. That's when the adrenaline let down and all the fear he'd been holding at bay while watching his precious Piper go through that godawful labor crashed over him. His eyes welled up with tears as he hugged his father and Genevra to him, ducking his head into their huddle.

It was the perfect moment for Jack McReady to make his grand entrance, shifting the focus from Vance's emotional breakdown to Missy's.

CHAPTER FORTY-SIX

Two weeks later, Thor reminded himself that Missy had indeed *begged* her parents to stay in Henderson for a few days after her father's landmark arrival. She wanted to spend quality time with them. She wanted to show them around town and introduce them to everyone she knew. She also wanted them to see her lacrosse team in action on the field Thor had built, as well as her new office located inside Duncan's law practice. Most of all, she wanted them to get to know Thor, and for Thor to get to know them.

No surprise that on Saturday—the day Piper was released from the hospital—the Evans family held a large brunch honoring their grandson as well as the McReady family. It was there Vance made a point of introducing four-day-old Vance, Jr. to his one-month-old Uncle Brody.

"Brody?" Missy's mom questioned. "I thought your son's name is Beau."

"It is." Genevra smiled. "But ever since we told Vance and Lolly we were pregnant, Vance declared he'd always wanted a brother named Brody. We assumed he'd get over it."

"You assumed wrong," Vance stressed, his forehead marred with a scowl.

Crain and Tansy Carraway flew in from Dallas, not wanting to miss out on all the excitement. And since Scarlett was stuck at Ole Miss prepping for finals, Davis took the opportunity to goad Crain once again as he proudly introduced Tansy to Mr. and Mrs. McReady as his *ex-lover*.

Fortunately for Pinks, Tansy's parents, Rye and Garland Langford, didn't show up in the middle of that introduction but just afterward. Garland bestowed all of her Southern charm on Missy's parents, claiming their daughter as one of her close personal friends. Missy wholeheartedly agreed, explaining their work with the Henderson Has-Beens and adding that, through Davis, Missy had crashed Garland's oldest daughter's wedding her first night in town, and then recently bonded with Garland's youngest daughter, Scarlett, over Scarlett's all-star girl power.

When her father looked to Thor for an explanation, Thor simply shook his head, turning the two of them toward Harry, who was, of course, tending bar.

Duncan and Annabelle arrived with "Aunt Lolly and Uncle Brooks" as Vance now referred to them. Lolly was accused of being a baby-hog, refusing to let anyone else hold her brother Beau. Of course, once Annabelle announced that the House of DuVal's debutante gowns would be unveiled the following month, Lolly tossed Beau at Missy, threatening not to go back to State for the last three weeks of her master's program because there was just too much work to be done before the line went public.

Though Genevra and everyone else (except for Hale, because Hale still relished seeing Lolly wound up) tried to talk Lolly down, Brooks jumped right on her bandwagon. He adamantly agreed there was no need for Lolly to return to school. He insisted she'd be just fine studying for finals or finishing up her graduate projects from home.

Thor leaned over, explaining quietly to the McReadys that Henderson's Golden Boy was at the end of his rope dealing with his woman living in Raleigh. Thus his complete willingness to chance her master's degree falling by the wayside.

Emelina flowed around the party, decked out in her usual Hollywood glam, claiming to all that she had a mystery date on the way. Thor couldn't have been more surprised, or pleased, to find his own buddy, Bryce McNally—better known as Picks—enter the party on Big Em's arm just before brunch was served. Picks claimed he wanted to shake Jack McReady's hand now that he was home safe, but Thor thought that might just be the excuse he used to get back to Henderson. Because thirty minutes after Picks showed up, so did that cute little number he'd had his hands all over the last time he was in town. From the satisfied smirk on Em's face, it appeared she'd had a hand in setting up the reunion.

The most intriguing part of all the merriment however, was watching a new *bromance* emerge. One between Hale Evans and Jack McReady.

Once the party started rolling, the two of them talked exclusively, moving from the kitchen bar to the outside grill, and then seating themselves at the tall kitchen countertop while the rest of the guests ate in the dining room or out on the patio under tall heaters. Much, much later, Thor found them with Pinks in Hale's study, the three of them sharing a well-aged Scotch and no doubt discussing potential business alliances in hopes of benefiting Henderson.

Missy joined Thor at the threshold as he stared into Hale's home office, begrudgingly admiring how Davis Williams managed to fit in fucking everywhere. "That's quite the scene," she commented.

"Who are they talking to on speaker?" Thor asked quietly.

Missy listened for a moment and then smiled real big. "Davis's father, Arthur Williams. He and my dad are best buds."

They listened in, unnoticed by the three now smoking cigars and trading war stories. Finally, they turned away and let the business tycoons be.

"Missy, you know I love you, right?"

"Yes," she grinned up at him.

"And your parents, well, they are great. Truly."

"They are," she agreed.

"But, I'm just not certain I can take one more rah-rah Balti-moron moving to Henderson."

Missy busted out laughing.

"Seriously. Your parents, Pinks's parents, they are welcome here any time. But, let's not suggest they move to Henderson permanently. I know that's the campaign and all, but you and Pinks are about as much Baltimore as any good ol' North Carolina town should have to handle."

"Since I have no control over who actually moves into Henderson, I will personally promise to tamp down the Baltimore hype."

"I suppose that's all I can ask," he said, kissing her lips.

"I do a good rah-rah Henderson too," she whispered.

"True that," he said, wondering how long it would be until he could rah-rah her ass alone out on his plantation.

Two fucking weeks.

The McReadys were still in town two fucking weeks after Jack's infamous return. And it got worse, as Thor's unconscious mind must have known it would back on that fateful day at the Evanses' brunch. Because, yep, Mr. and Mrs. Pinks had come to town. With fanfare in the form of a big, *glorious* dinner party at the club. Where all of the Pride of Baltimore's fans descended in order to pay homage to the loins from which Pinks had sprung.

Ho-ly hell.

Thor had not gotten laid in two weeks.

Oh, Missy hadn't stopped touching him, that was for damn certain. She touched him whenever they were together, making him sweat more often than not. Whether or not the girl had any idea of the torture she was putting him through—because he didn't put it past her not to be conducting some form of erotic revenge—it had to end.

It was going to end.

Tonight.

Tonight was the big Get-The-Hell-Out-Of-Henderson Event, otherwise known as Thor and Missy's *Party at the Plantation.*

Missy had begged her parents and the Williamses to stay on long enough to attend their come-dressed-as-your-inner-farmer event and then gathered a team of women who had been on his property for three straight days placing hay bales, setting up bars, food stations, the works. All of this while lacrosse practice continued at his place so that the girls and their parents couldn't help but take note of the party preparations. Now, about one hundred more guests had been invited, causing Missy to go into a panic and recruit Annabelle into all of the shenanigans.

With Missy and Pinks's moms rolling up their shirtsleeves the day before the party, Thor's backyard was swirling with feminine creativity. Knowing what was good for him, he fell right back into military form, taking orders and not asking any questions. The only saving grace was that Picks was still in town, so he was toting and fetching and yes ma'aming right along with him. Right up until party time.

The night before the party, when Thor once again couldn't convince Missy to stay the damn night even though she'd already blabbed to her father that they'd been intimate, he and Picks camped out on a prime piece of land that backed up to the lake. Frankly, it felt good to sleep on solid ground away from all those high voices and their OMG-let's-do-this ideas.

"So, the Ranger X Games?" Picks asked.

"It's on the list," Thor told him. "Right there with organic farming, which Jack thinks could eventually turn into something called an *Agrahood* and make me a bloody fortune. But this was your idea, your vision, so I'd want you to be the voice and face of the Ranger X Games."

"I could live with that," Bryce told him.

"Could you? Really? Trade in real bullets and hostages for paint pellets and a flag?"

"Just tell me where to sign." He clinked his bottle against Thor's.

"Sexy, little Shannon coming out to the party tomorrow night?" Thor asked.

"Sexy, little Shannon and all of her totally foxy friends."

"You let Cox and Balls in on this?"

"I wouldn't be surprised if Coxie and Balls make a showing."

Thor laughed, taking a sip of his beer. "It'd be good to see them regularly. Especially if you're here."

Picks simply nodded, eyeing the land around him, apparently dreaming his own dreams.

Thor didn't have to do much to dress for his own party. He could have put on his own flannel and denim, but he wanted to honor the true farmer in him. So he went into his pop's closet and took out the stuff he remembered his pop wearing most. Most of it didn't fit, his pop being of slighter build. But Thor managed to find a thermal undershirt that didn't hurt his image if it was stretched a little tightly across his chest, and an old flannel shirt he left open over it. He grabbed his old John Deere cap as well and hit the back door just in time for the entourage of Baltimoreans to arrive.

They did not disappoint.

Jack McReady, Arthur Williams, and their wives must have decided they grew racehorses on their fictional plantation, because they came dressed for the Kentucky Derby, as did the entire Dallas contingent.

However, his Melissa showed up as a smokin' hot cross between Elly May and Daisy Duke, with her tightly curled blond pigtails and the curve of her waist nicely displayed by tying up a red gingham shirt high above her belly button. Thor thought that if he were Jack McReady, he wouldn't have let his daughter out of the house in those crazy, low-riding jeans, but hey, who was he to judge?

In retrospect, the evening should have been called *Showdown at the Hoedown* because once it got dark, and the young ones and the old ones and the married ones headed home, the swinging singles started to … swing.

On the tire swing.

The one Missy had made him set up.

As often happens when idiots and alcohol combine, it became a contest of sorts, seeing who could swing the highest and then leap the farthest over a set of hay bales without killing themselves. There might have been one sprained ankle in the group, but that was nothing compared to what happened when the idea of tug of war entered their heads.

Tug of war over the fire pit.

Yeah, it was miraculous that the paramedics only had to show up once that night.

But it was fun. In fact, it was good, old-fashioned fun with a completely adolescent revival of cow tipping, which involved everybody trespassing onto the adjacent farm, all sanctioned by a blond, curly-headed cop.

Yep, tales would be told in the morning. Tall and otherwise. Folklore and legends came out of nights like this, Thor thought as he looked around for Missy, wondering what the hell time it was. The last he saw her, she was dancing on a hay bale. But right now, she could just as easily be at the top of the hill ready to ride his old Radio Flyer wagon down, or have slipped inside the house to begin formatting the next Henderson Happenings newsletter. Because plenty of pictures had been taken before and after the party had dissolved … or *evolved,* as the case may be. The details would definitely be digging down and tickling the roots of all past Hendersonians.

Thor caught Picks's eye, motioning that he was heading into the house.

He found Elly May Missy face down on his bed, fully clothed, dried mud on her ankles, arms, and cheek. She must have heard him come in because without opening her eyes, she licked her lips and said, "That was epic."

Thor laughed, standing at the foot of his bed, every part of his body aching with overuse. Except for one. "Epic indeed."

"Country Club Set meets Hicks Gone Wild," she groaned.

"You got that right," he said, stripping off his thermal, which was as dirty and dusty as if he'd truly been working in the fields all day. "Round one looked like a Ralph Lauren photo shoot for one of their Polo ad campaigns. I was sure my Army buddies were gonna give me some hell for that."

"Oh, but round two," Missy said, flipping over to her back, "was more their style. Like an episode of Backwoods Survivor."

"Yeah," he said, grabbing her ankles and pulling her down the bed toward him. "And now we're finally getting to round three."

"What's round three?"

"Daisy Duke does the God of Thunder."

Missy choked up a tired laugh. He put one knee on the bed so he could lean over far enough to kiss her lips, holding his dirty, sweaty body above hers. "You and I throw a great party together," she said quietly.

He nodded. "We make a great team." Then he kissed her again. "Come get in the shower with me."

"Okay," she said, giving him her shy Missy smile. "I've missed you."

"I've missed you too." Thor helped her sit up, pulled her into a standing position, and led her by the hand toward the bathroom.

"I was too tired to take off my clothes."

"Not a problem," he said, starting the shower.

She leaned back against the sink's countertop, letting him work at the knot in her shirt. Allowing him to discover the skimpy bit of red lace she wore underneath. "Damn," he said, coasting his hands gently over skin and lace. "Had I known this was waiting for me, I'd have had you in the shed between tug of war and cow tipping."

"You like red." Missy shrugged the shirt from her shoulders and arms.

"Absolutely my favorite color." Then his gaze shifted from her gorgeous tits spilling over the red lace up to her face. "Next to the color of your eyes." That Caribbean blue still slayed him. "You got red underwear on too?" he asked against her lips.

"Maybe," she said coyly.

He grinned, locking their eyes as his hands drifted down to the snap of her jeans. He held her gaze as he unzipped her pants, tucked his thumbs into the waistband at her hips, and began pushing the denim down. "You put a lot of thought into your outfit tonight?" he teased.

"I've got a lot to make up for. And since you really have an aversion to pity sex—"

He outright laughed at that.

"—I had to think of something else."

Thor moved back, giving her room to step out of her clothes. His gaze drifted down, down, down, until it finally landed on a sexy red G-string. "That's a helluva change from your Nikes," he said, his tongue feeling thick in his mouth. He shed his jeans and boxers and pulled her toward the shower.

"I'm still young enough to learn a few new tricks. Besides, surprising you is fun. Everything about you is fun."

Thor backed into the shower, protecting Missy from the spray. "It's been a long time since I've been accused of being fun."

"You and I have been having fun since the night you stole me from the Cowboy," she said, wrapping her arms around his neck.

"Yeah, but back then you didn't know you were kissing a farmer."

"Back then, *you* didn't know you were a farmer. You thought you were just another random superhero without a cape."

Thor's hands drifted over the lingerie that was slowly being soaked. "I love you, Missy," he said softly, honestly. "Cape or no. I still wanna be your hero."

When round three was done, and then round four, Thor laid in bed on his back worried they were moving on to round five by the way Missy was crawling up his chest. If so, this was definitely going to be the knockout round. The one to knock him out cold.

But Missy gave him something he hadn't expected.

"Thor," she whispered over his chest.

"Yeah, Pretty Girl?"

When she hesitated, he opened his eyes. Watched her lick her lips.

"I know you and Bryce are talking about a business venture, and that you've committed land to the Garden Club. And I think the farm-to-table thing is a good fit for you and will benefit Scarlett's restaurant even if it never develops into that whole agra-whatever stuff my father keeps talking about. But I also think you, Big Red, and I should consider going into business together."

Thor smiled, closed his eyes, and drifted his fingertips over her naked back. "You worried Big Red and I won't have time to tote lacrosse goals and whatever else you need for your party-planning business?"

"Not exactly," she hedged.

He tucked an arm under his head and looked into her eyes. "You'll always come first, Pretty Girl. No matter what's going on with the plantation, you're always gonna come first."

She grinned real big and stretched her neck up to kiss him, but then went on. "The acreage closest to your home? It would make a perfect venue for outdoor events. We just proved that."

Thor stopped stroking her back and lifted his head. "You're serious about this."

She nodded.

And then her sweet mouth went into its typical overdrive, running on and on about what they could do with certain parts of his land. Assuring him in between listing a myriad of ideas that he didn't have to do it simply because she was asking, but that she wanted him to consider it along with the rest of his options. She kept going on about how she'd be fine with whatever he decided, one way or the other, it really didn't matter to her—

Until he shut her up.

The way he liked to do.

Shut her up long and hard and gave it to her so good that when he was finished, she just sighed, laying her head on his chest. Eventually, he heard her whisper, "I can't believe I ever thought you were Mr. Wrong."

And his heart ate that up. Because after hearing those words, Thurgood Lewis Watson III was finally ...

All right.

I hope, like Missy, you fell in love with Thurgood. When I realized he was an actual Army Ranger, I made myself conduct heavy research wanting to make sure I'd do justice to the men and women who serve the United States of America with their brains, bravery, brawn, and tireless dedication. I felt the need to get this character right.

Two special real-life heroes offered their assistance. Captain Lowell H. Patterson, IV, a Ranger himself and the son of some of my closest friends, Cathy and Buddy Patterson, provided so much fascinating information at such a high level that as I listened to him, I thought to myself, "Wow, we are in really good hands if Lowell is representative of who is serving our beloved country."

Zach Billingsley came into my life as I began writing *Mr. Wrong*. I cannot thank him enough for being so open, honest, and compelling as he shared personal experiences of his deployment in Iraq and his return to life as a civilian. Presently he continues to serve in the Army Reserves and evidence indicates that he's just as romantic as Thor.

A heartfelt thank you to both of these outstanding men.

Thanks so much for reading *Mr. Wrong*.

All of my Heroes of Henderson novels and novellas are complete romances in and of themselves and do not need to be read in any particular order. However, it's a little more fun that way.

Heroes of Henderson full-length Novels
Good Cop
Bad Cop
Top Dog
Tempting Vivi
UnderDog
Mr. Wrong

Heroes of Henderson Novellas
Playin' Cop
Taming Molly
Kissing Cooper ~ A Christmas Quickie

The Heroes of Henderson Series
Listed in Order

Countdown To A Kiss
A New Year's Eve Anthology

Playin' Cop
Heroes of Henderson ~ Prequel
Previously published as
The Keeper of the Debutantes in
Countdown to A Kiss

Good Cop
Heroes of Henderson ~ Book 1

Bad Cop
Heroes of Henderson ~ Book 2

Taming Molly
Heroes of Henderson ~ Book 2.5
A DuVal Cousins Quickie

Top Dog
Heroes of Henderson ~ Book 3

Tempting Vivi
Heroes of Henderson ~ Book 3.5
A DuVal Cousins Novel

Kissing Cooper
Heroes of Henderson ~ A Christmas Quickie

UnderDog
Heroes of Henderson ~ Book 4

Mr. Wrong
Heroes of Henderson ~ Book 5

Mr. Wright
Heroes of Henderson ~ Book 6
Coming in 2017

Sign up at *www.LizKellyBooks.com*
to be alerted when new books are released.

About the Author

Growing up every summer in a place where dancing and romancing are literally part of its theme song, Liz Kelly can't help but be a romantic at heart. And since her favorite author, Kathleen E. Woodiwiss wrote some of the world's greatest romances, she's just trying to give the world a little more of that. (Okay, maybe a little sexier that, but we are now in a new millennium after all.)

A graduate of Wake Forest University, where she met her handsome golf-addicted husband, (who is now sporting dark glasses everywhere he goes) Liz is a mother of two grown sons (also sporting dark glasses) and a miniature Labradoodle named Isabelle. They split their time between The Windy City of Chicago and the Fountain of Youth, a.k.a. Naples, FL where dancing and romancing continues on ad infinitum.